Praise for the Novels of
Jane Porter

EASY ON THE EYES

"Jane Porter writes endlessly entertaining and yet deeply thoughtful novels. EASY ON THE EYES is a perceptive, tender page-turner—a joy to read."

—**Laura Caldwell, author of *Red Hot Lies***

"A page-turning novel about love, loss, friendship, aging, and beauty (not necessarily in that order). I couldn't put it down."

—**Karen Quinn, author of *Holly Would Dream***
and *The Ivy Chronicles*

"Jane Porter knows a woman's heart as well as her mind. EASY ON THE EYES is a smart, sophisticated, fun read with characters you'll fall in love with. Another winning novel by Jane Porter."

—**Mia King, national bestselling author of**
Good Things* and *Sweet Life

"Witty and observant—Tiana's search for love and meaning amidst shallow celebrity will stay with you long after you've finished reading."

—**Berta Platas, author of *Lucky Chica***

"A fun, poignant story about searching for life and love on the other side of forty."

—Beth Kendrick, author of *The Pre-Nup*

MRS. PERFECT

"Great warmth and wisdom…Jane Porter creates a richly emotional story."

—*Chicago Tribune*

"Porter's authentic character studies and meditations on what really matters make *Mrs. Perfect* a perfect…novel."

—*USA Today*

"Thrills and laughs."

—*Kirkus Reviews*

"Porter scores another home run."

—*Romantic Times BOOKreviews Magazine*

"Fans will appreciate Ms. Porter's strong look at what happens to relationships when the walls come tumbling down."

—*Midwest Book Review*

"More poignant than the standard mommy-lit fare."

—*Publishers Weekly*

"Jane Porter understands women. This is the kind of book you'll want to share with your best friend."

—Melanie Lynne Hauser, author of *Confessions of a Super Mom* and *Super Mom Saves the World*

"Jane Porter strikes a fine balance in the follow-up to her hit *Odd Mom Out, Mrs. Perfect*, a novel about losing 'The Good Life' only to discover what the good life really is—funny, thought-provoking, affecting... and highly recommended."

—**Lauren Baratz-Logsted, author of *Secrets of My Suburban Life* and *Vertigo***

"Porter does a spectacular job of creating... characters that resonate in the hearts of moms everywhere."

—***South Jersey Mom***

"Compulsively readable... a delicious treat."

—**BookReporter.com**

"Real life hits trophy wife right in the Botox, in Porter's empowering page-turner!"

—**Leslie Carroll, author of *Choosing Sophie* and *Play Dates***

ODD MOM OUT

"Jane Porter nails it poignantly and perfectly. This mommy-lit is far from fluff. Sensitive characters and a protagonist who doesn't cave in to the in-crowd give this novel its heft."

—*USA Today*

"A poignant critique of mommy cliques and the plight of single parents."

—*Kirkus Reviews*

more . . .

"Funny and poignant...delightful."

—**Stella Cameron**

"Best of all is Porter's take on mother-daughter dynamics."

—*Newport News Daily Press*

"*Odd Mom Out* is an engaging tale that examines important issues of today's world. Behind the entertaining, witty prose are insightful observations about real life."

—*Woodbury Magazine*

"Marta is an intriguing heroine."

—*Publishers Weekly*

"Keenly emotional and truly uplifting."

—*Booklist*

FLIRTING WITH FORTY

"A terrific read! A wonderful, life- and love-affirming story for women of all ages."

—**Jayne Ann Krentz,** *New York Times* **bestselling author**

"Calorie-free accompaniment for a poolside daiquiri."

—*Publishers Weekly*

"Strongly recommended. Porter's thoughtful prose and strong characters make for an entertaining and thought-provoking summer read."

—*Library Journal*

easy ^{on} _{the} eyes

Also by Jane Porter

easy ^{on} _{the} eyes

★★★

Jane Porter

NEW YORK   BOSTON

5 Spot
Hachette Book Group
237 Park Avenue
New York, NY 10017

Visit our website at www.5-spot.com.

5 Spot is an imprint of Grand Central Publishing.
The 5 Spot name and logo are trademarks of
Hachette Book Group, Inc.

Printed in the United States of America

First Edition: July 2009
10 9 8 7 6 5 4 3 2 1

Library of Congress Cataloging-in-Publication Data

Porter, Jane
Easy on the eyes / Jane Porter. — 1st ed.
p. cm.
ISBN 978-0-446-50940-4
1. Women television journalists—Fiction.   2. Self-realization in women—Fiction.   3. Widows—Fiction.   4. Chick lit.   I. Title.
PS3616.O78E27 2009
813'.6—dc22
2008048332

Book design by TexTech International
Cover design by Elizabeth Connor

For Mary Katherine Porter
My sister, inspiration, and best friend

Acknowledgments

Thank you as always to my superb agent, Karen Solem, who makes me believe I can do anything.

Thank you to my editor, Karen Kosztolnyik, who works tirelessly on my behalf, nurturing every book from inception to publication.

To all at Grand Central Publishing, from the fantastic editorial department, to the creative minds in the art department, to savvy marketing, to my publicist Melissa Bullock, to the fantastic sales team—thank you for working so hard on my books' behalf.

To Megan Crane, Liza Palmer, Lilian Darcy, and Christine Fugate, thank you for the hours and hours you spent reading this manuscript and generously sharing your time, talent, and opinions. I wouldn't have found the end, or the middle, without you. I loved the brainstorm, the edits, and even the rants.

To my guy, Ty Gurney, and my boys, Jake and Ty Gaskins, thank you for giving me such a wonderful life away from the writing life. You make me feel very loved and happy.

And lastly, to my readers. Thank you for embracing my stories. You are the reason I write.

easy ^{on} _{the} eyes

Chapter One

"Tiana, how do you feel about a co-host?"

Only a couple minutes into the closed-door meeting with my boss, Glenn, the executive producer of *America Tonight*, and he drops that bombshell.

How can he be so casual about something so huge?

And something so *bad*?

"Co-host?" My voice doesn't wobble, but I'm stunned. Horrified. For nearly six years I've been the sole host of the show. It's a show that debuted with me as the host, a show that's earned me the nickname America's Sweetheart. "Why would I do that, when it's my show?"

He hesitates, looks at me, thick sandy eyebrows shot with gray, before answering bluntly, "Your show's in trouble."

I silently count to five and speak only when I'm certain I'm perfectly in control. "You said it was a temporary blip. You told me twice in the past few months not to worry."

"Unfortunately, I was wrong. The downward cycle hasn't reversed, and the network wants changes. They've brought in outside consultants who've done extensive market studies. The consultants believe that the best approach is to bring in some young blood."

The words *young blood* chill me.

I think of myself as a warrior. I've been to hell and back

with the death of my family and then my husband. I've battled to build my career and sacrificed a personal life to be where I am today. But the one thing I can't fight is time. I'm going to age. And apparently I already am.

But none of this matters. Nothing matters but ratings, stats, and demographics.

"Do you have any young blood in mind?" I ask, crossing one leg over the other under the hem of my bronze St. John skirt. I'd already changed for the *Larry King Live* interview and was just about to leave Horizon Broadcasting for the CNN studio in Hollywood when Glenn called me into his office.

"Shelby Patterson," he says.

"Shelby?" My voice comes out strangled. I not only trained Shelby, I helped develop the weekend show for her because I thought she had so much promise. I was right. And they wonder why successful women are afraid to mentor younger women.

"Her weekend show has strong numbers," he continues, "particularly with the younger viewers, demographics you desperately need."

Desperately.

Young blood.

He and I are both wordsmiths, and these are not good words. This is not a good conversation. I'm in trouble.

My heart races and I press a hand to my lower rib cage as if I could slow the mad beating. Max, my agent, should be here. Max, my agent, should be defending me, protecting me. This is my career. My life. God knows I don't have a life outside *America Tonight*. No husband, no kids, no hobbies or free time. Everything I have, everything I am, is invested in this show. "How good are Shelby's numbers compared to mine?"

"She's outperforming you by nearly twenty percent."

Oh. Stunned, I suck in a quick, sharp breath. Those are unforgivable numbers in any business, but here, in the delicate world of television market share, that's pretty much a catastrophe.

"We think the solution is to bring Shelby onto the weekday show and make Manuel the sole host for the weekend show. You and Shelby would be co-anchors, like Mary Hart and Mark Steines on *Entertainment Tonight*." Glenn gets up from behind his desk and walks around to sit in the gray chair next to me. "Nothing's been done yet. I just wanted to get a feel for your reaction before it became formal."

I open my mouth to speak, but nothing comes out. I feel as if I'm on a plane that's going down and I can't stop it. Can't exit.

But I can escape this. I can survive. I just have to focus. Be calm, because I know how this goes. I've watched it happen a hundred times. You add a co-anchor to boost ratings and eventually the new young talent replaces the mature talent. I'm being phased out. He doesn't need to say it, but if I'm not damn careful, this is the beginning of the end. "Have you considered other correspondents for the position? Like Manuel, for example?"

"He's thirty-four. Shelby's twenty-eight. She's youthful. High energy. She'd bring a new dynamic to the weekly show and pull in some of those numbers we've lost."

"You're right, she's great on camera, and she's definitely high energy, but she doesn't know how to write a story. She just delivers—"

"We have writers who can write. We need charisma. Beauty. Poise. Charm. Youth."

Youth. There it is again. Young blood, desperation, youth.

"I'm too old?" I ask quietly.

He squirms ever so slightly. He can't answer that directly because he'd be sued, but he knows what I'm asking. "Our decisions are dictated by the viewing public," he says after a moment. "American audiences don't mind watching mature men on television, but they object to mature women. And by adding Shelby, we can keep you on camera."

"You've considered replacing me, haven't you?"

His expression changes, grows sympathetic. "I haven't, no, but I can't tell you that the subject hasn't been discussed. You are up for contract renewal in March." He hesitates for a moment before adding, "You're also expensive compared to Shelby."

"That's because I'm good," I say, smiling, and that's to hide the fact that my eyes are burning and I'm horrifically close to tears.

I love my job. I *need* my job. I can't imagine what I'd do or who I'd be without the show.

"You are good. You're very good. Which is why I don't want to see you go."

"When would she join the show?"

"If she joins the show, it'd be after the holidays."

Silently I digest this. It's hard to take in, and I don't know what to say. I don't know what to feel, either, as I bounce between anger and denial.

"I know it's a lot to think about," he adds, "and we'll talk more about this later. I just wanted you to be aware of the discussions we're having here right now and some of the proposed changes for the New Year." He stands, returns to his desk. "Now, if you're going to make it to CNN on time, you'd better go. With Thanksgiving just a week away, traffic could be a bitch."

I drive in a state of shock.

They've discussed replacing me. They're interested in promoting Shelby from weekend host to weekday co-host. My God. I had no idea that for the past six months my future with HBC has been the subject of discussion. I know market studies are done all the time. Consultants are always being hired, brought in to revamp a show, make some changes, try a new direction. But until now, no one had had a problem with me.

Hands shaking, I call my agent. Max Orth is the reason I'm on a national syndicated TV show. My first job out of Stanford was in Boulder, Colorado, and I would stand on mountaintops during snowstorms and report on road closures and freeway pileups. I'd wait at the Boulder airport to interview family members reuniting after years of separation. I'd race to the outskirts of town when a body was found. And as much as I wanted to be a serious journalist, hard news stories and I never really clicked. Maybe I asked the wrong questions. Maybe I was too sympathetic. Inevitably my pieces came out soft, cozy, human interest. Pieces editors and producers derisively termed fluff.

It didn't help that I looked fluffy, too. Beauty queen, they called me at the station, beauty queen with pageant hair.

Three months into my job with KKPQ, I cut my hair into a sleek, studious chestnut brown pageboy, and that was when big hair was fashionable. After six months, I overhauled my wardrobe and tossed out color. No bright blue blouses or greens. No red coats or pink scarves. Brown and black with gray. But even then the camera loved me, loved my light hazel eyes that looked gold in some light, greenish brown in others, my debutante high cheekbones, the dimples at the corner of my mouth.

Even though my pieces were fluff, the ratings went up at the station. We were just a little station, too, but KKPQ was a Fox affiliate and some of my pieces were picked up by other Fox affiliates. And before I knew how or why, I was sitting at the news desk as a weekend anchor, and then within a year I was hired away to co-host the morning news in Tucson.

It was in Tucson I met the two most influential men of my life: Keith, my future husband, who only ever saw the best in me. And Max, my future agent. Keith, ten years my senior, was a weathered, world-traveled, award-winning reporter working for CNN. We met on the scene of a devastating freeway accident—I still can't stand to remember that one, as a mom and her two children died that day.

And Max? Like everyone else, he saw the photo of me pressed to Keith's casket after he was killed, and unlike everyone else, he didn't call or send flowers. He flew in to Tucson to meet me. He said I was going to be big. He said I had a huge future.

I expect to get Max's voice mail, but he answers. "Hey, doll, I was wondering when I'd hear from you."

"Did you know Glenn was going to talk to me this afternoon about adding Shelby to the show?"

"I knew there's been talk about making changes to the show."

"Why didn't you tell me?"

"Because there was nothing to tell you, and I didn't want to upset you without cause."

The lights on Santa Monica blur. Cars stream past. I feel

unbearably sad. "You should have warned me. I should have been prepared."

"What did he say?"

"That my numbers are really down and it's hoped that Shelby will help bring them back up." I brake as the traffic light turns yellow and then red. "I don't want to share the show with Shelby. It's my show, and why Shelby of all people?"

"She's twenty-eight, ten years younger than you, and she's proactive. She's already had her eyes done to look even fresher on camera."

The horrible sick, sinking feeling is back. "Is that what this is about? My age?"

"For the record, I told you a year ago that a little work wouldn't hurt you."

He did, too.

I rest my elbow on the door and press my fingers to my temple. *For the record*, I heard him, and I didn't ignore his advice last year. I consulted a dermatologist, and she recommended laser light treatment to stimulate the collagen in my face. She said it'd keep the skin around my eyes from growing too thin, and then I did a chemical peel to get rid of some of the finer lines.

"You should have listened to me then, babe."

"I'm not into cutting and stretching, Max. That's not me."

"Then kiss away your career."

"No one can make me do it."

"No one can, no, but no one will renew your contract, either." He sighs. "Come on, get real, you and I both know this industry. If you don't renew your contract, you'll be reduced to a celebrity correspondent for some cable show for a year or two until you're too old for even that."

"You're saying I'd be washed up at forty if I don't get work done."

"I'm saying you'd definitely be washed up at forty if you don't get work done. Because frankly, and this is coming as a friend and as your agent, for your line of work, you're looking old."

Could he hit any harder? Could he hit any lower? My throat, already thick with emotion, threatens to swell closed. "Max, I'm walking into CNN. I have to go."

"Call me after the show."

I hang up, blink. I can't cry, it'd ruin my makeup and I'm about to go on live TV.

Besides, I'm not old. I'm only thirty-eight.

An *LKL* intern shows me to the green room, where I check my makeup in the bright lights to make sure it's dark enough for the bright lights on Larry's set. I'm just applying a darker lip liner when the intern returns with another guest in tow. I look up, into the mirror, as the intern and guest appear in the green room.

Dr. Hollywood.

My breath catches in my throat and my heart falls. Not him, not tonight. I can't cope with him on a night like this. Gorgeous, famous Michael O'Sullivan, plastic surgeon to the stars. And the hopefuls. And the has-beens.

Michael's gaze meets mine in the mirror. He's tall, dark, and handsome, which is such a waste of genetics, as I find him impossibly shallow and superficial. He's always being photo-graphed at the big fund-raisers and parties and nearly always with a different woman on his arm or at his side. I don't like plastic surgeons, so you can imagine my loathing for a plastic surgeon who's also a player.

"Dr. O'Sullivan," I say coolly.

"Tiana," he answers with a mocking smile. "How are you?"

"Good."

"I'm so glad."

Theoretically he hasn't said anything wrong, but I'm already gritting my teeth.

Why do I detest this man so much? Is it because he's become a bigger celebrity than many of his celebrity patients? Or is it the fact that last year he starred in his own reality show, appropriately named *Dr. Hollywood*? Or is it that he's rich, ranked by *Los Angeles* magazine as one of the five wealthiest surgeons in Southern California, and I hate that he makes millions every year off of women's insecurities? Or more appalling, *People* magazine had the gall to make him one of their "50 Sexiest Bachelors" last year?

"And you look rested," I said icily. "Is that Botox and self-tanner?"

Michael just laughs as though I'm an adorable child and heads to the refrigerator to retrieve a bottle of chilled water. He's wearing a dark, expensive suit, exquisitely tailored across the shoulders and through the chest. The man knows how to wear a suit, and with his open-collared white shirt he looks effortlessly elegant, which I also resent.

He's the only man I know who makes me feel emotional and impulsive. But then he's also the only man I know who pokes fun at me and my ambition.

Michael twists the cap off his water bottle. "One of my patients saw you on the Air France flight from Paris. Have a nice trip?"

"I did, thank you."

"What were you doing in Paris? Work or pleasure?"

"Pleasure. I went to see—" I break off, stopping short of mentioning Trevor. I've been dating Scottish actor Trevor Campbell for six months, and it's not a secret, but I don't want to talk about Trevor now, not with Dr. Hollywood, who is notorious for dating skinny blondes with big boobs and cotton candy for brains.

"A friend?" Michael supplies, trying to keep a straight face. Why I amuse him is beyond me, but Michael thinks I'm hilarious, and he has ever since our very first meeting nearly four years ago at a Christmas party somewhere. I don't remember the party, but I remember Michael. I thought he was gorgeous and funny, and then later someone told me he wasn't Michael O'Sullivan but Dr. O'Sullivan, and my heart sank. I loathe plastic surgeons, particularly plastic surgeons in Beverly Hills. They're slick doctors who like to position themselves as experts on aesthetics and the female form, using surgery to cut and sculpt an idealized look that's more Barbie doll than authentic beauty.

"Yes," I answer, "he is a friend." I don't even realize I've lifted my chin until I catch my reflection in the mirror. Warm brown hair, flushed cheeks, overly bright eyes. I look as excited as a gawky preteen talking to a cool boy.

I curse my transparency and head to the sink to wash my hands. "We must be on the same expert guest list," I add crisply, soaping my hands and rinsing them beneath hot water.

"How fortunate." His lips twist. "We always have such great chemistry."

I've faced Dr. O'Sullivan twice before on *Larry King Live*, and what we have is tension and dissension, not chemistry, great or otherwise. But for some reason, the *LKL* producers love to square us off, pitch one against the other, and even if an army of guests and experts has been booked, the show's fireworks always come down to Michael and me.

I reach for a paper towel. "At least we know each other's positions." My eyes meet his in the mirror. "You'll talk about the pressure doctors feel to make miracles and I'll talk about the pressure celebrities feel to be young and beautiful."

"And then you'll get personal," Michael adds, his voice dropping. "You always do."

The suddenly husky note in his voice makes my stomach do a little flip. I'm rattled despite myself, and my cheeks burn hotter. I hate how he throws me off balance. "Because you always defend the greedy doctors—"

"That's exactly what I mean. Why must doctors be greedy? Why can't they be compassionate?"

My gut clenches even as my shoulders tighten. "Was Jenna Meadows's surgeon compassionate? He performed the surgery out of greed, and he subsequently destroyed her body."

Michael folds his arms across his broad chest. "He advised her not to increase the size again."

My eyebrow lifts. "So it's her fault that the implant displaced?"

He doesn't take the bait. "Jenna knew the risks. She had complications with her first augmentation, experiencing early capsular contracture. There was additional surgery to remove scar tissue. She never was a good candidate for increasing to 650 mL."

"Then the surgeon should have said no. He can say no, right? Or must the doctor dance every time a patient speaks?"

"We say no more often than you realize."

"So why didn't her doctor refuse?"

"Why did Jenna insist?" He looks down at me, dark lashes concealing his expression.

Impatiently, I crumple the paper towel and toss it away. I so wish I weren't here. I so wish I were home in my sweats eating a bowl of cereal. "But still, you have to admit your industry thrives on insecure people."

"And your industry glorifies celebrities to a point that ordinary men and women feel ugly in comparison."

"Well, thanks to Jenna's botched surgeries she'll never work again. Her breasts are completely disfigured."

"No surgery is one hundred percent safe."

"Ahem, kids, be nice," Allie, the segment producer, admonishes as she sticks her head into the green room. "Are you two at it already? You're supposed to save it for the show, and it's going to be a great show, too. Jenna's on live feed from New York, and one of the guys will grab you in five to get you miked. See you soon."

She disappears, and Michael and I look at each other for a long moment before I reapply my lipstick. My hand shakes as I run the color across my lips.

"Want some water?" he asks me. "It'll help cool you down."

I shoot him a sharp glance. "I'm not hot."

"No need for false modesty, Tiana. You're America's Sweetheart. Queen of tabloid news."

For a moment, I can think of absolutely nothing to say. Is he paying me a compliment? Even if in a roundabout way?

Then I see his expression. Michael's making fun of me.

Embarrassed, I snap the cap on the tube of lipstick, toss it into my makeup bag, and zip it closed.

What a jerk. He's such a jerk. Michael O'Sullivan personifies everything I despise.

One of the *LKL* production assistants retrieves us from the green room and escorts us to the studio's soundstage. As we walk, I smooth my skirt and tug down the fitted knit jacket. Bronze is supposed to be a good color for me—brings out the gold in my eyes—but only now do I remember it's not a great color for the *LKL* set.

Oh, hell.

Suddenly I'm exhausted. The twelve-hour flight has caught up with me. I should be home showering and getting ready for bed. I should be anywhere but here, getting ready to spar with Michael O'Sullivan on *Larry King Live*.

On the set, the sound technician runs the microphone cords up beneath our jackets and clips the head to our lapels. Larry had been going over some notes, but seeing us, he walks over to shake Michael's hand and give me a kiss on the cheek.

"We just got word that Jenna's not going to be on tonight," he says. "Her lawyer advised her not to do it, so it's going to be just the three of us and then we'll open the phone lines."

"Great." I muster a smile. "We'll still have a good show."

Larry wags a finger at me. "Working too hard again? You're looking tired."

Ouch. Two hits tonight. I'm aging and I look tired. My God, these men are brutal.

"Too much fun in Paris," I say, fighting for a cheeky smile, projecting as much youthful zest as I can. "Probably should have slept on the way home instead of working all through the flight."

"Good trip, though?" Larry asks as we take our seats on the stools around the set table.

"It was great." I catch Michael's arched eyebrow and turn my head away. His picture should be next to the definition of "annoying" in the dictionary.

The technician steps over to adjust my mike. Someone else powders Larry's nose and smoothes down a stray hair. Michael just sits there in his dark suit, cool as a cucumber. I bet the man doesn't even sweat. He's probably Botoxed his armpits to keep from perspiring.

A minute until we go live.

Larry chats with Michael about his wife and their plans for the holidays. He wants a white Christmas and cozy fire. She wants beaches and sun and time by the pool.

I can't believe the holidays are already approaching again. Is Thanksgiving really just a week away?

Thirty seconds until we go live.

As a kid, I loved Thanksgiving. I don't anymore. I hate being alone on Thanksgiving, but even worse is crashing Shey's family celebration like an orphan. An orphan...

Fifteen seconds.

I take a deep breath, sit straighter, shoulders squared.

Ten seconds. Larry smiles at me. I smile back. Piece of cake.

Five seconds.

Michael leans toward me. "If you need any recommendations for a good plastic surgeon, just call me. I'll get you squared away."

And we're live.

Asshole.

Chapter Two

★ ★ ★

I leave the building, shoulders slouched, absolutely exhausted.

That was a disaster, I think, unbuttoning the top button of my jacket and exhaling hard.

Michael made mincemeat of me. I don't know how he did it, either. He's never bested me before. Maybe I didn't feel enough sympathy for Jenna Meadows. Maybe I was preoccupied with Glenn's devastating news. But still, I'm a professional. I can't lose focus, not on national TV.

I drive home without seeing anything, drive lost in my world of disbelief. First Glenn drops his bomb and then Michael pummels me. Ridiculous.

Hard to believe that only two days ago I returned from Paris and felt as if I were on top of the world. Now here it is Thursday night and I'm facing what? Unemployment?

Fighting panic, at the next red light I text Shey in New York to see if she's still awake: *"R u up?"*

Shey is one of my closest friends, and we go way back, all the way to our high school days when we met in boarding school in Monterey County. Back then we were the Three Amigos. It was Shey, Marta, and me. And we were tight, really tight, and we still are, although due to the fact that we live in separate corners of the country, we don't see as much of each other as we'd like.

My phone rings almost immediately. It's Shey. Shey's a former model and co-owns Expecting Models, an agency in Manhattan devoted to pregnant models and new-mom models. She still models from time to time, and she deals with image all the time. I think she'd relate to my conflicted feelings.

"Tell me I didn't wake you," I beg her, knowing that as I am the only unmarried left, we have very different schedules and demands.

"It's not even ten here, sugar, and I'm a night owl," Shey drawls into the phone, her Texas accent still present, although not nearly as strong as it was when she arrived at St. Pious as a willowy sixteen-year-old. "How are things?"

"Crazy busy." I hesitate, dig my nails into my Jaguar's leather steering wheel. "And just a word of warning, I'm pissed off, so you're going to hear me rant."

"Has Marta already been subjected to the rant?"

"No, I called you first. Marta won't be sympathetic, not to this."

"Ah, it's about your love life then."

"No, although that needs help, too." I pause, searching for the right words. "It's my face."

She smothers a laugh. "What's wrong with your face?"

"*Exactly.*" Hard to believe I'm even having this conversation and I clench the steering wheel tighter. "There's nothing wrong with my face and I think it's bullshit, absolute bullshit, that they're even pulling this on me."

"Who? What?"

"The studio heads. They want to promote Shelby to co-anchor." Just saying the words aloud makes me sick.

She hesitates. "Isn't Shelby the host for the weekend show?"

"Yes, and she apparently has phenomenal ratings."

Another hesitation, and this coming from Little Miss Ray of Sunshine. "How are yours?"

"Not so good." I take a deep breath. "And Glenn didn't come out and give me any specifics other than Shelby's young and fresh and high energy."

Shey is quiet a moment. "Maybe they just want to shake the format up, try something new after six years."

"Maybe."

"Or maybe they don't want to replace you but they want a younger, fresher you." She seems to be choosing her words with care. "Have you considered that this might be their way of telling you it's time to get some work done?"

I never thought of it quite like that. But it's possible. I'm not wrinkly, but my face is softer than it used to be. I've noticed at certain angles there's definitely a bit of a droop near my mouth. If I'm smiling it's not a problem, it's just when I'm caught without expression. "I don't suppose they could come out and say get a face-lift, or else."

"It'd be illegal, and discriminatory, but it might be what's behind the drop in ratings."

"No way. People aren't that shallow. My viewers tune in for me. They're women like me. They can't expect me to never age—"

"Oh, sugar," she interrupts softly, "you of all people can't play ostrich."

"What does that mean?"

"You know what it means. It means you're in an image business and image is king. It always has been, always will be."

"So you think I need work done?" I demand belligerently.

"As a woman? No. As a friend? Never. As one of America's most watched faces? Maybe."

"No!"

"TV, media, magazines, it's all a numbers game. Ratings equal advertisers. Advertisers equal profitability. Profitability equals livelihood. I'll tell you the same thing I tell my models—you do what you've got to do to stay alive."

I exhale, hard. So it's not my imagination. Those droops do show. People are noticing. How infuriating because I don't *feel* old. I don't feel droopy or flabby. I feel amazing. At least I felt amazing. "A face-lift?"

"Not a full lift, sugar. Maybe just the eyes, and some filler to soften the lines around your mouth and plump the hollows beneath your eyes."

Idling at yet another red light, I snap down my visor and open the mirror to inspect my reflection. I frown. Hard. A few lines appear around my eyes, but nothing significant. "But it's not absolutely necessary, is it? I don't look bad—"

"Of course you don't look bad. You're Tiana Tomlinson, and you've been in *People* magazine's 'Most Beautiful People' issue how many times? Three?"

"Four," I correct in a small voice. "And the last time was just two years ago—"

"But you and I both know that two years is a long time in this business. And face it, Tits," Shey says, using my high school nickname, Tits, short for Tiana Irene Tomlinson, "high-definition TV has changed the game. Until recently, great makeup and lighting camouflaged a multitude of sins, but not anymore. Every wrinkle, every pimple, shows. I'm going through this with my models. It's not just you."

I'd love to argue, but I can't. I am where I am because of my face. My curiosity, tenacity, and smarts made me a good journalist. But it was my photogenic properties that propelled me to bigger and more successful networks, eventually resulting in my current position. Sad as it sounds, Max wouldn't have found me appealing on Keith's casket if I weren't attractive.

"Tiana, if that's what the studio is saying, I'd listen." She hesitates. "Unless you want out?..."

Out? Out to where? Out to what? I'm thirty-eight and single. All I have is my career. Since Keith died I've poured myself into my work, and I love my work. I live for my job. It's who I am.

My phone beeps. I've got an incoming call. I check the name and number. Max. "Shey, it's my agent to give me more doom and gloom."

"Talk to him and call me later if you want to chat some more."

I hang up on Shey to take Max's call as I pull up in front of my house. "It's got to be upsetting, doll," Max says.

I sit outside my house, engine still running. There's not much curb appeal to my house, other than the trailing hot pink bougainvillea, but the facade isn't the appeal. It's what lies on the other side of the exterior wall that I love: 3 bedrooms, 2.5 baths, 1932 Mediterranean-style home with high-pitched beamed ceilings, wood-burning fireplace, terraces and balconies on a secluded woodland lot with views of the city and canyon. I fell in love with the house the moment the agent opened the front door. Unfortunately it's always so empty once I step inside.

"Upsetting is putting it mildly," I answer tightly, feeling so angry and yet unable to articulate any of it. I'm not good at expressing my feelings. I'm a doer, not a dreamer. If I want something, I go for it. And I have gone for it, heart, mind, body, and soul. I worked night and day to make *America Tonight* a top-rated show. How can that suddenly mean nothing? How can I suddenly be worth so much less?

"But you know nothing's done, no decision has been made. You said Glenn was just testing the water."

I put the car into park, turn off the engine. My street's narrow and dark without my headlights. My head aches and I press my fist to my temple to stifle the pain. "I don't want to share the job with anyone. It's *my* job, *my* show."

I realize that sounds arrogant, but I'm on call 24/7. When I'm not taping a story, I'm researching, writing, following up on leads. And when it's not *America Tonight*–related, I'm usually speaking somewhere to some group. My speaking schedule just gets busier, too. Everyone wants to hear my story, how I'm a veritable phoenix from the ashes.

People can't get enough of my life story. American girl achieves the American dream. Only I'm not your typical American girl. My father was American, but my mother was South African, and I was raised in South Africa. It's where my mom and dad settled after they married. It's where home once was.

But the public knows nothing about my childhood. They just see the face on TV, hear the accent I've developed, and they embrace me. I could be them. One day I was just a lifestyle reporter for a paper in Tucson, and then months later I was host of a new national television show. That's the Cinderella story the public loves, rags to riches, nobody to somebody.

"If it does come to job sharing," I continue flatly, "I don't want to share the job with a woman ten years younger than I am who will just make me look even older by comparison."

"That's a good point. But it sounds like they're serious about improving the ratings—"

"Oh, they are. I don't doubt that. But there have to be other options. We haven't even discussed those. Glenn didn't seem interested in those. But I suppose I could look into getting some work done." My voice cracks. "Or we could bring on a co-host who's not a younger woman. Maybe we bring on a younger man. All I know is, it can't be Shelby. I can't lose my job to my protégée."

I don't sleep well that night. I toss and turn and strategize. If there's anything I've learned from being orphaned at fourteen, it's that only the strong survive. Punching my pillows, I vow to survive. I will survive.

I just need a plan.

The next morning, brittle with fatigue, I arrive at the studio's conference room at eight fifty-five with my hair still damp and my new Paris mug filled with coffee. Every morning, the writers and producers meet for an hour to plan the day's show, but Fridays are big planning sessions and I usually attend those.

Although I'm five minutes early, most of the team has already arrived. I sit at my place at the end of the board table. Glenn always takes the opposite end, and the writers and segment producers take seats in between.

I chat with the staffers sitting around the table. Mark, Jeffrey, and Libby have been with the show several years. Harper's been here only two months. Glenn's the only one missing. And then he arrives. With Shelby in tow.

What's Shelby doing here?

I stiffen as they enter the room, my shoulders tensing. Glenn looks like his harried, rumpled self, while Shelby is immaculate in a pink Chanel-style suit, her sleek blond hair a shade lighter than the last time I saw her.

Shelby spots me, wiggles her fingers, and smiles.

"Good morning, everyone," Glenn greets us as he pulls forward one of the empty chairs so it sits next to his. He rolls out the chair for Shelby. She gives him a grateful smile. I try not to throw up in my mouth.

Glenn looks at me. I hold his gaze. He doesn't appear the least bit apologetic, which just makes me angrier.

When I flew out to Paris a week ago, I was on cloud nine. I felt strong and successful, beautiful and invincible. I had a young, hot boyfriend. An exciting life. A challenging career.

It was all a mirage.

Glenn starts the meeting right away. But it doesn't take long for me to feel the strongest sense of déjà vu. I swear to God we just do the same stories over and over, even though the writers and producers change.

Does Katie Holmes feel too much pressure as Mrs. Tom Cruise?

Is Nicole Richie starving herself again?

Is Angelina adopting again?

Instead of listening, I find myself watching Shelby. On the surface she's sweet and glamorous, always immaculate, hair and makeup constantly camera ready. She's obviously a lot smarter than I gave her credit for, because she's here, in my show planning session, and she's the one who execs want to co-anchor with me.

Just thinking about the proposed change in format makes my chest squeeze tight. I'm feeling so much anxiety and fear, it's hard to breathe. Why didn't Glenn tell me just how bad the ratings were before? Why didn't Max insist on getting those numbers? I used to study the reports all the time. It was the first thing I did when I arrived in the morning. But I've gotten comfortable. I've lost that edge that made me hungry like Shelby.

"Tia?" Glenn prompts. "I like the idea. What about you?"

I try to remember what Mark was talking about before Glenn's question, before I zoned out. What was it?

The lesbian prison wedding scandal. Right.

"Do we really need to do this story?" I ask, keeping my tone friendly because I don't want to step on Mark's toes, and Mark is very tight with Shelby. But really, lesbian prison wedding scandal? "I can't help but think it's too *National Enquirer* for us. We are news—"

"Human interest news," Mark jumps in, protective of his story. "And this is colorful. Six guards have been disciplined, and two of those might lose their jobs. And then there are the brides—they've been separated, punished, because prisoners are forbidden to have sexual relations with each other."

It's all I can do to not shudder. "I think it's beneath us," I try again. "It turns my stomach."

"It's a good story," Mark says defensively, "and with the right tease we'd get a huge audience."

"I love it," Shelby interrupts. "Can I do it?"

I don't even try to hide my shock. "Are you serious, Shelby?"

"Why not?" She shrugs. "It's heartwarming."

"It's not heartwarming. It's bizarre, and we'd only be running it for shock value. If we want real human interest stories, I have plenty I'd like to do—"

"Like one of your feel-good stories that touch the heart?" Mark asks sarcastically, getting a laugh from everyone.

"Which our viewers need a lot more than sensationalistic pieces like lesbian weddings and prison scandals." I check my tone, soften my voice. "How will this benefit anyone? Will our viewers feel more empowered? Happier? More at peace?"

"We're not a yoga center," Mark says, tapping his pen impatiently. "And if viewers want to be uplifted, enlightened, or empowered, they can head to *The Seven Hundred Club.*"

"It's all about ratings," Shelby adds as though I'm an intern and she's here to show me the ropes.

I smile, although on the inside I'm anything but sunny. There is no way in hell I will share the anchor position with this woman. I turn to Glenn. "I don't want to do this story on my show."

"I already said I'll do it." Shelby's giving me the same smile I just gave her. The gloves are off. She's not my protégée anymore. She's my competition and she's gunning for my job.

"Thanks, Shelby, but as you know, the weekend show isn't in trouble," Mark replies. "We're all here trying to figure out how to save Tiana's ass."

The conference room falls silent. Everyone looks at Mark and then Shelby and then Glenn. But not one person looks at me.

The silence stretches, endless. Jeff coughs. Shelby studies her nails. Harper shuffles paperwork. And I stare at Mark until he finally turns to meet my gaze.

"What was that?" I ask quietly.

He rolls his eyes. "Oh, come on, Tiana. Your numbers have been crap all year and you know it—"

"Glenn, may I have a word with you?" I say, interrupting

Mark and looking at him hard. "Everyone, can you give us five minutes?"

Glenn doesn't speak, but everyone's on their feet and heading for the door. I may have lackluster ratings, but I still have clout. I wait for everyone to file out.

"Glenn, what's going on?" I demand as the door closes. "What is Shelby doing here?"

"The execs thought it'd be a good idea to have her sit in, get familiar with the weekday format."

"Why?"

"We had this conversation last night."

"Yes, and last night you said nothing had been decided, which made me believe an offer hadn't yet been made."

"Not officially, no."

My stomach's in knots again. This is bad, and it's getting worse. "So what's the unofficial word?"

Glenn holds my gaze. We have this odd love-hate relationship, and it's been this way for the past six years. He's good at what he does. "You can't carry the show anymore."

"So that's it? I'm toast?"

"You're not toast."

"I am if you haven't even given me a chance to address the problems and you've turned control over to someone else—"

"We need input."

"Great, then come to me. Talk to me. Ask me. Instead you've spent months telling me everything's fine, when nothing's fine. You insisted it was temporary, a blip, and even though I asked if we could sit down and brainstorm some ideas, you said no, not to worry." I swallow hard. "But I should have worried." I realize now how irresponsible it was not to worry.

Why did I stop being proactive with my career?

Why did I think I was secure?

Glenn leans back in his chair. "You don't like the party piece, or the prison wedding scandal. You don't like the stories that the viewers do."

"What happened to real news, Glenn? We don't even attempt news stories anymore."

"America loves its celebrities."

"And children love sweets. But that doesn't mean we let babies eat only candy."

He smiles.

"Glenn, do you know how long it's been since we did a really interesting story? One that made people feel? One that made people care?"

"Is this about your Alicia Keys profile again, because I did run it by the heads, but they don't think a story about antiretroviral medicine will help the ratings."

"You didn't even let me present the idea."

"AIDS stories overwhelm your average American."

"It might overwhelm us, but it's killing Africa!"

He just looks at me.

"Glenn, we'll run stories on how young Hollywood parties, but we won't show Alicia Keys's involvement with Keep A Child Alive, a nonprofit that's saving lives?"

"It sounds bad, I know."

"It is bad. Come on, fight with me on this one. What about a show for Christmas or the New Year featuring celebs with heart? Stars who are involved with life-changing charities, and we'll run one story every day leading up to Christmas."

"Would it be bouncy? Fun?"

"There was a time we had an award-winning show and

produced award-winning stories." I'm referring to the Emmy Awards that Glenn and I both earned four years ago after doing a story on the heartbreaking decline of a former A-list star. No one knew where he'd gone, but after a tip, I tracked him down in Camarillo. The former star, a man who'd made thirty films over twenty years and won an Oscar and been nominated for three, had been abandoned, penniless and senile. His children, named custodians of his estate, dropped him off at the home and that was the end of that.

Until I showed up with my cameraman and microphone.

"Let's do good stories again, Glenn." I clasp my hands together. "Let's not be like the other shows. Let's be what we're meant to be."

Glenn's smile fades and he looks at me for a long moment. "Are you not happy here anymore, Tiana?"

I shift impatiently. Life isn't black or white, it's full of shades of gray. "Of course I'm happy—"

"Then let's stick with the format that earns us the best ratings, which means Hollywood banter and celeb chatter."

Meeting over, I head downstairs to the Starbucks in the lobby for a proper cup of coffee. Usually Madison offers to run down for me, but I need to get out for a few minutes, get some air. Hollywood banter and celebrity chatter. Oh, my God. Is this what I aspired to be?

I can't even imagine Keith's reaction to the stories we do. Lesbian prison wedding scandals. The best bikini bods. Reality TV stars.

He'd say it was crap. And I agree. We weren't always so soft on real news. It's only lately, as we try to keep up with the other shows. But I think we can do both—Hollywood gossip and human interest stories. People enjoy both. The human interest stories just have to be good.

Grande soy latte in hand, I'm crossing the gleaming glass-and-marble lobby, passing the kiosk that serves as a newspaper stand, when a magazine cover jumps out at me.

COUGAR HUNTING!

The magazine's caption screams in huge lurid yellow font. But it's not the caption on the glossy cover that grabs my attention. It's the photo. It's Trevor and me.

I stop in front of the newspaper stand and stare at the cover and wonder how in God's name did they have our Paris pictures on the cover already? It should be impossible to have our photo on a magazine before I've even unpacked.

But there we are, in Paris, both of us dressed in black. It's raining and I'm holding a red umbrella and he's smiling down into my face and I'm smiling up at him. The photo's cropped, but I know exactly where we're standing. We've just left Stresa after dinner, and my hair is pinned up and loose bits are falling around my face. I'm wearing big gold gypsy earrings, and I look so happy that it makes my chest hurt.

I nearly pick up the magazine, intrigued by this smiling, beautiful couple who have actually very little to do with me.

Is that what I look like? Am I really that happy?

It's strange to see me look like that. It's not how I feel on the inside. It's not who I am anymore. Haven't been happy like that since Keith died.

For a moment I'm lost, trying to remember what truly happy feels like, trying to figure out if I even miss happy, when an arm reaches past me, bracelets jingling, and takes a copy of *Us Weekly* and then scoops up an issue of *Life & Style*, which also has a photo of Trevor and me on it, but this one screams, SHE'S GOT IT ALL!

I keep my head averted as the girl pays for her magazines.

So this is what I've become. Tabloid fodder. In some ways, it's funny. Not that Keith would find it funny, or my family. My father was an American intellectual living abroad. My mother was a brainy South African beauty queen. They raised us kids apart from society, teaching us to be different, to think for ourselves, to question people and systems. Maybe that's why I fell for Keith. He reminded me of my dad. Both wanted to change the world. Both died too young.

I glance at my watch, wondering if I should call Trevor and alert him that our Paris rendezvous made tabloid news. It's eight hours' difference between L.A. and Nice right now, so he should be done with work and back in his hotel room.

Back at my desk, I punch in his number and wait to see if he'll answer.

As the phone rings, I tell myself everything's fine between us. Just because we've talked only once since I've returned from Paris doesn't mean there's a problem. We're both just busy. And he's a twenty-six-year-old man co-starring in a movie with Kiki Woods, Hollywood's sexiest, wildest starlet.

And then he answers. "Good morning, beautiful," he says, yawning. "What's new?"

I don't know if it's his yawn or his voice, but I smile. He is hunky if nothing else. Hazel green eyes. Dark blond hair. A lock falling forward, giving him a distinctly James Dean appearance. These last six months we've had a good time—he's fun—but we'll never be serious. There's too much distance between us, never mind the twelve-year age difference. "You're dating a cougar, you know," I say.

"That's right. We're on some magazine covers."

"You heard?"

"Max called me."

Of course Max would. Max represents both of us, and he was the one who brought us together during the Cannes Film Festival last May. We were all attending the same party, and Max walked Trevor over to meet me. It's the thing managers and agents and PR people do, but I don't think even he expected us to begin a six-month romance. Trevor is, after all, a young hunk in Hollywood. He's the type I interview, not the type I sleep with, but here we are approaching the holidays and we're together still.

Not that we actually spend all that much time together, as Trevor's usually away filming.

"So how do we look, Tia?"

It's been a year since I made the cover of a national magazine, and I barely remember the details. But the first time. I'll never forget that. A photographer snapped a picture of me lying on Keith's coffin at his funeral. I was inconsolable. The next week, the photo ran on the front page of *Newsweek*. I was still a newlywed, and suddenly my very private grief became part of popular American culture.

Excruciating.

Worse, the photograph continued to show up everywhere. I couldn't go online without seeing it at MSN. Couldn't turn on the TV without hearing it discussed on *The View*. Overnight I became a national figure. Because my beloved husband, Pulitzer Prize–winning journalist Keith Heaton, was dead. Shot by a sniper in Afghanistan.

"Darling, you still there? You haven't fallen asleep on me, have you?"

I put a hand to my eyes. Although dry, they burn. I can see Keith—the gleam in his eye, that cocksure smile of his. He was brave, so brave, and so foolish. I once loved his bravado. His sense of immortality. He was larger than life, and it enchanted me. Nothing would happen to Keith. Nothing could. And because of that I learned to live larger, too, taking risks I never would have taken before. But now those risks appear to be backfiring. Everything I worked so hard for is about to be yanked away. I could lose everything all over again.

Eyes stinging, chest burning, I take a deep breath and then another. Dammit, I don't want to feel this way. I hate feeling this way. Too much of my life has been sad. Too much of my life has been spent grieving.

"Not asleep," I answer huskily, sitting upright and struggling to inject some life into my voice, even as I remind myself that covers of magazines must be heady stuff for Trevor. He's young and he's hungry for fame. "You look like a movie star."

Madison, my assistant, pops into my office. "Hey, cougar," she mouths, dropping yet another magazine on my desk. It's one I haven't seen before, *Star*, and they've got the same shot of Trevor and me, and this one's headlined COUGAR ON THE LOOSE!

I glance up at Madison and roll my eyes. She reaches up to claw the air like a big cat.

Shaking my head, I try to push away the magazine, but she opens it up instead to a two-page spread with more photos from our weekend. Trevor and me cuddling on the Seine riverboat. A photo of us lip-locked in the rain. Another shot of us disappearing into our hotel.

It's so weird, because I never saw one camera this trip. I

didn't feel anyone's eyes, didn't feel much of anything except pleasure that I was out of L.A. and in Europe and just free. Free to be a kid. Free to play.

But now my weekend in Paris has been turned into a celebrity photo spread with saucy captions.

"Trevor, something's come up. Can I call you back in a few minutes?"

"I'm heading out for the evening, but why don't you try me before you go to bed."

"Okay. Have fun."

Off the phone, I hand the magazine back to Madison. "Keep it or I'll toss it. I'm not interested."

"Don't you want to see what they say?"

"I saw enough."

"There are more photos, too, on their Web site." She pauses, then growls, raking the air with another imaginary claw. "Cougar."

"Madison, you're fired." I make a shooing motion. "Now go away."

She just laughs and opens the magazine again to read aloud, "Who's Purring Now?" She pauses to look down at me. "Hollywood hottie Trevor Campbell and veteran entertainment anchor Tiana Tomlinson continue their romance in the City of Love. With displays of affection like this, can the pitter-patter of little cubs be far behind?" She stops reading, looks at me. "Cute."

"It's revolting and you know it."

"You have to appreciate how hard they're trying to run with the cougar theme."

"No, I don't." I grimace, seriously nauseated by the piece. "Now do go away before I do fire you."

"You won't fire me. I'm your Valium. I keep you sane."

"Uh, not right now."

Madison leans over my desk, plants the open pages in front of me. "You have to admit he is yummy. Look at him—"

"*Madison.*"

"Everybody says he's the next Brad Pitt." She straightens, snatches back the magazine. "Oh, and what I came to say was that Glenn wants to see you."

I'm instantly on guard. I've already had one tense meeting with Glenn. I'm not ready for another. "Why?"

Her thin shoulders shift. "Why do you think?"

"Why don't you just tell me?"

"He wants to know why every magazine and show is running this story but us."

My phone buzzes and I pick up. Madison waves good-bye and I watch her leave, noticing she's leaner than ever.

When Madison first started interning at the station two years ago, she was your typical midwestern college grad: smart, honest, earnest, and hardworking. She also looked like a healthy, normal American twenty-one-year-old. After two years in L.A. her hair is blonder, straighter, and she's lost probably twenty-five pounds. Five, ten pounds ago I complimented her on her transformation, but now she's just skinny. Not good. L.A. already has too many bobble heads.

The call is from Andrea, Glenn's personal assistant. "Yes, Andrea?"

"Glenn wants to know why you're not already in his office," Andrea announces cheerfully. "He said to tell you that no woman makes him wait the way you do."

"Tell him it's good for him." I take a deep breath, inject warmth into my voice. "And let him know I'm on the way."

I grab a bottle of water from the break room and head for Glenn's office. His door is open, and he motions for me to sit down.

"I want to run the story and photos, Tia," Glenn says without further preliminaries. "He's hot, you're ours, and everyone else is talking about your trip. Why can't we?"

Good old Glenn. Tall, thin, with curly graying hair, he's smart and tough and a great producer. But it's not his life he's wanting to put on the seven o'clock show.

I cross one leg over the other. "Because it'd be like discussing your daughter's sex life on TV, Glenn." I smile sympathetically. "It's just not right."

"Trevor's not my daughter."

"And I know I'm not your daughter, but where are our ethics? Journalists aren't supposed to make the news, they report the news." I lean back in my chair, smile pleasantly. Glenn's an old bat, but we've been through a lot in the past six years, not the least being his son's suicide and his wife's battle with ovarian cancer. Thank God he still has his girls. The twins are twenty and smart and loving, and they completely dote on Dad. "But I'm feeling generous, Glenn. We can make a deal. You keep Shelby off my show and I'll agree to gush a bit about sexy import Trevor Campbell."

"Can't make that deal, but I do want to run with some Paris romance on today's show."

Clutching my bottle of water, I close my eyes, hold my breath, and tell myself I'm not a sellout. This is business. This is what I have to do to stay alive.

And then I think about the show idea I've been working on these past few months in my free time. A show profiling extraordinary women, women with courage, strength, passion, and heart. Those women have to matter. Real women must matter.

Jaw set, I look at Glenn. "Will there ever be a place for real human interest stories in our format again? Or are those days long gone?"

"I don't see those stories working with the new format, no."

My heart sinks. Not just a proposed co-host, but a new format, too. I can't believe it's all changing so quickly. I can't believe I have so little control. "What is the new format?"

"Hollywood buzz, high energy, lots of fun."

"But we do that already."

Glenn looks at me from beneath his bushy brows. "And you don't like it. If you had your way, we'd be CNN and you'd be Anderson Cooper."

He's right, and I wrinkle my nose. "Would that be such a bad thing?"

"Not if you were a man on a news program. But we're not the news, we're entertainment, and we've got to entertain the folks, Tia, and that's the part you have a hard time doing."

But I didn't always. "I'm still fun," I say without too much conviction.

"Maybe it's time you took a break. Did something different for a while—"

"No." I get to my feet, give him a tight smile. "I don't want to leave and I don't want a break. This is my home."

Home, I find myself repeating during the taping of tonight's show. Home. A sensitive topic for me.

I was fourteen when everything changed. Fourteen when I learned that life is precarious and death just a shadow beyond our doorstep. We'd just spent the day at the beach and were driving home. I was mad at the time, I forget why, and wasn't talking to anyone. But I remember being mad, remember saying over and over beneath my breath that I hated them all, that I couldn't wait to grow up and move away, that I couldn't wait for my real life to begin.

And then in one instant it all changed. In one instant I lost them all—Mom, Dad, Willow, and Acacia. Willow, sixteen and the oldest of us, was at the wheel, but they say the accident wasn't her fault, that it was the other car that swerved into our lane. I can't help thinking though that if Dad had been driving he might have had better instincts. He might have braked or swerved the other way instead of plunging off the road and down the cliff.

I also can't help thinking that if I hadn't been so mad, if I hadn't said I hated them, if I hadn't wanted another life to begin, they'd all be alive today.

"Tia, thirty seconds," Kevin, the floor director, calls out.

I blink, look up, returning to the set and the teleprompter and the next segment I'm introducing.

My heart aches, the old grief swamping me, pulling me back down. Grief is my biggest enemy. I've spent too many years missing. Missing my family. Missing my husband. Missing me. Hating me. Won't go there again.

My head lifts, and I smash the sadness, smash the emptiness, smash all the bad feelings. Good feelings, I tell myself, good thoughts.

Marta's Eva, who makes me laugh. Hiking with Christie in the canyon. Shey's gorgeous Texas drawl.

Good feelings. Only good feelings.

But God, it's hard. It's hard when I'm so afraid it's all about to be taken away again and I can't let it happen, I can't. I'm done losing in life. I'm done hurting. I'm done feeling numb and dead and empty. *America Tonight* is all I have. It's all I am. Don't they see that? Don't they get that?

Kevin holds up a card. Ten seconds.

Ten seconds and I'm falling apart. Can't fall apart. I'm Tiana Tomlinson.

I force a smile despite the gritty sensation in the back of my eyes and the raw panic burning in my throat. Smiling that fierce white smile, I drag the good in and up, from the tip of my toes through my knees to my belly and my chest, turning on for the camera and my audience of millions. Because this is my family now. These are the people who matter and this is the place I now call home.

Chapter Three

✦✦✦

I'm meeting Celia Ramirez tonight at Grill on the Alley in Beverly Hills at a quarter to six. I'm tempted to cancel, as I'm exhausted and tomorrow's going to be a nightmare with three events in one day. But I can't cancel on Celia. We're friends, but she's a bit like Shelby. When with her, I'm always aware that I've got to watch my back. Too many of my relationships in this town are like that.

I arrive at Grill five minutes late because of traffic, and Celia's already at our table against the brick wall, texting furiously. A senior editor for *People*, Celia works nonstop, but that was what brought us together. We were both fiercely ambitious, and as it turned out, we both were running from our past.

Raised in Selma, California, daughter to immigrant farmworkers, Celia has worked hard to make sure Hollywood sees her beauty, not her Latina past. She's self-made, too, excelling in school, becoming the first Hispanic girl to hold all three positions—Student Body president, head cheerleader, and homecoming queen—her senior year of high school. She was offered a full scholarship to UCLA, where she promptly made the dean's list each quarter, while cheering at UCLA's football games every weekend.

I work hard, but I've never worked as hard as Celia, and

I don't think Celia would ever stab me in the back. But she might prick me with a fork. The entertainment industry is cut-throat, and a girl has to do what a girl has to do.

"Hello," I say, arriving at our table and bending down to kiss Celia's cheek. "Sorry to keep you waiting."

"No problem. I've had plenty to do." Celia finishes her text, presses send, closes her BlackBerry, and looks up at me with a smile.

Celia is beautiful. Jennifer Lopez meets Catherine Zeta-Jones beautiful. Tall, slim, olive skinned, with long thick, glossy black hair, Celia has learned to work not just the red carpet, but life itself, and I admire her for that. She's one of those women with a take-no-prisoners attitude, and in that respect, she reminds me of Marta. Marta has never apologized for being beautiful or brilliant, and maybe other women don't always immediately warm to her, but she has confidence and peace. She knows who she is, she knows what she is, and she's good with that.

I'd like to have that kind of self-acceptance, but between the pressure of my industry, where everyone's always judging and criticizing, and my own inner demons that don't let me forget what a bratty, self-centered kid I once was, it's hard to feel good about myself.

I know that growing up, all kids go through a bratty phase. But that doesn't change the fact that I was at the height of my hatefulness when my parents and sisters died. It doesn't change the fact that for years, I secretly believed it was my hatefulness that killed them.

I'm old enough now to know that's just survivor's guilt, but they did die without knowing the real me. They knew the self-ish, preoccupied me, the one who wouldn't talk, the one who didn't want to spend time with them, the one who expressed contempt every time they opened their mouths and told me what they thought.

And this is the part that haunts me.

My parents were good people. Wonderful people. And they will never know how sorry I am for being selfish and treating them as if they weren't important.

They will never know that I've worked hard to become who I am to make up for who I was then.

I know I was just fourteen, but still, I was wrong to be rude and to always act so irritated with them. I was wrong to walk away when my mom was talking to me and my dad was trying to explain things. I was wrong to tell them that I didn't love them and I couldn't wait to leave home.

But I can't even tell them that. Can't even say sorry.

"Tiana, you okay?" Celia's looking at me over her menu and her expression is concerned.

"What?" I say blankly, my chest tight and heavy. I'd still do anything if I could just make amends. I'd do anything to bring them back. And I'd do anything to have them know I love them and miss them with all my heart.

Celia gestures at my face. "You're uh, crying."

Frowning, I reach up, feel damp lashes. So I am. I had no idea. I force a smile, the smile that makes the world think I'm just so damn lucky and happy. "It's the smog," I say, nonchalantly wiping them dry. "I've had that problem all day."

The waiter appears at our table to take the order, and once he's gone, Celia's thoughts are in a different direction. "I confess I have an ulterior motive for meeting you tonight." She looks at me, one black eyebrow arching. "I wouldn't bring it up if I weren't concerned."

"What is it?" I ask, wondering if this is about Trevor and the Paris stories.

"It's your girl Shelby. Rumor's on the street that she's taking over your anchor chair the first of the New Year." Celia pauses to wave off the basket of bread the waiter has brought us. No point in having temptation sit on the table and stare you in the face. "Didn't know if there was any truth behind the talk or not."

We both know there's nearly always a kernel of truth behind gossip. Even if it's a very small kernel, and in this case, it's not so very small. "She wants it, that's for sure."

"But it's not hers?"

"Not as long as I have any say."

"Do you have any say?"

I flinch. I've known Celia too long to object to the question, but it's a hard one, and it further undermines my increasingly shaky confidence. "I don't see why I wouldn't. I'm still the host. My contract's not up until March."

Celia looks at me for a long moment and then shakes her head. "Shelby's hungry."

"I know."

"Be proactive. Don't wait for the other shoe to drop. It'll only get worse if you do."

Dinner over, I drive home, park in the garage, and enter the house through the side door. I stand in the hallway off my kitchen, clutching my briefcase. It's so quiet.

It's always so quiet.

For a moment I droop, fatigue rushing over me in waves. I can feel the weight of my computer in my briefcase, the hard adobe tiles beneath my heels, the pinch of my thin, snug bra straps. Standing there, I can feel the quiet night like arms wrapping me, holding me, and it's suffocating. Suffocating and lonely.

Keith.

For the first time in a long time, I miss him. Badly.

If only he was here. He'd know the right thing to say. He'd give me a hug, and a kiss, and tell me that everything's going to be fine. He'd remind me that I have to be a fighter, and strong. And then he'd give me another hug, and kiss me and offer to get me a glass of wine.

I try to smile but can't.

I wish he was here. I could use some Keith Heaton advice. Keith was great at giving advice. Sometimes he gave a little too much advice, and sometimes his advice was a little too black and white, but in the end, it's what attracted me and kept my respect. Keith knew what was right. And even though he was ambitious, he had this incredible inner moral compass. He was a man who couldn't be bought, couldn't be had, and that's a rare find in our society.

Throat aching, I walk slowly to the hall table and put down my briefcase and look around a house I bought for Keith and me. Of course he was dead already, but I knew he'd love this house. I could see us in this house.

I kick off my heels, one and then the other, then shrug off my coat and drop it on the back of a living room chair. Even though it's almost Thanksgiving it's a warm night, and I head for the French doors and push them open. The potted Meyer lemon tree on the patio is in bloom, and the heady citrus scent perfumes the air.

It doesn't happen very often anymore, but sometimes at night I dream Keith's still here, still with me, and then in the morning I wake and roll over, warm and happy, and it comes back to me. He's gone and he's never coming back.

Which is why I date and why I want to fall in love again. But Keith will be a tough love to replace.

He was beautiful—a blond Graeco-Roman soldier—and smart, so incredibly smart. I loved looking at Keith while he worked. I loved looking at Keith when we were sitting having coffee and reading through a dozen papers every morning. I loved watching him sleep, whether it was in bed or in his chair, where he wrote and edited. He was warm and self-deprecating, funny, heroic. The only thing he feared was not getting the story right. Not getting the truth.

He taught me more than anyone else and in the shortest amount of time. After that meeting on the side of the highway, I didn't see him again for months, until we were seated across from each other at an industry awards dinner. We were both attending the dinner with different people, and yet there we were, directly across from each other, and every time I looked up I somehow caught his eye, and every time I did, I smiled.

I couldn't help it.

There was something in his face, something gentle and intelligent, kind and loving, and the best way I can describe it is think of the actor Greg Kinnear. He had that kind of face. Open and curious and yet most of all kind.

Kind. So very kind to me. So full of love, and God knows how much I needed it. How little I've had of it. How much I still want it.

And here I am, in my beautiful little historic Mediterranean bungalow, alone. I'm so sick of alone. Which is why I've continued dating Trevor. Even though he's far away, and even though we'll never be soul mates, he makes me feel that I matter. He fills the time, if not the space. But he doesn't challenge the memory of Keith. No one does, and I suppose I've liked it that way. Keith's memory is safe. No man who enters my life can compete.

But it does limit the personal life. It means that my home is quiet. It means that I live with ghosts instead of people. Makes it tough to have a family. Or kids. Which I do want.

If only Keith had made me pregnant. If only he'd left me with a piece of him before he died.

Because I want a life that begins when I open the front door. I want voices here in my house. I want conversation and lights and activity. Hugs. Talk. Laughter.

I want.

Catching myself, I turn around and head for the kitchen, where I open the stainless steel fridge door and take a look inside. Two prepackaged meals delivered by In the Zone delivery, a Tupperware of trimmed radishes, celery, broccoli, and carrots, a bottle of pomegranate juice, and an opened bottle of white wine.

I reach for the white wine and pour myself a tiny glass. Wandering out of the kitchen, I grab my phone and dial Trevor's number. It rings five times before kicking into voice mail.

"Trevor, it's me. Just wanted to hear your voice before I went to bed." *I want to hear someone's voice before bed. I want someone to say good night to me, someone to say "I love you" to me.*

But that's not the relationship Trevor and I have. Ours isn't love. It's sex and passing time and keeping company. But that has to count for something.

More brightly, I add to my message, "I'll be up another half hour to an hour, so call me if you can. Otherwise I'll talk to you tomorrow. Night."

I hang up, sip my wine, and look out the living room's open doors to the sparkle of lights on the valley floor. I take a last sip, finishing the minuscule amount I poured myself. I never drink too much because I don't need the calories, but tonight I want the taste. I want the warmth.

And there it is again. I want. Ah, the evils of wanting. I shouldn't want.

I have more than most.

Except for love and family, I have everything.

The morning comes too early. I wake up and look at the clock. Six-fifty a.m. And then I remember it's Saturday and I have nothing to do until eight, when Dana, my trainer, arrives for my (ugh) workout.

I flop back down and tug the covers up higher, wishing I were starting the day without a workout. But there's no room for error here. Weight, face, and image must be perfect.

After ten minutes of not being able to fall back asleep, I roll over onto my stomach and reach for my BlackBerry, which has been on the bedside table charging all night. After unplugging it from the charger, I check my calendar for my weekend schedule, which I already know will be crazy busy.

8:00 AM Workout with Dana

9:15 AM Fittings with Shannon

10:00 AM Hair appt

11:30 AM Baby shower brunch thrown by pal indie film-maker Christie Hern at Shutters Hotel on the beach in Santa Monica

2–5 PM Pediatric AIDS fund-raiser hosted by producer Mel Savage and his wife, Meg, at their home in Brentwood

　　7–11 PM Political fund-raiser at the Getty with a pre-party
　　　at 6 hosted by CAA king Steve Lehman at his house for a
　　　hundred of Steve's closest friends.

I could possibly sneak out of attending the political fund-
raiser—I already paid—they don't need me physically there.
But the pre-party at Steve's is important. Steve is one of Max's
closest friends and very dialed in, which means I have to go.
I'm there not for me, but to make my agent look good, so today
wardrobe and hair really matter.

But then, I think, climbing from bed, when do I have a day
when hair and wardrobe don't matter?

Dana arrives at eight on the dot, arms full of stretchy bands
and huge vinyl balls. She sets them down in the living room
and heads back to her car for her medicine ball, and I drag
my stationary bike from the hall closet (this is L.A., we don't
own a lot of coats) and unfold the treadmill that's in the living
room corner.

But back in my house, Dana swiftly shoves my sofa back and I
move the coffee table and we have our workout space.

For the next sixty minutes, I do weights and reps between
two-minute bursts of intense cardio. Sprints on the treadmill
are followed by a hundred lunges (seriously). Two minutes
cycling as fast as I can at the hardest resistance I can bear is the
precursor to forty pushups. More treadmill and then squats
with the medicine ball. More bike and then shoulder presses
and bicep curls and tricep kickbacks.

By the time she's done with me, I'm sweating profusely
and every muscle quivers. My legs shake as I push the bike
back into the closet and head for the shower. I'm still trying

to recover when Shannon, my stylist, arrives fifteen minutes later.

Years ago, I learned the value of a good stylist after choosing my own evening gown to wear on the red carpet during the pre-award interviews. I thought I looked beautiful and I felt like a princess in the salmon silk gown and with my hair curled. Instead I ended up being horribly skewered by Joan and Melissa Rivers in their post-awards fashion roundup. They mocked me for looking more like Cinderella's pumpkin carriage than Cinderella herself. My dress was the wrong color, the skirt too full, the sleeves too puffy, my hair beyond absurd. Apparently, I was the show's fashion travesty. Didn't I have a mother to dress me? Joan asked.

I don't, haven't since I was a teen, but that's not the point.

The point is, I don't have good taste. There are women with an innate sense of style, but I'm not one of them. I now employ a stylist for all appearances related to my position as host of *America Tonight*. Happily, it's an expense Max got covered by the studio in my last contract, and that's helped considerably. Best of all, I haven't been a fashion victim again, although Marta and Shey find it hysterical that I need so much help just getting dressed. In my defense, unlike them, I don't have an artistic bone in my body, which is why my bedroom is still white and my dream of a terraced garden with a pool remains but a dream.

And it is rather funny that I—who can do so much—can't get dressed without help.

As the doorbell rings, I wonder what a weekend in Los Angeles without events would be like.

Two days without hair, makeup, wardrobe. Two days without cameras and paparazzi.

Opening the door, I welcome Shannon and take a couple of the garment bags slung over her arm. Shannon's a tall, willowy redhead, a former costume designer who understands fabric and fit, two things definitely beyond my scope.

The dresses are all beautiful, but there's a clear standout, a fitted Grecian gown in an unusual hue, the color somewhere between plum and eggplant, by designer Naeem Khan, topped by a stunning thick silver collar that's so ornate it might have been worn by an Egyptian queen.

Shannon's zipping my gown, and the zipper sticks for a split second. "Suck it in," she commands.

I do and the zipper goes the rest of the way up.

"You might want to step up your cardio," Shannon suggests. "You're putting on a little weight."

So it's not just my imagination. She's noticed it, too. "I'm working out just as hard as I used to. Maybe harder."

"You're getting older. Metabolism slows. You've just got to cut back on the food."

"I hardly eat as it is!"

"No one said being thin is fun." She steps back, studies me. "I like it. What do you think?"

I pivot to face the full-length mirror and admire the way the dress hugs my curves and kicks out at the hem. "I love it."

"The fit's great and the color's gorgeous on you. What about your hair? You're leaving it down tonight?"

"I've got a blowout scheduled."

"Good. Keep it simple. Just the bangle on your wrist, and the evening bag. Nothing else."

"Got it." I start to unzip the gown and then notice Shannon is still studying me closely, a frown creasing her brow. "What?" I ask.

She hesitates. "Glenn's assistant, Andrea, called me early last week. The show wants me to start working with Shelby Patterson. Apparently she could use some help, too."

I go cold and clasp the unzipped dress to my chest. "Did you say yes?"

"It's good pay." She gives me a quick smile. "But I'm still your stylist. There's no reason I can't dress both of you."

She leaves with the extra garment bags, and I stand in my bedroom feeling naked although I'm fully clothed.

It's a familiar feeling. I've felt it at numerous times before.

Keith's funeral.

Arriving at St. Pious in Northern California at sixteen.

My first day at Epworth, the boarding school my grandmother sent me to one week after my family died.

But of all days, that day at Epworth was the worst. Epworth is in Pietermaritzburg, Natal, the most English of South Africa's four provinces. I'd never been to a boarding school before. I'd never even gone to public school or worn a uniform in my life. But there I was, still cut and bruised from the accident, in a shapeless blue cotton dress two sizes too big, wearing white ankle socks and black Mary Jane shoes. I was a week shy of fifteen and dressed like an orphan. But then I was an orphan, and my only living relative had just dropped me off at this strange boarding school, even though I'd just lost my parents and sisters days before.

I cried for months in my narrow Epworth bed, my pillow over my head to muffle my sobs.

I missed my mom and dad, missed Willow and Acacia, missed our farmhouse in Stellenbosch, missed being homeschooled by our mother, missed my father at the kitchen table, grading papers.

Missed everything. Missed everyone. Missed me.

That me, that innocent me, died with everyone else that day, and it's never come back. That me, that little girl, died in that car crash, too.

I blink and tell myself I can't feel sad, can't feel bad, can't change the past. Life happens. Even when we don't want it to.

So I do what I've done for years—smash back the memories, smothering the feelings and needs, and focus on what needs to be done. And as always, there's so much to be done. Appointments, fittings, meetings, tapings, appearances. Being Tiana Tomlinson is a full-time job.

Baby gift in the backseat of the car, I race to my blowout at Neil George, then head straight to Shutters Hotel in Santa Monica in the festive beach casual attire requested for the baby shower brunch. I had no idea what festive beach casual meant, but Shannon assured me that the outfit she selected (slim white pants, orange silk tunic with red, orange, and gold embroidery accents, and pretty gold sandals) would be chic and fun.

Fun is big right now, because I dread, dread, baby showers. I like them about as much as funerals and wouldn't be attending this one if Christie hadn't asked me.

For years I had two best friends—Marta and Shey—but Christie's snuck into my heart and managed to take up some serious real estate there along with Marta, Shey, and their children.

Christie, an independent filmmaker, and I met four years ago at the Sundance Film Festival, and what was merely a business connection has turned into a very close friendship. Christie isn't just funny and authentic, she's also unbelievably talented, and I'm a huge fan of her documentaries. She also juggles motherhood and art like no one else I know.

Traffic is light heading toward Santa Monica, but it's a traffic jam in front of the hotel as Shutters' entrance is small, snug, more like a house than a luxury hotel, and everyone seems to be arriving at once. Jaguars, Bentleys, and Rolls-Royces jockey for position as valets take keys and move cars as quickly as possible.

I use the time to check messages. Madison has sent me a few e-mails updating me on my schedule for next week, and Marta wants me to call her, as they've decided to reschedule Zach's baptism for after the holidays and they need to know when I'm free. I move from e-mail to my voice mail, and as I listen to messages I flip down the visor and open the lighted mirror to examine my face.

I have an oval face framed by thick chestnut brown hair, delicate arched eyebrows, good cheekbones, no lines at my mouth, the faintest of creases near the eyes. But there is a hint of a shadow between my eyebrows that could use a Botox touch-up.

What else? I frown at my reflection and then squint and smile, and yes, there are faint lines on my forehead. Those probably could use an injectible, too, but hell, it's a face. It's skin and muscle, and I'm not rushing out to Dr. Raj every other day. I have a standing appointment every four months, and that's enough.

Thank goodness it's my turn to hand over my car keys. I scoop up the baby present wrapped in yellow polka-dot paper and tied with an enormous yellow-and-white ribbon, take the ticket from the attendant, and head inside, wearing my favorite pair of sunglasses, a huge black Jackie Onassis style that covers half my face.

A blonde, tan dynamo, Christie spots me right away and

links her arm through mine. "Three cancellations all at the last minute," she whispers to me, "and twelve people who never even bothered to RSVP. What is that all about? Don't people know what RSVP means?"

"If you were Steven Spielberg, everyone would have RSVPed," I say cheerfully, giving her a quick hug.

"Thanks. That makes me feel a whole lot better."

"Thought so." I grin. "Who's everyone? Do I know anyone?"

"Brooke's here, and Kate Beckinsale. Nancy O'Dell and Lindy Becker as well."

"Good. I'll go mingle. Let's catch up later if we can."

I join Lindy on the patio overlooking the ocean. Lindy hosts *Hello, Hollywood,* and over the years we've worked the red carpet together. We have our favorite shows. In terms of fun, we love the Golden Globes, but the Oscars, not so much.

Lindy's talking with a woman I don't know. Not wanting to barge in, I take a moment to admire the view. Today the sky is one of those rare perfect shades of blue that happen only when the Santa Anas blow or after a hard rain. It was breezy last night, which explains this morning's gorgeous blue sky. The water itself is darker, a murkier green blue that lightens in waves to foamy white crests.

Having grown up in South Africa, I had a hard time getting used to the cold water off the California coast. The water off the cape is incredible. While growing up, we went body boarding almost every weekend in the summer months, but I don't swim here.

Lindy spots me and interrupts her conversation to include me. "Tiana, do you know Eve Frishman? She's a vice president over at Sony TV? Eve, this is my good friend Tiana Tomlinson, host at *rival America Tonight.*" Lindy hits the word *rival* play-fully hard.

I shake Eve's hand. "It's good to meet you. I've been hearing exciting things ever since your move to Sony."

"It's been busy," Eve agrees, "but it's a great fit for me."

"You've been here four months now?" Lindy asks Eve.

"Almost six," she answers. "Hard to believe. Time is moving so fast."

"I know. I can't believe how big my little girl is getting. She's not a baby anymore."

Eve looks at me. "Do you have kids?"

"No." Somehow it seems so inadequate. I always wanted kids. I never thought I'd be thirty-eight and widowed and childless. I came from a family of three. Keith and I had wanted children, too.

"That's okay," Eve says kindly. "Motherhood can be over-rated. Not every woman has to have children."

Eve's trying to smooth things over, but she doesn't know how much I want a full house, a big family, noise and love and chaos when I come home. "I do want kids. It just hasn't happened yet." My face feels warm, I feel warm. My tunic now sticks to my back and grows tight across my shoulders. "It's just turned out harder than I expected."

"Don't give up," Eve says.

"I won't," I answer jovially, when on the inside I'm scream-ing because I never planned to lose everyone I loved. I never wanted to lose my family and then my husband. I never wanted to be afraid to love again, or need again, or feel safe with some-one. It was hard enough trusting life to fall in love with Keith, but then to lose him, too... it's absurd. Beyond absurd.

A woman in a white pantsuit comes up to speak to Eve, and

Lindy takes my arm and draws me a few steps away. "I heard there's an opening on your weekend show," she whispers, her voice low. "Do you know who's leaving?"

They're advertising Shelby's job? I swallow hard, rattled all over again, and smile. It's how I cope with everything. Smile and pretend to be serene when on the inside I'm all pins and needles. No wonder I have problems sleeping.

Christie saves me from having to answer. She comes up behind me and grabs me by the waist. "Can I steal Tiana?" she asks. "I've got somebody I want her to meet."

Thank you, God.

I say good-bye to Lindy and walk with Christie back inside, whispering on the way, "You saved me, girl. I was dying back there."

"Too much mom talk?" she guesses, squeezing my hand. She's mom to three, and I've spent plenty of weekends at her house in Laguna Beach attending recitals, birthday parties, and bat mitzvahs. "You'll get your baby," she adds with another quick squeeze. "It'll happen."

That might have been my concern a week ago, but suddenly babies and my ticking clock are less relevant than keeping my job. "Lindy told me *America Tonight* is looking for new talent," I tell her as we approach a young brunette.

"Whose job is on the line?"

"I think it's mine."

"What?"

I nod. "We'll talk later."

Christie swallows her shock and introduces me to Liv, a pretty woman in her early twenties who has worked for Ashley Judd for the last year as her personal assistant.

"Liv," Christie says, "Tiana is the best news reporter in this business, and I know she'd be interested in hearing more about Ashley's involvement with YouthAIDS. I know Ashley's been the global ambassador since 2002, but I don't think the rest of the world knows how active Ashley's been with them. Maybe you can fill Tiana in?"

I look at Christie, and my heart just brims over. This is why I love the girl. She's always thinking of others, always looking out for me. In a world that can be callous and self-absorbed, Christie is a breath of fresh air. She's sunny and strong. She's creative and brave, and she's the first one to open a door, especially if it's for another woman, and for Christie I would do anything. For Christie I'd drive three hours in traffic just to watch her youngest dance for three minutes.

Two hours later, the shower winds down and Christie walks me to the lobby. "So, what's this about your job? I haven't been able to stop thinking about it since you told me. What's going on?"

"I don't know. It all just happened Thursday. Glenn pulled me into his office to talk about adding Shelby as a co-host to my show. He said my ratings are down, hers are up, and they're hoping she can lift my ratings."

Christie winces. "Ouch."

"Yeah, I know."

"Is she good? Would she make a good co-host?"

I shrug. "She's dedicated. She's already had her eyes done."

"How old is she?"

"Twenty-eight."

"Is that scary, or what?" Christie just shakes her head in disgust. "The industry's soulless."

"Unfortunately, the execs are proud of her for doing it. I think it's what they want me to do."

Understanding dawns. "They're scaring you into getting a face-lift."

"I know this happens," I say as we step outside to give my valet slip to the attendant, "but I just didn't expect it to happen to me."

We watch the valet run off to get my car. "I think that's the problem," she says after a moment. "We know intellectually we'll age, but we're still surprised when it happens to us."

That's for sure. I honestly never thought I'd get old. My mother was thirty-eight when she died—my age now—and she's forever frozen in my mind as young, laughing, beautiful. Most children find their mothers beautiful, but my mom was a true beauty queen who took second place at the international competition behind Miss Venezuela. My mother stopped men in their tracks. But to me, she was always my mother, a mother who smiled, laughed, and chased us about the garden.

"How's Trevor?" Christie asks as my car appears.

I look at her, but I'm still thinking about my mom and family, and my eyes fill with tears.

Christie sees, and she puts an arm around me. "Oh, hon, no. What's wrong?"

I shake my head. "All this talk about thirty-eight being old hits a little close to home. My mom was my age when she died—" I break off, look away, bite my lip to get control. "And the studio is making me feel old, but thirty-eight isn't old. Thirty-eight is still just a beginning."

Christie's arm squeezes my shoulders. "Do you want to come to my house for dinner tonight? I've got nothing planned. Simon's working."

"I have more events. Two more, to be precise." I reach up to hug her back. "But thank you. I appreciate the offer."

She looks at me hard. "You need fewer appearances and more downtime. You need a personal life, someone to love you. A good someone. Someone who would appreciate you. Not these ridiculous men you date—"

"Oh, Christie."

"It's true." Her eyes blaze blue fire. "You want love, need love, but the men you date are the ones you'll never love, and they'll never love you back."

"But at least this way if they die, I won't mind," I joke.

"Tiana Irene Tomlinson!"

"I'm kidding," I answer, giving her a hug and motioning to the valet attendant that I'm on my way.

Christie follows me to the driver's-side door. "But you're not kidding. That's why you date these dingbats, and they're all the same, handsome but shallow."

"Trevor's not shallow—"

"Then tell me one thing you have in common besides sex."

I slip the attendant a ten and slide behind the wheel. "He's fun?"

"My dentist would be fun if I only had to see him now and then."

"I see Trevor every five or six weeks."

"And that's not a relationship. It's casual sex."

"You yourself told me sex was beneficial."

"It'd be even more beneficial if it came with a healthy, happy relationship. Let me introduce you—"

"No!" I swiftly, firmly close the door but roll down my window. "Don't even think about another setup. Understand? I love you, but honestly, Christie, I don't like your taste in men."

Chapter Four

─────── ★★★ ───────

The fund-raiser's pre-party is at Steve Lehman's house, and his five-acre estate is high above the city in elegant, affluent, exclusive Bel Air.

There's been a breeze all day, which has blown the smog out of the valley, leaving the city glittering like white fairy lights on a Christmas tree.

Cocktail in hand, I walk slowly around Steve's enormous Grecian-style pool, which glows with a hundred floating votives. An orchestra plays beneath a white canopy as fountains tinkle and beautiful people laugh and talk and mill about while keeping an eye out for someone more important to talk to.

From the corner of my eye, I see Tom and Katie appear and be welcomed to great fanfare. Across the pool, Jessica Biel is talking to Kirsten Dunst. I knew it'd be one of those "who's who" parties, but I thought I'd find an ally before I felt insignificant.

This is where it gets complicated.

The very fact that I'm here will put plenty of stars' teeth on edge. If I were a different TV host, I'd work the party, say hello to the famous faces that I've interviewed in the past; but I can't stand it when they give me that little look. The sneer. The half-annoyed, half-pitying glance that says you don't belong.

I had enough of that at Epworth. Although I was raised in South Africa, I never had a proper South African accent, and I don't know if that was my dad's doing since he was American, but the girls at Epworth teased me for sounding like a Yank, and they made it clear that as a Yank, I was merely tolerated, not accepted.

There were times I was tempted to name-drop. I had impressive connections. The girls would have loved that my mother was a former Miss South Africa, and her mother was Lady Hollingsworth in England but dropped the title when she moved with her new husband, Lord Hollingsworth, to what was then Rhodesia. But I never did. Maybe it was the rebel in me, but I wouldn't share my past, wouldn't share my strength, wouldn't give them access to me.

My father always said I was the secretive one, but I'm not secretive. I'm just reserved. Contained. Willow was the one who wore her heart on her sleeve. She was emotional and tender, just like our mother. But just because I didn't laugh or cry as easily didn't mean I didn't feel.

I feel. I feel so deeply that it scares me.

I don't let many people in because when I do, I'm wide open. Completely vulnerable. The problem is once you're in my heart, you stay.

Even when you're dead. Even when you're gone.

Feet already aching, I scan the crowd of expensive suits and elegant gowns, and while I know many of them by sight, none are friends like Christie or Celia from *People* magazine. My friends aren't A-listers, we're the industry's worker bees, and I'm here only because of Max.

It was Max who helped me through the first year following Keith's death. After signing me to a contract, he had me move straight to Los Angeles. By the time I arrived with my car and trailer full of possessions, his assistant had found me a sunny one-bedroom apartment in a nice neighborhood in Santa Monica within walking distance of the beach.

Those first three months in L.A. were disorienting. Max knew my history, knew I had no one else, and he was always reminding me to get exercise and sleep and to make sure I ate right.

As I settled in, Max introduced me to people. Sent me to meetings and lunches. Got me invited to parties. And then came the offer. HBC was developing a new show and they needed a host. They wanted someone special, someone readers would take into their hearts, and they wanted me.

Me. Tiana Tomlinson, nobody's girl.

Six-plus years, here I am, sipping a sidecar and wearing a Naeem Khan gown on Steve Lehman's lawn. If this isn't success, I don't know what is.

"It's Ms. America," drawls a horribly familiar voice, sending a shiver down my spine.

Michael O'Sullivan. Satan himself. And yet as I turn to face him, my spirits lift ever so slightly. I've been a little too blue and introspective today, and sparring with Michael should give me something fun to do. "Hello, Hollywood."

He's smiling at me, laughing at me, as amused by me as if I were just a floppy puppy. "*Dr.* Hollywood," he corrects with a glint in his eye, looking ever so 007 in his tuxedo with his thick dark hair slicked back to a glossy shine and his jaw freshly shaven.

It really is tragic that he's this good-looking. Must fool most people into thinking he's likable. I like that I find him unlikable. I like that I can resist him. Too many women can't. The man's far too popular in this town for his own good.

"Have you recovered yet?" he asks, rocking back on his heels. "Or are you still licking your wounds?"

"I'm licking nothing, Dr. O'Sullivan."

A tiny muscle pulls in his jaw, and I see a flash of white teeth. "Then perhaps you need a good licking."

I blush deeply, my face burning from my collarbone to my hairline. "Dr. O'Sullivan!"

"I love that frosty tone. You do it so well."

I tell myself I hate him. I tell myself he's the worst company in the world, but my heart is beating a little too hard to believe that. "Don't you have a date somewhere needing your attention?"

Laughter lurks at the corners of his mouth. "She's getting me a drink."

"How chivalrous of you."

Light flickers in his dark eyes, and I realize his eyes aren't dark brown but the darkest shade of blue. No one has eyes that color. They must be colored contact lenses, which makes me think that he must have done other things. O'Sullivans don't have chins like his, or nearly perfect noses and jaws, either.

"As a plastic surgeon, you're an advocate of plastic surgery." I pause. "Have you had work done yourself?"

"No, I haven't. Are you considering work?"

"That wasn't my question."

His lashes lower as his gaze scrutinizes my face and then drops even lower to take in my body. It's a slow inspection, his gaze traveling ever so leisurely over my breasts and then down my waist to my hips and to the thighs. I grow hot beneath his inspection but hold still, unwilling to turn chicken now.

His lashes lift and he looks into my eyes. "Are you asking for my professional or personal opinion?"

I flush hotter. "Why would I want your personal opinion?"

The very air seems to sizzle as he looks down on me. "Why wouldn't you?"

This is my cue to leave. I ought to spin on my heel the way heroines in my beloved Mills & Boon romances used to do. But I don't. I'm foolish and proud and reckless, and I stand there, chin up. "I do not find you attractive. I am not impressed by your money. And I loathe plastic surgeons."

He looks down at me, and then he smiles a slow, wickedly provocative smile. "But you do like my body."

For a moment I'm speechless. I don't know what to say. He's horrible and impossible, and my heart races too fast. "Goodbye, Dr. O'Sullivan."

"It's Michael, to you."

I give him the dirtiest look I can and then walk away briskly to the other end of the glowing Grecian pool, where floating candle boats gleam on the aquamarine surface. My heels sink into the lawn, and I can feel the weight of soil cling to the high, lean spikes. I hate him. I hate him. I hate him. And yet I could have kissed him, which makes no sense, especially as I hate him so very much.

Tucking my tiny clutch bag, I struggle across the lawn, wishing I'd stuck with the flagstone pool deck, wishing my shoes weren't so high, wishing I hadn't been on my feet all day. But most of all wishing Michael didn't affect me like this. He makes me too aware of me, the real me, the one who isn't hair and makeup. The one who lost her family at fourteen. The one who lost her husband at thirty. The one who's worked relentlessly since then to not feel, want, need, dream.

But he makes me feel. No man other than Keith has made me feel. And that scares the hell out of me.

After another hour at Steve's, I text my driver. I have two drivers and they're both named John, but tonight it's Russian John and I let him know that he can pick me up now.

Once I'm in the back of his limo on the way to the Getty, I check my phone. Trevor called. I missed his call. I try him, but now I go to voice mail.

In the dark I close my eyes, press fingers to my brow, and stifle the rush of longing.

I could have handled being a widow better if I'd been married longer. I could have handled being a widow if I'd had a baby.

Christie's right. I am too alone. If I'm not on camera, I'm off at events, and with Trevor so far away I attend most of those on my own.

The bottom line is that this long-distance thing isn't working. I'm too lonely and am just getting emptier by the day. I need to talk to Trevor, but I'm not good at sharing feelings. Which might be one reason I'm a reporter. I ask the questions. I don't have to answer them.

We're climbing Getty Center Drive, and it's a steep climb to the top of the mountain, where the sleek, stark Getty Center was built ten years ago.

I'm not easily awed by theatrics anymore, but my breath catches as I step inside the museum's largest exhibit hall. The museum's glass, marble, and metal surfaces have been transformed by floor-to-ceiling tents, with the billowy fabric sheathing the walls. I'm no longer in a modern museum, but outside in the middle of a Sonoran desert sunset.

Keith loved the desert. Tucson. Morocco. Afghanistan. He'd get a kick out of this, I think.

I spend the next hour working my way around the room,

making cocktail conversation. Familiar to nearly everyone, I have plenty of people to talk to, and I'm happily surprised when dinner is announced.

Gown swishing, I thread my way through the tables with their deep violet cloths and glowing candlelight, looking for Max's table, dazzled all over again by the decor. The fabric walls capture the undulating hills of the desert shadows while the fabric ceiling is that of a soft night sky.

Max spots me before I see him. He lifts an arm, signals to me. He's been in conversation with his wife and another couple but breaks away to speak to me.

"Love the dress," he says, giving me a kiss on the cheek.

"Thank you. If only my feet weren't killing me."

He glances around the table until he finds my seat. "Here you are. Seated between Greg Breese and Alex Frost."

He pulls out my chair for me, and with a grateful sigh I sit down, setting my little black clutch on top of my plate. It's been a long day on my feet.

"Enjoying yourself?" Max asks.

"It'd be more fun with a date," I admit.

"Too bad Trevor couldn't be here."

Trevor's attended only one event with me in the six months we've been seeing each other, so it's difficult to imagine us as a couple despite the media frenzy of the past few days. "It's a gorgeous party. Clever to do a wildlife conservation theme. Reminds everyone that Democrats care about the environment."

"So how is he?" Max persists.

"He's fine."

"Yeah?"

What else does Max want me to say? What does everyone

want me to say? Trevor is sexy. Trevor has gorgeous hair. Trevor has a muscular body. Trevor has six-pack abs. And Trevor lives in London. He flies to L.A. every couple of months, but usually it's me doing the flying around, me putting the stress on my body. Truthfully, I'm tired. I've been tired for a long time, and I'm not sure I can keep up this lifestyle. "Yeah."

Max drums his fingers on the table. "You like him?"

Yes, I like him. But he's not Keith. He's definitely not Keith, and I want to find a Keith. Someone I can fall in love with again. Someone I can believe in again. But I suppose to do that I have to stop dating men who live thousands of miles away. "Yes, Max."

"Good. When do you see him again?"

"I don't know. As you're aware, he's on location in France. I work here. It's not an easy commute."

"So you're going to leave him alone with Kiki?" Max asks shrewdly, knowing, as I do, that Kiki has a reputation for seducing her co-stars.

"Max, I have a career, too. A career that might be in trouble—"

"Yes, and Trevor's good for you."

What Max really means is that Trevor has upped my fair market value. I'm a hotter, more exciting commodity with Trevor attached to my name.

So maddening. So L.A. But also so true.

Dinner is finally served at nine o'clock. Everyone has taken their places at our table save for two, and I'm delighted when the salad course appears. I have never in my life been so happy to see field greens with beets and crumbled feta cheese.

The empty chair next to me scrapes back, and heads lift at our table, everyone pausing to welcome the final couple, Alex

Frost and his date—only Alex isn't a man. Alex is a very tan, very sexy blonde, and Alex's date is none other than Michael O'Sullivan.

Lightning, apparently, can strike twice. Lucky me. Alex takes the chair next to the gentleman on her right, leaving the chair to my right empty, which means Michael and I are going to be sitting next to each other for the next couple of hours.

How is this possible?

I detest this man, yet he keeps turning up everywhere that I am. And of course his date, Alex Frost, is a voluptuous blonde poured into a red beaded gown with a keyhole opening at the sternum, showing the firm magnificence of her breasts.

"I'm sorry we're late," Michael apologizes to the group as he helps Alex with her chair. "Alexis was paying homage to Jessica Simpson's hairdresser."

Is he serious? Or is this a joke? But Alex beams. "I adore Ken Pavés," she says.

I guess he was serious.

"She's a huge fan of his work," Michael says, grinning, as he sits next to me.

"We're just glad you're here," says Irene, Max's wife. "As I'm a huge fan of your work."

Irene explains to the table that Michael is Dr. O'Sullivan, the renowned Beverly Hills plastic surgeon. "I owe everything to Dr. O'Sullivan," she adds, holding out a slim, bejeweled hand to Michael. "A couple years ago he gave me my pre-baby body back, and then this year he erased the ravages of time."

Max catches my gaze across the table and gives me a significant look.

He deliberately put Michael and Alex next to me. Max is hoping that by putting me close to Michael O'Sullivan, surgeon to the stars, I'll suddenly find plastic surgery less offensive.

I shake my head at Max and look away, catching Michael's eye instead.

"Lucky us," Michael murmurs, taking his napkin from beside his plate and spreading it on his lap. His arm bumps mine, sending little frissons of feeling up my arm and down my spine. My chest constricts and I take a quick, surprised breath.

Why does he do this to me? I don't like him. I don't want to like him, but he has so much energy, such vitality, that I can't help but be aware of him.

"Someone's laughing somewhere," I answer flatly, trying to ignore the way his body takes up all the space, trying to ignore the way my body responds to him. Not even sexy Scottish Trevor makes my skin feel hot and my nerves scream. I shuffle to my left to put more space between us.

Michael notes my sideways maneuver. "Uncomfortable?"

"Not at all," I lie.

He muffles a laugh and leans toward me, his tuxedo-clad shoulder nearly brushing mine. "You remind me of my favorite Sunday school teacher, Miss Littleton," he says softly, his voice pitched so low that I feel as if he's telling me something very serious. "She was twenty-one and beautiful and very, very virtuous."

He pauses, dense lashes lifting, revealing those deep blue eyes that aren't natural at all. "And then she ran away with the priest Father Flaherty." Michael clucks. "Tragically, Father Flaherty was excommunicated."

"And what happened to her?" I ask, curious despite myself.

"She became Mrs. Flaherty and had five little Flahertys."

I don't know if it's the hint of an Irish brogue in his voice or the glint in his eyes, but I blush. "That's not a true story."

"It is. Every word of it."

Alexis suddenly wants to be part of our conversation, and she laces an arm through Michael's and leans across him. "What's not a true story, darling?" she asks, her blue gaze fixed on me.

In her mind I'm competition.

If only I could tell her I loathe her man.

"Father Flaherty and his five little Flahertys," Michael answers with a half-smile.

She frowns, arched eyebrows flattening. "I don't understand."

Michael introduces us instead of attempting to explain. "Alexis, this is Tiana Tomlinson. Tiana and I were on the Larry King show Thursday night. Tiana, this is Alexis Frost, an expert on cosmetic surgery."

Obviously, I think.

Alexis looks at me critically. "Are you considering having work done?"

I smile, but it feels brittle. "No. I'm not a fan of plastic surgery."

"Why not?" she asks.

Michael gestures to her. "We met on the show—"

"His show," Alexis interrupts. "*Dr. Hollywood.* You're familiar with it?"

This is torture. I can't believe I have to sit here next to these two for dinner. "I'm familiar with it, but I never had the chance to watch it. It was on for only a year, wasn't it?"

"Yes, but it's in syndication now." She glances at Michael. "I had a guest role on an episode. One thing led to another, and here I am."

And here she is. A work of art.

Michael's gaze meets mine. A smile tugs at his mouth. I'd love to ask him what he sees in Alexis. I'd love to ask him why he—by all accounts a brilliant surgeon—is with a blonde bimbo, but I know the answer to that. Men love beauty, even if the beauty is brainless, which means even brilliant, charismatic surgeons can be shallow.

I'm feeling very shallow the next morning when Trevor calls me and we struggle to find something to discuss other than his movie.

I'm sitting curled up on the couch with my morning coffee, sunshine streaming through the windows, the phone tucked between my chin and shoulder as I leaf through the Sunday papers while we chat.

"I can't believe it's only been a week since you left," he says. His voice is rough, and he sounds tired.

"Long week?"

"Very." He yawns and then adds with a grumble, "Sometimes I hate the long-distance thing."

"Me too."

"So when will I see you again?"

"When is your next break?" I ask.

"I don't know. We're behind schedule. Two of the producers are here this weekend, and they're tearing into the director as we speak."

"That's not going to help things tomorrow, is it?"

"No, but the money people don't care."

And just like that we run out of things to say. Again. Always. I struggle to come up with a new topic and grab at the first thing that comes to mind. "So how's Kiki?"

"Why do you ask?" His tone is less friendly now.

I try to make a joke of it. "Everybody keeps teasing me that you're on location with Kiki Woods."

"And what does everybody say?"

He's not laughing. He's angry. I swallow hard.

"What are they saying, Tiana?"

"Nothing."

"Come on, don't be coy now."

"They say she's a man stealer," I answer defiantly.

"Then they have it wrong. Kiki doesn't steal men. I don't know why you'd repeat gossip."

I close my eyes, press my fingers to my brow. "I'm sorry."

He's not mollified. "I don't know why you'd believe garbage like that."

"I was trying to make conversation. I'm sorry."

We say good-bye and hang up, and I sit for a moment feeling profoundly empty.

This is not the relationship I want. This isn't going anywhere good. I should just end it with Trevor. Break it off. Be done with it.

But if I break things off, then I'm completely single again, and I don't like being completely single. Being single means you have to start dating all over again and looking for someone new and being open and vulnerable. I'm not good being vulnerable. Not good opening up and sharing.

Don't think about it, I tell myself, reaching for the newspaper again. Don't think about Trevor or dating or men.

It's while reading the *New York Times* "Style" section that I spot an article on the rise in plastic surgery in the United States and fold back the newspaper to read the article in its entirety.

The article doesn't say anything I don't already know. A year ago, I attended the American Society for Aesthetic Plastic Surgery's annual, just after Kanye West's mom's death. I'd gone to do research for a story on our American culture's obsession with self-improvement.

The products repulsed me—chin implants, breast implants, lipo needles, sponges, drains, forceps, dissectors, retractors—but I was fascinated by the professional education offered. Workshops covered the newest medical tips and techniques, including how to up sell your "client" to generate more income.

It was a lightbulb moment for me, the realization that medicine had moved from the necessary to the elective and that doctors must not just compete but actively solicit for business.

A great plastic surgeon isn't necessarily a gifted surgeon, but a brilliant businessman.

One of the workshops I sat in on was titled "The Malpractice-Free Practice," run by a former physician who founded an insurance company for physicians. Dr. Krupp urged every physician to brush up his or her bedside manner. "Communicate," he lectured, "become a good listener. Make sure you understand what it is your client wants. Don't ever assume, and don't—whatever you do—don't play God."

Setting aside the paper, I realize I can't fight it anymore, can't relax. I need to be busy, get researching. I carry my laptop downstairs to my terrace with the wrought iron table and chairs. Thanks to wireless technology, I'm able to sit in the warmth of the sun and research everything I can on women, beauty, image, success, and self-esteem.

There's a lot to be found.

I'm still reading when the clock on my mantel strikes noon, and I suddenly feel like Cinderella about to miss her own ball as I rush into the bedroom and look for the dress Shannon suggested I wear to the Pixar film premiere. It's a chocolate shirt dress with a wide belt cinched at the waist. She accessorized it for me, too, so I throw on the wooden bangles and the gold hoops and do a quick makeup and comb through before heading out the door, where Polish John, my other driver, waits.

While John drives, I wonder if more women would have work done if they could afford it. Is the idea of being cut not as frightening to other women as it is to me?

Maybe it's time I did another piece on plastic surgery, and this time not on the industry itself, but on the impact surgery has had on women's lives.

I know the bad stuff already. I know those who've died from undergoing the knife. Kanye West's mother. Olivia Goldsmith, the novelist. Ordinary women hoping for a make-over. But there are hundreds of thousands of people who have undergone successful procedures without complications. I want to talk to those women, real women, who've had work done and find out why they did it and if they're happy with the results. Did they get what they wanted? Are their lives better now for having done it?

As the limo pulls up near the theater, I double-check my lipstick in my compact mirror and swipe a fingertip beneath each eye to catch smudged liner.

I study my reflection for a moment longer.

Would I be a different person with a different image? And who would I become if I did allow myself to age?

Chapter Five

$\star\star\star$

Max's assistant calls me Monday morning to schedule a late lunch for that afternoon. We're to meet at the Bel-Air once I'm done taping tonight's show.

It's a good choice, I think, arriving at one and handing over the keys to my car. As I head to the restaurant, I'm soothed by the myriad archways, the gurgle of fountains, and the purple bougainvillea draping from pink stucco walls. I love this hotel and stayed here for a weekend once when my house had a broken pipe. I suppose I didn't have to stay here for three nights, but it was so luxurious and I felt so pampered that I hated to go back to my empty house with moisture problems.

We eat on the Terrace with its terra-cotta pavers and elegant stucco arches. My fish entrée is perfect, and the service is superb. As my plate is cleared and the pink linen tablecloth is scraped of crumbs, I can't help wishing this was how life really was. Beautiful. Calm. Peaceful.

I wonder if this is how the public imagines my life. Glamorous. Pampered. Luxurious.

It's funny, but Hollywood is the least glamorous place I know. It's a creation for the cameras, achieved with lights and makeup and special effects. Turn off the lights, put away the cameras, and what we do becomes just another job.

"I have some good news," Max says, waving off the waiter with the dessert tray.

"What's that?"

"Last week *America Tonight* trumped its competition. Glenn just gave me a breakdown of the week's numbers, and as expected, those numbers were highest on Friday with all the tabloid press about your trip to Paris with Trevor." He looks at me, and there's a gleam in his eye. "I think the secret is keeping you and Trevor in the news."

I totally disagree but am careful expressing my opinion. "Manufacturing ratings?"

"It's done all the time."

"I know, but I haven't succumbed to a steady diet of sensationalistic news yet."

"Which is why your show needs Shelby," he answers bluntly. "She understands that this is business, and sex and scandal sell."

"So I'm to date a progression of hot young actors to keep my name in the news?"

"We can't milk the cougar thing forever. We need a long-term plan as well." He drums his fingers on the table. "I see two options. The first is a complete but discreet make-over. Face-lift, drop ten pounds, and a new wardrobe. And the second is the make-over coupled with a new show format. Partner you with a sexy young male co-host. New high-energy stories. A new fun set to showcase your youth and chemistry and sex appeal."

"You know plastic surgery scares the hell out of me. I *like* my face."

"And so do I, but I like you even better employed." He pulls out his iPhone and opens the calendar icon. "What's your schedule like? When could you schedule the surgery? It'd need to be done prior to your contract renewal. I'm thinking late December is slow, which would be ideal. You could take the last couple weeks of December off to recover and be back on the show early to mid-January. Depending on the swelling and bruising, of course."

I don't have my desk calendar here, but I can see it. The spaces are packed with dates, times, appointments. I use a huge desk calendar along with my BlackBerry to keep track of my commitments. "Max, I don't have time to pee, much less take three to four weeks off for surgery."

"You're missing the big picture here, Tia. You deserve a nice break. Think of it as a paid vacation. A spa thing."

"Spas don't hurt."

"Spas can hurt. My wife went to one—not the Golden Door, I think she liked that one—but she said it was the most miserable experience of her life. Worse than childbirth."

I arch an eyebrow. "You do know you're not helping your argument, don't you?"

He closes the calendar and reaches into his jacket pocket to retrieve a business card. "You were sitting next to Dr. O'Sullivan at the party. I noticed you didn't talk much, but I hope you got a feel for him. He's a great surgeon, one of the best, and you should at least go see him for a consultation." Max hands me the business card, and it's Michael's. "Call him, schedule an appointment, okay?"

I'm just leaving the Bel-Air Hotel when my phone rings. It's Madison on the line. "Where are you?" she asks frantically.

"Leaving the Bel-Air."

"Get here fast. The studio execs have been hanging out with

Shelby for the past half hour and now she's going to tape your tease for Wednesday's show."

"Why is she going to tape my tease?"

"I think they're testing her tease, checking numbers." Madison gulps a breath. "Tiana, what's happening? Are they replacing you?"

"No." My voice is firm, no-nonsense, belying my own inner panic. "It's just a numbers thing," I continue crisply. "It's sweeps month, so the studio heads are always looking for a new gimmick to punch the ratings up."

I'm at the HBC tower in twenty minutes, but the execs are gone by the time I arrive. Shelby has already tracked Wednesday's teases and is just stepping off the soundstage.

Shelby spots me as I enter the room and comes over to greet me. "I hope you don't mind that they asked me to tape. We had some really fun headlines, too."

She smiles, and nothing moves on her face except her lips as they part to reveal very straight, very white veneered teeth.

"What was one of the headlines?" I ask.

She smiles even more brightly and straightens her shoulders, about to deliver the line the way she would on camera. "Jamie Spears's baby already on Prozac? The doctor's orders, on the next *America Tonight*!" Her on-camera voice and posture drops and she looks at me, giggles. "Good, isn't it?"

Good? Jamie Spears's baby's on Prozac? That's the big tease for Wednesday's show? "Who wrote the headline?"

"Mark."

"But Jamie's baby is two and he's definitely not on Prozac."

"Of course he isn't." She laughs. "But it's juicy and people will tune in to hear what's happening in the Spearses' household."

And okay, this is snippy, but is this really the job I'm fighting to save?

Maybe what I need to fight to save is the show itself. Maybe it's time to take back our programming. Women, our key demographic, must want more. I know I want more.

Although I could conference call in for the nine a.m. production meeting Tuesday morning, I put in an appearance instead. With a four-day holiday weekend looming, I want to make sure everybody remembers that I'm still the host of this show and plan on remaining the host, too.

Upon arriving at the office, I find that the books I ordered on plastic surgery from Amazon are here. I take a couple of the books into the production meeting with me and pitch the idea of doing a series of stories in the New Year on plastic surgery. I tell them I'd like to interview men and women who've had work done and see if they're happy.

I draw the *New York Times* article from a folder and slide it across the table so everyone in the meeting can see. "This just ran in the Sunday *New York Times*. Cosmetic surgery is a two-billion-dollar industry and growing. So are people who are spending the money happy with their decision to get work done? Did surgery give them what they want, and need?"

"Tyra Banks just did a show like this last week," Libby answers. "Most of her guests had disastrous experiences and terrible scarring."

"But she probably solicited for the horror stories," Harper points out. "I think Tiana's wanting a more balanced view."

She looks at me for confirmation, and I nod. "That's just it.

Are most people happy with their decision? Are they not just physically, but psychologically, satisfied?"

"Is there a celeb angle?" Mark asks bluntly.

"No," I answer honestly. "I was looking at interviewing ordinary men and women, people like our viewers. In fact, I thought we could use our Web site blog and ask viewers to share with us their experiences." I glance at Glenn. "But I'm sure we could sprinkle some celebs into the piece. That would be easy, and I think that's a great idea, Mark."

Glenn nods. "I like it. Just hammer out the logistics and let me know who will handle the screening, the number of segments you intend to do, and what week you anticipate the stories running."

I smile, feeling victorious. "Will do." Finally a story I like, a story that's appropriate, and a story I vow to make good.

Back in my office, I flip through the plastic surgery books while returning phone calls. I closely study the before-and-after photos of everything from lipo thighs to breast lifts to breast reduction to eyelids and necks and full face-lifts. There are photos and surgeries for everything. Upper arms. Inner thighs. Tummy tucks. Nose jobs. Chin implants. Labiaplasty.

Labiaplasty.

My stomach churns as I read about the procedure—the prep, the recovery, the technique. Normally not squeamish, I find it difficult to look at the before-and-after photos. I can understand doing the surgery if one honestly can't walk or function, but for beauty's sake?

Is it something I'd seriously consider?

No.

Marta calls me while I'm typing up my ideas for the feature. I haven't talked to her in ages, and I sit back in my chair, happy to hear from her. "Happy almost-Thanksgiving. How are you?"

"Great," she answers, and in the background there's a loud screech. "That's Zach," she explains with a good-natured laugh. "He's discovered the joy in vocalizing."

"I can't wait to see him again."

"He's grown so much. He's a brute."

"Just like his dad?" I tease, as Marta absolutely adores her husband, Luke, who is a gorgeous specimen of a man at six feet seven, with the coloring of a Celtic warrior.

She laughs appreciatively. Marta with her long, straight dark hair is biker tough on the outside, but on the inside she's fiercely loyal and almost too tender; her children and husband are her Achilles' heel.

God, I want this for myself. A baby. A family. People I belong to. People who belong to me.

I used to think I should do what Marta did to conceive Eva and just go to a sperm bank and make a baby. But unlike Marta, I don't think I could be a single mom. I want a partner—a lover—to be there to raise a child with me.

"We have a new date for the baptism," Marta says, "but before we confirm it and invite everyone, I wanted to make sure it'd work for you since you're going to be the godmother."

I reach for my desk calendar. "What's the date?"

"The morning of Sunday, December twenty-eighth. We hoped you could come join us for Christmas and then just stay on for the baptism. That is, unless you have something else planned for Christmas...?"

Trevor flashes to mind, but I don't see us spending Christmas together. I'm not good with holidays, never have been, and I tend to spend them with friends who really know me, friends like Marta, Shey, or Christie. "December twenty-eighth sounds great, and Christmas could work, but let's leave that loose for now, okay?"

"But December twenty-eighth for the baptism is a go?"

"A definite go."

"Eva will be so glad to see you. We all miss you. Aunt T is really loved around here, you know."

I swallow the ache of emotion. "I miss you, too." And it's so true. For it's when I'm with friends who've known me forever, since we met at St. Pious when I was sixteen, that I feel the real me emerge. And the real me isn't glossy and glam, but driven and hungry and sometimes just damn confused.

Life hasn't been what I thought it'd be. I've achieved far more than I ever expected, but it feels like so much less than I wanted.

"What are you doing for Thanksgiving, Tia? You do have plans, don't you?"

For the first time I hear a note of worry in her voice, and it touches me. Marta isn't touchy-feely, but she sounds almost maternal now. Being a mom has definitely softened her edges. "Christie, my friend in Laguna Beach, has invited me to join her family for dinner. She has three girls and numerous in-laws, so it keeps things lively."

She hesitates, then adds gently, "I know it's not an easy day for you."

For a moment I say nothing, my insides hot and excruciatingly sensitive. When it comes to Thanksgiving, my heart's perpetually bruised. I got word on Thanksgiving Day that Keith had been killed.

"Seven years, isn't it?" she adds even more gently.

Marta knows these things. She and Shey were my bridesmaids. Keith and I married on Valentine's Day. It would have been eight years this coming February. Instead he died three months before our first anniversary.

For a moment I can't speak. Even now grief is huge. Loss goes so deep. It's like the ocean, vast and dark and endless. I am here, on the other side, only because Marta and Shey swam me across. "I love you, Ta," I say huskily. "I don't know what I'd do without you."

"You don't have to do without me. I'll always be here. Shey, too. You're ours."

I blink, wishing I could jump on a plane right now and fly up to Seattle for a hug. "Give Eva and Zach a kiss for me, and give my best to Luke."

"I will. And Tiana, see you soon."

After hanging up, I bury my face in my hands and squeeze my eyes shut to hold back the emotion.

I have read every book I could on grief, trying to come to terms with death and dying. People used to tell me that time would heal. Time didn't heal. Time just made me numb.

I go to the window and look out at the tidy towers and plazas of Century City and the wide boulevards below. I take a deep breath. I hate being thirty-eight and yet feeling like a child instead of a woman. I hate the fear. I hate the emptiness. I hate the inability to trust.

I don't want to be like this. I don't want to date only distant, shallow men who don't challenge me or ask for my love. I don't want to always be alone.

But if I love again, if I dare to love, I risk not just my heart but my sanity.

I can't lose anyone again. I can't go to that dark place again.

I'm not that strong a swimmer. I'm tired, and God forgive me, but this time I'd drown.

Thursday morning I don't have to go to work, as Manuel's handling the Thanksgiving show, and I close my eyes to sleep for another twenty minutes. The next time I open my eyes it's an hour later, and I'm groggier than ever. No reason to get up, I think, pulling up the covers. But then, there's no reason to stay in bed, either.

Sleepily I climb from bed, stagger into my robe, and head to the kitchen to start coffee.

While coffee brews, I turn on the kitchen TV to watch Macy's Thanksgiving parade. For three years I co-hosted HBC's parade show and it was always freezing cold, but it was also good for me as it kept my mind off the day. I don't like having time on my hands on this day.

I was worried when they didn't ask me to host the show this year. I kept waiting for them to ask, but they didn't. In the end I phoned Max and had him find out what was going on, and it turned out HBC decided to drop their parade coverage. I was relieved. I know it's spiteful, but better they drop the coverage than ask Shelby to host.

Dressing for today's Thanksgiving dinner at Christie's should be easy. It's a simple family dinner, but I struggle with what to wear, eventually settling on a brown Michael Kors blouse and pants and a turquoise, coral, and silver necklace; but then I struggle to get motivated to do my hair and makeup. I'm getting sad despite myself. I'm thinking of Keith even though I vowed not to.

I'm feeling brittle as I drive down the canyon toward the

freeway entrance. There's no traffic and the sun is hazy and my eyes burn. Seven years without Keith. Several days without a call from Trevor. Why am I seeing him? Clinging to this long-distance relationship? It doesn't work, it'll never work, but God, it's so much better than being alone.

I hate being alone.

I hate dating even more.

There's no traffic as I merge onto the freeway. Everyone's already somewhere preparing to eat turkey. This is the first year in five years I've had a proper Thanksgiving as I usually host specials or attend parades around the country.

To keep from thinking, I drive with the stereo blasting, the songs from the CD player on shuffle, and it's a hodgepodge of Aretha, Coldplay, Snow Patrol, and the original cast album from *Rent*. It takes only one song, the song "Without You" from *Rent*, to bring me to my knees.

"Without You."

I reach out to push skip but can't make myself. My song. How many times did I play this after Keith died? How many times did I cry trying to understand how life can just go on without him?

I lower my window and let the wind rush through the car. And then the song comes to an end and I hit repeat.

I drive crying. I drive letting the music unbury the grief, letting the music dust off my love.

This album is my Keith album. This is the one that reaches into my chest and rips my heart out. I shouldn't be playing it today, not now, not on my way for turkey and cranberries. But in a way I'm glad to be here, in this place, in this deep, aching grief where it's real and honest and true. Where I am real and honest and true. So much in my life isn't real, or true.

But love and loss are.

And Keith was.

Although Keith would be disgusted that I call *Rent* my Keith album.

I crack a small, watery smile.

We saw the show together in New York in September, a month before his final trip to Afghanistan. He hated it. I loved it. *Loved it.*

I was on my feet during the curtain call, applauding like mad, and Keith, my Mr. Nonemotional, looked at me as though I were an alien, which made me laugh, and I have never been so full of emotions as I was that night. I was laughing and crying, singing, clapping, dancing, and I remember thinking, This is what life is. Messy and huge and brutal and beautiful.

Keith died seven weeks later.

I stop at a McDonald's ten minutes from Christie's and go inside to repair my makeup. My eyes are still pink despite the new mascara and eyeliner. And looking into my reflection in the McDonald's ladies' room, I still see Keith in my eyes.

The bathroom door opens and a little girl runs in. I turn from the mirror and smile. I will only ever show the world my happy face.

I arrive at Christie and Simon's just after two. One of the garage bays is open and Simon's red convertible is missing, so I park on the far side of the drive to give him access when he returns.

Their two-story concrete block of a house looks severe from the outside, but the interior frames the spectacular view perfectly. The house sits high above the ocean and every window on the west side overlooks the water, revealing cocoa cliffs, sapphire waves, and the sandy cove below.

Christie opens the door and greets me with a hug, mindful of my bags and platters. "Happy Thanksgiving!" She's wearing a brown-and-white animal-print tunic with a chunky bead necklace, and her necklace crunches against my collarbone in her quick hug. "How was the drive?"

"Easy. Fast."

She looks at me closely. "You okay?"

"Yes. Wonderful."

She's not entirely convinced, but she doesn't press. "Let me take some of that," she offers, reaching for the three ceramic platters and flowers.

I'm happy to share some of my burden, and I follow her into the house, closing the door behind me with my foot. "Where's Simon?"

"He got called in to the hospital. But we're hoping he'll be back by dinner."

The girls come rushing down the staircase, screaming and feet pounding. "Tiana! Tiana's here!"

I set down the bags and hug each of them in turn. Christie's girls, just like Marta's Eva, always make me feel like a rock star.

"Hey, girls." Hands on my hips, I grin and take them all in. They've grown again, and at eleven, nine, and seven they're as opposite as opposite can be. Melanie's a little Simon, brown hair and brown eyes. Melissa's the spitting image of her mom, blonde hair and blue eyes. And Kari with her red curls, well, she must be the milkman's daughter. No one knows where her dark red curls came from.

"We're setting up Disney Princess Monopoly," Melissa tells me. "Come play!"

"You have to play, Tiana," Kari adds.

Disney Princess Monopoly. If that doesn't get the heart pumping, I don't know what would. "Maybe later?" I say, catching Christie's smirk. She finds it very funny that I can't say no to her girls. "But first I need to help your mom in the kitchen. She's got a lot to do today."

"But we already counted out your money," replies Melanie, the youngest.

"And it'll be boring without you," Kari, the eleven-year-old, adds. She's in a phase where everything is now boring and babyish for her.

"I will play," I promise them, "but first let me put together the appetizers I brought and lend your mom some help in the kitchen." When the girls protest again, I hold up a hand. "Unless you all want to help your mom in the kitchen instead?"

They scream and run back up the stairs, feet pounding once again, and Christie makes a face and reaches for one of my grocery bags. "Something tells me I'm not raising them right," she says.

We head to the kitchen with the flowers and groceries. I slip the bottle of white wine into the fridge to chill and start unpacking the bags, placing platters on the counter along with the ingredients for my fruit-and-cheese tray.

"That's all right," I console her, unpacking the Tupperware containers with my ingredients for the baked mushroom caps and stuffed Brie. "You've got me."

"Great. The girl that doesn't know how to cook."

"I know how to cook." I see her expression. "Appetizers."

She laughs and returns to the preparation of her stuffing. "So what's the latest at *America Tonight*? Are they serious about making Shelby a co-anchor?"

I open the package of thawed puff pastry for my baked Brie. "All the big network bosses were there Monday, for one hour." I exhale and begin unwrapping the wheel of Brie. "The *one* hour I wasn't there on Monday."

"Was Shelby there?"

I look at her, nod grimly. "I'm trying to keep my cool, but it's hard when it feels like I suddenly have no control."

"So why all the Shelby fanfare now?"

"I'm skewing older and the bosses are worried that I've forever lost the younger audience."

Christie grimaces. "Which is key."

I nod again.

"So it really is about age," she concludes.

"The one thing we can't fight," I answer, reaching for a baking sheet.

"I can't imagine they really want to replace you. You're so good, Tiana. You're skilled, talented, professional. Experience does count." She gives me a hard look. "Would you consider plastic surgery?"

No. But I shrug philosophically, far more philosophically than I feel. "I think I have to."

But Christie doesn't buy it for a moment. "You wouldn't. You don't even like Botox. You freaked the time they asked you to try collagen in your lips—"

"It hurt."

"Face-lifts hurt."

"I've heard, and to be honest, the idea of being cut *freaks* me. Having my skin cut, stretched, lifted, and restitched? That's a Freddy Krueger movie."

"Thank God not everyone's so squeamish, huh?"

I laugh weakly. But she's right. I wouldn't go under the

knife, not unless I had no other choice, and I'm not out of options, not by a long shot.

"I'm not against cosmetic surgery, though," I add, and tell her about the feature I'm researching and all the books with the before-and-after photos. "The after photos look great, but there is still something sad about the body being treated like a lump of clay. I'm not judging those who do it, I'm just saying I don't understand it."

"You don't understand because you can't." Christie leans against the counter, pot mitt on one hand. "You're extraordinarily beautiful. You were born beautiful, and thanks to fate and great genetics, you live a life the rest of us mortals only dream about."

"Knock it off."

"Tiana, your looks do more than secure a fat paycheck. They get you reservations, great tables, great service. You're photographed, admired, envied. You wouldn't have a clue what it's like to be average, or ugly."

"Neither do you!"

Christie scoffs, "No? Then why don't I work the red carpet? Why don't I get asked to host televised events?"

"Because you're a writer and a director."

"I used to be a writer like you. But no network would put me in front of a camera. I realized I wasn't ever going to work if I didn't find work for me to do. So I got damn good at being behind a camera."

"This has nothing to do with looks," I answer, setting aside the baking sheet and beginning to prepare the baked cheddar mushroom caps appetizer.

"Cut the bullshit, Tia. It has everything to do with looks. I'm not ugly—I work hard to make sure I don't fall into that category—but I'll never be beautiful. Not even pretty. I score okay on a good day—"

"*No.*"

"And attractive on my very best day." She stares at me pointedly. "Beauty is power, Tiana, and most women don't have enough of either."

"So if you were me, you'd have a face-lift?"

Christie turns to look at me hard. She studies me for a long moment and her expression changes; her mouth softens and emotion darkens her eyes. "No."

"No?"

"You're still beautiful. And you have more goodness and love in you than anyone knows. You're more than your face, and if the show execs can't see it, then screw them. They don't deserve you."

I try to smile but can't. Instead I go to her and hug her. Hard. "Thank you," I whisper. "God knows I needed that."

She hugs me back. "I mean every word of it. You're wonderful. And don't you forget it—no matter what they tell you, or try to sell you."

"Don't make me cry," I warn, giving her a last quick hug and a smile before stepping away. "I'm already an emotional wreck. If I start crying again today, I don't think I could stop."

She shoots me a side glance. "Keith?"

I nod. "And then I had to torture myself by playing sad songs the whole drive down."

"But if it made you feel better?"

"I don't know that it did. Keith wouldn't want me this sad. He wasn't an emotional guy."

"That doesn't mean you can't be an emotional girl." She

flashes me a smile. "But you're here and we're thrilled you're here, so let's get cooking!"

We spend the next twenty minutes chopping, sautéing, and mixing, and I've just begun spooning the cheddar filling into mushroom caps when the doorbell rings. Christie is elbow deep in hot, soapy water, washing pots and pans, and I offer to answer the door. "I can get that."

"Would you? I bet it's Michael." She glances at me over her shoulder. "You know Michael O'Sullivan—"

I freeze. "*Dr.* Michael O'Sullivan?"

Christie looks at me strangely. "He's a close friend of Simon's. Why? Is there a problem?"

The last twenty minutes of warmth and comfort desert me, and my spirits plummet. "You know we don't get along."

"No, I don't. I knew you squared off on Larry King, but I figured that was just for television." She frowns at me, rinses her hands, and reaches for a dish towel. "Are you serious? How can you not get along with Michael? He's one of the best people I know."

Chapter Six

From the kitchen, I hear Christie open the front door and welcome Michael. Michael's deep voice answers in reply. She drops her voice, says something to him I can't hear. He laughs, a low, husky sound, and she laughs in return. Aren't they cozy?

Irritated, I march to the double ovens in the wall and shove the tray of cheddar-stuffed mushroom caps into the top oven, the one without the roasting turkey. Christie could have said something to me about her other guests earlier. A little warning would have been nice.

I'm still fuming when Michael makes his way into the kitchen. He's dressed in a black linen shirt unbuttoned at the collar and crisp khakis. He has a bottle of wine tucked under his arm and a pink bakery box in his hands.

"Happy Thanksgiving, Ms. America," he greets me, setting the box on the counter and adding his wine to the refrigerator before giving me a dazzling smile.

His smile is pure charm, and it throws me. I take a step back, frazzled beyond belief.

I was planning on a quiet Thanksgiving, a relaxed Thanksgiving, which means a Thanksgiving without Michael O'Sullivan. "Happy Thanksgiving to you, too," I say coolly, wondering where the hell Christie's gone. First she invites

Michael here and then she disappears, leaving us alone? "Where did Christie go?"

"I think she ran upstairs to check on the girls."

Needing something to do, I rinse out my prep bowls. "I didn't know you were friends with Simon," I say, giving my orange Tupperware bowl an unusually vigorous scouring.

"We go a long way back."

"Christie's never mentioned you."

"At a brunch, Simon brought up Jenna Meadows's lawsuit, I mentioned Thursday's Larry King show, and Christie remembered you and I had been on the show together. Small world."

And getting smaller.

I begin scrubbing the sink. "Is that when they invited you for turkey?"

"I actually invited them to my house for dinner, but they said they'd already invited guests to theirs."

I look at him, surprised. "*You* cook?"

"Turkey's pretty basic."

Not to me, but I don't see the point in telling him it's something I haven't yet mastered. Sink sparkling, dishes washed, I'm forced to turn off the water. "Alexis couldn't make it today?"

"She's at a conference in Quebec."

I face him. "Thanksgiving weekend?"

He's leaning against the counter, watching me. A crooked smile curves his lips. "The Canadians celebrate Thanksgiving in October."

"What kind of conference?"

"Cosmetic surgery."

"Really?"

Christie bustles back into the kitchen, a heavy folded table-cloth in her arms. "Alex is a plastic surgeon, too," she says cheerfully. "She's a brilliant woman, and she'll find the right guy someday. Michael's just not the right guy."

My jaw drops so hard, I'm sure it smacks the floor. I shoot Michael a swift look. "Alexis is a surgeon?"

"You didn't know that?"

No. Those breasts... the very blonde hair... the red sequin dress. "Why didn't you introduce her as a doctor?"

Michael's expression is strange. "I did. I said she was an expert in the field of cosmetic surgery."

"I didn't know you meant—" I break off, shake my head, cheeks hot.

"You didn't what?" he asks.

My face warms. I thought she was a bimbo. I took one look at her, noted the packaged sex appeal, figured she was brain-less. Figured Michael was shallow. Figured I was superior.

Oh God, I've goofed again. Seems like I'm getting more wrong these days than right.

What's happening to me?

Ashamed, I focus my attention on the empty platter on the counter, a platter I need to fill with crackers and fruit to accompany the baked Brie.

Christie comes up to me, wraps an arm around my waist, and whispers in my ear, "I thought she was a *Playboy* Playmate the first time I met her. Turned out she's Mensa and her IQ's about a hundred points higher than mine. Awkward."

The front door opens, slams shut. "I'm home," Simon calls out. "Let's get this party started."

Michael leaves the kitchen to meet Simon, and I whisper to Christie, "They're not a couple?"

Christie steals a red grape, pops it in her mouth. "Nope. Haven't been for about six months. Apparently she's having a hard time letting go."

"Then maybe he should make it easier for her by not taking her as his date to black-tie functions."

"You mean the Getty fund-raiser."

"She was clearly into him."

"Alexis knows he's dating other women. I wouldn't call him a playboy, but he's definitely popular with the ladies."

I shudder. "Gross."

"What's so gross? That women find him attractive?"

"I don't know. The whole thing. His fake charm. His excessive good looks. His money. Is it really necessary?"

Her brow furrows. "The same could be said for you."

"But I'm not fake, and I don't lead men on!"

"So what is the relationship between you and Trevor? Soul mates...true love...recreational sex?"

"You're comparing apples and oranges. I'm nothing like Michael. I don't use men."

"Why are you so critical of him?"

"Have you heard the way he talks to me? He's always making fun of me—"

"He's teasing you." She shakes her head. "Playing with you. Where's your sense of humor? You've always been able to laugh at yourself."

"Not anymore," I answer, knowing it's true. I don't laugh like I used to. I'm far more tense, as well as intense. I never used to be this stressed about my work, but success has become more bitter than sweet. Even one year ago Mark would never have slammed me in a staff meeting the way he did last week.

The show's ratings have never tanked. I've never needed saving. I've always done the saving.

I want to be the invincible Tiana Tomlinson again, the girl wonder who couldn't get it wrong.

Now I can't seem to get it right.

I suddenly sniff. Something's burning. My mushroom caps. I completely forgot. I rush to the oven, grab a hot mitt, and retrieve the tray, but they're blackened. Inedible.

Holding the tray, I look at Christie and she's looking at me and I'm so mad because this is what I'm talking about. I don't burn stuffed mushroom caps. I don't get distracted. I don't fall apart. But my eyes are welling with tears and there's a huge, dark hole opening up inside me. "You don't suppose I could serve them anyway?" I ask wistfully.

"You could try." Christie smiles. "Maybe no one will notice."

I glance down at the baking sheet with the charred puffs. "Or maybe I could just give them to Michael. They'd go nicely with his black heart."

Christie laughs and then wags her finger at me. "Tiana, I'd be careful if I were you. Karma's a bitch!"

Thankfully, the baked Brie turns out golden and flaky. Surrounded by crackers, grapes, and pear slices, it's a glorious appetizer and I carry it toward the living room, where I hear the sound of a televised football game. Simon's from Oklahoma, went to Texas A&M, and is a diehard Dallas Cowboys fan. I enter the living room expecting to find Simon and Michael in front of the enormous flat-screen TV. Instead, Simon's watching the game alone.

"Where's Michael?" I ask, setting the platter on the low glass coffee table.

Simon waves to the stairs, his gaze glued to the screen. "Upstairs, playing Princess Monopoly."

I climb the stairs and follow the raised voices to Kari's room, where the door is partially open. Melissa's apparently upset about how someone's playing. I stick my head around the door to see the girls and Michael clustered on the floor, but they're not playing Princess Monopoly; instead they're gathered around Barbie Queen of the Prom, a game Melanie got last year for her birthday—and loved—much to her mother's dismay.

"That's my boyfriend, Michael. You have to get your own," Melissa is explaining to him with exaggerated patience. "You have to land on a different square."

"But I need a boyfriend to go to the prom," he protests.

The girls are in fits of giggles.

"Yes, but you can't have mine," Melissa answers, trying to be severe and failing.

Melanie is also trying to keep a straight face. "You'll just have to go on a date again."

"Again?" he exclaims.

The girls are laughing harder. "Well, I wouldn't," Kari says. "Skip the going on a date, and try to go to the class party, otherwise you'll lose too much time and never make the prom."

"But don't I have to go steady before I go to the prom?" Michael asks, bewildered.

"*Yes*," they chorus loudly.

He sighs heavily, clearly overwhelmed by the trials of being a girl in 1961. "Going to the prom is a lot of work."

"And yet to Barbie, so worth it," I say, stepping into the room and taking a seat on the edge of Kari's twin bed. Kari's just had her room redone from pinks to lime green and chocolate brown, and I love the fun, fresh colors. They're perfect for a young tween.

Michael looks up at me, dark blue eyes creasing at the corners. He's in his element here, playing a board game with three little girls who clearly all have a crush on him. "Have you played this game before?"

"Many times."

Melissa looks at me. "We let Michael take your place," she says apologetically. "Sorry."

"It's okay. He probably needs to practice his dating skills." I meet his gaze, smile a little.

"Actually, I'm quite good on a date," he defends himself, holding my gaze. "It's the shopping for a dress I'm struggling with."

My lips twitch. I can't help it. He's such a contradiction: On the one hand, he's Mr. Sophisticated in his black linen shirt, yet here he is stretched out on a green carpet playing the Barbie Game.

He sees my amusement and his smile deepens, the light back in his deep blue eyes, and there's something in his smile that reaches into my chest and squeezes tight.

Keith. Keith's smile.

That's how Keith used to smile at me. Smart, laughing, loving. Wicked and wonderful. Mostly wonderful.

I breathe in so hard that my chest constricts again and I stumble to my feet. Need air. Must get air.

Descending the stairs, I hear Christie talking to Simon and I slip down the hall for Simon's study with its balcony overlooking the ocean.

I push open the sliding door and step outside. Clouds have moved in, partially obscuring the sea, hanging low and gray over the rocks and sea and sand. It's colder, too, the temperature dropping with the thick clouds. I shiver and gulp in air.

Michael's not like Keith.

They're not at all the same. Not the smile. Not the values. Guilt assails me. I don't know why I'd even compare the two. No one's like Keith, no one.

But then I hear the sliding door open and I look over my shoulder and see Michael walking toward me.

My stomach falls. Not him, not now.

I swiftly reach up and wipe my eyes, hoping he can't see any of what I'm feeling. I'm usually so good at hiding my emotions, but I'm too raw right now and far too tender.

"Nice view," he says, coming to stand next to me, resting his weight on the balcony railing.

I nod, gaze out at the ocean where the clouds hang above the waves' white foam tips.

"You all right?" he asks quietly.

I nod again.

"Simon told me this isn't an easy day for you," he adds even more quietly. "I'm sorry."

He doesn't sound like a shallow playboy, and his simple words bring a lump to my throat and fresh tears to my eyes. "It's okay," I say thickly.

"No, it's not. Death's a terrible thing. No one understands it, do they?"

And suddenly I'm crying again.

I rest my elbows on the railing and cover my face and cry hot salty silent tears into my hands. I *loved* Keith. I loved him as much as I could love anyone and it didn't keep him alive. I loved him with all my heart and soul and it wasn't enough. I gave him all of me and it couldn't protect him. How the hell are we supposed to love when it doesn't last? How are we to love when life is so capricious that love can be taken away at any time?

This is the grief I can't bear anyone to see. This is the pain that shadows me when I'm alone, yet here Michael is, witness to it all.

He closes the distance between us and wraps his arms around me and holds me as I cry. He says nothing, and a little voice inside me insists I push him away, but I can't. I've been lonely and too full of grief for far too long. Besides, he's warm and solid and he keeps me from toppling down, which is something.

The tears finally stop and I step carefully out of his arms and away from him even as I wipe my eyes dry. "Sorry about that."

"You loved him," he says.

My eyes sting, my throat aches, my voice is hoarse. "More than anything."

"He was lucky, you know. Not everyone gets loved like that."

I look at Michael warily. I don't trust him. I won't ever trust him—he is Dr. Hollywood, after all—but his tone is sincere and his expression is serious, and after a moment I nod. "We just didn't have enough time. There should have been more time."

"But that's how it should be, shouldn't it? We should be greedy with life. It's so damn short."

I search his gaze, not sure what I'm looking for. Mockery? Sarcasm? Cynicism? But I find none of it. "Too short," I agree.

"He's been gone how long?"

"Seven years today."

"And you've never married again."

"No."

"You don't want to marry again?"

I can't answer that. I don't even know the answer. Part of me would love to fall in love and marry, but another part of me, a big part of me, is too scared to take the risk. And I don't want to forget Keith, don't want him to be wiped away completely. "You don't know if they've opened any wine, do you? I think I could use a glass."

"I do remember seeing a very nice white wine chilling in the fridge. Let's say we open that."

I smile, grateful that he's allowing us to move on and away from this painful subject. "Yes, please."

I don't return from Laguna Beach until close to ten. At Christie's insistence I've brought home a plastic container filled with turkey, stuffing, potatoes, and gravy, along with another container of pie. Upon entering my house, I go straight to the kitchen to put away the leftovers.

I change for bed, wash my face, and as I apply the necessary lotions and potions to keep Father Time at bay—lotions and potions more critical now than ever before—I think about the conversation I had with Michael on the balcony. It was a Michael I'd never seen before. A Michael I hadn't known existed.

But maybe it was just a facade. Maybe that was smooth, charming Dr. Hollywood talking. The man who can sweet-talk any woman into doing any procedure. I don't want to ever fall for a man who's superficial. Keith had substance. If I ever fall in love again, it's going to be with a man of substance, too.

Still mulling over our conversation, I think about the men I've dated since Keith's death. There haven't been many. I didn't date for years after his death, and then when I started to go out again, it was brutal. Painful. Obviously no one was going to be Keith, but no one came even remotely close to having his wit, intellect, and passion.

But I promised Shey and Marta that I'd keep trying. I told them if I was asked out, I'd go out, at least once. Few men lasted more than a single date, although there were a few who became brief relationships.

The entertainment lawyer I saw for three weeks. The retired football player for two months. The UCLA heart surgeon for a month. The Laguna Beach artist for five months. Trevor.

Trevor.

I make a face at myself in the mirror. And Trevor isn't exactly the answer to my dreams, either, is he? But maybe that's the point. As long as I date men who are lightweights, I'm protected. As long as I date men who don't touch my heart, I won't get hurt.

Better not to hurt.

Better to just keep killing time.

Or so I try to convince myself as I get into bed and turn out the light.

I'm relieved when Monday comes because it means I can go back to work. After four days off, I need to work, and after arriving in Century City, I discover Celia is at the studio today, filming a segment that will be taped to air tonight. Once every two weeks she comes in and does a feature on celebrity lifestyle just the way I appear on Larry King as a celebrity expert. I find it ironic that so many of us in this industry make a living being celebrity experts.

Celia pops into my office when she's done. She stopped by earlier, but I was still in a production meeting then.

Celia spots the pile of books on the corner of my desk. *"Beauty Junkies: The Smart Woman's Guide to Plastic Surgery* and *Secrets of a Beverly Hills Plastic Surgeon."* She looks up at me. "Thinking of getting some work done?"

"No." *Yes.*

She sits in a chair, props her boots up on the edge of my desk with a decisive plunk, and studies me. "How was your weekend?"

There's a note in her voice that tells me it's not a casual question. I look up, into her eyes. "Good."

"You're sure?"

"Yes, why?"

For a moment there's only silence in my office, and then Celia reaches over to her bag and draws out a magazine page and hands it to me. "Thought you deserved fair warning."

"What is it?" I ask even as I look at the photo. It's a blown-up picture of me behind the wheel of my car. The photo's been taken through my windshield, but you can still see that my face is puffy and my nose is red and there are traces of tears on my cheek.

"Heartbroken and Betrayed!" screams the red caption above the photo, and yes, I do look devastated in the picture.

I frown, trying to figure out when the photo was taken. I'm wearing my brown Michael Kors blouse and a turquoise, coral, and silver necklace. Thanksgiving. I was on my way to Christie's.

"It's in this week's issue. It'll hit the stands tomorrow. I thought you'd want to know. Sorry."

I don't answer, as I'm reading the story's subtitle: "A heartbroken Tiana flees her house after discovering that boy toy Trevor Campbell is sleeping with Kiki Woods!"

"This is ridiculous," I protest. "It's totally untrue. There's nothing wrong between Trevor and me—"

"It doesn't look like it."

"This," I say, shaking the photo, "is private. I was sad about something that's personal that has nothing to do with Trevor. You can't run this."

"It's done."

"It's a fabrication!"

"You're sure?"

"Goddammit, yes!" I almost never yell, but I do now, and I slap the article onto my desk so hard that my hand stings. Madison suddenly pops her head around the corner, and I give my head a slight shake. She wisely disappears. "Celia..." I drop my voice. "Trevor and I are fine."

"*OK!* magazine is running a story this week with photos of Trevor and Kiki frolicking on a yacht."

"So?"

"Kiki's topless."

I don't say anything.

Celia gives me a sympathetic look. "I'm sorry, and maybe I shouldn't have told you, but I wanted you to be prepared."

My hand shakes as I read the article to appear in *People*. There's not much to the story other than I am apparently devastated after learning through an unnamed source that Trevor's been having a hot affair with his sexy co-star. "They couldn't keep their hands off each other," the source adds.

It doesn't even matter if the story is true or not, it's humiliating knowing that millions of readers will see it and believe it.

Celia waits for me to say something.

In the end, I crumple up the tear sheet and toss it away. "Thanks for the heads-up."

Celia leaves, and I'm called to the soundstage to go through the show one last time. They keep the studio at a chilly forty-seven degrees because once the lights go on, the temperature rises, and even though I'm wearing a sweater over my slim knit dress, my teeth keep chattering.

I'm always cold on the set before the lights go on, but this morning I'm absolutely freezing. I know it's not just the cold studio getting to me. It's Celia's revelation. Is Trevor seeing Kiki? If so, why wouldn't he just tell me? Why wouldn't he just break things off with me first?

I tried to call Max after Celia left, but he was tied up in a meeting so I left a message. I tried to call Trevor, but he wasn't answering his phone, either.

I force my attention back to the teleprompter, making sure I'm familiar with the names and introductions, but I can't stay focused.

Trevor isn't sleeping with Kiki.

Trevor isn't involved with Kiki.

Trevor's seeing me.

The stage director gives me the signal that we're ready to tape, so I peel off my cardigan sweater and hand it to Harper, who is standing off to the side with her clipboard and headphones.

Vanessa, my makeup artist, is called to touch up my décolleté with a hint of bronzing powder. She strokes the brush across my cheekbones, complaining that I'm too pale. "You're not coming down sick, are you?" she asks, brushing another light dusting of bronzer down my nose and then across each of my shoulders.

"No."

"It's that time of year, so start taking lots of vitamin C, zinc, and echinacea."

I promise her I will, and she steps off the stage. The floor director signals that we're a minute away.

I check my mike. The three cameras, all robotics, are focused on me. I glance at the teleprompter, make sure it's where we're supposed to be, and then once we're taping, I get through the show by the skin of my teeth.

Done taping, I try Max again. Max is still not available. His assistant says he's tied up in meetings for the rest of the day. I take a deep breath to keep myself calm. "Let Max know it's about Trevor and Kiki and a story breaking today in *People* magazine."

I hang up, thinking I'll hear from Max within the next fifteen minutes. He calls me in ten. "What's up, doll?"

It takes under a minute to fill him in. The photo, the story, the caption. Max is silent for a moment, then laughs. "You've got paparazzi staking out your place. Which means there will be more stories."

He's pleased. He likes this. "Max, this is bad. It's sordid—"

"Hell, it's publicity, and you of all people know that bad publicity is better than no publicity."

Not necessarily. Not when it comes to my private life. "Do you really think he's seeing her?" I ask, a catch in my voice. "Would he do that to me?"

"He's a man. Men do shitty things."

"Not all men."

"Most men."

"*No.*" I refuse to believe this, refuse to listen to this, although I'm the one who delivers the news on celebrity cheating and broken hearts every night at seven.

"You're dating an actor," Max says with an exasperated sigh. "It comes with the territory."

"He could have ended things with me first."

"But why should he if he can have his cake and eat it, too?"

I don't know if Max is trying to help or if he even cares if his brutal honesty hurts, but I feel worse than I did earlier. "Obviously it's over."

"You don't know that yet."

"If he's screwing Kiki Woods, it is!"

"But you don't know that, either."

"Have you heard about the *OK!* story? The one with the photos of Kiki topless?"

Max doesn't answer, which means yes, he has.

"Have you seen the photos, Max?"

"She's beautiful, she's young, and she loves attention, Tiana."

"What does that mean?"

"It was only a matter of time before Trevor fell into bed with her. To be honest, I'm surprised it took him this long."

I hang up on Max. I have to, it's that or drive my car into the nearest tree, and that's not a viable option. I'm Tiana Tomlinson and I'm a good girl and I don't do reckless, self-destructive things, although drinking the bottle of wine in my refrigerator sounds like an excellent idea right now.

But at home I don't drink. I kick off my shoes, retrieve my phone, and turn it on to dial Trevor's number. It rings before going straight into voice mail. Heart thudding, I leave a message: "Call me. Tonight. Please."

There's more I'd like to say, but I pause, consider whether it's wise. Then I can't stop myself and the rest tumbles out: "They're running a story in this week's *People* that has an unnamed source claiming you and Kiki are lovers. Call me."

As I hang up, my eye falls on the cluster of antique silver-framed photos on the bookshelf in the living room. My wedding photo, one of Marta, Shey, and me at Marta's wedding in Banff last year, and then the picture of Keith.

It's my favorite picture of him, taken in Afghanistan just a week before he died.

He's on horseback and wearing traditional Afghan garb, a long white-and-black scarf tied loosely around his neck, and a multitude of cameras around his neck. He's grown a beard, and his fair hair is hidden beneath a knit cap. His white horse's gray mane is tangled and Keith's brow is beaded with sweat, but he's grinning and he looks so damn happy to be alive that just looking at it makes my heart hurt.

This is what it means to be alive.

This is what it's all about.

I keep this photo out because it reminds me of the promise Keith and I made to each other. We were both so ambitious, and we complemented each other in our fierce drive and determination to succeed. We were going to go for it. Go big or go home, Keith said one night, kissing me in bed.

Go big or go home, I repeat. Live every day until we die.

The sick feeling in me shifts, changes, softening to something deeper, stronger, tougher. It's part protection, part self-preservation, and part pure grit.

I will not go down without a fight. I've been through so much, this is nothing I can't handle.

My chin notches up, and I focus on all that I am instead of what I'm not. Things haven't been good lately, and I have a feeling they're about to get ugly, but I can do ugly. I'm a woman. And damn tough.

Chapter Seven

———— ✦✦✦ ————

Despite my conviction that I can handle whatever life throws my way, I toss and turn much of the night, waking up every hour or so and glancing at the clock. Eleven forty-five. One-twelve. Two-twenty. Four-ten. Five. And then finally my alarm at seven.

The moment I wake up, the sick feeling returns harder than ever.

I dread the day, knowing how it'll unfold. The other entertainment shows will jump on *People*'s story. The coming week will be filled with gossip and endless commentary. Poor Tiana. How shocking. How embarrassing. Did she know? Did she suspect?

There will be tabloid segments where I'm pitied and segments where I'm mocked. Perez Hilton will say I had it coming. *TMZ* will dig for dirt. *Talk Soup* will no doubt have some horrendous photo and sarcastic put-down.

I go to the French doors in my room and open them wide. It's cold for Los Angeles, bracing, which is exactly what I need. The sharp smell of oak and eucalyptus trees makes the air pungent. Today is going to be rough. I might as well be prepared.

Driving to work, I do nothing but field phone calls from the office, from rival shows, from journalists at tabloid magazines.

The issue of *People* hasn't hit the public mailbox yet, but the newswire has the article and every station and every producer has seen it, and everybody wants a comment. Would I care to respond to the *People* article? Did I know Trevor was involved with Kiki? Am I still seeing Trevor? What is the future of my relationship with Trevor today?

Madison is downstairs in the HBC tower lobby to meet me as I take the elevator from the garage, a leather folder clutched to her chest.

"That bad, huh?" I say, seeing her expression.

"They're going nuts upstairs, especially Mark. He's frothing at the mouth." She exhales, blowing blonde wisps of hair from her face. "By the way, cute coat."

I can't help grinning. "That's what I like about you. You know how to keep things in perspective."

We step into the elevator together, and she flips open the leather folder and retrieves the copy of *People*. "Celia had this couriered over. I take it you knew about it?"

I nod.

"Is it true?" she asks.

"I don't know. You're the Trevor fan. Is it?"

Her eyebrows lift. "Wow."

"What?" I answer as the elevator doors open and we step out into our reception area. "Was that the wrong thing to say?"

Her eyebrows just arch higher, and together we walk to our desks, backs straight, shoulders squared. And I have to say, it's kind of nice to have someone walking next to me. I need an ally right now, and Madison, even though young, is exactly who I want on my side.

Harper is pacing outside my office as I arrive. She follows me in and over to my desk and chair.

"I want the story," she demands, "the real story. This *People* article is pathetic, and it makes you look pathetic. I've never once seen you like this. And this face"—she flicks the blown-up photo with her finger—"what does this even mean?"

I slide off my red swingy car coat, which shows off my slim black sheath dress, and hang up the jacket on the back of my door. "Good morning, Harper."

"Are you serious?" She pivots on her three-inch black heels to face me. "Is that all you've got for me?"

I roll out my chair, sit, and reach for my laptop. "I don't know what you want me to say." I open my laptop and look up at her. "I don't know what the story is. I don't know what the truth is. I don't know if Trevor was unfaithful. I don't know if he's madly in love with Kiki. I don't know anything."

She drops into the chair facing my desk. "Do you know how stupid this makes you look?"

I grimace. "Thanks."

"You know what I'm saying. I'm looking out for you, Tiana. You're our star. You're my number one girl. You've got to give me something we can run with for today's show. Some rebuttal, or comeback, something to fight this idea of you being the broken, pathetic victim—"

"A little heavy-handed, don't you think, Harp?" I interrupt with a fierce white smile.

She looks at me a long moment. "Your numbers are up."

I sit back in my chair, surprised. "That's good news."

"They're up quite a bit, too, not just with the younger audience, but all across the board."

She's pleased, pleased but clearly surprised, and I know she hasn't figured out why there's been a jump in my numbers. But I know why.

"They're up because of Trevor." I reach for the issue of *People* that Madison handed to me as we exited the elevator. I open the magazine to the big photo of my face and feel a pang that my grief is there in living color.

"It's all the Paris magazine covers and subsequent stories," I add idly, an idea starting to form, although I'm not yet ready to share it. "Our younger viewers love him, and they're watching me right now because of him."

"You're right. I didn't think of that." She pauses, frowns. "And without Trevor, you'll lose the numbers?"

"Maybe. And maybe not." I think about how fickle audiences can be and how easy it is for boredom to set in. I think about our teases and headlines and the lengths we go to in order to pique viewer interest. "I guess it depends on the next couple of weeks and how we follow this story up."

Harper looks at me with interest. "So you're seeing it as a story?"

"I'd be a fool to think of it in any other way—"

I'm interrupted midsentence when Mark barges into my office, waving a sheet of paper in my face. "Your boy toy's defected," he says, shoving the paper even closer. "He's doing an interview by satellite with Mary Hart over at *Entertainment Tonight* today."

I yank the paper from his hand and read the e-mail from Paula, one of the *ET* producers, to Mark. Everybody knows everybody in this business, and depending on the story, we'll sometimes share tips, leads, and sources. Paula is positively exultant that Trevor's agreed to do a satellite interview from Nice. They've got a French broadcasting studio taking care of the logistics.

No wonder Paula's chortling.

I'm one-third of the equation, yet I don't even have an active part in the story. I'm an accessory.

And that's going to change starting now.

Harper and Mark leave and, gathering my courage, I go online, type "Keith Heaton obituary" into the Google tool bar, print off the first of the obits that pull up, and then type "Keith Heaton funeral" into Google images. Dozens of photos from Keith's funeral appear, half with my body lying on top of the casket.

I avoid looking at the photos, avoid reading the obituary. Instead I gather everything I've printed and head to Harper's desk. She and the other producers and writers all work in a large open space just a wall away from the studio and control booth.

Harper is on her computer, and I set the photos and obituary in front of her to get her attention.

"I have a story for you," I say. "I wasn't crying over Trevor. Trevor's out of my life—good riddance. I was crying because Thanksgiving marked the seventh anniversary of my husband's death. I was thinking of him and missing him. Here's his obituary. And here are pictures from his funeral." I jab the body in one. "And that's me on his casket."

Harper just looks at me.

"I can't compete with whatever story Trevor will give Mary. I only know what's true. And what's true is this—I never loved Trevor. Sex was good. He was fun. But he was a fling. My heart has only ever belonged to one man, and it was my husband. My hero."

Harper rolls back from her desk, her brown gaze speculative. "You want me to make this a story?"

"Yes. And make it a good one." I pause. "Can you?"

"Yes." She thinks for a moment. "I'll have Manuel cover the story. He'd be good. He could even interview you, just a few questions about your late husband. Is that all right with you?"

I nod. "Let's get him in here." I start to walk away but stop. "And don't believe Mark or Libby if they say I don't care about this show. Since Keith died, this show has been my life."

It's a push today to write all new copy, get photos and text edited correctly, plus tape new teases to run before the show—never mind actually filming the show itself. But we do it, and we're done by one.

Manuel arrives a half hour before we're to tape, and he and I sit together on one of the soundstages doing our mini-interview. The camera loves Manuel—with his dark, soulful eyes, he's perfect on sympathy pieces. Ten minutes later, we're changing and preparing for the show.

We're opening with the Tiana-Trevor-Kiki-Keith story, a story that's beyond convoluted, but somehow Harper makes it all work by tackling the issue immediately and hitting it hard:

"What's the world coming to? Tabloid news at its worst!"

There's going to be a big-screen shot of me in one of my publicity shots, then the *People* photo, followed by an even bigger shot of Keith smiling in Afghanistan—a different shot from the one I have, but maybe even more effective, as he looks rugged and sexy and oh, so handsome—and finally the funeral photo with me lying on his casket.

With the photos making a dramatic backdrop behind Manuel, he'll tell the fairy-tale story of girl meets boy, and how boy loves girl, but then boy dies and girl must try to move on with her life in a mean world filled with underhanded, unethical people.

It's very in-your-face and the text is a little controversial for my tastes, but the photo sequence makes it emotional and magical, which makes it work. Especially the photo of Keith kicking back with his beer, boots on the table, smiling. What a smile. Irresistible.

I'm standing offstage watching the segment—they need only one take, too, which is downright miraculous, as Manuel has a tendency to misread the teleprompter—but today it works, and even I am moved. The segment is powerful, telling a story of love and loss, and I know this is something our viewers will respond to. They want emotion. Elation. A vicarious thrill. And the story tonight gives it to them.

No matter what happens over at *Entertainment Tonight*, no matter what Trevor says to Mary, I know we've done what we needed to do. Maybe not for Trevor, but for the show. And me. And maybe that's the most important thing. In the fight for ratings and audience share, it's easy to overlook that I matter even more than the show.

That evening, I watch *Entertainment Tonight* from the safety of my living room sofa. Trevor is live by satellite, and to be fair, he looks golden and bronze, just the way a movie star should. Mary opens the interview by attempting to ask Trevor hard questions about his relationship with Kiki, but Trevor has her eating out of his hand.

"Kiki's an amazing woman, and I have the utmost respect for her talent," he says, deflecting the question from the personal to the professional. "Can't say enough good things about her."

"So you two are involved?"

"She's my co-star, and any man would be proud to be seen with her."

"Which brings up the photographs in *OK!* showing the two of you on a yacht in the Mediterranean and Kiki's topless."

"I find this subject interesting because it's really one about cultural differences. Women don't sunbathe topless in the U.S. I believe Americans see it as dirty, pornographic, but it's natural in Europe, and women in the South of France frequently swim and sunbathe without their tops on."

Mary nods. "How is Tiana doing, Trevor?"

"Great. We just spoke yesterday and things couldn't be better."

"So you're still together?"

"As much as we've ever been."

I sit riveted by this interview and rather fascinated by Trevor's smooth lies. He and I never spoke. Things could be a lot better. And we're definitely not together.

"So the photo in *People,* the one of her crying…she doesn't look okay there," Mary presses.

"She was upset, but I've reassured her that everything is fine and things are fine."

I grab the remote, turn off the TV, and throw myself backward on the couch. Trevor, you are such a shithead. Why didn't I see it until now? What did I like about you?

But this is bigger than Trevor. This is about me, my choices, my life.

What have I been doing these past six months?

My show is in shambles. The content's crap. The numbers suck. My writers and producers are near mutiny. Why am I seeing this only now? How long have things been like this?

Where have I been?

What *am* I doing? And why am I sleepwalking through life?

I don't know what happened or why it happened, but I do

know this: I'm through sleepwalking. I'm awake now. And things are going to be different. Starting with axing Trevor from my life.

I grab my phone and dial his number, and when I get voice mail I leave a cool, curt message: "Trevor, it's been fun, but it's time I dated men with a little more backbone and a lot more integrity."

And then I hang up.

One problem down. Only half a dozen more to go.

I oversleep and don't wake until the doorbell rings. It takes me a moment to figure out it is my doorbell making that god-awful sound, too.

Yawning, I stumble from bed and make my way to the front door, where I find Dana, my personal trainer, on the doorstep with her basket of torture gizmos. "You still sleeping?" she asks in disbelief.

I nod. "First decent night's sleep in a long time."

"Well, honey, go change because it's time to wake your ass up."

I dash to my bedroom to put on sweats and workout shoes and think I'm finally getting the message.

Time to wake my ass up.

How long has God been sending this message? And how long have I been ignoring it?

Working out on an empty stomach sucks, and Dana's ruthless, pushing me harder than usual, determined to teach me some proverbial lesson.

As I cycle madly, I think there is a method to her madness. My heart's pumping. My muscles scream. Sweat drips from every pore. I hurt so bad, I know I'm alive. Painfully alive.

I crack a wry smile as Dana shouts, "Faster! . . . Faster!" Better that than painfully dead.

At the studio, Glenn drops by my office to tell me our ratings last night went through the roof.

"What about *ET*'s?" I ask.

"Theirs were strong," he admits, "but we enjoyed a big jump, and that's on top of last week's impressive numbers. You have to feel good about that."

"I do. So who won last night?"

"Last night they won, but that was just a battle. We're going to win the war," he says, leaving my office.

I pump my fist in the air in solidarity, but after he's gone I bury my face in my hands. The ratings boost is related to Trevor, and Trevor and I are through. So how are we going to win this one? What rabbit do I pull out of a hat next?

I'm busy over the next few days, fielding phone calls from everyone but Trevor. I want him to call, needing an apology, but knowing that if I can't get an apology even a good-bye would help. All the losses in my life make me crave closure, but as the days pass and I hear nothing, I realize I'm not going to. Trevor's not going to call. He's gone.

I'm done, too, I remind myself as I do a half dozen interviews with rival magazines and shows—*Yes, Trevor was fun, but it's better he's with a woman his own age. And no, I wasn't devastated when it ended; this was mutual and a long time coming.* But the rejection gnaws at me and I'm grateful to be busy. In fact, I'm so busy smiling and feigning personal and professional joy that I totally forget Shey's arriving from New York to spend the weekend with me until Thursday afternoon's call from her.

I'm at my desk just about to turn off my computer and I have to listen to her voice mail twice before I realize tomorrow's Friday. She's here tomorrow.

I can't believe I forgot Shey was coming. We originally were supposed to convene in Seattle for Zach's baptism, but the date was changed. Instead Shey rebooked her flight to head to L.A. to spend a girls' weekend with me.

And now she'll be here tomorrow and I'm craving a girls' weekend as well. A good one. Decadent, relaxing, *fun*.

I instant message Madison, who ducks into my office to see what's up. "Can you see if you can get me a reservation for a two-bedroom suite at the Parker in Palm Springs for two nights?" I ask her. "The hotel also pulls up as Le Parker Méredien. I'd love the Gene Autry guesthouse but don't know if that's available."

"New romance?" she asks, waggling her eyebrows.

"With my best friend."

"Oh, fun. I'll get right on it."

Madison dances her way back to my office ten minutes later with a reservation confirmation. "You got the Gene Autry residence and they love you." She places the printed confirmation in front of me. "No, seriously, they looooove you and have promised to spoil you rotten. Daily morning coffee service. Spa treatments. Dinner at Mister Parker's. I wish I was going."

"If that's what you want for Christmas...?" I answer, slipping the confirmation into my briefcase.

"Really?"

"Unless you have a better idea."

"I'll do Palm Springs!"

"Smart girl."

*   *   *

I'm practically singing my way through Friday morning's taping. I'm so excited about the weekend with Shey and thrilled to be leaving the city for a girls' getaway in Palm Springs. I was so jealous when I heard that Marta and Shey had their own getaway in the San Juan Islands a few years ago. I haven't done anything like that with either of them since I started at *America Tonight*—my fault, not theirs, as it's my schedule making things difficult.

We're done taping by noon, and I'm in my car and rushing to the airport. I'm just five minutes away when I get the text from Shey saying her plane has landed and she'll be heading toward the curb as soon as they reach the gate.

I'm circling Arrivals in my Jag when I spot Shey emerging from the terminal. Nearly six feet tall and a gorgeous, willowy blonde, she'd be hard to miss, too.

I pull up to the curb, shift into park, and jump out to greet her with a hug and a laugh. I feel like a midget hugging her, but then I am barely five three.

"Are you shrinking, Tiana?" Shey teases me as she gives me a squeeze.

Oh, my God, it's good to see her. Her voice, her warmth, her Texas twang. "I was just asking myself the same thing," I answer, opening the trunk to put her luggage in the back. "How was the flight?"

"Uneventful."

"The best kind of flight."

"How's life?" Shey asks as we climb into the car and close the doors.

"Could be better, but you know I love a good challenge."

"You've certainly been in the news a lot."

"Not by choice," I mutter as I pull away from the curb.

"This new guy of yours, Trevor Campbell, he's gone? Out of the picture?"

"Yep."

"What happened?"

"Not entirely sure, but I think he started sleeping with his co-star."

"Is that what he said?"

I glance at her. "He hasn't returned my calls in a week."

"But he appeared on *ET*—"

"Spouting lies." I shrug indifferently, but then my brave face crumples and I feel the sting of rejection all over again. He never did call. Never did care. "To be honest, I feel like a fool. I guess it wasn't much of a relationship, and I should be relieved it's over. I guess I'm relieved—"I break off, gulp a breath. "Sort of. No, not really, because now I have to start dating all over again."

Shey arches an elegant brow. "Why do you hate dating so much?"

"Because the whole Tiana Tomlinson identity trips men up."

"How?"

I wave a hand as I change lanes and prepare to enter the freeway. "I think they fall for the package and don't realize there's a real me beneath all the hair and makeup and celebrity appearances, a me who's considerably different than the TV persona."

"Are you different?"

I shoot her an accusing glance. "Of course I'm different. You know I'm different—"

"Not if you're dating actors like Trevor Campbell for six

months! Did you really think he'd fall in love, settle down, and be ready to start making babies before your biological clock runs down?"

I'm staring straight ahead, concentrating on the 405's bumper-to-bumper traffic, but I also hear every word she's saying.

"T, you need someone your age or older, someone settled, someone mature, someone not in the business." Her tone softens. "But if you don't want the marriage and kids, then admit it, and just be done with it. But that's not what I hear from you. I hear you still want a family...?"

I know she's looking at me, and I just tighten my grip on the steering wheel. Of course I want a family. It's normal for a woman to want a family. But most women aren't widowed at thirty, either.

Shey leans toward me, taps the back of my hand where it clenches the wheel. "You know, if Keith hadn't died, you'd be a reporter in a small city, juggling assignments between making cookies and driving kids to music, dance, and sporting events."

I see the I-10 intersection ahead, knowing I want to go east.

"You'd already started collecting baby clothes, remember?" she adds.

"One outfit and one blanket, not exactly an entire layette."

"But you know what I'm saying. Having a baby was a top priority once Keith returned—"

"But he didn't, and I haven't met anyone close to Keith, so the baby blanket and onesie are long gone and my focus has been on work."

"Okay. We'll drop the subject...for now." She grins and slides her seat back to give her more legroom. "I do have some big news, though. Well, it's actually not my news. It's about Marta."

I glance at her again. "Yeah?"

Shey's grinning. "Do you know why Zach's baptism was postponed from this weekend until the end of the month? Marta's pregnant."

"What?"

Shey's grin grows. "Marta's just hit her second trimester, but she's still really sick."

"Zach's not even a year old yet."

Shey just laughs her throaty laugh and tucks a wave of thick blonde hair behind her ear. "But that's not all. She's carrying twins."

I let out a screech, and Shey laughs again. "Eva let the news slide when I called the house last night. Marta doesn't know we know yet."

"We've got to go see her. I know the baptism has been postponed until the twenty-eighth, but we should just surprise her—" I break off, bite my lip as I realize this is Marta we're talking about. "She doesn't want anyone to see her sick, does she."

Shey shakes her head. "Apparently she can't keep any food down and she's lost a lot of weight—"

"Not that she needed to lose any," I interrupt.

"Eva says Luke's been worried about her, but according to the doctor the pregnancy's fine."

"Wow." Marta pregnant with twins. Incredible. Just two years ago she and Eva were an island, and now Marta's married and a mom to little Zach and expecting two more.

Shey casts a sympathetic glance my way. "I promise, if you want it, your turn will come, Tits."

I force a smile. "I know." But I don't know, not anymore.

Shey's right about Trevor, though. Trevor would have never married me or had children with me, nor would any of the last few men I dated. But those are the men I date. I'm not attracted to the kind, salt-of-the-earth men—and those men do still exist. I just avoid them. Just like I avoid being hurt.

"Good things come when we least expect it," she adds.

I roll my eyes. Shey can say that because she's known only good things. She comes from a stable, loving home. Her modeling career fell into her lap. Her brilliant, wealthy husband pursued her hard for two years before she capitulated. She has adorable boys, an Upper East Side apartment, a country estate, and a thriving business. In short, she has it all.

"I hope so," I whisper.

Shey reaches out and squeezes my arm. "I know so."

I glance at her, and she looks so serious and so sure of herself that some of the tension in me eases. How can I not believe Shey? Shey has a huge heart and more strength than any woman I know.

"So do you want to know where we're going?" I ask, shooting her a quick smile.

"We're not going to your place?"

"Nope."

"Why not?"

"Thought we needed to do something totally escapist and self-indulgent."

Her eyebrows lift. "Are we going to a spa?"

"In Palm Springs."

Shey lets out a whoop and pumps her fist in the air. "Road trip!"

Chapter Eight

——— ★★★ ———

Our hotel, the Parker, has enjoyed an impressive list of owners and names, first as Gene Autry's Melody Ranch Estate, then as the Merv Griffin Resort and then the Givenchy Hotel & Spa, and now the Parker. The villa walls are pale pink and draped with bougainvillea, and the gardens are as lush as a desert oasis. Restyled by designer Jonathan Adler, it's also hip, stylish, and popular among celebrities fleeing Los Angeles for sun and fun.

Shey and I tumble onto the slipcovered living room couch with happy sighs. The doors to our private garden and pool are open. Fresh flowers and chilled champagne greet us. We even have our own "butler" on call for the next two days.

"It's forty-five degrees in New York," Shey says, wiggling her bare toes. She's been talking about changing into her swimsuit to go lie out by the pool, but she still hasn't moved from the overstuffed sofa. "My kids would die to be here. They'd love the pool."

"The boys are good swimmers, aren't they?"

"For city kids, yeah." She stretches, yawns. "I love my boys, wouldn't trade them for anything, but God, sometimes it's all so much. Sometimes it seems like everyone needs so much from me."

Shey turns her head, looks at me, her expression unusually

serious. "You don't know how badly I needed this. Two days of nothing. Two days to be lazy. Two days where I can just take care of me for a change."

After an hour by the pool, we finish off the afternoon with massages and oxygenating facials before changing and making a ten-minute drive into downtown Palm Springs for dinner. The sun set behind the mountains an hour ago, and the desert city sparkles tonight. The night is calm and clear as we arrive at one of my favorite restaurants.

The maître d' knows me on sight, welcomes me warmly, and finds us a table almost immediately. Not long after we're seated, Brett, the owner, appears table side with a kiss for me and a complimentary bottle of champagne.

I introduce Shey, and he swears he recognizes her. She laughs, demurs, and then he snaps his fingers. "*Sports Illustrated* swimsuit issue 1991."

"Yes," she admits, cheeks dusky pink.

"I knew it. Green bikini in the waterfall. And then there was the lizard-skin one-piece against the sand. Right?"

Her jaw drops a little. It's been a long time since she's been recognized as a *Sports Illustrated* swimsuit model. "That's impressive, sugar."

He just grins. "I have two of the most beautiful women in America dining at my restaurant. Am I a lucky man, or what?"

As he walks away, Shey shakes her head. "That never happens anymore."

"It's because you're always with your husband. Men aren't going to trip over themselves in front of John."

The exchange with Brett reminds me of my conversation

with Christie on Thanksgiving when she told me that beautiful women get better reservations, tables, and services. They get attention and eye contact.

I tell Shey about the conversation Christie and I were having in Christie's kitchen, and I ask Shey if she'd ever consider getting work done.

"Probably, at least my eyes," she answers without much hesitation, but then adds, "But Marta would kill me. She's so antisurgery, so anticaving to societal pressure."

"You've discussed cosmetic surgery with Marta?"

She nods. "Marta just about took my head off. Wanted to know what kind of role model would I be for Eva? What kind of example was I setting for other girls?"

"Easy for her to say. She's not in front of a camera, not like you or me."

"Which is why she was livid I'd consider it. Apparently I'd be perpetuating Madison Avenue's propaganda, that only young and beautiful women are valuable."

A little heavy-handed, but that's Marta for you. And although heavy-handed, Marta's usually right. I don't know if it's because she's the mother of a daughter or a rebel at heart, but Marta just doesn't succumb to society pressure the way many beautiful women do. But maybe that's what makes Marta beautiful. She's strong, different, unique.

"If you were to take Marta out of the equation, surgery wouldn't be an issue then? You'd have the surgery tomorrow?"

She starts to answer and then stops, shakes her head. "No. Not tomorrow. Maybe in five years, maybe ten. I'd do it when I wanted to do it, when I felt comfortable with it. I certainly wouldn't do it because I was being told to do it."

"I don't want to be told to do it, either. It's one thing to want to do something. It's another when it's forced on you. Besides, I don't want to be a clown."

Shey shudders. "There's that. I've seen some bad work, too. I guess the bottom line is that people should feel good about themselves, and that includes taking responsibility for themselves. There's nothing worse than being unhappy and blaming everyone else for your unhappiness." She looks up at me, and her gaze meets mine. "If you're not happy, fix it. Life's short, you know?"

The expression in her eyes is sad, and I realize we're not talking about plastic surgery anymore. I reach out, take her hand, and give it a squeeze. Something's going on with Shey, but she's clearly not ready to share. Shey might be our sunshine, but she's also damn stubborn. When she's ready to talk, she will, but until then, I'll just keep letting her know I love her.

After dinner we return to the hotel, where we change into PJs and lounge around the living room with the TV on mute so we can talk. Shey and I haven't had this kind of time alone in years, and we make the most of it. She brings me up to speed on her boys and some of the issues they're facing in school. The youngest one is very tall and very thin, and kids make fun of him for having a stork neck.

"It brings back all the feelings of inferiority I had as a girl growing up. Giraffe, stilts, daddy longlegs." Shey shudders and runs a hand through her blonde hair, thick and tawny as a lion's mane. "Being a kid was horrible. Did anybody have a good time growing up?"

"I hear a few people did. But for the majority it's rough."

"Can you imagine being pretty and popular in school?" She laughs her low, husky laugh, and then her laughter dies. "It's funny how just when you get old enough to take the hits, the hits go to your kids instead, and they don't know what the hell to do." She sees my face. "Am I going on too much about the parent thing?"

"No. I like it. You make me feel normal again." And it's true. It feels so good to be around someone who has known me for over half my life. It feels even better to be myself and accepted and understood. No matter what I do in life, no matter what career I choose, I'll always have Shey and Marta. Real friends, true friends, are worth their weight in gold.

"Ah, honey, you are normal. It's your industry that isn't."

She gives me a crooked smile and it's a little country, a little cowgirl, and I love it. It's her real smile, not her model smile and I suddenly lay all my cards on the table. "Maybe it's time for me to retire."

Shey looks at me for a long moment, her blue eyes narrowed. "You don't really mean that, do you? If you were to ask me, I'd say you're just pissed off right now."

She's right. I am pissed off. How can I be valuable only if I look young and unlined? How can they really replace me just because I'm closer to forty than twenty?

I roll over onto my back, cross one leg at the knee, and swing my foot. "Why didn't I see any of this coming? During the summer I thought I had it made. Hot guy, great career, steady income. But it was an illusion. I'm in trouble."

"What would you do if you weren't with the show anymore?"

I pause, think. "No idea."

"But you've always had a plan. Even back in high school, at

St. Pious, you were the only one of us who knew for sure what she wanted to do."

"I knew what I wanted to be, not do." My lips twist ruefully. "I was going to be famous. I wanted everyone to know me." Who knows why I thought being a celebrity would solve anything.

"And everyone does."

"And now look where I am."

"Sugar, maybe that's what this is really all about. You met your goal. You're famous. You've spent ten years on TV. Perhaps it's time to change direction. Make some new plans."

"Leave *America Tonight*?"

She reaches out, strokes my hair, smoothing it as though I were a little girl. "There are other shows, and you could do more than just TV."

"But I like TV. I love TV."

"Then at least you have part of your answer."

I turn my head to look at her. My gaze holds hers. "I'm glad you're here, Shey. I needed this."

"I'm always here for you, and Tits, don't worry so much. You have a great brain and amazing drive. You can do whatever you want to do. You just have to know what you want to do."

The next morning, we get trail maps and directions from the concierge and head off on a hike in the San Jacinto Mountains.

It's a cool morning and we're both bundled up, but in layers so we can strip down as we heat up.

We've been walking about fifteen minutes when Shey glances at me. "Do you really miss Trevor? It sounds as if you've taken the breakup hard."

"I don't think I miss *him*, but I do miss being in a relationship."

"Even if the relationship doesn't work?"

"The real question is, when do you know it's not working? How long does it take to figure out that things just won't ever get better?" I unscrew the cap from my bottle, take a quick drink, and put it back on. "What's sad is I didn't feel that happy with Trevor, but I don't think I would have been the one to end it. I liked believing someone, somewhere, cared for me. I liked pretending I'm not alone."

"But you're not alone. You have friends who love you to pieces."

I flash her a smile. "Call me greedy, but I want both. Friends *and* romance."

"I get that." She unzips her green jacket and ties it around her waist. "And we should have both in our lives. Men are great, but they're not women. Men will love us, but they'll never really understand us, not the way our girlfriends do. And our men see us and love us in a way our girlfriends can't. That's why we need both."

"Research shows that women with close friendships live longer and healthier lives than women without. Spending time with girlfriends is supposed to be one of the best stress busters out there."

"I believe it." Shey takes a long drink from her water bottle. "I already feel a hundred times better than I did when I arrived in L.A. Just hanging out talking about life makes life easier. Less overwhelming."

I study her profile with the high, strong brow, straight nose, prominent cheekbones. Her face is one of those genetic wonders, yet there's no drama attached to her, no air of superiority. She's still a country girl at heart. "You've never found life overwhelming. You're the most grounded woman I know."

She turns to look at me, and her eyes are clouded with emotion. There's a hint of panic in her voice when she answers, "I think I'm losing my bounce! Those little things that never used to bother me, they don't seem so little anymore."

"Like what?"

"Everything." She laughs, but the sound is hollow. "What do you say we pick up our pace, really show these mountains a thing or two?"

Two hours later, back down off the mountain we stop at the Coffee Bean & Tea Leaf in downtown Palm Springs for iced chai tea and sit on one of the low brick walls, sipping our tea and relaxing. The temperature is perfect, mid-seventies, with just a hint of a breeze. I don't remember when I last felt so good, so happy.

"Let's do this again tomorrow before we leave," I say, flexing my toes to savor the stretch in my calves. "That was amazing. Exactly what I needed."

"Such a different feeling than running in Central Park," she agrees. "I need to get back to nature more than I do."

I tip my face to the sun, lashes closing. "I used to. For a couple years Christie and I hiked once a month in the Santa Monica Mountains, but we've gotten out of the habit. Between trying to meet up with Trevor on weekends and Christie working on her latest film, we stopped scheduling the hikes, but I'm inspired to make it a priority again."

She pushes up her sunglasses. "Me too. I think I better step up my workouts. Exercise is a great way to cope with stress."

"So enough of this. Talk to me. What's going on at home? What's making you so sad?"

"I don't know. But everything's just off. My family doesn't feel like my family. And I can't stand to have the boys bullied like this at school. Nothing John or I do seems to make a difference, and we've had endless meetings with the principal."

"All three boys are being bullied?"

"Mainly Coop. But then Bo tries to stick up for him and he gets made fun of, too. Makes me crazy, the name calling, the ridiculing. What's wrong with kids? Why do they have to do it?"

I think of Eva and how she struggled in her Bellevue school the first couple of years after moving from New York to Washington. Marta was sick with worry. Even tried to become a PTA mom to help Eva fit in. "Kids can be horrible. Remember how Eva suffered after they moved?"

Shey nods. "At least Eva was plucky. Cooper's not. He's withdrawing more and more, and we've talked to the school and talked to professionals and everyone's doing what they can, but he's disappearing right before my eyes. John says it's a phase and that eventually this will pass, but I don't know. I feel like I can't breathe."

"How long has this been going on?"

"For the past year. It gets better, then it gets worse. New York's so different from where I grew up. Boys are different. They're just so competitive and everything is about status and money and that's not how I was raised. Sometimes I fantasize about packing us up and moving us back to Texas. It'd be good for the kids to grow up on the ranch. They'd realize that God gave them hands for things other than Nintendo games."

"Can you do it?"

She laughs incredulously. "John leave New York? Never. He loves the city. He'd die of boredom in the country, and now that he's transitioning from being a fashion photographer to owning his own gallery, he's even more into the arts and culture scene."

Shey and I didn't just go to St. Pious together, we roomed together at Stanford. I know her better than I know any woman, and I've never heard her sound like this. Not about her marriage. Or her kids. "Are *you* okay?"

She doesn't speak. Eventually she nods. "Yeah."

But she's not. "This is more than the boys, isn't it."

Her chest rises and falls as she takes a deep breath and then another. "No one ever said marriage would be easy, right?"

"Right."

She forces a smile. "We're going to be fine. It's just a blip, a bump in the road. We've had them before. Nothing to worry about."

I smile back, hiding my worry. "You're tough. You can handle whatever life throws at you."

"Of course I can. Piece of cake." She stands, tosses her now empty plastic cup in the trash bin. "I say a visit to the spa is in order. Whirlpool. Sauna. Maybe another massage."

"I say, *yes.*"

Shey doesn't bring up John or the problems at home again, and although I'm worried, I don't press, waiting for her to talk when she's ready.

So instead of talking, we hike, swim, suntan, and eat. And we eat a lot. Shey has the fastest metabolism of anyone I know. She can eat what two men can and not put on an ounce. Marta and I once talked about Shey's ridiculous metabolism and we agreed if she weren't so funny and warm and wonderful, we'd hate her. Sad fact, but true.

Sunday afternoon I drive her back to LAX for her flight. Shey, who rarely gets emotional, gets choked up when it's time to say good-bye. She hugs me extra hard. "Thanks for the best weekend ever," she says, her voice husky. "It's exactly what I needed."

"Me too." I hug her back. "Call me if you ever want to talk. I can be a good listener."

"I know you can. Love you, Tits."

"Love you, too. See you in Seattle in a couple weeks."

And just when I think she's going to walk away, she puts her hands on my shoulders and gives me a little shake. "We can't lose faith. We don't always know why life happens the way it does, but we can handle it. We are strong enough. Right?"

"Right," I agree, and as she walks into the terminal I know those words were for her as much as they were for me.

When I return to work Monday morning, I discover the show's art directors have unveiled our holiday set and Clarence, our stage manager, wants my feedback. I love it. The stage looks like fantasyland with decorated wreaths and Christmas trees, candy canes, and nutcrackers. There is even faux snow outside the faux window. It looks deliciously wintery—and feels that way on the stage with the forty-degree temperature, too.

This week I start the plastic surgery feature interviews, and I'm only halfway done with the celebrity tradition segments, too. Several years ago, I interviewed stars about their favorite holiday memories and family traditions, and viewers loved them so much that the holiday stories became a show fixture. The only drawback to the celeb segments is that we shoot them close to the holidays in the celebs' houses and hotels to capture the season, and it means rushing all over the city with our cameraman in hellish traffic when everyone's temper is painfully short.

We have a sixty-minute production meeting at nine, followed by an in-studio interview with Harry Connick Jr., where he shares with me his Christmas traditions in his beloved New Orleans. I change into a different outfit, fix my makeup, and have my hair touched up before Mike, my favorite cameraman, and I race across town to meet Dennis Quaid and his wife, Kimberly. I have Mike film Dennis and Kimberly playing with the twins in front of the Christmas tree before Dennis sits down with me to share his holiday memories.

We're back at the studio by noon. I tape another segment with Dwayne Johnson, aka the Rock, at twelve-thirty, and this isn't a celeb holiday tradition story, but an in-depth interview promoting his new film.

We wrap Dwayne's interview in time for me to tape tonight's show, and then it's another wardrobe change, back to hair and makeup, and then I'm on our festive stage, shivering in the cold in my flirty dress and strappy four-inch-heel sandals, and we're filming segments for the hiatus show.

But the day's still not over. I promised Joy I'd put in an appearance at her holiday party at the Sunset Tower, and I make one more change, this time into black slacks, a white satin blouse, and a little silver shrug.

Joy Kim is a talented young clothing designer whose line, O Joy, has become wildly popular with the beautiful people; we became friends after she sent a dress for me for the Cannes Film Festival last May. I was wearing her slinky barely-there metallic bronze gown the night I met Trevor. The neckline plunged, the back plunged, the fabric molded to my breasts and hips so that very little was left to the imagination. Photos of me in the O Joy gown were splashed all over the Internet and in the tabloids of the foreign press.

The extensive press coverage helped launch O Joy internationally, and once I was back from Cannes she sent two dozen white roses and lilies to thank me for wearing her gown on the film festival's red carpet.

After pulling up to the hotel, I hand my car keys to the valet and take the elevator to the penthouse floor, where Joy's throwing the party. It's a young crowd hanging out, and I recognize a few faces, mostly young actresses, a couple of musician types and their girlfriends, and some reporters from rival entertainment shows.

I find Joy, hand her the hostess gift I've brought, and chit-chat for a few minutes until her next guest claims her attention. I slip out of the penthouse suite and down the hall to the elevators, and as the doors open I breathe a sigh of relief. God, I felt old and overdressed in there. The young trendy crowd is so not my scene.

I'm waiting for the valet attendant to bring my car around when I hear my name called. I know that voice pretty well by now.

Slowly I turn to look behind me, and there is Michael, leaning against the building, smiling.

"What are you doing out here?" I ask, drawing my coat closer over my shoulders. The days might be warm, but the evening definitely cools off. "Coming, going…?"

"I had a call. Couldn't get good reception at the party."

"Joy's party?"

Like me, he's overdressed, dark slacks and a long-sleeved

white shirt with the cuffs rolled back on his forearms. The crisp white cotton fabric speaks of money. The shirt is probably Frette. His leather belt and shoes are equally pricey. "I saw you arrive," he answers. "And you're leaving already?"

"It's a young crowd."

"You're young."

"But not nineteen."

He smiles at me, and my pulse quickens and my spine tingles. "Thank God. Women with a little life experience are infinitely sexier."

I walk toward him, one slow step at a time. "Have you abandoned your date again? Or is she off foraging for drinks?"

His smile deepens, warming his eyes. "I'm pulling a Tiana Tomlinson. I'm facing the party scene alone."

"Oh my. You do live dangerously."

"You don't know the half of it." His deep blue gaze wraps me, holds me, warming me from the inside out. "I'm barely civilized, Ms. America."

"That's no surprise. I could have told you that."

He just smiles down at me, his lips crooked, his eyes darkly blue and lit with amusement.

Once I hated that he found me amusing. Now I almost enjoy his sense of humor. Almost.

And just admitting that truth, I feel heat flaring inside of me. How annoying. He makes me feel so much, and it's strange, so strange, after seven years of feeling nothing like this around men.

I probably would like Michael if he didn't make every alarm in my head sound.

My car's headlights appear in the driveway. "That's me," I say as the attendant parks the car in front of us.

"Tiana," Michael says as I hand the valet attendant a folded ten-dollar bill, "if you should ever need a date, I'd be happy to clean up for you."

I hesitate next to my car. "I've seen you in action, Doctor."

"Have you?"

I nod once. "You'd abandon me at the first opportunity."

"Never."

My gaze meets Michael's and holds. "Don't make promises you can't keep."

"I never do."

The heat in his eyes scorches me. Unnerved, I climb in behind the wheel and start the car even though it's already running. The car squawks in protest. Heart hammering, I pull away from the curb and head home with Michael's words, *I never do,* ringing loudly, if not a little ominously, in my head.

Chapter Nine

——— ✦✦✦ ———

Home, I wander restlessly around my house, unusually hyped. Michael always throws me. He just has that effect on me.

I open the fridge, see the new bottle of white wine chilling, close the fridge. Don't need liquor tonight. I'm drinking more than I should. I'm sleeping less than I need.

After changing into my pajamas, I climb into bed with my laptop to prepare my interview with Susie Fleming tomorrow, but I find Michael popping into my thoughts as I read through my notes for Susie's interview.

But I don't want to be thinking about Michael, and I don't want to be distracted.

Susie was one of the show viewers who answered my blog when I asked if any of my Los Angeles–area viewers had had plastic surgery and if they'd be willing to talk to me on camera about their experience. Within a day, the comment box was flooded with nearly a hundred volunteers. Some of the volunteers never had work done and just wanted to be on TV. Others were aspiring actors and actresses who'd undergone cosmetic surgery to improve their appearance and hoped to share their story on TV. Those I also weeded out.

Libby and Jeffrey screened the volunteers and pared the list to twelve. I talked to all twelve on the phone and will interview five on camera. Susie is the first interview.

I check my e-mail before I open my Word program and scroll through the in-box. Madison has forwarded an e-mail to my personal account from an organization in Tucson that wants to honor me with a lifetime achievement award at their annual black-tie fund-raiser in February. Every year they select a member of the arts to recognize, someone from Tucson or who started their career in Tucson, and this year they've selected me.

I read it through twice and then forward it to Madison with a note asking her to get more info on the event. Who were some of the past honorees? How visible is the group? And then, putting everyone and everything out of mind, I begin typing up possible questions for my morning interview, because that's what's important now.

Glenn sees me Wednesday morning in the break room as I'm pouring myself yet another cup of coffee. "Good interview with the Rock on Monday," he says. "You had a nice rapport."

"Thanks."

"Tia, your numbers are still up. Substantially up."

"Good."

"Network heads are noticing."

"Great."

"This is the kind of attention you want."

I just smile.

"So how's the cosmetic surgery feature going?" he asks.

"First interview's today. Susie's coming in here. We're using *This Morning*'s set for the interview so it looks cozy."

"Good. And keep up the good work."

I report to makeup forty-five minutes before I'm due to meet Susie.

As I sit in the makeup chair and Vanessa clucks over my tired, stressed face, I wonder what will happen when the rise in numbers starts to fall. Because they will fall. Maybe not plummet, but at the first drop, will everyone panic again? Will Shelby become overnight co-anchor?

I wish I liked Shelby better. Maybe I wouldn't resent her success quite so much if she cared about the news, but Shelby isn't interested in news, she's interested in ratings and fame. She's interested in my job. Maybe more interested than I've been lately.

Vanessa mists my face and wipes off old makeup to prepare for the new, and I find myself wondering if I'd feel differently about being at this crossroads in my career if I had more, like a husband and children. Would I be more or less satisfied with my success? Would the drop in ratings feel different?

Success is so bittersweet. The more you achieve, the more you expect yourself to achieve, so that the quest to do more, be better, and reach higher never ends.

As Vanessa preps my face for the spray-on foundation, she tells me the big bosses stopped by to chat with her. "That was a first," she adds. "But then they were talking to quite a few of us today."

My eyes are closed and my lips shut so she can get an even spray, but I make a sound in the back of my throat so she knows I'm interested in hearing more.

"I don't want you to take this the wrong way," Vanessa adds as the cool makeup hits my face. She sprays in small, even circles from my brow down to my collarbone. "But they were talking to the lighting guys about redoing your lights to try to take some years off. Apparently new research shows you're skewing older and they don't want to lose the key, younger audience."

The spray goes off. I wait a moment for Vanessa to inspect the work before I open my eyes. "What did they say to you?" I ask her.

She shrugs uncomfortably. "Nothing much."

"Come on, Vanessa. We've worked together too long. Tell me the truth."

"They wanted to know how I liked working with Shelby."

I clench my teeth together, livid all over again. I have worked so hard and my numbers are finally up, and the studio heads are noticing, and yet it's not enough. They still want me younger. Hell, I'd like to be younger, but I'm not. I am who I am and I'm just beginning to realize that *America Tonight* could hit number one but that won't satisfy the network heads. They want me to get the work done. This is more than ratings. This is about image, and youth, and the fact that I am—like every human being—aging.

Vanessa begins applying glue to the delicate strip of black false eyelashes. "I told them she was fine," she adds briskly. "But I like you better." When I open my mouth, she holds up a finger. "Don't say anything. Just don't cry. I'll kill you if I have to take off the foundation and start over."

I manage a smile and begin mentally reviewing my notes for Susie's interview.

Susie's cosmetic surgery was to address her breasts, which were different sizes. Her right breast was a C cup and her left breast not even an A. She'd spent thirteen years trying to hide the fact that her breasts were so very lopsided. She didn't swim, wouldn't go to the gym, wouldn't wear snug clothes. Her whole life revolved around hiding something she had no control over.

Hair and face camera ready, I head to the stage to greet

Susie. She ends up being an easy interview. The words tumble from her. Her embarrassment, her shame, her inability to date or let any man close. The feeling that everyone stared at her, or worse, laughed at her. The difficulty buying proper bras, having to fill one cup with everything from tissue to foam to silicone pads.

"The surgery changed all that," she says, pausing for breath. Her cheeks are flushed, but she's not ashamed, she's happy. "I'm not afraid to meet people anymore. I'm going to Cabo for Christmas, and I've never been to a beach resort before. I wouldn't do a trip like that before the surgery. But now I feel like I have a whole new life. I can do anything." Her blush deepens. "I'm even dating a really nice man and it's getting serious."

"Does he know about your surgery?" I ask.

Her blush extends to her hairline, but she's smiling broadly. "He knows. He didn't until I told him. But he says I have a great body. He says I'm hot." Susie's smile turns shy. "No one has ever said that to me before."

She's thirty-two going on eighteen. It's as though she's just discovered life. I wish I could embrace plastic surgery the way Susie has. Her work has made her hopeful and eager, innocent and new. But her surgery was to correct a wrong. My surgery would be to roll back time. It would be an end, not a beginning, because once I start down this slippery slope, where do I stop? Where do the tweaks and fixes and lifts end?

It's not just the cutting and stitching, either, it's the mindset, the attitude. I will have caved to the pressure, caved to conformity. But I don't want to cave. I can't cave. Because honestly, no one can fake youth and beauty forever.

We wrap up the interview and I return to my office to check

in with Madison, who was trying to reschedule a lunch date I'd made weeks ago that won't work now thanks to a reshuffling of some of the celebrity holiday stories.

I stop at Madison's desk. "Lucy Liu's holiday segment is today. Where am I meeting her?"

She makes a sad face. "Her publicist had to cancel."

"Again?"

"It's a nasty bug. Her publicist assures us we wouldn't want it."

I close the door to my office and sit at my desk and tap my keyboard, waking my computer from sleep mode and clicking on my in-box. My in-box has thirty-one new e-mails; many are holiday greetings and e-vite reminders for holiday parties, plus an e-mail from Shey thanking me for a great weekend, and then a follow-up from the Tucson group that wants me to join them in February for their fund-raiser. They're hoping I can confirm my attendance soon. Madison got me info on the event.

I flip through my calendar, note a rather light February, and type a response: "I'm delighted to join you, please send me details when possible."

I'm hitting send when there's a light rap on the door and Madison pops her head in. "Do you want a latte? I'm making a Starbucks run."

I shake my head. "I'm good. I'm just going to work until I leave for the Mario López segment. Then I'll return to tape the show."

Mario is so easy to talk to that I arrive back at HBC in record time, which is a good thing since Libby had forgotten to tell me she'd bumped Helene's interview from noon to eleven.

Helene, the second of my cosmetic surgery features, is an attractive, bright brunette, a mix of Greek, Dutch, and Italian heritage, and her story moved me before I even saw her photos.

Despite her college degree and strong oral and written communication skills, Helene had struggled to find a job. She finally landed a bookkeeping position even though math wasn't her forte, and she kept the books for a small construction company in Apple Valley. Although she hadn't been hired for public relations or sales, she made numerous suggestions to the company's VP of marketing, ideas that were used and ended up greatly benefiting the company. When a position in sales and customer service opened, a position that paid ten thousand a year more than she was getting, she applied for it, thinking she would be a great fit. Instead they hired a young recent college grad with no job experience. Helene was devastated. When she asked why she'd been passed over for the position, one she knew she was more than qualified to do, the VP had said, "Juliet's personality makes her better suited to the job."

It was then that I looked at Helene's before photos. The pictures reveal a somber, dark-eyed brunette with big eyes, long black eyelashes, a humped nose, and no chin. The lack of chin made her face look top-heavy and contributed to the appearance of an overbite.

I can see how someone might form an opinion that she wasn't socially adept based on the photo. Worse, she doesn't appear bright or confident. Much has been documented on how quickly we form opinions, and we form these opinions in a split second or less. We use appearances and impressions, and in the blink of an eye we might judge someone attractive, confident, intelligent, successful, or plain, slow, mean-spirited, humorless.

I haven't seen Helene's after photos. Instead I'm going to just meet her live, and I'm looking forward to this interview.

I pop into makeup and then I'm on the set getting miked when Libby walks Helene onto the stage. Helene greets me with a smile and outstretched hand, and she radiates energy and warmth. Her brown eyes sparkle and her handshake is firm. "It's very nice to meet you," she says earnestly.

"Thank you for agreeing to be part of the story," I answer, amazed that this is the same woman from the photo. She's actually quite striking, and I start our interview with the question uppermost in my mind: "Are you still with the same company, or do you have a better job?"

"I have a better job."

"Good. Your story really upset me."

"It was tough, but things are so much better now. I'm a human resources manager for a Fortune 500 company based here in Los Angeles—"

"Hoping it's a better salary."

She smiles. "Twice the salary I had before, plus two weeks' vacation, great health benefits, and perks like travel and free gym membership."

"Did you go back to school, take new course work?"

"No."

"So how did this happen? What changed?"

Helene looks me in the eye. "My face. I had a chin implant and this part"—she puts her finger to the bridge of her nose—"shaved down. The doctor suggested braces to help with my overbite, but I didn't do that. I didn't think it necessary."

"You're happy with your decisions?"

"Thrilled," she says quietly. "People now see me the way I've always seen myself. This person"—and she gestures from the top of her head all the way down—"was here the whole time, but most people couldn't see past my profile, or lack of."

"Any regrets?"

Her expression grows wistful. "I just wish I'd done it sooner."

Harper's standing by the cameras with her clipboard as I detach the mike after the interview. "That's brilliant," she says, walking with me toward the decorated show stage where we're scheduled to tape tonight's show, including the new lead Harper's been working on.

"Thank you." I slip off the chestnut blazer I wore for the interview, revealing a slim sheath dress.

"Do you ever think you don't belong here, that maybe this isn't the best format for you?"

The glow I'd felt at her compliment quickly fades. I shoot her a sharp glance. "I like what I do."

"Yes, but you're really good one-on-one in interviews, as good as Meredith or Katie—"

"Harper, this is my job. And if memory serves, we have a show to do." My voice is clear and steady. My tone is professionally crisp.

But Harper isn't fazed. "Glenn's mentioned a special you want to do. Field stories. Investigative pieces."

"They'd actually be human interest," I correct, wondering why Glenn mentioned my idea to her. "When did this conversation takes place?"

Harper stands to the side as the teleprompter is rolled forward and different lights come on. I take my place in one of the tall director chairs as everyone does a sound and light check.

"I brought the subject up." She steps over black cables as

the robotic cameras move. "I told him I thought HBC was underutilizing you. That's when he mentioned your show idea."

"Did he seem open to my idea?"

"Noncommittal. But I'd like to hear more about it sometime. I think it's a great idea. I hope you're able to make it happen." She glances at her clipboard and then exclaims, "Speaking of making it happen, tonight's new lead is pretty big. Not sure if you're going to be comfortable covering it."

"Why not?"

"Mark's been on the phone for the past hour checking sources, but apparently Kiki's pregnant—"

"Kiki? Trevor's Kiki?" My voice cracks and I can't hide my shock.

He had been lying . . .

He was sleeping with her . . .

That explains why he didn't call. But it also feels so much worse.

Harper's scrutinizing my face, reading my reaction. "We have a new opening for tonight's show. It's the big story. Can you handle it, or do we need to call in another anchor? Shelby's around, I believe. . . ."

Her voice drifts away, and I know what she's asking. Am I tough enough, strong enough, to report dirt, particularly dirt on my former boyfriend? Am I the kind of anchor who would cover a story like this?

My conscience screams. Keith would scream. He'd be disgusted by the very idea, and I'm against this messy, sleazy form of journalism. But this is also my show, and I won't have everyone running to Shelby every time my scruples are smashed. "I'll do it," I say, smashing my doubts and misgivings.

"You're sure?"

"Yes."

"Here's the new copy, then. We tape in five."

That's all the time we have as someone from wardrobe comes running out with a chunky gold necklace to add visual interest to my hunter green sheath dress.

David smoothes my hair, flattening the flyaways before spritzing with spray while I skim the text that will be on the teleprompter. Vanessa powders my nose and applies a peachy pink gold lip gloss, and then I'm back on the stage, standing on my spot.

Harper's on the side with Libby and Mark. The floor director is counting down time. The three robotics zoom in. I'm given the signal, and smiling, I look straight into the camera. "You heard it here first! An exclusive—breaking news! Kiki and Trevor's love child."

By the time we've taped tonight's show, and tomorrow's tease as well as the tease for the hiatus show, I'm drained, and just plain nauseated. I haven't eaten since breakfast, although I did have a grilled chicken salad in the break room fridge waiting for me. It was too hectic with the interviews and back-to-back shows, never mind the news that Trevor and Kiki are having a baby together.

A *baby*.

I shudder and shove the image of a pregnant Kiki out of mind as I really don't want to think about him, them, or the baby anymore.

At home I wash my face, eat a bowl of cereal, and climb into bed telling myself that tomorrow can't be as hectic, or mind-numbingly awful, as today.

But tomorrow begins worse.

Somehow in the rush of interviews and taping and anchoring I'd forgotten that today was the announcement of this year's Golden Globe nominations, and when my phone rings at five-twenty a.m. and it's still dark outside, I'm certain something terrible has happened.

But it's only Max waking me up with the news that Trevor has just been nominated for his first Golden Globe.

I prop myself up in bed, shove a heavy fistful of hair from my eyes. "You woke me up to tell me Trevor's up for an award?"

"A *Golden Globe*. And you've ruined it."

I'm really not in the mood for this now. "What are you talking about?"

"His nomination. Everyone should be focused on his performance and the Globe nomination, but instead the only thing people are talking about is Kiki's pregnancy."

"It's true, then?"

"Jesus Christ, Tiana!"

I don't know why, but I smile. Max sounds so outraged, so upset that his golden boy's golden moment has been tarnished. But I don't feel bad for Trevor. Trevor's a shit, and he shit on me. "Well, if that's all, I'm going back to bed."

"That's not all. You owe him—"

"*Owe* him?" I interrupt, outraged. I sit all the way up in bed, knees bent, heart thumping. "Did you really just say that, Max?"

As if realizing he's pushed me too far, he backpedals just a little. "Maybe an interview will suffice."

I laugh out loud. I am so sick of being kicked around. "I'm not interviewing him. I'm not interested in him or concerned with furthering his career."

"Not even if it furthers your career?"

Max has me there, and he pushes his point. "Every time your name is linked with Trevor's, your show ratings go up. You know it, and doll, whether you'll admit it or not, you need him—"

I hang up. My phone rings immediately. I'm about to turn it off when I see it's Harper calling. Harper rarely calls me when I'm at home, which makes me think she's just heard about Trevor's nomination.

"Morning, Harper."

"Trevor Campbell's up for his first Golden Globe, for best supporting actor."

"I've already heard." I throw back the covers and slide into my robe. "Why are you up so early?"

"I always wake up early to hear the list of nominees," she says primly. "How did you hear?"

"My agent. Max reps both of us."

"Did he expect you to celebrate with him?"

I smile, relax a little, liking Harper more and more. "He thought I'd want to interview him. Apparently it'd be good for show ratings."

"You need a different agent."

"I've been thinking the same thing." I head to the kitchen to make much needed coffee.

"You're not going to do the interview, are you?" she asks.

I fill the pot with water. "Max said I need him, but Max is wrong. I don't need Trevor, and I don't need Max, and I don't need a man to make my life—or this show—great."

"Preach it, sister! It's about time."

*   *   *

The two weeks leading up to Christmas are frenetically busy. We're taping shows back to back, and everyone is in overdrive. I'm just counting down the days until December 22, when I begin my nine-day break. It's my longest vacation of the year, five workdays sandwiched between weekends and holidays.

Friday morning, my last morning before my break, Glenn calls me into his office. When he tells me to close the door, I have an unpleasant déjà vu sensation and flash back to the day last month when Glenn told me the show wanted to make Shelby my co-host.

As I sit down, I cross my legs and wait. He doesn't waste time.

"They want to introduce Shelby as co-host when we return to live shows the first of the year."

My lips part, but I make no sound. Instead I squeeze the water bottle I carried in with me, gripping it so hard that my knuckles shine white.

"Because your numbers are up so much, the execs thought it best to add her soon, while you're pulling in the viewers." He talks quietly, unemotionally, and the words just keep coming. "We're going to have you tape a series of teases this afternoon letting viewers know something big is happening on January second."

I squeeze the bottle until it pops. I jerk at the sound.

My good numbers have worked against me. My increase in viewership did nothing to protect me.

And then it hits me: They made their decision weeks ago. Nothing I could have done could have prevented this.

Glenn shuffles a few papers in front of him. "And there's one more thing. The network is dividing the awards coverage among the show hosts this year. You will still cover the Academy Awards. Shelby will work the red carpet with you—"

"We're sharing the Academy Awards?"

His gaze meets mine and holds. "And she's hosting our Golden Globe pre-show with Manuel. It hasn't been decided who will cover the SAG Awards. It might be Manuel, or it might be him with one of you girls."

One of us girls. Love it.

I stand. "Is that all?"

"Tiana, you've done a good job here. We're all big fans of your work. We think adding Shelby will make your job easier. It'll give you someone to chitchat with. Enjoy a little banter."

Chitchat and banter. I smile so hard that my cheeks ache. "Fabulous."

"This isn't a demotion—"

"Of course not. It's a wonderful opportunity. Right?" I look him in the eye. " You know, on second thought, I need a break, Glenn. I'm sure Shelby can cover for me in my absence."

"How long will you be gone?" he asks, clearly stunned.

I've never threatened to quit before, nor have I ever asked for time, and as impulsive as the decision is, my gut says it's also the right one. It's what I need. I need time to figure out what I want and what I need. For too long I've made the show my top priority, but it's time I become my top priority.

It crosses my mind that this could be the end, too. If I leave, I want to go out on top, and my numbers are strong. My viewers are back. "Four or five weeks."

"Four or *five*?" He's shocked.

My gaze falls to my hands, which are relaxed for the first time in a long time. I nod, exhale.

"So you'll be back in time for the SAG Awards?" he asks.

I stand. "I'll let you know."

Chapter Ten

———— ✦✦✦ ————

It rains as I drive home. It rarely rains in L.A., unlike in Seattle, where Marta lives. But it's coming down now, cool, hard, decisively, and the weather mirrors my emotions.

My moment of calm dissolves in outright panic. What have I done? What in God's name was I thinking? Leave of absence, now? Just before contracts? Just before awards season?

But I'm not thinking. I'm reacting. No, acting. I'm making a change. Change is good. Change is necessary.

At home, I strap on my iPod and put on a baseball cap and zip a thin L.A. Lakers windbreaker over my jogging bra and shorts and go for a run.

I refuse to cry as I run.

The words—*I need a break*—came out easily enough, but confronting the reality of what I've said and what I need is something else.

I'm terrified. Terrified of failing. Terrified of suffering. Terrified that I'll fall in love again and I'll lose him just the way I've lost everyone else.

Every time I think I want to give in to tears, I push on faster. I run and run despite the rain. I run, splashing through puddles, sprayed by passing cars. My shorts and ponytail are soaked through. My shoes drip water with every step. I'm so far from the house and I don't have a dollar to my name or I'd call for a cab and have it take me home.

I finally stop moving. For a long minute I just stand where I am, sweating and shivering at the same time.

I have to go back now. I've been running for over an hour. It'll take just as long to get back, if not longer since it's going to be all uphill.

If only I had my cell phone and could just call for help. Russian John or Polish John or even Harper. I'm sure she'd come. But I don't have my phone and I don't know any numbers by heart. Besides, I'm soaking wet and I can't climb into someone's car like this.

I'm alone. I start back for my house and I do what I do when I'm overwhelmed. I stop thinking, stop feeling, and focus on the moment. I focus on just moving, on putting one foot in front of the other. It's the way to get through a crisis. It's the way to get through loss. And it might just be the way to get through a breakdown.

One step at a time.

Marta had invited me to join them for Christmas but there's no way I can get on a plane on Tuesday, December 23. Better to stay home and get my head together so that by the time I arrive for Zach's baptism, I'll be good company.

But the 28th is five days from now, and I'm not sure how to fill them until I turn on my computer and see the file with Sveva's name on it, Sveva being the crusader in Kenya who caught my interest.

I open the file, see my rough notes begun last September. I was once so excited about the possibilities in this story. I can be excited again. I need to find whatever it is that's missing, because it's something that's missing in me.

Wednesday I head to Santa Monica to get breakfast but end up walking on the beach instead.

Hands burrowed in the pocket of my sweatshirt, I walk and walk and let my imagination run, but the tragic thing is, my imagination's stunted. I can't seem to see the possibilities I used to, much less a future beyond the Horizon Broadcasting tower and the artificially decorated *America Tonight* set. I've been part of tabloid television so long, I don't know where I could go or who would have me.

Eventually I leave the beach, cross the street, and head for the little indie coffee shop on the corner. It's warm inside and the decor is artsy-funky with a bit of faux Christmas greenery thrown in. I order a mocha with whip to go.

When I get back home, my phone is filled with voice messages. I scroll through the text messages and then the voice messages. They're mostly all from my girlfriends calling to check in on me, wanting to know if I'll join them for Christmas, wanting to make sure I won't be alone.

But I will be alone. I'm okay alone, and I flop down onto the bed and toss the phone on the mattress next to me.

At the last minute on Christmas Eve, I decide to attend a service at the Downtown Mission.

I love the California missions. The thick, whitewashed adobe walls. The red roof tiles. The towers with the bells. It can be blistering hot outside, but inside the mission it's always cool and dark and quiet. Some of the church interiors are plain, while others are a glorious riot of red, yellow, and blue color or a palette of elegant, sophisticated golds and blues.

I haven't been to a service at a mission in a long time, probably not since Keith and I were married at Carmel Mission nearly eight years ago. It was a beautiful service. Mystical.

I'm underdressed when I arrive for the midnight service. I'm also early, yet the church is already nearly full. I find a middle spot in a middle pew and squeeze past people to kneel to say my prayers.

Sitting back on the dark wood bench, I'm almost immediately overcome by emotion. My throat threatens to close and I fight for control. I can't cry. The familiar Christmas hymns have started. Must not break down until we're asked to sing something properly heartrending, like "O Holy Night."

The lights above are dim, and white pillar candles glow on the altar and in the alcoves and before the stained-glass windows. Fragrant pine boughs arch above the windows and through the Advent wreaths.

Emotion rushes through me again, and I squeeze my hands together, nails pressing into skin. Can't cry. Can't. But something's growing wild in me, something I'm not sure I can control.

I miss them all. My family. Keith.

The organist plays, and I concentrate very hard on the altar.

I used to play games after the car accident, pretending I was God and I could save just one of them from the wreckage. Whom would I save? Which one would live?

My sisters, Willow or Acacia? I'd tell myself that it should be one of them. They were young like me. They had as much right to live as I did. But then I'd remember my mom and how she gave the best hugs and kisses and every night told fantastical bedtime stories.

I'd pick Mom.

I want Mom. I want Mom even now. I feel as though I never had enough of her hugs before she died. Never had enough love. It's a painful thing when you go through life feeling needy for love.

The organist plays the first keys. I know this song. Everyone rises to their feet.

The emotion I've fought all night returns, surging hot and wild through me. "Silent night, holy night..."

Tears fill my eyes. I would give anything to be a child in my mother's arms again.

"All is calm..."

I would give anything to have lived with more love and less grief. The grief is huge and unending, and it is always there, in the back of my mind. Death can come at any time. Death can steal everyone we love.

"All is bright..."

I can't stop the tears. I cling to the back of the pew, my heart on fire.

"Round yon Virgin, Mother and Child..."

God, I know I don't talk to you often, but help me be not afraid. Help me be strong. Help me face all challenges with courage and calm.

I'm awake even before my alarm goes off and then I realize there is no alarm. There's no need for an alarm. There's nowhere to go, nothing to do. I lie in bed for another twenty, thirty minutes, half dozing, and then when the memories come rushing back again, memories of my family and Keith, and every memory is tinged with sadness, I throw back the covers and go to the bathroom.

I catch a glimpse of myself in the mirror. The mirror reveals just how little I slept. Red, bloodshot eyes. Shadows beneath the eyes and a puffy brow bone. Christ. I really need an eye job now.

My house isn't very festive. This year I didn't purchase a tree or even poinsettias. I make a face at the stark interior, and after putting on the coffee, I make quick calls to Marta and Shey to wish them a Merry Christmas, then phone Christie to wish her a Happy Hanukkah, and then turn off the phone and settle onto my couch to watch my collection of Christmas movies.

I start with *Miracle on 34th Street* and then move on to *It's a Wonderful Life* before finishing with *White Christmas*. And that pretty much takes care of Christmas Day.

Now I just need to figure out what to do with the next few weeks.

On December 27, I board the Alaska Airlines flight to Seattle for Zach's baptism and spend the first hour of the flight working on my laptop, putting together story ideas I could pitch to other networks if the situation came to that.

I'm in the middle of typing when the man next to me faces me. "I know who you are," he exclaims. "You're on that show. *Entertainment* something or other. You're her...." He shakes his finger at my face. "Come on. I know your name. T...T... Tiana! Tiana something. Right?"

I save my work. "Yes. Tiana Tomlinson, *America Tonight*."

He sits back in his wide leather seat, smug. "I knew I recognized you."

I smile briefly before turning my attention back to my laptop screen, anxious to use the last hour of the flight as effi-

ciently as I did the first. But my seat mate now seems inclined
to talk.

"I'm Bob," he adds, propping his left elbow on the armrest
to lean closer to me.

"Hello, Bob. Nice to meet you."

"You know, it was the glasses that threw me. You don't wear
glasses on TV."

"Not that often, no." I frown at the screen, trying to remember
where I was on this story I would just about kill to produce.
It's about Sveva Gallman, a young, slim, blonde warrior
of a woman born in Kenya to Italian parents. I had the pleasure
of hearing her speak in Baltimore four months ago at the
Maryland Women's Foundation and she dazzled the audience
with her intelligence and fire and passion for Africa.

Sveva and I were both there being honored that night for
our work. She, for working to preserve Kenya's cultural heritage.
Me, for bringing six years of celebrity news into America's
homes.

I told no one, but I was mortified to share the same stage.
Mortified that I don't make news but present it in tiny cheerful
sound bites.

Once I wanted to change the world. Once I thought I could.

But Sveva's passion touched me, and I felt the first stirring
of an idea: a show devoted to extraordinary women, women
who do heroic things not because they're paid to, or because
they're photographed or even thanked, but because they
believe they can make a difference. And they do.

I worked on the concept last September for an entire weekend,
but then it got put away. And it's only now, three months
later, that I've returned to it, although I did put in some time
during my Paris flight.

I'd start the show with the segment on Sveva. I'd go to Kenya and interview and film her there. I don't know that I could get my show producers to sign off on me heading to Africa, but if I funded my own trip, they wouldn't have a lot of say....

Heck, if I'm no longer employed in a month, they'd definitely have no say.

Not that I necessarily want to just quit my job outright, but I do want an opportunity to do fresh stories, inspiring stories. I believe there's a place in news for empowering stories, too.

"What are you working on?" Bob asks, peering at my screen.

My fingers hover above the keyboard. I glance at Bob. He's in his late fifties or early sixties and channeling George Hamilton with the white pin-striped shirt, orange tan, Botox brow, and dark pomade hair. "A human interest story."

I begin typing again, but he's still staring at my screen, trying to read what I'm writing, and I stiffen, my mind blanking in protest.

I flex my fingers, reread the last paragraph I've written. Unfortunately, Bob sees this as an opportunity to converse some more.

"But don't you have people who do that for you? Aren't you just the host?"

Just the host.

My jaw clenches. He's hit a definite nerve. Once upon a time, I was considered a good writer. Call it what you will—talented journalist, respected reporter—I researched, wrote, and produced my own stories. But that's been so long ago, I don't even know what I am anymore. Other than famous.

"I have a journalism degree from Stanford," I say evenly,

gaze glued to the screen. "I spent nine years as a reporter before *America Tonight*."

What I don't say is that joining *America Tonight* opened me to criticism from my former colleagues. It took me less than sixty days to discover that my new salary and star power cost me dearly. The media demoted me, stripping me of my intellect.

And it's funny, but Bob's comment brings the old anger roaring back. I am not merely a host. I am still a journalist, and a good one. I can put together a great story, and I know the right questions to ask in an interview.

Just a host?

Hell, no.

Thank God we land on schedule. Even better, Shey's already at the airport gate, waiting. Her hair is pulled back in a ponytail, and she's dressed in jeans and a black turtleneck and wearing oversize sunglasses. I've never seen Shey wear sunglasses inside a building, and I'm about to tease her that she's gone Hollywood on me when I catch a glimpse of her eyes from the side.

Her eyes are pink. She's been crying. In twenty years, I've seen Shey cry only once and that was at Keith's funeral when she held me as I cried on Keith's casket. She cried that day. And she's crying now. What the hell is happening in her world?

"You okay?" I ask quietly.

She nods, but her lips are pressed thin.

My heart knots. I'm scared, scared for her, because this isn't Shey.

We walk through the Sea-Tac terminal and down the escalators to baggage claim, where we find a driver in a dark suit holding a sign with Shey's name on it.

It's not until we're in the back of the town car, our bags stowed in the trunk, and the driver's heading for the freeway that Shey finally pulls off her glasses. Her eyes are red-rimmed and swollen. "John and I have separated. He moved out last weekend."

I don't know what to say. John and Shey were perfect together. I know there have been problems lately, but they were an amazing couple and very much in love. "Why?"

Her thin shoulders shift. "We grew apart."

"Shey."

Her lower lip quivers and she bites ruthlessly into it.

I reach out and put my hand on her arm. "This might just be temporary. Things will work out. They always do—"

"I don't think so. Not this time."

I don't want to hear this. Don't want to believe this. Shey and John's relationship is solid. Rock solid. I hold them up as my ideal, and if they can't do it, who can? "Why not?" I cry, and I sound childish, almost desperate. But I loved them together. I needed them together. I need to believe people can stay together.

She doesn't speak. Tears film her eyes. Blindly she reaches up to wipe the tears before they fall.

My fingers squeeze her forearm. "Shey, you can't quit! Don't give up—"

"It's not me, though. I don't want this." She's struggling to catch the tears before they fall but failing miserably. "John's the one who changed—"

"No."

"He loves the boys. He says he loves me. But he's not in love with me anymore."

"Is he seeing someone else?"

It takes her a long time to answer. "I can't talk about it."

"Yes, you can. This is me. Tits. Your best friend in the whole world," I say fiercely even as tears fill my eyes.

"It's just so impossible...so painful."

I wait, blinking tears.

"Tiana, it's...it's...Oh God—" She breaks off, gulps a breath. "It's another man. A designer. John thinks...he thinks..." She swallows hard. Her voice drops so low that I have to strain to hear her. "He thinks he might be...gay..."

"Gay?"

She looks at me, her expression haunted. "He wants to tell the boys, and I'm terrified. Coop's already struggling. He's already self-conscious about his height and how thin he is. Bo's dealing with depression. This will devastate all of them."

How could it not?

I'm beyond dumbfounded, and we lapse into silence. I'm grateful for the silence, struggling to process everything. This isn't the world as I know it. It's not the world as I want to know it. I can't even imagine Shey's pain. She's such a traditional girl. So small town and wholesome values. Her parents were married for fifty-three years. There's never been a divorce in her family. She never looked at another man after she met John.

If Shey's rock-solid marriage has come to this, what hope is there?

What relationship lasts?

Ten minutes from Marta and Luke's new Medina waterfront house, Shey puts in some eyedrops and applies fresh makeup.

By the time we arrive she's smiling, and she keeps up the cheerful smile as Marta opens the door and welcomes us with fierce hugs.

"How are you feeling?" I ask Marta as Luke enters the hall with Zach in his arms.

Marta pats her stomach, her long hair tumbling over her shoulders. "Good. Better now that I've hit the second trimester."

She does look good, and clichéd as it might be, she has that glow.

Eva arrives a minute later and lets out a scream as she throws herself at me and then Shey. A couple of years ago, Eva practically shaved her head in a fit of frustration, but her thick dark hair, the same shade as Marta's, has grown and now hangs below her shoulders. She's a sixth grader now and still lanky thin, but she's so sparkly and full of life that I don't know any girl more beautiful or wonderful.

We head to the living room, and we don't move for hours. Luke has Chinese takeout delivered, and we sit on the floor of their living room eating and talking while baby Zach sits in his swing rocking back and forth.

I must admit, I'm smitten with Zach. He's a big, bouncing boy with wide blue eyes and soft apricot cheeks. His hair has a touch of red in it, and as he gurgles and waves his baby fists, you can see his dad in him.

This is what I want, I think, entranced by Zach's gurgles and coos. Family, home, baby. With a man I love. A man who loves me for me, the real me, not the one everyone sees on TV.

Marta sees me watching Zach. "You can take him out of the swing, if you want. He'd probably love a chance to grab your hair."

I don't need a second invitation. After stopping the swing, I undo the strap in front of Zach, unhook the harness, and lift him into my arms. He's heavier than he looks, and his forehead puckers as he gazes into my face. I bounce him a little. His expression clears. He likes that. I bring him closer against me, my arms snug underneath his padded diaper bottom. The top of his head grazes my cheek. He's warm and smells of baby powder. "Aren't you gorgeous, Zach Flynn?" I whisper in his ear.

He coos. He's so firm in my arms. So sweet.

My heart turns over.

And then I look at Shey. She's curled up on the couch, talking earnestly to Eva, and my heart turns over again.

This is so life. This is how it is. Up and down and rough and smooth and good and bad. It's wonderful and terrible and forever unpredictable. And I don't mind unpredictable as long as it doesn't hurt my friends. But right now it is hurting Shey, and it doesn't seem fair that just when Marta gets her dream, Shey's world falls apart.

Late that night, I lie sleepless in my guest room bed. I'm sharing a room with Shey, but Shey's finally, thankfully, asleep.

I'm worried about Shey. She barely ate, and even though she kept smiling all evening, I could see the confusion and shock in her eyes when she thought no one was watching. She reminds me of me after I got the call that Keith had been killed. I couldn't believe it. I couldn't believe it was happening. Keith had to come back. He said he'd be back. He promised.

And John adores Shey. He has since they met on the *Vogue* photo shoot, and that was what? Fifteen years ago?

I know affairs happen. Mistakes get made. But this…this… how could he now love a man instead? It doesn't make sense. People don't change like that.

Do they?

And what happens to Shey and the boys now that John wants to try something new?

The baptism Saturday morning at Sacred Heart in Clyde Hill is beautiful. It's a big modern church with large modern stained-glass windows and a soaring ceiling. Zach squawks when he's dipped into the baptismal pool and then howls when his head is touched.

That afternoon, once we've returned from brunch I log on to my computer to check my e-mail and discover a message from Peter Froehlich, a German member of the foreign press. He's e-mailing to ask if I'd be interested in attending the Globes dinner and awards ceremony with him on January 11.

Peter's a lovely man in his fifties and very kind. We met at a Golden Globes pre–awards show dinner my first year hosting *America Tonight* and hit it off and have been friends ever since.

I'm not sure I should say yes, though, not after I've taken a hiatus from *America Tonight*, but before I can answer, I get a call from Max. He's just returned from a Swiss ski trip and discovered that I took a leave of absence from *America Tonight*.

"Have you lost your mind?" he roars. "Are you mad?"

Eva is sprawled on the bed next to me, and I bend down, kiss the top of her head, and head out of the bedroom and out the front door, where I can talk without anyone hearing us. It's raining, a steady gray cold drizzle, and I bundle my arms across my chest. "I'm sorry, Max. I didn't think I needed permission to take a break for a couple weeks."

"You have to know this is the worst time possible to take an extended vacation. Contract negotiations are just beginning.

The award show season is about to descend. This is when you need to be present and visible!"

"I'm not sure I want to return to the show." I sit on the front step and stretch my sweater over my knees. "I'm using this time to consider my options."

"What options?"

"I think, Max," I say carefully, "that is your job."

"You have a great gig going, doll. People would kill to be in your shoes."

"Maybe I'm ready for a new challenge."

"Like what? Where would you go?"

"I don't know. That's the whole point of this exercise."

"I'm going to call Glenn first thing on Monday and I'm going to tell him it's hormones, a perimenopausal thing, and that you'll be back to work start of the New Year—"

"*No.*"

"Are you listening, doll? You hearing anything I'm saying?"

"Yes, every word, and I think I've heard enough. This isn't working."

"What?"

"This isn't working. I think we've come to a fork in the road and I'm ready to head in a different direction. I appreciate everything you've done, but—"

"You're firing me?"

"—I no longer need you to represent me."

He's finally speechless. Good. About time I shut him up. "But I thank you, Max, and I'm glad we had these years to work together."

He finds his voice. "You can't fire me! I got you that job, I made you Tiana Tomlinson—"

"No, Max, you didn't make me. It's my work. My talent. I

made me who I am. I'll follow up with a formal letter, but I think this is it for us. Good-bye." And resolutely, I hang up the phone.

A moment later I appear in the enormous living room, cheeks flushed, emotions high. Marta's nursing Zach, and Shey is sitting next to her on the couch. They both look up at me. "I just fired Max," I say brightly.

Shey's grim expression eases, and she looks happier than I've seen her in the last two days. "Yeah?"

"Yeah."

She jumps up and gives me a high five. Our palms smack so loud that Zach pops off Marta's nipple and looks around with interest.

"I hated him," Shey says. "He was a jerk."

"I know." I glance at Marta, who is trying to get Zach to latch back on, but he's smiling a milky smile at me. I suddenly laugh with relief. With hope. Things are looking up. Which reminds me: I need to e-mail Peter back. I think I'm going to go to the Golden Globes after all.

Back in Los Angeles, my stylist, Shannon, comes over the first week of January to show me several gowns that would be good options for the Globes. One is a pretty strapless orange pleated gown, rather Grecian and very soft and flowing, and the other is a bold corseted gown the color of spilled red wine. The deep red gown's beaded bodice is intricately designed, tightly fitted, with two hidden zippers and dozens of little hooks. The neckline plunges low, and the skirt is smooth to the top of the hips and then turns full. A hint of fine black tulle peeps from the gown's hem.

I think of Max, who had to control me. I think of the show's executive producers, who want to minimize me by adding Shelby as my co-star. I think of Trevor, who played me while he was sleeping with Kiki.

And then I think of Michael, who watches me with that glint in his eye and that sexy crooked smile. I can't imagine Michael ever telling me to be good, be quiet, be silent, be grateful. He'd tell me what Keith used to tell me: Go big or go home.

My fingers caress the soft orange Angel Sanchez gown and then the primal crimson Oscar de la Renta.

I'm wearing red.

Chapter Eleven

★★★

Eight a.m. Saturday morning, the day before the Golden Globes, Christie calls to invite me to go skiing with her family. They're heading to Snow Summit at Big Bear, and they'll meet me where Interstate 10 East intercepts Highway 38. We've done this before, where I'll park in a lot on Orange Street and then jump in their massive luxury Range Rover and Christie's husband will drive us the rest of the way. I'm not very confident driving in snow and ice, although Christie said conditions are good today.

Skiing should be the last thing on my mind. I should be working on story ideas and then primping properly for the awards by getting a spray tan, a blowout, a manicure and pedicure. But all I've done for the past seven years is primp and work, and doing something fun with Christie is hugely appealing.

"I'd love to," I tell her. I haven't skied yet this year, but I know where all my equipment is. I keep it together in the garage, the skis and poles in the cabinet and my boots and clothes in a big Roxy duffel bag. "What time did you want to meet?"

"Soon. We're almost ready to leave." She hesitates. "But you need to know that Simon's meeting Michael on the slopes. Michael has a cabin at Big Bear and he's already up there. Is that going to be a problem for you?"

My pulse does a little jump at the mention of Michael, something I find infinitely annoying. I don't want to like him. I have no interest in the man. There's no reason for me to react like a girl in high school.

"It's not a problem," I answer calmly, glancing at my watch. "And if I leave in the next half hour, I could meet you at the Dunkin' Donuts around nine-thirty and we'd be on the slopes by eleven."

"Perfect. See you there. Call me if you hit traffic."

It's a clear, sunny day and no traffic since it's Saturday and all the college football games have ended for another year. I like driving on days like today and with my music loud—no sad songs today, just good driving music, my favorite oldie mix on my iPod of Supertramp, Abba, and Heart. It's not the kind of music that you want to be caught listening to in public, but in the privacy of my own car I sing as loud as I can and it feels so good.

I feel good.

Who knows what will happen at work, but I don't have to think about work right now. For once I'm going to give it all up, surrender to play. I'm going to hang out with Christie. Ski. And check out Michael's action on the slopes.

Wonder if he's any good. Hope he's not one of those men who have all the great gear but can't ski for anything.

The edges of my mouth lift.

I hit Redlands in just under an hour, giving me time to stop at the Starbucks next door to use the restroom and order a latte to go.

My cell rings and it's Christie outside, saying they've arrived. I dash out to meet them, and as Christie hugs me, Simon takes the gear from my car and stows it in his. I climb into their SUV, hug each of the girls, and take my seat in the very back—and we're off, with a very motivated Simon at the wheel.

The girls are all enrolled in ski school, and while Christie takes them to their classes, I slip on my boots and carry my skis to the base of East Mountain Xpress, the quad chairlift, where I'm supposed to meet Christie and Simon once the girls are all checked in. Christie arrives ten minutes later, tells me that Simon's already hooked up with Michael and they've headed to the freestyle park, Westridge.

With two hours before the kids are returned to us, we take the East Mountain Xpress and spend forty-five minutes enjoying a surprisingly uncrowded run down Miracle Mile. Christie's boot is bugging her, though, and back at the base, she begs off the next run to see if she can't figure out why she's getting a blister. I'd like to get in another run before the kids join us and am heading for the chairlifts for Log Chute when I spot Michael all dressed in black ahead of me.

I slide into line behind him and poke him in the butt with the tip of my pole.

His head turns sharply, and then he spots me. I make a face at him. "Hello, Dr. Evil. How handsome you are in all black."

His smile is rueful. "A Mike Myers fan?"

"I did like the Austin Powers movies."

"Then you should know—Dr. Evil wore gray."

"How do you know that?"

"How can you not?"

I make another face.

His dense black lashes drop. "Are you on your own? I thought you were skiing with Christie."

"Her boot's bugging her. I told her I'd take a run and then meet back up with her. Where's Simon?"

"He's at the top waiting for me. I had a call regarding one of my patients."

"So you do actually work?" I tease.

"Just a little bit."

We end up riding the chairlift to the summit and part ways at the top, as Michael likes the triple black diamond runs and I'm more comfortable on the intermediate slopes. As he heads off, I take one of the cat tracks past View Haus for Miracle Mile, which is my favorite run here at Snow Summit. I'm enjoying myself, executing smooth, flawless turns and feeling very skilled, when I make a little turn and realize I've made the wrong turn.

I'm no longer on Miracle. I think I'm on Dicky's, Dicky's being one of the advanced terrains, and I hit a rough icy patch and go sailing over a mogul and career wildly toward the bowl. I'm beginning to panic as I slip and slide faster and faster.

I'm scared. This out-of-control feeling is something I don't ever want to feel. It's turbulence when you fly. It's a car hurtling too fast around a tight corner. It's danger and imminent disaster.

And I don't like disaster.

"You okay, Tia?" It's Michael back at my elbow, and I dig my blades into the mountain as hard as I can to come to a complete stop.

I turn to Michael, terrified and yet relieved. "I can't do this," I squeak. "I don't have enough control—"

"I've been watching you. You're doing great."

"I keep falling."

"You've only fallen once. And you did great over that last mogul. You were flying."

"*That* was a mistake! I didn't even see it until it was too late."

He grins. He knows it was. "I'll ski you down."

"Please."

Michael skis in a graceful zigzag down the mountain, and I focus on his back and the smooth pattern of his skis as they cut through the snow. Little by little, I relax and lean into the mountain when he does and crouch lower in my skis on turns, and the tension and fear ease. We reach the bottom and he's waiting for me, goggles off, a light in his dark blue eyes. "You did it."

"Thank you. That was not fun."

"You're a good skier, Tiana. You just need more confidence."

I grimace, lift a hand off my pole, and show him how it's trembling. "You think?"

"Let's get you a drink. You've earned it."

I don't argue.

We leave our skis and poles outside and clomp upstairs to the bar, where we find two seats at the crowded wood counter.

Before I place an order, the twenty-something bartender looks at me and then does a swift double take. "You Tiana Tomlinson?"

I nod and the young bartender whistles. "You're even hotter in real life. Drink's on me." And with a wink he turns to make a special cocktail.

Michael looks at me. "He doesn't even know I'm here."

I laugh a real laugh. "Sorry."

"No, you're not."

I grin. "Okay, I'm not."

"So, Roxy skis? I didn't know they even made skis."

"That's because you're one of those K2 Apache Outlaw kind of guys. All performance and image."

"They're great skis, and performance matters."

The bartender returns and with a flourish places a steaming coffee cup in front of me that's topped with whipped cream and chocolate sprinkles. "A Summit Xpress. Chambord, vodka, Godiva liqueur, and espresso. Total liquid courage."

He waits for me to try it.

I lift the cup, take a tiny sip, and *wham!* the liquor-soaked espresso hits me. It's strong. And sweet. And strong. "Wow."

The bartender, a fairly hot young guy, leans on the counter and smiles into my eyes. "Good, huh?"

"I think I'll try one of those, too, but without the sprinkles," Michael says. Then he turns to me and gives me a look that I don't know how to decipher. "I'm dying to ask you questions I have no business asking."

I arch a brow. "And you haven't even had a drink yet." I push my cup with the tips of my fingers. "This is strong, too."

"How strong?"

"If I have a couple of these, I might actually like you."

His cup arrives with its tower of whipped cream, and Michael knocks off half the whipped cream before taking a sip. He whistles. "That's a stiff girlie drink."

"Eyes watering?"

"No, but I've got more hair on my chest already."

"Ew." I wrinkle my nose.

He laughs, lifts his glass mug, and clinks it against mine. "It's good to see you, Ms. America. How are you feeling now?"

I'm about a quarter of the way through my cocktail and beginning to feel nice and relaxed. "Good."

Laughter lurks in his dark blue eyes. "You're a lightweight, aren't you?"

"Mmm-hmmm." I rather like the rush of heat in my stomach and the warm, lazy weight in my limbs. It's been a long time since I felt lazy and sexy, yet sitting here with Michael, I feel downright dangerous in a good way.

"Were you in love with him?" Michael asks bluntly.

"Who?"

"Trevor."

"No."

"How long were you together?"

"Six months."

"That's some serious time."

"If you're in high school."

He laughs. I drink. And then drink again. I'm definitely feeling more relaxed now. "The thing is," I add, "it was all long distance. We didn't really see each other that much. We didn't have that much in common."

Two seats open up by the fireplace, and Michael gestures for me to snag them while he puts his credit card on the counter for the bartender. The chairs are big and sturdy, and I curl my legs up under me, the cup clasped in my hands to keep them warm. When Michael joins me, he stretches his legs out with a sigh. He's like Johnny Cash, the man in black in his black North Face ski pants, shirt, and jacket, except he has blue eyes, not brown.

In the glow of the firelight, he looks hard and strong and alive, and I watch his face as he smiles at me. He's confident and male and primal, and I feel my pulse quicken in response. He's always been handsome, but I've never felt this intense physical attraction before.

I tell myself it's the fire and the drink, but as I cross my legs, I'm aware of how my heart beats and my hands shake. I'm totally turned on right now, which makes no sense at all since we've never gotten along and I've spent years hating the sight of him.

"So why don't we like each other again?" I ask, sipping from my cup.

He looks amused. "I like you. You don't like me."

"And why is that again?"

"I'm shallow, superficial, greedy, materialistic..." He pauses, thinks. "I think those are the big four."

Heat rushes through me. Heat and desire and more. I'd like his hands on me, on my face, on my body, in my hair. "So if I've disliked you so much, why don't you dislike me more?"

Grooves bracket his mouth. "I knew it was just a matter of time before you realized that you used anger and disdain to mask your true feelings."

I'm feeling so very pleasantly tingly, and I lean toward him. "My *true* feelings?"

His lashes drop, partially concealing the blue sheen of his eyes. "You like me." He leans forward so that we're just a foot apart. "And you want me."

My gaze meets his and holds. There's more than laughter in his eyes. There's heat. Fire. A shiver of feeling races down my back, and my fingers curl into fists as I respond to this crazy dizzying chemistry. "I'd never want you, Doc." Yet my voice is as warm and husky as whiskey, summer, and sin.

The corner of his mouth lifts and his lashes lift. His eyes burn. *He* wants *me*.

In part of my mind, I know Trevor never once looked at me like this. Trevor never once made my brain and body ache at the same time. And my body does ache. My lower belly is tight and my skin tingles and every sense is so heightened that I feel a little mad.

But how many women has he looked at this way? How many women does he do this to?

He reaches out, touches the curve of my cheek with his thumb. "You're very beautiful and very delusional."

A shiver dances down my spine at his touch. The lines come to him so easily, don't they? "You're delusional if you think I'm enjoying this," I say, voice suddenly very husky.

"Maybe I am. But I've never seen you smile this much before. I like you like this."

I don't know if it's his words, the tone of his voice, or his expression, but I feel a yearning for this whole life I haven't yet lived. A life of love and connection and emotion. A life where I'm cherished. Wanted.

Impulsively, I lean forward and kiss him.

His lips are cool. His breath is warm. I put my hand against his jaw and feel the bone and shape of his face. It's a strong jaw, rough with stubble, and he feels like a man. A man who would know how to love me properly. And even if it's all misleading, for a moment I cave, giving in to the pleasure.

The kiss deepens, and emotion and sensation rock me hard. I haven't felt anything like this in forever.

I drop my hand to his shirt and hold tight. I have to hold tight. I might never feel like this again.

And then from far away, I hear Christie's voice. Yet I don't pull away. It's Michael who lifts his head, ending the kiss.

I look at him mutely. What the hell did I just do?

"Does this mean you like each other?" Christie asks, smiling smugly as she stands in front of us, hand on her hip.

I blush, mortified. Michael laughs.

"You were supposed to meet us for lunch," she reminds me. "Everybody's waiting."

"Right."

I get to my feet, legs tingling and boots heavy. Michael's talking easily to Christie, but I can't look at either of them. I feel like a kid caught making out under the bleachers.

What is his secret? How does *he* get *me* to kiss him? God, he's dangerous.

While they talk I gather my jacket, goggles, and gloves and follow them to the cafeteria, where the rest of Christie's family is waiting, although I'm far from steady on my feet. I'd like to think my dizziness is due to one potent cocktail, but my gut tells me it's Michael's kiss.

Lunch is loud and chaotic, which suits me just fine, as Melissa's tears and Melanie's hurt feelings keep the conversation bouncing all over the place.

I notice Christie looking at me every now and then, trying to figure out what the hell she saw in the bar.

I'd like to know what the hell happened.

I've never done that. Not in years. Don't know why I did that today. Just threw myself at him. So wrong. So not me.

I tune back in to the conversation at the mention of Africa. Simon's asking Michael when he's leaving for his Rx Smile mission in Zambia.

"Less than two weeks," Michael answers.

"How long will you be gone this time?" Christie asks. "Your last mission was nearly a month."

"Ten to fourteen days. The return date's not set, as I might be heading to Cairo to speak at a medical conference. I'm very much looking forward to being back in Africa."

My interest is piqued. "I didn't know you volunteered with Rx Smile."

"That's how I met Simon," Michael answers. "He was part

of the first mission to La Paz, and that was what? Six or seven years ago?"

"Eight." Christie nods at Melanie. "I was pregnant with that one and worried I'd go into labor while you were gone."

"I've been thinking about going to Africa, too. There's a woman in Kenya I'd love to interview. She'd be a wonderful story. I've sent an e-mail to her this past week trying to get in touch."

Michael's lips curve. "You should come to Zambia. Do a story on Rx Smile. I guarantee you'd be amazed, and touched."

"Participating in Rx Smile in Bolivia was one of the best things I ever did," Simon concurs, "but also the hardest. There you are, ready to help, and then you realize you're not going to be able to help everyone. I found that frustrating. I was there. I wanted to do even more."

I feel a surge of adrenaline even before Christie turns to me. "You should go to Zambia, Tia. Here's your opportunity. You said you've taken the month of January off. Go when Michael's there. He'll introduce you around. Make sure you get the story you need."

"It's an interesting idea," I say, my mind spinning. I'd love to do it. I'd absolutely love to go. Finally, the chance to travel somewhere, see something I haven't seen, create something I've never done. "Who would I contact? What are the costs? Would they even let me film the mission?"

"I could put you in touch with the director of public relations for Rx Smile on Monday," Michael says. "Since it's a volunteer organization, I imagine you'd have to pay your own expenses getting to and from Lusaka, as well as lodging and meals. But if you were willing to do that, they'd be open to having you there. In fact, they'd be grateful to have you. It'd be a wonderful opportunity for them as well."

My heart's jumping. I'm excited, really excited, and mentally I go through my finances, as well as my experience with cameras. It's been a long time since I did my own camera work, although in the beginning every reporter learns how to do a one-man stand-up. "Yes, I'd love a name and number. Definitely interested."

Driving back to Redlands late that afternoon, Christie asks me if I'm serious about tagging along on the Zambia Rx Smile mission, and I tell her I'm very serious.

"This is what I've been dying to do. It was hard skiing this afternoon because I kept thinking about all the logistics, wondering if I can combine Sveva's story with the Zambia mission, wondering if I can manage to interview and film. I'll need to look into travel requirements as well. See if I need any visas and vaccines—" I break off, gulp a breath as my pulse quickens. "Wow. It'd be incredible if I could pull this off. I really want to do it."

She glances at me over her shoulder. Smiles. It's her smug Christie-knows-best smile, and I pretend I don't see.

It's not until I'm in bed that I finally let myself think about Michael and the kiss in the bar.

I really can't believe I did that. I don't know what in God's name I was thinking. Michael's a player. I don't need a player. Obviously I wasn't thinking. Obviously that can't happen again, especially in Zambia.

Shame. Because nothing has felt half as good as that kiss in a long, long time.

Chapter Twelve

★★★

I wake up Sunday morning feeling happy and very, very relaxed. And then yesterday starts to come back to me in embarrassing pieces.

Skiing. Michael. Drinks. Talking. Flirting. Kissing.

Kissing.

Kissing Michael O'Sullivan. I press my pillow to my face, groan into the feathers. Can't believe I did that. Can't believe I'd fall for his charm. He's so blatant. So obvious. You'd think I'd know better.

First thing—there'll be no more kissing. And if I do go to Africa when he's there, I'll keep my distance. There'll be very little contact and no moonlit conversations and definitely no canoodling. Africa is business. Work. Only work.

I'm pouring milk on my cereal when Christie phones to check on me. "How are you doing?"

"Good." I play with my spoon. "Excited to talk to Michael's contact at Rx Smile tomorrow. I can't stop thinking about the trip. Do you know how long it's been since I've done something like this?"

She laughs. "I'm more interested in hearing about Michael. What's going on between you two?"

"Nothing," I say, hating the twinge of anxiety. This is exactly what I don't want or need. Michael isn't what I want or need.

"That's not what I saw."

I'm reminded suddenly of how I felt kissing him, how there was something so right being near him; but then there was that horrible painful embarrassment after. "The kiss was a one-time-only thing. We were joking around, being ridiculous, and then it just happened. But it won't happen again."

"Oh." She sounds so wistful.

"Now I'm going to hang up because my cereal is getting soggy. But I'll call you later this week and let you know what's happening with Zambia, okay?"

"Deal."

After my tan, nail, and hair appointments, I rush home to meet Shannon, who is literally sewing me into my dress. The dress is beyond gorgeous, but it's tight, very, very tight, and the snug corset of a bodice is going to mean I eat and drink very little tonight.

Shannon also helps me apply my false eyelashes, and once she's gone I deal with the rest of my makeup, which goes on quickly. Finished, I stand back to examine my face and hair with the dress. It all looks good. I look good.

And then something else happens. I don't see me. I see my mom.

It's the strangest jolt of recognition. This is what my mom looked like when she died. She was my age, thirty-eight. Leaning close to the mirror, I stare at my face, into my eyes, searching for my mother.

There were times after the car accident when I envied my sisters for going with her. Envied that they all went together. I didn't want to be left behind.

I used to tell myself there was a reason for being left behind.

I've still been searching for answers, for that elusive reason why I survived when no one else did.

Shaking the whisper of sadness, I smile at myself and my deep dimples come and go. The dimples weren't my mother's. Those I got from my father. He said they were unmanly. We children loved to put our fingers in them. Smile, we'd say, climbing on him, arms circling his neck. Smile. And then we'd gouge the dimples and laugh.

He acted as if he hated it, but his eyes laughed with us.

Two hands to the mirror, I try to capture them, the people I lost, the people I miss. It's futile, but it doesn't change it or make it easier. You'd think after this many years the grief would sleep. And it does, sometimes for weeks, even months, life goes on, but then something wakes it and the sorrow returns, resting on my rib cage, riding my heart.

I push away, take a deep breath, settle my shoulders. Time to go. Time to shine.

The Golden Globe Awards are given out each year by the Hollywood Foreign Press Association and are the favorite awards for those of us in the industry who work the red carpet. The awards are a combination of the Oscars and the Emmys, as they recognize outstanding performances in both motion pictures and television.

When I first started working for *America Tonight*, the awards were held at various theaters around town, but now they're a steady fixture at the Beverly Hilton Hotel. Unlike the Oscars, where everyone sits in theater seats, the Globes ceremony is a seated dinner.

With twenty-five different categories, the Globes are also shorter than the Oscars, but the fans still descend beforehand to get a glimpse of the big names attending the party. However, bleacher seats for the Globes aren't free, as they are for the Oscars; instead, they're sold as part of a guest room package at the Beverly Hilton Hotel, and the package price starts at around two thousand dollars.

I know from working the red carpet that stars begin showing up at the hotel around three-thirty, although I used to arrive between noon and one. Because Peter is not running the gauntlet of international journalists and American entertainment reporters, tonight we don't actually arrive until five, but that's due partly to the backup of limousines inching toward the hotel entrance.

I have butterflies as our limousine pulls toward the hotel curb. I don't get nervous often anymore, but I'm certainly nervous tonight.

There could also be some butterflies because I'm about to step from the relative safety of the limo and into the lion's den.

Peter, a senior writer for *Die Welt* as well as a regular columnist for German *Vogue*, pats my hand. *"Du bist sehr schön,"* he says.

You are very beautiful.

The driver puts the car in park and comes around to open our door. Photographers press toward the car. Peter reaches for my hand and nods once at me. I nod back. And then he's stepping out and assisting me.

I straighten as dozens of lights flash around us. I've never been in the middle of such a crush of photographers before, but I'm used to cameras, I know what to do with cameras. I tilt up my chin, drop my lashes ever so slightly, and smile.

*   *   *

We walk the length of the red carpet; lightbulbs flash and publicists escort the stars to some journalists and past others. I see Shelby and Manuel interviewing Tom Hanks. Nancy O'Dell's talking to Trevor. George Clooney is chatting with Pat O'Brien. It's a crowded red carpet, and it takes us several minutes to make our way inside.

Our table is way in the back, and we're packed together like sardines. The front tables with the stars seat eight to ten. Our tables are squished with twelve, and here and there you can count fourteen. Fortunately, members of the Italian and French press are quite lean.

I've always enjoyed working the carpet outside before the show, as well as the post-awards interviews, but I'm having a wonderful time at our table, which is mostly German, Swedish, and Finnish, with a Latvian journalist thrown in. There's quite a bit of drinking and joking, but once the awards begin, everyone quiets down. These awards are taken seriously and often viewed as a precursor for the Oscars, although it's said that the foreign press tend to favor their own.

NBC's huge cameras roll back and forth to capture the presenters walking to the microphone and then the award winners as they move through the ballroom to the stage.

I'm having such fun with Peter and the gang that I forget all about Trevor until his category, "Best Performance by an Actor in a Supporting Role in a Motion Picture," is announced and my stomach falls.

The camera zooms in on each nominee, and there are five in his category. Trevor's table is filled with fellow actors and actresses from the nominated film, and they applaud him as his name is read.

"And the Golden Globe goes to..." The envelope is opened and the presenter glances at the card and then smiles at the audience. "Tom Hanks."

There are cheers, and Tom is accepting congratulations at his table, and as he stands and heads for the stage, people continue to clap.

I'm clapping, too, yet I'm suddenly sorry that Trevor didn't win.

Twenty minutes later, I duck out the back and head for the ladies' room. My gorgeous dress is so snug that it makes using the bathroom a challenge. I'm just exiting the ladies' room when a hand lands on my shoulder.

I turn.

It's Trevor. He's golden and bronze and devastatingly handsome in his tux with a drink in his hand. He smiles, and it's all white teeth flashing, but there's no warmth in his eyes. "Max said you were coming. Enjoying yourself?"

He's definitely had a few drinks. I smile, but I'm wary. "It's been fun."

"Happy for Tom?"

"I was hoping you'd win," I answer.

"Of course you were. You're such a fan."

I smile tightly. "It was good to see you, Trevor. Best of luck—"

He grabs my arm. "You're the lowest of the low. Celebrity leech. A bottom-feeder—"

"Let go."

But he won't. He grips my arm tighter. "You only mattered because I made you matter—"

I finally wrench free. "Good-bye, Trevor." I walk away as quickly as I can, conscious of the cameramen in the lobby.

Trevor's either too drunk or too angry to care. He shouts

after me, his voice filling the hall: "You need help, Tiana. You're sick! You know that, don't you? You're sick."

I'm shaking as I return to the table, yet I keep a smile fixed on my face as I take my seat, aware that I'm sitting surrounded by members of the foreign press. Peter stands as I sit, and I turn my smile on him and thank him. Yet inwardly I'm just stunned. Trevor's behavior wasn't just hurtful, it was frightening. Aggressive. Nothing like the man I dated for six months. How strange to think that just weeks ago we were a couple. And then *boom!* It all fell apart. I didn't even see it coming. Tabloid sensation to tabloid disaster.

Peter's hand brushes mine. "Are you all right?" he asks me.

I nod. "Wonderful," I answer with a dazzling smile before leaning forward to hear the joke one of the Finnish journalists is telling.

Bright, shiny, happy, I tell myself over and over during the next hour and a half.

That's all I have to be, that's all I have to do. And it's a good thing I've had fifteen years of broadcasting, nearly six of those on national TV, because if there's one thing I can do well, it's fake a bright, shiny, happy mood.

My composure holds during the drive home. Peter thanks me for attending the awards, claiming that all the other tables of foreign press were insane with envy. They had to sit with one another's ugliness, but he had the beautiful Tiana Tomlinson at his table.

As the limousine pulls up in front of my house, he takes my hand and squeezes it. "*Gemutlichkeit.*" He looks into my eyes, my hand still in his. "This is what I wish for you."

I know the word. It's a German noun that means cozy, happy, peaceful, well-being. It's used to describe a warm family room or a wonderful holiday like at Christmas. But it's also a personal state of being, like a state of grace where everything is warm and cheerful, happy and good.

He is wishing for me all things good.

A lump forms in my throat, and I squeeze his hand back and lean forward to kiss his cheek. "*Danke*. Thank you."

Then I'm walking the short distance from the curb to my front door and letting myself into my house.

My shoes are off right away, and then, dress swishing, I lock up, turn off lights, and head to my bedroom to get out of my clothes. It's not easy. In fact, it might be impossible. Shannon hooked and zipped and stitched me into this gown, and now I can't get it off.

I'm beginning to sweat as I struggle to reach the second zipper. I want out of the gown. The bodice is tight and my waist is squeezed, and I try and try to twist around and find a way to open the gown without tearing it—but there's no way to get it over my head or down my hips, not without the zipper unfastened and the hooks undone.

Where is the second zipper? Why won't the hooks open?

Hot and frustrated, I tug at the fabric. I tug and tug and hear threads snapping, seams threatening to give way, and I let out a frustrated cry.

I've had enough. Really, I've had enough.

I got drunk and threw myself at Michael last night. Trevor humiliated me tonight. And now I can't get out of my dress.

Trapped. Trapped. Trapped. I wrestle with the gown, absolutely ruthless. With a violent yank, I manage to pull it over my hips. I ignore the tearing sound. I keep twisting, wriggling, right, left, arms up, pinned to my head.

I hate this, all of it. The dress. The shame. My life. When did I become the stuff of jokes? When did I become ridiculous?

Hot, flushed, I finally yank it over my head and toss it onto the bed.

I see myself in the full-length mirror, red-faced, eyes watering. I've lost weight these past few weeks, and my hips are gone again and I'm back to very thin, which looks sexy and svelte in a size two awards show gown, but naked I feel freakish.

Big head. Skinny body. Flesh-colored plunging bra and thong against a dark bronze spray-on tan.

All this primping and pimping. Hundreds of hours, and thousands of dollars, spent to look glossy and flawless on camera, as if real women are glossy and flawless.

As if Hollywood is about real women.

I go to the bathroom to wash off my flawless face. The mascara runs down my cheeks in inky rivulets. It's a hideous moment, a moment of complete and utter self-loathing, and then I stop it. I stop the hurt and the self-hate.

I am not this. I am so much more.

For the first time in weeks I sleep soundly, sleeping all the way until eight-forty. I wake up and roll over and feel a moment of utter well-being. And then I remember who I am and where I am and the status of my life.

But before I spend any time thinking, I'm definitely going to need coffee.

Maria, my housekeeper, doesn't arrive until ten, so I have time to sit on my couch and be lazy. Coffee and papers in hand, I sit on the living room couch and open the papers, flipping to the entertainment section for a round-up of last night's awards. But along with the awards is a photo of Trevor, his face contorted. SUPERSTAR MELTDOWN! reads the headline.

Heart thudding, I skim the short text. Apparently, an intrepid photographer caught the interchange between Trevor and me.

If this made the paper, it probably made the morning news. I turn on the TV and flip through channels, checking to see if any of the morning shows are discussing last night's awards ceremony.

Live with Regis and Kelly at nine a.m. does not disappoint me. The opening dialogue is all about the Golden Globes. They mention some of the stars in attendance along with those notably absent. Regis mentions a beautiful gown Jennifer Aniston wore. Kelly cracks a joke about the number of babies Angelina wore.

"But the big news last night was Trevor Campbell's meltdown," Regis segues, turning to face Kelly. "You saw it?"

"I did. Ouch!" Kelly pulls a face. "I bet Trevor Campbell never expected that to end up on the national news."

Regis shakes his head. "I admit, I feel for Tiana Tomlinson. But she handled herself like a lady."

Kelly's expression grows earnest. "This is a tough business, Reg. Not a lot of love or loyalty at times."

"We both know her, don't we?"

"She's been a guest host here on the show with you, hasn't she, Reg?"

"Several times."

"You liked her."

"Great host. Lovely lady."

Kelly leans forward and speaks to the camera. "Tiana, we just want you to know we're on your side."

Regis crosses his arms over his chest. "And you're welcome back anytime. Come see us. We love you."

They cut to a commercial and I sit on the couch, thinking but not thinking, feeling but not feeling.

They were good to me. They didn't beat me up. If anything, they protected me.

Emotion washes through me. They didn't have to be nice. But I'm glad they were.

Glenn calls just before noon and asks if I can meet him for lunch. "I'd like to talk to you. Could you meet me at the Terrace at one?"

"Glenn, I'm not ready to come back."

"I'm not going to talk to you about coming back early. I just have an idea you might actually like."

Interesting. This I want to hear. "I'll see you at one."

The Terrace restaurant at the Sunset Tower has the best view of Los Angeles, and unlike some other area roof restaurants, it's never too blazingly hot to enjoy your meal.

I'm just about to go for my standard uniform of black T-shirt and black pants when I realize I refuse to look as though I'm in mourning. There's nothing wrong with my health, and there's nothing wrong with my career.

An hour before lunch, I shower and dress. Feeling feisty, I select a rather wild Dolce & Gabbana print dress. It's a modern twist on the sixties, and I take a leather belt and cinch it at my waist the way Shannon showed me. I pair it with a twig bracelet and chunky bead necklace, and with strappy leather high heels I look confident and casually sexy. Definitely sexy. Sexy's good. I give my reflection an approving nod.

It's not a long drive to the Sunset Tower, but there's a ridiculous amount of traffic and I valet my car just minutes before one.

Glenn's already upstairs waiting at our table, and he stands as I appear in the doorway and lifts a hand to acknowledge me. I smile and, conscious of nearly every head turning as I move toward the table, I slow my pace and make it a catwalk stroll. I'm not hiding. I'm not running away. Feel free to stare.

Our table's near a potted palm tree, and we have the luxury of light shade.

"You look good," Glenn says, surprised.

"I've had a couple weeks off."

"Mike and B.J. had photos of you from last night. I have to say I loved what you wore. The red gown was perfect. Very powerful and yet feminine."

"Thank you." I don't bother telling him it was difficult to put on and a nightmare to get out of.

"You're still using Shannon?" He sees me nod. "Good. I'm going to send her a bonus. She dressed you just right. It's exactly the image you want to be presenting right now. Beautiful, poised, sophisticated, and warm."

I'm not sure where Glenn's going with this, so I wait.

"Have you been following the news this morning?" he asks.

"I watched a little TV this morning, but other than that, the TV's off and I've tried to stay offline." As God only knows what might be being said over at Perez Hilton or *TMZ*.

Glenn studies me, his eyes narrowed, his expression contemplative. "There seems to be a bit of a backlash."

"I'm not surprised. Trevor's everybody's golden boy—"

"Against Trevor."

My eyes widen.

"Something's happened in the past twenty-four hours. Not sure if it was Trevor's tirade, or the way you carried yourself, or the fact that you sat with members of the press, but certain members of the media are rallying around you."

My throat grows tight. I take my napkin and make a show of spreading it across my lap.

"Regis and Kelly," Glenn says.

"I did see them."

"But they weren't alone. Ellen DeGeneres. And Barbara Walters on *The View*."

I look at Glenn, overcome.

"Not many women in this business have that kind of support, not from their peers." He hesitates. "This is obviously very good, and I want to use it to our advantage." He hesitates a moment, as if formulating what he's about to say next. "I want you back. I want you where you belong, as host of *America Tonight*."

Half a dozen emotions flood me. Exultation. Hope. Happiness. Doubt. Anger. Frustration. "What about Shelby?"

"The studio wants to keep her as co-anchor."

I open my mouth in protest, but Glenn holds up a finger to buy himself time. "But maybe that's good," he continues. "Maybe we can use Shelby in the studio and you in the field. You've said you wanted to do more stories again, real stories. Maybe this is how we do it. Your plastic surgery pieces were wonderful. Our viewer feedback has been terrific. Perhaps we can have you do more features, in-depth profiles, and one-on-one interviews."

I close my mouth and let him keep talking.

"Sweeps month is next month. I'd love to run some more of your stories throughout the month. I could provide you with a cameraman, but you'd be in charge of writing and editing and producing."

This is getting interesting. "I like the sound of it."

"Good. I hoped you would. Is there anything you've been working on?"

"Africa."

He sighs. "Besides Africa."

If he wants me back, if he wants my stories, then he's going to have to meet me halfway. "I want to do the Africa stories, and I've got a great lead. Beverly Hills plastic surgeon Michael O'Sullivan is part of the Rx Smile mission to Zambia. He's done these missions before, has promised to put me in touch with the organization's PR director. Best of all, they're leaving in less than two weeks. The timing would be perfect for February sweeps."

"I have to be honest, I'm not excited about Africa stories. But if you can make us care, and you can get people to tune in, then I won't tell you that you can't do Africa."

Victory. It's all I can do to keep from grinning.

Glenn drums the table with his fingers. "The stories you choose are important. Think about each interview. Make sure every segment conveys your warmth and charm and wit."

"Not easy to do when you're talking about malaria or the millions of children left orphaned by AIDS and HIV," I say.

"Then maybe you pick happier stories. Or pick an angle that can be happy. As you know, people in this country are struggling emotionally and financially. We've been in a protracted war. In the past several years Americans have experienced floods, fires, and storms. Families have lost crops, homes, loved ones. It's not an easy time for people. When our viewers turn on the TV, they want to forget."

And I, of all people, can understand that. "So how does this work?"

"Soon as you've got your plans made, our travel agency will handle flights and hotel arrangements. But we need your itinerary, and I need a rough outline of stories that I can expect to air when you return."

My head spins. "So theoretically, I could be on a plane to Africa in a week."

"Theoretically, yes." He allows himself the smallest of smiles. "Oh, and by the way, I heard you're no longer with Max. Who's your new agent?"

"Don't have one yet."

"Even though your contract's up for renewal soon?"

"Yeah, I know, but one thing at a time. And my first priority is this trip to Africa."

Chapter Thirteen

———— ✦✦✦ ————

I arrive home and discover a gorgeous floral arrangement in ravishing raspberry red and strawberry pink on my doorstep. The flowers are beyond beautiful.

Setting the vase on the hall table, I grit my teeth and then open the small white envelope to read the card.

Trevor's an ass. I'll beat him up if you want me to. Michael
P.S. This is Alice's number at Rx Smile. She's expecting a call from you.

I study the card for the longest time, smiling and smiling again.

Trevor is an ass, and I love the idea of Michael teaching him a thing or two. Even better, I've got Alice's contact info for the Rx Smile office.

I move the flowers into the living room, where I can see them while I dial Alice's number. She answers personally, and we spend the next half hour discussing my objectives as well as Rx Smile's objectives. As I listen to her describe the mission—the first in Zambia—I can't help but imagine all the possibilities.

We end the conversation with Alice promising to overnight me literature on the organization and a video from previous missions, and she'll e-mail me travel details and information regarding the Zambia mission so I can get my flights booked and the necessary vaccines.

After we hang up, I stretch gleefully and head for my laptop. I feel good. Better than I have in a long time.

I shoot an e-mail to Marta and Shey, letting them know my plans. And then I look up Michael's business number, call his office, and leave a message:

"Let Dr. O'Sullivan know that Tiana will see him in Lusaka."

First thing the next morning, I head to HBC in Century City to work. As I near my office, Madison leaps up from her desk and launches herself into my arms with a squeal. "You're back!"

She walks with me into my office, and I give it a curious once-over. It looks different. There's an orchid on the corner of the desk and some crystal writing accessories that aren't mine. "Has somebody been using my office?"

Madison flushes. "Shelby."

Good old Shelby. "Have they given it to her, or was it just on loan?"

"It's your office. She was just using your desk and phone."

Such a Shelby move, I think, but I say nothing aloud, not wanting to be antagonistic my first day back after several weeks away.

Instead I update Madison on my plans as I turn on my laptop, letting her know Glenn has asked me to develop a series of show segments for sweeps month and that I've decided to head to Zambia to do a series on Rx Smile as well as several features on inspiring women in Africa.

I tell her I hope to fly out in less than two weeks' time, but I have to organize my ideas, outline some stories, contact my subjects, and get this info together in such a way that the company's travel agency can handle my hotels and flights.

"I'll help," Madison volunteers. "Give me a list of people and places and I'll get to work. I don't care what you need me to do—research, set up interviews, look into visas or required vaccines. You name it, I'll do it."

"Thank you," I say, pausing in my setup to look at her. "I appreciate it."

"My pleasure."

She holds my gaze a moment longer, then smiles and walks out.

I sit and stare off into space for several moments after she's gone.

Madison hunted down a huge map of Africa at the UCLA bookstore, and by Tuesday afternoon it's pinned on my office wall and I'm covering it with little stickie notes on areas where I have potential stories.

Nairobi, Kenya. Kenya again. Tanzania. The Congo. Malawi. Zimbabwe. Zambia. Chad. Somalia. Ethiopia. South Africa.

The stories and causes are huge. I've done my research these past few months, too, reading and watching everything I can from Jay-Z's documentary, *Water for Life*, to extensive *Wall Street Journal* interviews with Melinda Gates (I've interviewed her as well, but not necessarily on Africa), Kenya's First Lady Lucy Kibaki, and actress Terry Pheto of South Africa.

Poring over the story ideas brings my South Africa childhood vividly alive. I haven't been back to South Africa since I left at sixteen for St. Pious. I didn't even go back for Grandmother's funeral, but that was her wish, not mine, although truthfully I was relieved I didn't have to return.

Studying my story ideas, I make the decision not to go to South Africa this trip. I lift the stickie note off South Africa with a silent apology to Terry Pheto. But even removing one stickie doesn't reduce the size of the project. Africa is a vast continent, and traveling from one country to another isn't like traveling in Europe. The distances are huge and the travel options limited.

There is also the matter of my budget. And safety.

In the interest of safety, I limit my stories to countries that are currently stable. I don't want to take a cameraman with a family at home into an area that's unpredictable.

One by one, I pluck off the stickies until I have narrowed the continent to Zambia, Botswana, Kenya, Malawi, and Tanzania.

Libby stops by my office late Tuesday afternoon as Madison and I go through the remaining stories, trying to see if we can't narrow them further or at the very least create a value system and assign them each a priority.

"Can I listen in?" she asks.

"Sure," I answer, and Madison and I continue discussing the various possibilities.

Madison wants happy stories, but stories with heart.

I've been leaning toward deeper stories, hoping to educate as well as entertain, although I'm mindful of Glenn's caustic comment a month or so ago that "we're not PBS."

We both agree that we should offer hope.

Libby stands before the map and reads each of the stickies. I can tell she's forming opinions, but she doesn't interject her point of view. After ten minutes, she picks up some of the folders on my desk to review my notes.

With a list of tentative subjects in hand, Madison returns to her desk to begin attempting to contact the various people, including Sveva, whom I still haven't managed to reach. I've sent her several e-mails in the past two weeks but haven't gotten a reply yet.

Now Libby's gaze travels across the map. "I know you have quite a few stories in Kenya, but are you sure you want to go there?"

"I'm avoiding the Great Rift Valley. My interviews are down near the Masai Mara National Reserve, and there hasn't been any trouble in the region for years."

"Just be careful."

"I am."

Libby heads for the door and turns partway out. "Oh, and I totally forgot. I came by to tell you that you have a cameraman for your trip. Howard's volunteered to go."

"Howard *Schnell*?" My jaw drops. Howard has the most sensitive stomach of anyone in our office. He lives with Imodium tablets in his pocket. "Does he know he has to get all the vaccinations and take the malaria medicine and everything?"

"Says he's looking forward to the adventure."

"Great."

Libby cracks a smile as she turns again to leave. "You're going to have an adventure, too," she says on her way out.

She knows Howard's going to get sick before our flight even touches down.

*   *   *

That night, I wake up around three and can't fall back asleep.

It's been years—twenty-two years—since I've been home. Not that Africa's home, but I was born and raised in South Africa, and South Africa's heritage is my heritage.

I leave bed and go to the kitchen to make a cup of chamomile tea, and as the water boils I stare out the window at the lights of Los Angeles. Africa's countryside will be dark, very dark. I've heard that even in the big cities there are frequent power outages.

Tea in hand, I return to my room, but I can't make myself sit down. I pace the floor.

I'm nervous. Anxious. Excited. Mostly excited. I just want the trip to start. I just want to go. *Now.*

Hell, I'll just start packing.

In the end, I have to pass on interviewing Sveva, as Sveva e-mails me to say she'll be in Italy for the next several weeks. So I focus my story ideas in and around Zambia.

Harper is wonderful at nailing down the final details and logistics. She's the one who locates a pilot and guide for me. His name is Chance van Osten, and he's apparently one of the best pilots in southern Africa. His family goes back five generations, and he calls himself African, although he's blond and blue-eyed. He's thirty-something, speaks *eleven* languages, has been flying commercially since he was seventeen, and knows Africa intimately. "He's your guide and a great story all in one," she says.

I'd be impressed if it weren't for the young, blond, and blue-eyed part. "Can't you get me an old guy? I don't want to have to deal with a thirty-something-year-old who speaks eleven languages and has been flying since he was in diapers."

Harper grins. "The fact is, Chance is the best, and he speaks so many African dialects—and apparently there are hundreds—you'd be fine no matter where you are."

Familiar with the Bantu language complexities in South Africa, I think this is the time to tell Harper I have ties to sub-Saharan Africa. Now is when I confess that my grandmother owned a huge sugar plantation in the province of Natal and that growing up, I learned Afrikaans as well as a smattering of Zulu. But I don't. I find sharing that part of my life almost impossible because it always leads to other questions, like "Why did you leave South Africa?" and "Where are your parents now?"

That night, I get a voice mail from Michael: "Looking forward to seeing you in Lusaka. We usually stay at the same hotel. Give me a call once you land."

I tell myself the goose bumps have nothing to do with Michael.

Nothing at all.

We fly out a week later to Lusaka—first on American Airlines to Washington, D.C., and then on a South African Airways jet for Johannesburg. During the flight, I flip through the travel guides and the binder of articles and essays instead of sleep, arriving in Lusaka just after ten at night. We've been traveling for over thirty hours now, and I'm dead on my feet. We deplane by stairs at the Lusaka airport, since there's no jetway here. The air is heavy and thick, and the sky is dark with clouds. Puddles cover the tarmac, and the night's so humid that you know it'll rain again soon.

The hot, moist air smells achingly familiar—earth and night and Africa. I'm suddenly aware that South Africa isn't far. My home outside Stellenbosch isn't far.

I've come back.

I'm back, and it only took twenty-two years.

But what I'm feeling isn't the number of years, but the changes in me, the person I've become. I left the continent a repressed, depressed sixteen-year-old, but now I'm back as an accomplished adult, a successful woman. Only my parents will never know what I've done with my life. They'll never know how hard I've worked to become who I am.

The need to reach them, the need to connect and make amends rushes through me, hot, heavy, insistent. I wish I could go back. I wish I could do it over again. I'd be a different daughter. I'd be more open, more accessible, more everything.

The longing for the life I lost fills me. My eyes burn and my throat swells closed.

I wonder if people, after they're dead, know how much they're loved and missed. I wonder if the people we've lost know how we think of them, and long for them, even years after they are gone.

In front of me, Howard holds the terminal building door and we duck in. An ear-splitting boom of thunder is followed by a fork of silver white lightning. Zambia, a landlocked country, lies just beneath the equator. This is the heart of the tropics. And this is home. Even without my family.

We clear customs close to midnight, and our driver is waiting for us near the rustic baggage claim. He doesn't attempt to make conversation during the twenty-minute drive to our hotel, a tall, modern-looking building that could be any Inter-Continental Hotel in the world. Turns out it is an Inter-Continental Hotel.

We check into our rooms, same floor just a few doors down

from each other. After stripping off the traveling clothes I vow to never, ever wear again, I fall into bed.

I sleep like the dead and am awakened by my alarm at nine. I call Howard's room to see if he's up, as we have our first interview at eleven at Darlene's art gallery in downtown Lusaka.

We agree to meet downstairs in the restaurant within a half hour. I wash my hair and blow it dry, and although it looks appalling, I'm so excited to be here and starting the day that I don't care.

Our driver's in the lobby by ten-thirty, and he has us at Darlene's small gallery office in twenty minutes. Lusaka might be the capital of Zambia, but it's small and cozy in size compared with Los Angeles.

Darlene is warm and welcoming and absolutely delighted to meet me. "I've been a fan of yours for years," she says, giving me a big Texas squeeze. "Before I moved here permanently, I watched your show every night. How're you doing? How was the flight?"

Darlene's incredible. The interview is electric. She's absolutely passionate about helping Zambian women support themselves and their family with handmade arts, and although she misses her friends and family back home, she's convinced she's doing what she's meant to do. And I think I've found my calling, too.

This is what I'm meant to do.

Real stories, real women.

I'm on cloud nine as we arrive at Zambia's Population Services International office after Darlene's interview. Richard Harrison, the director of the Zambia office, is out of the country, but his assistant Jean welcomes us warmly. I've read all of PSI's press materials on the flight, and as Howard sets up the camera and hands us both microphones, I ask Jean about PSI's programs.

"We're very focused on malaria, reproductive health, child survival, and HIV programs," she answers, taking a seat in one of two chairs we've put together for the interview. "Our objective is promoting products, services, and healthy behavior so that low-income and vulnerable people can lead healthier lives."

It's not until we're ten minutes into the interview that I realize YouthAIDS, the group for which Ashley Judd serves as ambassador, is affiliated with PSI.

When I mention Ashley, Jean's eyes light up. "She's been tremendous. She's a tireless ambassador, and her efforts are bringing needed recognition and funding to YouthAIDS and PSI services."

"Don't the statistics ever overwhelm you?" I ask.

She smiles again, yet her expression strikes me as both sad and wise. "They would, if I let them. But I won't give myself that luxury. Life is very short, and very precious. I feel a responsibility to my community. If I can help make a difference, then that is what I want to do."

"Where do you find the strength?"

She starts to answer and then stops. Her dark eyes glisten, but she waits to speak. "I look into the faces of children. They hope for so much. They're so innocent. They do not know all the things we know—" Her voice breaks and she waits again until she is sure of herself. "If I can help save one of them, then I have done a very good thing."

I don't even know that I have tears in my eyes until the camera is off and Howard is reaching for our microphones. I hand him the microphone and blink, and a tear falls.

"Good interview," he says.

I hug Jean.

Howard and I part ways on our floor outside our rooms. We're both thinking a nap sounds pretty good, and we make plans to meet for a drink before dinner in the lobby's lounge. Our pilot, Chance, is scheduled to join us for dinner and talk about our next few days at Victoria Falls.

I'm sound asleep when a door slams and wakes me. Startled, I sit up. It takes me a moment to place where I am. Hotel. Lusaka.

With a glance at the clock, I see I've been sleeping for hours. I have only a few minutes before I'm to meet Howard and Chance.

Chance, I repeat silently as I take a quick shower and change into my orange tunic and white slacks. It's the same outfit I wore to the baby shower at Shutters, only I've pulled my hair into a ponytail and am wearing flat sandals.

Howard's not in the lounge, but I spot Chance right away. He's leaning on the bar, talking to the bartender. Very blond and very tan, he's not a pretty boy. With his weathered skin and stocky, muscular build, he reminds me of a South African rugby player.

Chance spots me as I enter the darkened lounge, and he studies me for a moment before pushing off the bar.

"Chance," he says, meeting me halfway across the lounge. He's taller than me, but I wouldn't describe him as big. No, he's average height. Compact. Strong. With an open face and a friendly smile.

"Tiana Tomlinson," I answer, shaking his hand. "My cameraman, Howard, should be down soon."

"I don't know what kind of pictures you'll get with this," he says, gesturing to the windows, which are slick with rain. "Last year was the wettest rainy season in thirty years, and so far this year's not much better."

He has a distinctive accent, although it's neither English nor Afrikaans. "Where were you raised?" I ask him.

"Kenya."

"Is that where you live now?"

His smile broadens. "They told me you were a reporter."

A *reporter*. It's been a long time since I've been called that, and I flush with pleasure. "I'm sorry. I'm always curious about people."

"No, it's fine."

We walk back to the bar where Chance's beer sits, and he asks me what I'd like to drink. It's five-thirty here, which means it's cocktail hour. "White wine," I answer.

The bartender asks if I have a preference.

"The house white would be fine."

The house white is a Stellenbosch, from the heart of South Africa's wine country. The winery is less than ten miles from my home.

I'm again swamped by emotion—love and grief, longing and need. I lost my childhood overnight. Left my native country at sixteen. Reinvented myself as a smart, ambitious American young woman. It wasn't such a stretch. Dad was American, and I was ambitious. But now my mother's Africa reaches for me, and I want to fall into it, embrace it, reclaim my past.

They say you can't go home again. But what if you could?

Over drinks we talk about Kenya and South Africa, Zambia and Botswana. We talk about the rainy season—which is now—and the rise in ecotourism, trying to pass the time until Howard appears.

In midthought, Chance breaks off. "Is that your cameraman there?"

I turn to the doorway and the figure silhouetted against the light. "No."

But I know him.

I watch Michael O'Sullivan enter the dark lounge as though he were a gunslinger entering a western saloon.

He's dressed in jeans and a white linen shirt that he hasn't bothered to tuck in. A lock of black hair falls forward on his brow as he looks around, taking in the lounge seating, and then walks to a group of men gathered around a low table.

One of the men who were seated gets to his feet and vigorously pumps Michael's hand. It's a warm welcome, and the group is delighted to see him. They pull up a chair for him and he sits down, shaking hands with everyone as he does so.

"Fancy him, do you?" Chance teases as he leans on the counter to order another beer.

"I know him." And then as I continue to stare at him, Michael suddenly turns and looks straight at me.

I don't know what to do now. I can't exactly pretend I don't know him or that I haven't seen him. For God's sake, I kissed the guy.

So I do the only thing that I can do in this situation. I walk over to say hello.

"Michael."

He rises and then leans down to kiss my cheek. His hair is still damp, his skin is warm, and I catch a whiff of soap and shaving cream. "So you've arrived."

It's just a kiss on the cheek, but I go hot all over. "Safe and sound."

"Good."

And then he smiles, and I think he's never looked more attractive. Faded jeans that cling to his quads. Loose white linen shirt that shows off the makings of a tan. Strong hands. Great face. Dammit.

I become aware of the group of men waiting for his attention. "I'm sorry," I apologize. "I shouldn't keep you."

"No, please, let me introduce you, especially as you'll be seeing most of them during the next few weeks." He gestures to the men he's joined. "Tiana, I'd like to introduce you to my esteemed colleagues and very good friends. Dr. Paul Zarazoga, Dr. Ranjeev Kapoor, Dr. Jon Danovich, Dr. Marques Mukajere, and Dr. Tomas Voskul."

I shake hands with each. "You're all with Rx Smile?"

"I'm not," answers Dr. Zarazoga. He's the eldest, but his eyes are lively. "I live here. I'm on the staff at University Teaching Hospital."

"*On* staff?" Jon, one of the doctors, jeers. "*Chief* of staff."

"Years ago we all served Doctors Without Borders in one capacity or another," Dr. Kapoor explains. "Michael's the only one still working with Doctors Without Borders, but we still are all committed to providing medical care in Africa. Marques is director of a hospital in Zaire, Jon volunteers in Mozambique, and the rest of us work with various groups like Red Cross, Operation Smile, or UNICEF."

These men would be an interesting story. They're from different countries and are different nationalities, but they all want to do something positive, something to help. "So you've been friends for years?"

The fair-haired doctor, Tomas Voskul, makes a face. "I'm friends with them," he says, pointing to three of the doctors, "but not him," he says, gesturing to Michael. "I don't like him. He's not ugly like the rest of us."

Everyone roars with laughter.

I can't help smiling, too.

Tomas adds, "We were supposed to be on the bus for the mission site in Katete, but the roads are flooded thanks to the rain."

"Will the mission be canceled?" I ask, concerned.

"No," Michael answers. "But it's frustrating right now. We have folks already in Katete, others stranded in Lilongwe, and then there are those of us here in Lusaka waiting to jump on the express bus—if it would only dry out enough that the bus could run."

I can't believe he's here, and that I'm here, and that any of this is happening. "It's surreal seeing you here," I say to Michael. "It's like I never left home."

"Were you the one at the PSI office today?" Michael asks. "I heard there was an American TV crew filming there this afternoon."

I nod. "I interviewed Jean. Do you know her?"

"She's a lovely lady. How did you get on with her?"

"Great. I really like her. There's something about her, isn't there?"

Michael smiles at me, and it's different from his other smiles. This one's warmer, gentler.

Dr. Zarazoga offers to get me a chair so I can join them.

"I wish I could," I say. "But I'm meeting people for dinner and I should get back to them." I glance at the door, and yes, Howard's standing there, looking forlorn. "It was nice to meet you. Sounds like I'll be seeing some of you in Katete?"

I shake hands all around a second time, and then I'm heading to meet Howard. Chance meets us in the doorway, too. He's brought my glass of wine for me. We chat for a moment. Apparently Howard's not feeling very well. Chance thinks food might help and recommends the hotel's restaurant. We leave the lounge for the dining room, and as we walk out, I look back over my shoulder at Michael.

He's watching me.

I grow warm all over again, and a nervous fizz fills my stomach. I don't want to like Michael. I have no desire to like Michael. But it's going to be strange being in Zambia together.

"It rains almost every day here during the wet season," Chance tells us over dinner, "but we also get dry mornings and afternoons, too. Let's hope tomorrow will be dryer."

We sit with coffee and a custard-type dessert. I'd forgotten how much influence the English had in Africa with their puddings and only pick at mine, my thoughts straying to the lounge where I left Michael and his friends. I wonder if they're still having drinks or if they've left by now.

The last time I had a drink with Michael, I ended up kissing him. I still find that embarrassing.

I force my focus back into Howard and Chance's conversation and discover they're discussing our flight to Victoria Falls tomorrow. Howard's looking forward to the trip, but he's worried about flying in a little plane. "A six-seater, you say?" he repeats.

"I do have a bigger plane," Chance answers, "but it's experiencing engine troubles."

"But the six-seater—"

"My Cessna Skywagon."

"Your Cessna. It is safe, isn't it?" Howard presses, adding yet another teaspoon of sugar to his coffee.

"Haven't killed anyone yet."

I check my smile. I don't think that was the answer Howard was looking for. "Have you crashed before?" I ask.

"Many times. But that's part of being a bush pilot. Petrol stations are far and few, and control towers nonexistent. To be a good pilot out here, you rely on your control panel, use common sense, and luck."

"Luck?" Howard echoes, turning green.

Chance turns to me. "Are you a nervous flyer, too?"

"Not as long as we don't cr—" I break off as I spot Michael entering the dining room.

Michael heads our way. "We're braving the rain and going elsewhere for dinner," he says on reaching our table, "but it crossed my mind you might enjoy meeting Meg, our Zambia mission director, in the morning. It could get you some background for your story and it'd help her forget about the rain for a while."

"We're flying out in the morning," Chance says, leaning back in his chair. "Heading down to Livingstone."

Michael looks at him, then me. "Thunderstorms are predicted for the morning."

Chance gives Michael a cool once-over. "I'm aware of the weather."

Tension crackles at the table, and I quickly handle introductions. "Howard and Chance, this is Michael O'Sullivan, a doctor and friend from Los Angeles. Michael, this is Howard, my cameraman, and Chance, our pilot and guide while we're here."

Howard shakes hands with Michael, but Chance doesn't.

Instead Chance's expression is mocking. "What kind of doctor?"

"Plastic surgeon," Michael answers evenly.

"You're here for a safari?"

Michael's lip curls. "It's the rainy season." He pauses ever so slightly. "Although I do understand it's the new thing in tourism. Cheaper safaris. Come see the bush when it's in bloom. Are the tourism board's efforts working?"

"Wouldn't know. I don't work for the Zambian government."

Michael turns back to me. "Here's Meg's contact info. If you don't fly out tomorrow—and I hope you won't try to fly if the sky isn't clear—give her a call. She'd love to talk to you." He gives me a faint smile, nods at the others, and walks out.

Everything feels different after he leaves. Flatter. Grayer. Duller.

I wish he hadn't gone. I wish he'd pulled up a chair and stayed. I wish we were back in Big Bear and he was kissing me.

Chapter Fourteen

——— ✦✦✦ ———

It rains all night, and it's still coming down the next morning. We haven't yet heard from Chance, but there's no way we're going to fly anywhere, not with weather like this. However, Howard and I have packed our bags and checked out of our rooms in the event the weather changes, which is making the wait even harder.

"I'd die if I had to live in Seattle," Howard says glumly from his position in front of the lobby's picture window, where he's watching the rain.

"We need to do something. I think I'll give Meg a call."

"Good idea." Howard brightens immediately. He doesn't like sitting around any more than I do. The pace at *America Tonight* is frenetic. It's hard to grind to a halt here.

Meg ends up coming to us, and I quickly write a set of questions to ask her during the interview.

Meg's personality makes up for the gloomy weather. She shakes our hands, makes a joke about when it rains, it pours, and I marvel at her ability to stay so calm and sunny when a huge project is on shaky ground.

"It'll happen," she says confidently, sitting in one of the chairs. The microphone wire is hidden in her blouse, and she's ready to go. "It's just a matter of when."

"But isn't it a bit like a movie set?" I ask, getting the signal from Howard that my mike is working. "Every day people sit around is another day of wasted money."

"We have invested considerable finances and resources," she admits. "All of the medical professionals here are volunteers. These doctors, nurses, anesthesiologists, and paramedics have used their vacation time, or taken time without pay, to be here, so time is the most precious commodity right now."

She goes on to explain that the roads are the biggest problem. They're underwater, and in some places, roads and bridges are completely washed out. "Despite the weather, we already have close to one hundred people lined up at St. Francis Hospital, hoping to be selected. That's the part that makes me crazy. They're there and we're not."

"Where are they coming from?"

"From all over the Eastern province. St. Francis is a large rural hospital, and they've been advertising our mission outreach for the past year."

"And many come on foot?"

"They'll take buses as far as they can, but if buses aren't running, they walk, crossing the flooding rivers on foot, too, with their babies on their backs. And mind you, this is Africa. Those rivers are filled with crocodiles." She's smiling, but I see she's extremely worried.

"What would it take to get the mission under way? How many staff members are you short?"

"The doctors here—O'Sullivan, Kapoor, Danovich, and Voskul—and then there are five ER nurses still stranded in Lilongwe, Malawi. The nurses flew there instead of Lusaka as it's a shorter bus trip from there, but no buses are running to Katete, not with the flooded roads." She pauses to consider logistics and then nods firmly. "Once those nine arrive, we could probably begin, as medicine, supplies, and surgical equipment arrived weeks ago."

I wish I could do something. I feel compelled to do something, and then I realize I can. I have a pilot, and he has a plane. Instead of taking Howard and me to the Falls, I can have Chance flying Michael and the other surgeons to Katete and then, if possible, zipping to Lilongwe to grab the nurses. If the weather breaks today . . . if the weather holds for the day . . .

"Maybe I can help," I say, and tell her that I have access to a pilot and a plane.

Meg listens intently. "I can't tell you how much I love your generosity. But would your pilot fly into Katete? The commercial pilots we've talked to say the airstrip is in too poor a condition and they won't risk their aircraft."

I think about Chance and his swagger. He should be up for a challenge. "I guess the only way we'll know is if I ask."

It's a go.

I have to cajole Chance a bit and offer him a bonus, but he promises to fly everyone there the moment the weather breaks, and it breaks that afternoon.

Now the doctors and Meg are filing into Chance's car.

"Have a great trip," I tell Meg as she climbs into the car.

"We'll see you day after tomorrow?"

"As soon as Chance can get us there." I smile. "You've got my number. Call me if you need anything. Otherwise we'll see you at the end of the week."

She climbs in, leaving just Michael on the curb with me. He's wearing a black T-shirt and olive green cargo-style pants and looking very rugged and very male. It's a good look on him. Maybe even better than the expensive Italian suits.

"Look who saved the day," he says, gazing down on me. "Major brownie points, Tomlinson."

"Thanks, Doc. That means a lot coming from you."

He grins, white teeth flashing. "Do I detect a note of sarcasm?"

"Just a bit."

His expression sobers. "All kidding aside, we appreciate this, Tiana. You've done a good thing."

I flush, uncomfortable. I didn't do this to curry favor. I really did just want to help. "Get in the car, Hollywood, it's time to go."

Chance lays on the horn.

"I'll see you in Katete," Michael says, shouldering his duffel bag. "I'll look forward to your arrival. We do have some unfinished business."

And then he's in the car and the door is shut and Chance is pulling away. I stand at the curb and watch them go. I'm excited they're on their way, yet I feel this strange emptiness now that Michael's gone.

This has to stop, I think. I don't like Michael. I don't.

Or do I?

Howard and I spend the next morning with Jean from the PSI office, visiting the children's ward of the local hospital. Michael's friend Dr. Paul Zarazoga takes us on the rounds. The beds are filled with very young children, their mothers sitting on the floor since there aren't enough chairs. Despite the ceiling fans spinning, it's stiflingly hot. The large plain ward looks more like an army barracks than a hospital. In one bed at the far end of the room, a mother lies across a small blanket-covered body, weeping.

"Her five-year-old," Paul tells us. "It's her third child she's lost."

"HIV?" I ask, horrified.

"Diarrhea."

I stop abruptly, and Jean, who sees my horror, nods. "Twenty percent of children in Zambia die before they're five. Most die from malaria and contaminated water."

And both are preventable.

I gesture around the ward. Dozens of little bodies are dying in front of me. "Is that why they're all here? They don't have the medicine and clean water they need?"

"Pretty shocking, isn't it?" Paul agrees.

I swallow hard. My stomach is doing mad flip-flops. What I feel is inarticulate. It's beyond sad. It's revulsion. People are dying. Children are dying. And they could all be saved.

"The oral rehydration products...are they expensive?" I ask unsteadily.

"No. But we need the private sector—companies and people like you and me—to reach out. People think they can't do anything, that it's too much, but they aren't here. They don't see the difference one water purification kit or one mosquito net makes."

"One net can make that much of a difference?"

Paul explains, "Mothers sleep with their children, couples sleep together, sometimes grandparents sleep with grandchildren, so you can see how one net can save many lives."

"One net," I repeat.

Jean presses one hand into the other. "But it takes outreach and education to teach people how the nets help, and what they need to do. The same is true for water and reproductive health. Nothing's impossible. Not if we work together."

We just need to work together.

Just imagine what we could do with our love.

The night is stormy, and the sky explodes white with electric forks of lightning. Thunder booms and rolls as I sit on my bed, writing in my journal.

The thunder grows louder and closer, rattling the windows. One violent boom follows another. And then everything is black. Power outage. I'd heard it was common during the rainy season, but it hadn't happened yet. Fortunately, this is a four-star hotel, and the hotel should have a generator.

Within thirty seconds there's a blip and the lamp next to my bed fills the room with light again.

Power on.

I set aside my notebook and pen and leave my bed to go to the window and look out at the city, which normally is bright with streetlamps and traffic lights and buildings. There are no lights in Lusaka now. The city outside my window is almost pitch black, and the rain slashes down in relentless sheets. Thunder booms, and booms again. The thunder sounds so close.

Back at my bed, I pick up the hotel phone and call the front desk. "Yes, Miss Tomlinson?" the front desk answers.

"How long does the power outage last?"

"We have our own generator," he says proudly.

"I know, and that's very good, but for the rest of the city, for those who don't? How long will the power be out?"

"Could be an hour, could be all night," he continues cheerfully. "Our power comes from South Africa, and sometimes they shut it off."

"So the whole country is dark?"

"Yes."

"And the South African power company shuts it off, or the storm cuts it off?"

"Yes," he agrees happily. "Anything else I can help you with, Miss Tomlinson?"

He doesn't understand, and I don't have the energy to make him understand. "No, thank you. Good night."

"Good night."

Sunday morning, Howard and I are having breakfast when my international phone rings. It's Chance, calling from Katete to say he's on his way for us now. We're to meet him in two hours at the Lusaka airport, where he'll land and refuel. Then we'll take off immediately.

We do, too, and within forty minutes after taking off from Lusaka, we're flying low over the lush river valley, just three hundred feet above the ground. We can see the path of the dark blue Luangwa River and its tributaries and lakes. Then suddenly Chance is diving lower. He points to a herd of elephants crossing the river. There are at least three babies in the herd and two bull elephants.

They're huge and beautiful and mythic, and I can't believe I'm here, in a little Cessna, doing this. Just two weeks ago I was in Los Angeles, wondering if my career was over, but now I can feel my energy recharging. I feel new again.

Sometime between waking up and landing in Katete, Howard is hit with intestinal distress. He writhes near the end of the flight, the cramps hitting hard and harder. He's desperate for us to land. I'm desperate for us to land. Chance radios ahead to let them know that Howard isn't well. Landing in Katete, we discover one of the hospital's beat-up ambulances waiting for us. Michael O'Sullivan is also waiting at the airstrip.

"How are you?" Michael asks me, one of his arms moving toward me as though to protect me, making me feel as though I'm the most fragile thing on earth.

Strange, because men don't treat me gently, and I'm not sure why. Not even Keith was protective. In fact, he was the one who put me into the fire.

"Fine," I answer, putting a hand to my cheek to push hair back from my face. Clouds blanket the sky. It's suffocatingly warm, the air so thick with moisture that I find myself praying for rain just to lessen the humidity. "But Howard...I don't know. He was groaning pretty bad the last thirty minutes of the flight."

"We heard, and we've got the world's best nurses, doctors, and medics gathered here. Howard couldn't get better care at home than he will here."

Even as he's talking, two medics are lifting Howard from the plane and onto the gurney. A freckle-faced nurse takes Howard's pulse, and then, after a quick check of the rest of his vitals, she begins an IV.

Chance has unloaded our luggage and Howard's cameras and lights from the back of the plane and has stacked everything into a pile. "Is all that yours?" Michael asks.

I nod sheepishly. "Howard's and mine, but mostly mine. I overpacked."

Michael's eyes gleam. "Why am I not surprised?"

Once the gurney is in the back of the ambulance, Michael offers to give me a ride into town. We load the bags and cameras into the trunk of the ancient Renault Michael has borrowed for the airport run.

I turn to Chance to see if he needs a ride, but he's going to stay and tend to his plane. He promises to check in with me tomorrow to see what my plans are.

In the Renault we bounce along the rutted road, the earth a bright muddy orange brown and the trees a scrubby olive green. Michael frequently swerves to avoid puddles that threaten to swallow the car the same way they've swallowed the road.

I'm tired but relieved, and in the bumping, jostling car I close my eyes and just concentrate on breathing.

I was so afraid for Howard.

I was so scared that something would happen to him before I got him to Katete.

"You okay?" Michael asks.

Eyes shut, I nod, shoulders and back tight with tension. I take a deep breath, exhale, and force myself to relax. "This trip's harder than I expected."

"Why?"

"A couple months ago, Glenn, my show's executive producer, told me no one in America cared about real Africa. He said real Africa is depressing, and America doesn't care about the suffering in Africa because they're too busy suffering at home. Inflation, recession, school shootings, domestic violence, date rape—" I break off and glance at Michael. "I didn't agree with Glenn. I told him that Americans care. The problem is, they're overwhelmed by the news we get from Africa, all so negative."

"And now you're overwhelmed?" Michael guesses.

"I thought I could come here and do some stories and show the wonderful things being done."

"And you are."

"But it doesn't feel as good as I thought it would. It doesn't seem like it's enough."

"You're looking at the continent, not the child."

"There's so much dying here. So many children who won't make it."

He reaches over, covers my hand with his. "You can't lose sight of the miracles because of the shadows. Light is light. Every good thing matters. Just wait until you see the children we're screening. Wait until you see all the lives we change."

With Howard being taken care of at St. Francis Hospital, Michael delivers my luggage to the community center's guesthouse, where I'm to stay while here, taking a few minutes to give me the general lay of the land. According to Michael, most of the medical team is housed in hospital dormitories, tents, and the community center bunk beds. Meals are served cafeteria style in a central dining tent on the hospital grounds.

Tour ended, Michael is ready to head back to the operating room, where he's scheduled to be in surgery this afternoon.

"Can I go, too?" I ask, already digging through my bags for a notebook and pen.

"Isn't that why you're here?"

Each surgery to correct a cleft palate takes roughly an hour, and I wish I had one of Howard's cameras as I stand off to the side and watch the medical team work together to perform these life-changing procedures.

After three surgeries, Michael leaves the operating room and another doctor prepares to take his place. But Michael isn't on a break. He's just shifting to another role and, still dressed in his green scrubs, heads outside to meet with the children and parents who have been scheduled for surgery tomorrow.

I listen as Michael talks to nervous parents about the procedure. He's using a translator. No food or liquid after midnight. No liquid or food in the morning. The baby will sleep during the surgery and will not feel pain. But food or liquid could make him sick during the operation.

The translator tells Michael the mother is afraid. She's afraid her baby will die in surgery, but if he doesn't have the surgery, she's afraid he'll die anyway.

Michael assures her that her baby will not die and that it is a very short surgery. He will be out of surgery in an hour, and the moment he goes to the recovery room she can join him.

The mother nods. Wipes her tears. Asks if her baby will have a normal boy face when the surgery is done.

Michael answers yes.

The mother's tears fall faster.

Five minutes later, the mother goes and the scene is enacted again, and yet again, as he meets with the rest of the parents who have children scheduled for surgery tomorrow.

When the last of the waiting parents has been seen, Michael rises slowly, stretching, the thin green shirt clinging to his torso, revealing muscles and damp skin. He's hot and tired, but you wouldn't have known by the way he interacted with the parents and children. I've never seen a doctor so patient. He didn't rush anyone, and he took as much time as necessary to calm the parents' fears and answer the questions they had.

Michael turns his head and glances in my direction. "You're still here."

"That was incredible." And then because I can't help it and I've got a case of hero worship at the moment, I blurt, "You're incredible. You were wonderful with them. I've never seen anything like that before."

"Now you're gushing."

I blush and I can feel my cheeks go hot. "And you're back to horrible."

"But that's how you like me. Bad." He winks wickedly, and I shake my head and tuck my notebook and pen beneath my arm and walk out of the tent.

"Oh, and Ms. America," he calls after me.

I pause and turn to face him, one eyebrow arched.

"You look beautiful without all that makeup you wear in L.A. I like you natural."

"Thanks, Doc." And lifting my nose, I turn around and walk away even as my heart skips a beat.

I've got it all wrong, I think, pushing through the tent and stepping into the scorching heat. Michael was never the bad guy. Michael just might have been Prince Charming.

I check on Howard. He's still hooked up to an IV, but his color is better and they've given him a powerful antidiarrheal drug to try to calm his body. Still, it could be a few days before he's up and around.

He apologizes for letting me down, and I tell him that it's not a problem and then put a look of terror on his face when I ask if he'll allow me to use his camera tomorrow so I can film the assessments, preops, and surgeries.

"You want to film?" he asks.

I nod. "It won't be as good as anything you do, but I've used cameras before. Years ago I was a reporter in a one-person band. I can do it again."

"But you haven't had to light or photograph a story in years," he reminds me unhappily, struggling to sit up.

"Lie down. You're not strong enough to be sitting up."

"Maybe I can get up in the morning to film—"

"You're not going to do anything tomorrow but get fluids, maybe some food, and plenty of rest."

He groans as he settles back against his pillow. "I feel like I got hit by a truck."

"In the morning I'll familiarize myself with the camera and film my stand-up before the first interview. We can edit it all later."

Howard's not happy, but he reluctantly agrees.

Later that evening, after a simple dinner that reminds me of meals at Epworth, my South African boarding school, Michael invites me to join him and some of the other volunteer medical staff as they sit around the large dining tent relaxing after a long day working. The rain comes down, yet no one minds.

Michael's group is a collection of doctors, nurses, and staffers, and Michael is in his element, kicking back in his shorts and T-shirt, telling stories, making everyone laugh. Watching him, I get a strange fizz in my insides. A nervous but excited fizz that makes me feel and hope, and I'm not even sure what I'm feeling or hoping for.

Michael turns and looks at me. Our eyes meet. I get that nervous fluttery feeling again, and my hearts beats a little faster.

I like this Michael. He reminds me more than a little of Keith, casual, rumpled, relaxed. Happy. If I hadn't seen Michael in Armani suits in Los Angeles, I wouldn't have believed this is the same person. As it is, I'm having a difficult time reconciling this ruggedly handsome, very masculine surgeon with smooth, sophisticated Dr. Hollywood.

His gaze still holds mine and he smiles slowly, lazily, and I smile back. I don't even know why I'm smiling, but here everything is different.

I feel different. I feel as if all the superficial bullshit of Hollywood is falling away and the real me can breathe again. I'm finding myself and remembering what matters.

When the hospital van arrives on its final trip to the community center for the night, I try to slip away quietly from the group to get a seat in the van. But Michael sees me rise and reaches out to touch my arm as I pass. "Where are you going now?"

"Heading to bed."

His fingertips brush my forearm and my skin tingles, hot and electric. "Always running away."

I roll my eyes. "It's the last van of the night."

His dark gaze gleams. "Good night, Tiana. Sweet dreams."

Chapter Fifteen

———— ✦✦✦ ————

I feel alarmingly giddy during the ride back to the community center's guesthouse. Giddy as I wash my face and strip off my clothes and turn out the light.

Giddy, and hot, and restless.

I shouldn't be feeling this way, either. I should be smart. Focused. Honest.

Michael's a playboy. An Irish charmer. The compliments drop easily from his tongue, but does he mean it? Or are they just lines?

It rains now, and I climb into bed, listening in the darkness to the rain drum on the metal roof above my head. Even with the fan, it's oppressively hot.

If only I could just forget Michael. But I can't, and thinking of him just makes me warmer. I hate that I miss him and I've only just left him.

How funny. I barely know him, yet I already miss him more than I missed Trevor after six months of dating.

There's something about Michael that connects with me, touches me. But along with the hope is fear, and the fear is growing, too. Love never lasts. People either die or leave. Just look at Keith. And Shey and John.

No matter how interesting I find him, no matter how

appealing he is here, I can't want Michael. I can't love him. And I can't possibly let myself need him.

Keep it as friends, I tell myself, reaching up to touch the mosquito net cloaking the bed. My fingertips brush the fine net. He's safe, and I'm safe, as long as I don't let him close.

The van comes far too early to pick us up from the center for St. Francis, but I'm ready when it arrives and squeeze into the back with Howard's camera equipment and my notebook and pen. It's only a ten-minute drive and I'm wearing a tomato red sundress with spaghetti straps, but I'm still sweating by the time we reach the hospital grounds.

Fortunately, coffee and a hot breakfast await. After stacking the equipment in a corner of the tent, I get in line with everyone else for my eggs, potatoes, sausage, and bacon.

I see Michael at a table across the dining hall, and despite my resolve, my heart does a funny little jump. He's sitting in a sea of females.

With my eggs and potatoes, I go sit at a table near Howard's equipment to keep an eye on it. No one else is at my table, so I get out my notebook and scribble notes for myself about what I need to do today.

I'm halfway through my breakfast when Michael stops by the table. "Good morning, Ms. America."

My pulse quickens. "Good morning, Hollywood."

The corner of his mouth lifts. "You should have joined me for breakfast."

"You had quite a bit of company already."

His eyes spark. "There's no competition."

I blush, and I don't know why I'm blushing. It's silly that I suddenly feel nervous. "You're sounding very Irish lately, Dr. O'Sullivan," I say crisply to hide my uneasiness.

He sits on the bench across from me. "Hard not to. My mum and dad are both from Galway, on the west coast of Ireland."

"So you were born in Ireland?"

"La Paz."

"Bolivia," I say, making sure I understand.

His smile is crooked. "Travel's in my blood."

I'm even more curious now. "Was your father a doctor?"

"No."

"So why do you do what you do?"

His smile fades and he doesn't answer immediately, and then he raps the table with his knuckles and stands. "Because I can."

The camera's dead. I didn't think to check the battery last night, and now I scramble to find the plug and a converter and an available outlet. But just as I'm about to plug in the camera, Tomas, one of Michael's doctor friends, tells me to stop. "You'll fry your camera," he tells me. "You're missing a piece of the converter."

I'm embarrassed but grateful and have to go without filming until I can see Howard and find out where the missing piece is.

Michael is scrubbed in for surgery, and I'm in the corner of the operating room in a mask and robe with my notebook and pen, to make notes during the operation of questions I have and things I need to research.

In between procedures, Michael steps outside to drink water or talk with his surgical team. I keep my distance as the staff talks. They're truly on a mission and sharing something very special together. It's bonded them, turning a collection of international medical specialists into a team. They know they're doing something good, know they're making a difference, and their satisfaction is evident in their expressions.

I want what they have. I want to feel what they feel. I want to know I'm doing something good in my life.

The medical team is scrubbing up again, and Jon, Michael's friend, appears with a black box and plug. "This will work for your camera," he says. "And I moved some things around in the operating room. You'll find a free outlet against the wall by the door."

I'm surprised by the unexpected gift and thrilled. Impulsively, I lean forward and kiss him on the cheek. "Thank you!"

Red-faced, Jon leaves and I glance up to find Michael looking at me.

I lift the converter and plug to show him. He smiles and there's something warm in his eyes, something so good that I feel his warmth burrow all the way through me and into my heart.

If only he could be the right one...if only I could be brave enough...if only there could be some kind of guarantee that if I fall in love again, this time everything would work out....

During the next round of surgeries, I stand next to the camera and film with my best professional detachment, which is very hard to do in these circumstances. These patients are but babies, and Michael's hands are like those of a giant as he works inside, restructuring the palate and connective tissue and bone.

This "devil" of a man is gentle with the smallest and weakest.

*   *   *

I spend the afternoon filming the screening process. There must still be several hundred families waiting, and with only a week left to the mission, less than a fifth will be chosen.

I have the camera rolling throughout the afternoon as women stand patiently in line for their child to be evaluated. The mothers know only a few will be selected, and they all want one of those coveted spots.

Later, as the screening team of pediatrician, dentist, speech therapist, and nurse examines the candidates, I film an anguished father begging the doctors to help his son.

Tears spill from the father's eyes as he motions that his son cannot eat and is starving to death and if we do not help him, he will die. He will die.

Whispering into the mike, I repeat the father's desperate words, and I zoom the lens in on the father's face. It's difficult for me to keep my composure as the father's words are translated for the screening team's benefit.

I pan to the thin little boy with a hole where his lip and gums and teeth should be and then have to pause filming because my vision is too blurry to see.

They're not going to choose the little boy. I know they're not, and it undoes me.

Late in the day I see Michael, who is finally finished until tomorrow, and I ask him about the little boy who moved me so much.

"Will he be one of the ones chosen?"

"Not all children can be chosen."

"But some children who aren't helped will die."

He nods imperceptibly.

"How can you bear it?" I ask, my voice breaking.

"Because I've learned the hard way that we can't save everyone, so here we have to be careful, we must make good decisions. We evaluate the cases and choose the best possible candidates, children who are relatively disease-free and physically strong enough to tolerate the surgery. Children who can undergo anesthesia. Children without heart and lung problems. Children who won't die from infection afterwards."

"They're not going to pick the little boy, are they."

"If we were in an American hospital—"

"But we're not," I finish fiercely, and my anger isn't at him, but at the injustice of it all.

There has to be a way we can change things, improve things. There has to be a way to save the little boy, the only son of a weeping father, a father who has already lost his wife to childbirth.

"There has to be something I can do to help him."

"Tiana, he's a very sick little boy."

I fight to keep my voice calm. "Let me help him."

"We're not equipped to help all the ill children. We're limited by our mission, limited to doing what we can do—"

"Help me help him." I put my hand on his arm, and his skin is firm and warm. I can feel the muscle in his forearm. "Michael, you can find out what he needs. You're a doctor. You give me a list of medicines or treatment he needs, and I'll pay for it."

Michael covers my hand with his. "And what of the other hundred children who aren't chosen? Will you save them, too?"

I blink and tears fall. "Yes."

"It's impossible to save everyone. That's the first lesson they teach you in medical school."

"Then I'll help as many as I can."

His fingers press against mine. His voice drops. "You have a good heart."

"I have money—"

"Tiana."

"I want to help." I take a breath. "I need to help."

"You are by being here. You're telling the story that needs to be told."

I shake my head. "Children will die before the story even airs."

For a moment his expression turns bleak, and then it's gone. "They're dying as we speak."

I pull my hand away and avert my head to hide my rush of emotion. I hate what he said. I hate that he's right.

"Come…" Michael puts a hand out to me. "Let's get dinner. It's something we can do right now."

Michael keeps me close during dinner. It's an effort to eat the little I put on my plate. I'm exhausted. Flattened. And my mind is spinning trying to find solutions, trying to figure out how I can help the father's only son.

"It's hard to see so much suffering," Michael says to me quietly as he stacks our trays together. "And you, despite all your TV gloss and polish, are extremely sensitive."

My eyes burn, my chest burns. "I could not lose my child. I could not." And these people do. And they will. And it breaks my heart.

He's silent, studying my face. "I will have a look at the boy's file. I will look into the reasons he wasn't selected and see if there is anything I can do."

"You'll do that?" My voice catches.

"I promise."

I blink, sniff, but the tears fall anyway. "Thank you."

"Who would have thought little Ms. America had such a tender heart?" And then he puts his arm around me and holds me against him as I cry. And I cry. I cry for the mothers who lose their babies and I cry for the babies who lose their mothers and I cry for the losses I experienced too early, before I was ready to be whole and complete and able to stand on my own two feet.

As I cry against Michael's chest, I think I need those two feet now. It's time to be as big and tough and successful on the inside as I am on the outside. Fame doesn't mean anything. But confidence and strength do.

After my embarrassing crying jag, I want to return to my room at the community center, but Michael insists I stay and play games. So here I am, at a table in the dining tent, playing Yahtzee. In fact, the tent echoes with the sounds of cups slamming and dice rolling and shouts of laughter. Turns out Yahtzee is a tradition among Michael and his friends. They drink orange Fanta and play a mean game of Yahtzee. At least Michael plays a mean game.

"He's cheating," I say grumpily as he gets four fours and howls with delight.

"Get used to it," Tomas tells me with a long face. "He's very good at winning."

"Which is a good thing when you consider he's a terrible loser," Jon adds.

They laugh, and shaking my head, I glance up at Michael. He's looking right back at me, and what I see in his eyes makes me go warm even as my heart turns over.

He likes me.

Michael slides the plastic cup of dice toward me, and his fingers brush mine. "My parents were peace workers, Tiana. We didn't have a lot of money, and life in Bolivia was often hard, but compared to the pressure of life in Los Angeles, those years in South America seem like paradise now."

I inhale, breathless all over again.

I understand.

I understand that living in Los Angeles means never being good enough. No matter how young, how fit, how tan, how beautiful, there will always be someone younger, fitter, tanner, more beautiful. There will always be another young woman appearing on the scene, threatening to take everything away I've earned.

There's nothing wrong with how I am. I'm not the problem. The message is the problem, the message that we're not good enough or pretty enough or fit enough or smart enough. It's the message Madison Avenue has been selling us, and it's a message Hollywood packages and pushes with every bone-thin Botoxed actress they stick in our face.

It's a message I've perpetuated, too. But no more.

And last, I finally understand that Michael likes me.

Maybe a lot.

Today, with Howard finally behind the camera, we're staying out of the surgery room and focusing on preop and recovery. We've been told by Meg that it's the most emotional moment for parents. In preop, the fathers are usually stoic, but the mothers alternate between hope and terror. If preop is fear, recovery is pure joy.

Not just elated that their child has survived the operation, these parents are seeing their child for the first time with a whole face.

There is such wonder in their eyes as they reach for their children. The upper lip has been stitched closed and the palate has been restored. It's a miracle for the whole family.

After one particularly extensive surgery, Michael appears in the recovery room to check on the nine-month-old girl. The little girl's mother is practically a child herself, and she's overcome as she examines her baby's beautiful face.

Michael gives the sobbing mother a hug.

My chest grows tight. He's good. He's gifted. He's passionate. He's determined. He's the kind of man I always wanted, the kind of man who makes my heart beat harder, faster. Why didn't I ever see who he was? When I looked at him before, what was I looking at?

It's been years since I really loved, years since I let myself be loved. Can I do this again? Do I know how to do this again? Can I go for it without screwing it all up?

Midafternoon there's always a half-hour break for tea. Everyone spills into the dining tent for tea and coffee, rusks and slices of milk tart. It's a very South African tea and one I remember from my eight months in Natal.

Today I pass on the tea and head outside for a walk, needing the exercise to try to burn off some of my tension.

Despite the heat, I walk briskly, ignoring the perspiration beading my skin. I walk and walk, making circles around the brick hospital with its one-hundred-bed capacity.

I've just completed my third circle around the hospital when I hear, "How am I expected to sleep with you thundering about like a herd of elephants?"

I glance toward the shade provided by the lone hospital tree and see Michael stretched out on the ground, his arms folded behind his head.

I walk toward him, my nose wrinkling when I see him lying on an area that's more red dirt than grass. "Aren't you afraid of being eaten by ants?"

"I don't taste that good. They leave me alone." His smile is lazy. "I've been watching you march around the hospital. What's wrong?"

"Nothing. Everything. I love this. I hate this." My hands go to my hips. "I'm elated and emotional and excited and overwhelmed—" I break off, laugh unsteadily. "I'm so glad you challenged me to come here, to be here. I'm just so grateful."

He pats the straggly grass next to him. "It does give one perspective, doesn't it?"

I nod and sit cautiously. As I settle onto the ground, I get a look at Michael: The shadows beneath his eyes are even darker today. "You're not sleeping, are you."

"I don't tend to sleep well on the missions. There's so much to do and so little time in which to get it all done."

"Yet you're always so nice to everyone."

"You don't know the real me. I'm no saint. Just ask Alexis. She'll tell you."

"Did you cheat on her?"

"No." He laughs, gives me an odd look. "I didn't give her the attention she deserved. I don't try hard enough, don't listen enough, don't make her needs a priority."

"Is that true?"

He thinks, nods. "Probably."

"Did you go to counseling or try to work on the problems?"

"No."

"Why not?"

"We weren't ever supposed to get serious. It was just supposed to be fun. But of course it got serious, and...well, I'm an asshole."

I laugh. "I bet you can be."

"Oh, you know I can be."

I laugh again, shake my head. "You're proud of it?"

"No. But I am who I am, and I know who I am, and I know what's important to me. My work is important to me. Coming here, helping others, that's important to me. Parties, luxury cars, and first-class travel? Not so important."

"What about Alexis?"

He looks at me and then shrugs.

Not so important. Ouch.

"What about you?" he says. "What are your dark secrets, Ms. America? Or do you not have any?"

"Oh, God, I have hundreds." I see his expression, grimace. "Not hundreds, but dozens."

"Tell me one."

"The network has informed me I'm getting old," I say. "Between the not so subtle encouragement that I should get some work done, and the addition of a young co-host to the show, I'm feeling fifty-eight instead of thirty-eight."

"Max should nip that in the bud."

"Max was one of the forces behind the plastic surgery talk. He was pushing me to go to you to get a face-lift."

"Max is a dick," Michael says bluntly. "And he said a face-lift specifically?"

"Eyes, forehead, mouth, cheeks...pretty much tighten up the whole thing."

We sit in silence for a few minutes, and then Michael asks, "Do you think your face needs work?"

"Yes, and no." I feel like a traitor just saying the words. "Mostly no. I like my face."

"So do I."

I can feel his sincerity, and then I tell him a real secret. "My mom was thirty-eight when she died. I'm thirty-eight now—" I break off, take a quick breath. "And I know it's irrational, but there's this little part of me that tells me my face is all I have of her. If I change it, cut it, I worry I'll lose that connection to her." As well as having the work botched. I'm terrified of being turned into something clownish, something laughable. "Am I crazy?"

"No." He gives me a reassuring smile. "Paul Ekman, one of the world's experts on facial expressions, said our expressions link us to our families. As children we imitate our mother's smile, we stare fascinated at her expressions. Families look alike because they mirror one another's expressions."

"*Yes!* That's it. That's exactly it. I'm afraid I'll lose that family resemblance. With my grandmother gone now, too, there's no one left. There's just me, and it's crazy and scary." I chew on the inside of my lip. "What about your family? Are they still alive?"

"My mum's gone. She died of complications from cancer treatment when I was fourteen, and my dad sent me to live with friends of his in L.A. I ended up going to UCLA and then UCLA's med school and just never left."

"I'm sorry about your mom." I reach out and touch his shoulder near his chest. "I was fourteen when my mom died. It's a hard age to lose your mother."

"Very."

I'm quiet as I think about Michael's past and how we're far more similar than I would have imagined. His mom was Irish, and mine was South African. He was sent at fourteen to Los Angeles from Bolivia, and I was sent to boarding school in Natal. But within a year we both ended up in California. We were just at different ends of the state.

"Your mom's death influenced your decision to become a doctor," I guess, puzzling over the pieces of his life.

"Yes. I was so angry I couldn't help her, it was my duty to help others. Call it atonement—"

"You were fourteen."

"Still felt responsible. She was my mum. I was a man—"

"*Fourteen.*"

"My job was to protect her."

I fight for control. It takes me several moments and then several more. "Why not oncology, then, why plastic surgery?"

"Her double mastectomy was performed in a government hospital in La Paz. It completely disfigured her. She didn't heal properly. My dad used to say the grief of being turned into a road map killed her. I know now it was infection that wasn't treated right. But I vowed years ago to learn how to do it properly to make sure no woman would go through what my mother went through."

And I suddenly know who Michael is. Not the suits. Not the fancy practice. Not the ironic curl to his lip.

He's a boy who lost his mom, and he has missed her as much as I've missed mine. And his life has been shaped by her death.

"And I always thought you were about silicone," I say huskily.

"The show *Dr. Hollywood, Surgeon to the Stars* probably didn't help that image."

"No. But it's easy to forget that plastic surgery isn't always about vanity."

"There's nothing wrong with a little vanity. Beauty is important. It's valuable. It makes us feel good to see beautiful things. But too much vanity can ruin lives. I've met far too many women who spend their lives torturing themselves for not being perfect. But there is no perfect body. There never has been. And there never will be. Perfection doesn't exist."

My heart thunders in my rib cage. Perfection might not exist, but I can't help thinking this man just might be perfect for me.

Chapter Sixteen

The next few days pass in a blur of interviews and taping and editing, interspersed by meals and laughing and vicious Yahtzee games.

I feel as if I'm back in college. Fierce and passionate and so alive. I love being part of the group, and one lunch in the middle of a particularly intense debate, I grab Michael's arm and call him Keith. And then I realize what I've said.

Michael does, too.

He glances down at my hand on his arm, then up into my face. I shake my head faintly. I've never done that before. Have never called anyone Keith. Why did I do that now? "I'm sorry," I apologize. Part of me wants to run, yet another part needs to stay. I feel as though I've been running for a long time now, and I need to stop. I need to stay put. So that one day I can move forward.

"I think you must remind me of him." My voice is husky, and I don't know where to look. "And that's a compliment." I struggle to smile even as my heart pounds with raw emotion.

I could fall in love again. I could. But would it be safe?

But is love ever safe?

Suddenly he cups my face with his hand. "I hope you don't do it," he says quietly. "Don't get work done. You're beautiful. You're exactly the way you should be."

He's just paid me the most amazing compliment. "And that's your professional opinion, Doctor?"

His gaze meets mine. He drops his hand. "I'm not your doctor. Would never be your doctor. Couldn't. Not even if you paid me."

I smile slowly. "A man with principles."

"A man who could never do anything to hurt you."

I open my mouth, but I have no words, not when my heart races so hard that I hurt.

And I do hurt. Because there's so much I want and feel and need. Love, love, love.

"Tomorrow, would you be interested in going to dinner?" he asks. "There's a little restaurant in Chipata that serves some decent food. It's a fifty-minute drive, but it's going to be a dry night and it'd be fun to have a change of scenery."

"Yes. What time?"

"I'll pick you up from the center at six."

"I'll be ready." It's not until I'm in the van heading to the community center that I realize tomorrow night is our last night here. The day after tomorrow we head to L.A.

Michael picks me up at the community center in the old blue Renault again, and as he steps from his car I take a quick breath. The collar of his white shirt falls open at the throat, revealing taut muscles and tan skin. His khakis hint at strong quadriceps. This is a man I'd love to see naked.

When he sees me in the doorway of the center, he smiles slowly, and it's such a slow, sexy smile that I suck in air, remembering the kiss at Big Bear.

I remember the feel of his lips. And the shape of his jaw.

And the texture of his skin. Even tipsy, I remember that one kiss and remember how I didn't want it to end.

"You look beautiful," he says, opening the car door for me.

"You've cleaned up pretty nicely, too."

The beat-up Renault car lacks air-conditioning, so we drive with the windows down. My hair blows, and the windshield gets splattered with bits of sticky, flaky mud.

The drive is every bit as bouncy and bone jarring as I feared, yet with Michael at the wheel, the jolts make me laugh. Michael makes me laugh, and I push at my billowing skirt and tug at my hair.

"Is the air too much for you?" Michael asks, downshifting to avert a deep pothole full of pumpkin-colored mud.

"No. It's perfect."

Michael shoots me an amused smile, and I just smile back. But it's true. I wouldn't change a thing.

Not the bright hot twilight with the sky turning red above the burning sun, or the barely running car with the missing shocks, or my white sundress turning orange in places from all the swirling dust.

"Ever been married?" I ask, tipping my head back to look at him.

He swerves around another pothole, but the back tire hits a puddle and sends up a spray of dirty water. "I made the plunge once. It didn't work out."

"You're divorced?" I'm surprised, and I don't know why. "How long ago?"

"Seven years."

I look at him, trying to imagine him married, wondering what kind of husband he'd be. And having observed him in action here in Zambia, I think he would have been a good husband. A kind one. Patient, too. I've never once heard him raise his voice, and even when frustrated, he keeps his cool. "Did you like being married?"

Lines form on either side of his mouth as his lips compress. "No."

"Why not?"

One of his eyebrows lifts. "Am I being interviewed?"

"I think so."

He glances at me. "Turnabout is fair play. For every question you ask me, I get to ask one in return."

"Fine. Later. After my turn."

"Something tells me you could be ruthless as an interviewer."

"Well, we can't all be Yahtzee champions."

He laughs, and the warm glow in me just grows.

"So why didn't you like being married?" I repeat my question, as I know there's more to the story and I want the real story.

"I'm a better doctor than husband. My former wife would agree with Alex on a number of things. I'm not good at communicating, sharing, or letting people in. Oh, and I work too much."

I look at him for a long time, trying to see beneath the darkened jaw and shadowed eyes. There's a very complex man beneath the thick hair and solid bone structure.

I like this man. Even if his wife said he worked too much.

He probably did.

But I still like him, and I liked Keith even though he worked too much.

Hell, I work too much.

"I imagine she was beautiful," I say, my arm resting on the car door. Men are visual, and they sometimes fall with their eyes instead of their hearts.

"She was," he agrees flatly.

"Another aspiring actress, or a model?"

The corner of his mouth tugs. "A model who aspired to be an actress."

"The perfect combination."

Michael's eyes laugh, and little lines fan at the corners, deep creases that extend all the way to his temple.

I like his smile. And I like that his face isn't as smooth and perfect as I first thought it was. "You don't Botox, Dr. Hollywood?"

He reaches up to rub at his creases. "My nurses tell me I should. They say it's bad for business not to."

"I don't think your business is suffering too badly if there's a thirteen-month waiting list just to get in to see you."

His eyes crease again, and as he glances at me there's a light in them, as though he's swallowed a beacon and it's shining through him.

He's kind of magical, isn't he?

My heart turns over and I suddenly wish we could have a fresh start. That I was less banged up by life so that I could have met him with a young heart. I would have liked him sooner, faster.

"A penny for your thoughts," he says.

The light is still in his eyes, and he makes sense to me in a way no other man has since Keith. I can't help thinking that this is the man for me. That this is the man I want. This is the man I need.

My eyes suddenly burn, and the lump of emotion threatens to swallow me whole. "You make me wish I were younger," I say honestly, tired of pretending all the time, tired of keeping the game face on.

"But we probably wouldn't have gotten along if either of us were younger. You certainly wouldn't have liked me ten years ago. Getting knocked around a bit has taught me humility and forgiveness."

"You're humble?"

He grimaces. "Compared to the old days? Yes."

My eyes widen. I can't even imagine how horrible he must have been, but before I can ask him about the "old days," he changes the subject.

"Remember the little boy you were so worried about?" he asks. "Paul and I have been working on getting him the help he needs. The boy and his dad are already in Lusaka at the University Teaching Hospital—"

"Paul's hospital?" I interrupt.

He nods. "And if Paul and his team can't help him, we'll send him to Johannesburg."

"He's going to be okay?"

"Yes."

"His care—"

"It's covered."

"By whom?"

"It doesn't matter."

I know then it's Michael who played angel. My throat burns and my chest aches and I can't even articulate what I'm feeling. "Thank you," I whisper.

Michael just nods.

*   *   *

We arrive at a squat concrete building with a rusting metal roof. Michael shifts into park and turns off the engine.

The restaurant doesn't look much different from the center where I'm staying, and they, too, serve food. If we'd stayed there, we wouldn't have had to bounce along a muddy, treacherous road for an hour; but then if we'd stayed there, we would probably have been joined by the doctors staying at the center.

The interior of the restaurant is marginally more inviting than the exterior, although back home it'd be called decrepit, and that's relatively polite.

The restaurant's empty except for two old men sitting by the door. I know why they're by the door once we're seated. They're trying to get a breeze.

Perspiration beads on my skin, and I pick up my menu and use it to fan myself.

"The doctor who recommended the place said the food was good. He didn't mention the heat," Michael says with a glance at his menu.

"It's fine," I assure him. "I won't melt."

"That's probably because you're not wearing any makeup anymore."

"I guess I should have put on something more than lip gloss and mascara."

"I'm glad you didn't. Your foundation hides your freckles."

"I hate my freckles."

"I don't, and I'm the one looking at you." He cocks his head, studies me. "Did you like being married?"

"Yes."

"What was he like?"

I smile a little wistfully. "He was a good man. Smart, brave, creative, driven. And yes, I liked being married, but he died before our first anniversary, so I guess I don't really know what marriage is like. I was still in the honeymoon stage."

"Some people stay in the honeymoon stage."

"You think?"

His shoulders shift. "My parents did. My father adored my mother to the very end." Then he gets to his feet and heads to the very old jukebox in the corner.

I watch Michael drop in some coins and then punch his selections. The first song is "Billie Jean" by Michael Jackson, and as Michael returns to the table, I'm smiling. "Is this your kind of music?" I tease.

"There's not a lot to choose from."

"Not complaining."

I thought music signaled a change in mood, but Michael continues our rather serious conversation into dinner. As we eat, he asks about my mysterious past.

I take a sip from my glass of Zambian beer. The beer is warm. They don't serve many drinks cold here, as electricity is too expensive. "Why do you call it mysterious?"

"Your bio always starts with you graduating from Stanford. There's no mention of your life before. I now know your mom died when you were fourteen, but where did you grow up? What about the rest of your family? Where are they now?"

This is going to get depressing fast. "I didn't have your normal American childhood. You like to call me Ms. America. Well, my mother was *Miss* South Africa. The real one."

I concentrate on the broken lights of the jukebox as I collect my thoughts. "She was at Miss World in New Zealand when she met my dad. He was an American teacher, traveling. They fell in love and returned to the Cape, where he found a teaching job and she stayed home and had babies. Three babies, all girls. I was the middle one."

"And I thought my childhood was idyllic."

I smile at him, and then my smile fades as I wonder how to tell the next part, the not so idyllic part. "Just months before my fifteenth birthday there was an accident." I stop. "Everybody died. Everybody but me."

His brow creases. "How?"

"I was the only one not wearing a seat belt and I was thrown from the car. Everyone else, buckled safely, died." I'm staring hard at the red letters on the bottle. "How ironic that my act of teenage rebellion—refusing to put on my seat belt—saved my life." How ironic that everyone else who'd done the right thing perished.

"You lost everyone?" Michael's voice is filled with disbelief. "Mother, father, sisters?"

"All four."

"Where did you go?"

"For the first week after the accident I stayed with neighbors while people struggled to get funeral arrangements made. And then Grandmother, my mother's mother, arrived from Pietermaritzburg. I didn't even know she was my grandmother. She was tall and serious, rich and scary." I look at Michael, make a face. "We took an instant dislike to each other, which didn't help the grieving process."

The waitress stops by our table and asks if we'd like anything else. Michael orders another Zambian beer. I'm good with the one I've got.

"She hauled you home with her?" Michael guesses as the waitress walks away.

"Yes. Talk about culture shock. One day I'm being home-schooled in the Cape and weeks later I'm in a boarding school in the Natal province—" I break off. "But you know what culture shock is. You went from Bolivia to Los Angeles."

"Never had to go to boarding school, though. What was it like?"

"Awful. I knew my dad had taught at boarding schools, but I hated having to live, eat, sleep at school. There were so many bells and rules and impossible standards for behavior. I celebrated my fifteenth birthday seven weeks after I arrived at Epworth, and it was the strangest, loneliest birthday."

"Your grandmother must have come to see you."

"She sent a card—"

"Just a card?"

"We were strangers. She'd only just met me, and in her defense, I probably reminded her too much of my mom."

I look at Michael then, and his expression is so serious and so concerned that I can't bear it. I can't have anyone feel anything for me because it just makes it hurt worse. "Don't look at me like that. You'll make me cry."

He reaches out across the table, brushes hair from my cheek. "Tell me the story gets better."

"I eventually landed in a California boarding school where I met two of my best friends, Marta and Shey. They made it better."

"I imagine they're good people," he says.

I nod. "The best."

The next song on the jukebox is Journey's "Lovin', Touchin', Squeezin'." I haven't heard this one in so long, and I kind of smile.

Michael stands, extends his hand. "Let's dance."

I look around the restaurant of plain wood tables and metal chairs. A fabric wall hanging is tacked to the wall. It'd be cool if it were tribal art, but it's an ugly black velvet painting of a horse pawing at the moon. "Here?"

He takes my hand and pulls me to my feet. "And now." And that's how we end up dancing for the next half hour.

Journey, Cher, Stevie Nicks, and Elvis Presley. We dance like we're kids and it's our senior prom, my arms around his neck, his arms around my lower back, and our feet barely moving.

The only difference between now and high school is that Michael doesn't have a boy's body and I'm very aware as we dance that he's attracted to me.

It's not until we're in the car driving home that I remember that Howard and I leave for home tomorrow. I can't believe I've forgotten until now, especially as earlier, when I was dressing, it was the only thing on my mind.

I feel a flicker of panic. What if this is the end of everything? I know Michael's attracted to me. I know he enjoys my company. He also works just miles from my office. But that doesn't mean this will continue back home. That doesn't mean this is anything.

To be honest, I don't know what this is. What if I've fallen for him and he's just killing time with me? Isn't that what he said about Alexis? She was just supposed to be fun, but then things got serious and he doesn't do serious.

As if able to read my thoughts, Michael reaches out and touches the back of my head as he drives, his fingers tangling in my windblown curls before sliding to my cheek. He strokes my skin and then drops his hand. "I enjoyed tonight."

I shiver at how sensitive he makes me feel. "I did, too."

"You made this week special, Tiana. Thank you."

I dart him a quick glance. He almost sounds as if he were the one leaving tomorrow. "Is this a good-bye?" I ask, and my voice suddenly trembles.

"I have a symposium in Cairo tomorrow night. I leave in the morning, and then it's back to L.A. for me." He glances at me. "How about you?"

"Lubwe tomorrow—if the weather's good—and then on to Livingstone for a day, and then it's home after that."

"So we're both leaving in the morning."

Neither of us continues the conversation, and the silence stretches, engulfing us and the dark night. It's still hot, and the Renault's weak head beams barely make out the muddy, bumpy road in front of us. Driving to dinner, I felt so excited and optimistic. Everything had seemed magical. Now I'm just sad. What if this is good-bye?

I don't want to think about it. I want to enjoy these last thirty, forty minutes together. Make this everything, I tell myself, make this drive everything you want it to be.

I focus on the moonlight and the wild dog that runs across the road. I breathe in the smell of the warm humid air and the warmer fragrant earth. I glance at Michael as he drives, and he catches my gaze and smiles crookedly back at me. And just like that, my heart hurts and my stomach does a somersault.

I've fallen for him so hard. I've fallen for him in a way I never expected to fall for anyone again.

We arrive at the community center sooner than I'd like. He turns off the engine. I smile brightly, inject a cheerful note into my voice as I swing open the car door. "Here we are, safe and sound."

He's come around to walk me to the door. "I wouldn't use

safe and sound to describe you," he answers, taking my hand and assisting me out. "Ever."

I take a step around a puddle, and then I'm not sure how it happens or who makes the first move, but suddenly there's no distance between us, and his hands are in my hair, and I'm lifting my face to his, desperate to be kissed.

I have wanted him to kiss me since I arrived in Katete, and now I can think of nothing else. As his head dips, his gaze meets mine, and in the yellow light of the center, his blue eyes look stormy like the sea. I lean all the way in, press my lips to his, and feel his warm breath, and his firm skin, and nothing has felt this right in so long.

We kissed at the lodge in Big Bear, but that was different from this. That was liquor and adrenaline and nerves. This is need and emotion, and as his body presses against mine, his arm around my back holding me to him, I think, This is where I belong. This is where I should always be.

With his hand tangled in my hair, and I can't seem to get enough of him or his mouth or tongue. I can't remember when a man felt like this, can't remember when a kiss and touch and taste made me want to curl up, hang on, and just give in.

Home. Kissing him is home.

I need you.

He deepens the kiss and the heat flares and I feel so much everywhere. My lips, my body, my heart. *I want you.*

No one since Keith has made me feel this way. I don't even know if Keith made me feel this way. All I know is that I want to wrap my arms around him and hold tight, hold hard, hold forever, if only forever were true. If only forever could be.

The kiss ends eventually, and Michael lifts his head and

looks down at me. He strokes my cheek with his thumb, and I can see the dark splinters against the blue of his eyes. The creases in his skin. The exhausted shadows beneath his eyes. The grooves at his mouth. The texture of his lips.

"Come inside," I whisper. "Come to my room with me."

Our eyes lock, and there is a universe there, an entire universe of communication. He cares for me, he wants me, but he's not where I am. He doesn't feel what I feel. The warmth in me goes.

"I can't," he says. "Not that I don't want to—"

"Understood. You don't have to say more."

He stands there, watching me run away. "I have feelings for you, very real, very strong feelings—"

"No. Don't." I shake my head, unwilling to let him continue. He told me twice in two days that the women in his life say he's not there, not present, not communicative. The women in his life leave because he can't make them a priority. He works too much. He's too self-absorbed, too busy with his work and patients and career. "Let's not go there. I don't want to go there. I didn't mean to start this in the first place."

He just looks at me, and I close my eyes at the hot, livid stab of pain. The hurt is so sharp and deep, I think he's cut me. I was so close to falling in love again. So close to feeling safe again.

I take another step back, careful to avoid the next puddle. "Good-bye, Michael. Have a safe trip."

His jaw shifts ever so slightly, and then his dark head inclines and he's walking back to his car.

I go inside the guesthouse to my room and shut the door. I lean against the door for what seems like forever. But I don't cry.

Chapter Seventeen

——— ✦✦✦ ———

I've been home a week now and I'm still insanely jet-lagged, eating and sleeping at hours not at all conducive to good work habits.

In the past I've always dealt with jet lag the way I've always dealt with everything, by plunging into work. Unfortunately, my work is full of footage of Michael, and it's excruciating going through hours and hours of Michael working, talking, healing. All I can think of is how hard I fell for him, how much I wanted to be with him. I even invited him back to my room.

Oh God.

I spend the rest of the week working with Howard. During the day we're side by side in the production control room, and then at night I write my introductions and voice-overs and return to the studio in the morning to have one of the show editors help me piece together the final story.

Glenn, Harper, Libby, and Mark have all stuck their heads into the editing room during the past week to see what we have so far, and they've all been impressed.

Libby, someone I think of as very nonemotional, is teary when the Lusaka hospital piece with Jean is done. "They're dying from dirty water?" she asks.

Harper sees footage of Michael, and her eyebrows arch. "He's hot. Who is he?"

"Some doctor," I respond, turning my attention to the chimp story.

"He looks familiar," Harper adds, leaning low to get closer to the screen. "Why do I know him?"

"I don't know." I shrug, and Howard darts me a glance.

"I think he's familiar because he's an L.A. plastic surgeon," he says, shifting in his chair. "He had a show a couple years ago called—"

"*Dr. Hollywood!*" Harper exclaims triumphantly. "My God, he's hot. Look at that body! He's a total fox. He should be in *People* magazine's hot bachelor issue—"

"Harper." I give her a look. "If you want his number, I can ask Madison to track it down for you, but otherwise, can we get back to the story?"

Harper gives me a funny look in return. "You're crabby."

"I'm jet-lagged. I'm fighting a bug. And we've got just a few more days to get these stories together before I head to Tucson. Once I'm back from Tucson I have the big meeting with Glenn and the studio heads. Glenn says they're going to make me a proposal, but I don't think it's going to be one I like."

Near the middle of the week, Glenn appears in the production room and stands behind us, watching the video monitor wall where we've been integrating the videotape, graphics, still frames, and sound. We're just putting the final touches on Jean's segment, and Glenn's been observing for seven minutes without saying anything. The nearly finished story includes pieces of the interview I did with Jean at the PSI office and then touring the hospital in Lusaka with Dr. Paul, Michael's friend.

Jean's story is really about how one person doing just one

thing can make a difference. She's talking about a treated net, and the segment ends with the shot of a child in a Lusaka teaching hospital bed, sitting up and looking at the camera with huge shy eyes and a shyer smile. It was Howard's idea to use U2's song "One" in the background as we fade out. *"One love, One blood, One life, You've got to do what you should...."*

The studio goes quiet when the music ends. Howard and I just sit and wait for Glenn to speak. But Glenn isn't in a hurry to say anything, and his silence makes me nervous. "Hate it?" I ask.

"No." Glenn shakes his head. "It's heartbreaking and beautiful and hopeful." He pats each of us once on the shoulder and walks out.

Howard and I look at each other and smile. The boss approves.

We're down to just three days now before my trip to Tucson for the career lifetime award. Howard and I have finished the shows on Darlene and Jean at PSI, which just leaves the Rx Smile footage. And there is so much of it. Seven days, to be precise.

Seven days of Michael talking, working, comforting. Seven days of Michael and his doctor friends. Seven days of memories.

Africa changed me.

I learned so much about myself during my time in Zambia. I learned that I'm still a good writer and reporter. I learned that I still care passionately about people. I learned that I'm strong and yet hopeful. I learned that I have deep convictions.

I believe we each must try to make a difference, and there's not just one way to make a difference. Everything counts.

Everything adds up, big and small, because our efforts aren't isolated and we aren't alone, not ever, not even if we want to be. For better or worse, we're part of this community called life.

And in that vein, I concentrate on putting together the Rx Smile segments. I've mapped out three different shows, including two episodes that focus on the children before and after their surgery. The final episode of the three looks at the volunteer medical stuff. I'd interviewed the Irish nurses, the Canadian speech therapists, the international doctors and dentists. I have footage of them all working, too, and I weave their stories together, talking to me about why they're there, sharing their personal history, touching on how they came to be involved. What's interesting when you add up all the interviews is the one common element—the volunteers are there because it makes them feel good to do good.

"I'm here for purely selfish reasons. When I contribute, I feel good about me."

"Whenever I do something like this, I'm happier for months."

"Being on a mission changes you forever."

"I like me better when I'm reaching out to others."

"Helping these children makes you realize it truly is better to give than to receive."

Michael had so many pithy quotes that I struggle with which of his to use, but when I do select one it becomes the quote for the closing shot's final voice-over. The shot is of a mother leaning over her toddler as he wakes from surgery, and the baby boy is smiling and the mother is smiling, eyes bright with tears of happiness.

Michael's words are perfect for this clip: "I do what I do in my private practice so I can come here. I like being a surgeon, I'm proud of my practice, but this, this that we do here, it isn't work. It's joy."

I have tears in my own eyes as the story ends with Michael's voice and the mother's and baby's smiles.

He's right. What they did, that medical team, was joy. And being there, part of it, witnessing it, was my joy.

Friday morning, I'm sitting with my coffee and my stack of papers at the long counter that runs along the window of the Coffee Bean & Tea Leaf.

This is a rare treat for me—out early in the morning with nothing to do but sip my coffee and read the paper. Usually mornings are working mornings, hectic and shadowed with too much to do in too little time; but all our stories are in and done. I leave for Tucson later this afternoon, a day early so I can indulge in some much needed spa treatments at the Ventana Canyon Resort before tomorrow night's dinner fund-raiser.

And just look at this beautiful morning. The sky is a pale lucid blue thanks to the Santa Ana winds. Light gold sunshine reflects off the cars passing outside. And here inside the coffee shop I can smell the rich, dark aroma of ground coffee.

As I look back down at my paper, something in orange catches my attention. I glance to my left and see a little boy in an orange polo shirt with his nanny at a table just to my left behind me. The little boy has spilled his Mango Tango smoothie, and he's now drinking it off the table with a straw. The nanny is leaning forward whispering something even as she tries to scrape some of the smoothie back into the plastic bottle, but the boy pushes her off. He wants it all. He's not going to let it go to waste, and he drags his straw across the wood table, slurping it up.

It's both funny and awful. It's something only a kid would do, and I shudder to think of the germs on the table. I'm sure the boy's mom wouldn't approve of her son drinking his smoothie off the table, but mom isn't here and the nanny has given up and is calmly sipping her coffee and looking the other direction.

I laugh to myself and return to my paper. I'm still smiling when I hear a shout. I look up. A blue car flies at me through the window. There's no time to run or scream. Instinctively, I throw up an arm to shield my face.

I hurt. Everything hurts. I open my eyes. A woman in blue is leaning over me. She's holding my head and telling me it's okay, it's going to be okay, even as another woman stands above me, crying.

I don't know why she's crying. I can't see. Something dark blurs my right eye and slides down my face. I try to wipe it, but moving my arm sends such hot, sharp pain through me that I gasp at the shock of it.

"Don't move," begs the woman in blue.

"I can't see," I say, looking up at the woman holding my head. "Can you wipe my eye for me?"

She shakes her head, says something about an ambulance, and then I hear the siren. It's coming closer, and for some reason the sound comforts me.

Moments later the paramedics and police are swarming inside, and that's when it all gets blurry. There are men in black and men in blue and a blond woman in a navy jumpsuit with her hair in a ponytail who's taking my vitals while others talk to people standing around.

The woman in the blue shirt moves away, and as she steps back I see a huge stain all over her chest, the blue covered in dark red.

I stare at the stain, not understanding, and then as people talk, I realize it's blood. My blood. I close my eyes, and the voices rush around me. Someone's asking my name. Someone's giving my name. Someone's handing over my purse.

People talk to me, and I think I answer, am not sure I've answered, and then they're sliding a board beneath me, securing me before transferring me onto the gurney. As I'm wheeled toward the ambulance, I remember the little boy in the orange shirt. I hope he's okay.

The ambulance doors are closing. I need to tell them something. I try to tell them something. I don't know if anyone is listening. "Call Michael O'Sullivan." And then, afraid that no one has heard me, I move my right hand and pain shoots through me, stunning me all over again.

I nearly cry then.

The paramedic puts her hand on my shoulder. "You're going to be fine," she says, patting me again.

I know I'm going to be, but still, I want them to call Michael. Michael will know what to do. "Call Dr. O'Sullivan," I repeat. "He's my doctor."

And then I let go, sliding into sleep.

Her beautiful face . . .

Never the same . . . Tragic . . .

The voices whisper, yet I hear bits of the conversation,

the odd words reaching me and then floating away just as quickly.

All that glass . . . just cut too deep . . .

People move around me, and there's clinking noises and footsteps and lights, very bright lights, but I feel nothing. I'm numb. Foggy. I try to concentrate to understand what they're doing and saying, but I can't and I finally let go, sliding back into the dark.

But then later, I hear voices again. Older, quieter, male. They're calling him "Doctor," but it's not Michael.

I cry then. I cry because he didn't come. I cry because I have no one and someone is shushing me, comforting me, but I'm not calm. I can't be calmed. I need my family. I need my people. I need someone who belongs to me.

A hand touches my shoulder and stays there. "Tiana."

It's him. He's here. He came. "Michael."

"I just heard. I'm getting ready to scrub in. I won't let anyone touch your face."

"How bad is it?"

"I don't know. It's hard to say until I can get in there and take the glass out and examine the wound properly. But there's no rush. I'm going to take my time."

"Will there be a scar?"

"They'll be taking you into the operating room now, honey. The orthopedic surgeon will fix your arm and I'll take care of your face. I'll be with you the whole time. I won't leave you. I promise."

Something settles over my mouth and nose. The air smells different as it rushes at me. Panic floods me. "Michael!"

"Breathe through your nose, Tiana."

"Stay with me!"

"Honey, I am. Now just relax and breathe."

The mask feels weird on my face. I want to adjust it, but I can't. There's so much turbulence. The jet keeps lifting and falling. People are screaming. I want to scream, but I can't. Instead I close my eyes and pray. *Don't let me die, don't let me die, don't let me die.*

And then as the plane bumps and drops and shakes, the woman next to me turns to look at me. She looks like me but younger, prettier. Dark hair, blue eyes, heart-shaped face.

"Don't be afraid, honey."

I look at the woman again. "Mom?"

"Yes, darling?"

My chest squeezes so tight, I can't breathe. "Mom, is that really you?"

She reaches out and covers my hand with hers. "Of course it is."

I can feel her fingers and her hand and her skin, and she's warm. She feels so warm. "What are you doing here, Mom?"

"I came to be with you. You need me."

The tears are falling. They're falling so hard and fast that I can't see. "I do, Mom. I do."

Her fingers curl around mine, and she gives me the most wonderful smile. "It's okay, honey. Everything's fine."

The plane is still shaking, and it's making horrible shuddering noises as though it'll explode any minute. "Are we going to die?"

"No."

"But I'm scared."

"This is just turbulence. It's part of life."

"I don't want to die." I'm squeezing her hand so hard, partly because I'm scared and partly because I've missed her so much and I don't want her to go. "Please take me with you."

"But you want to live. You want to fly."

"But I am flying."

"Yes, you are. And isn't it amazing? Enjoy it, Tiana. Enjoy every second of it, every bump and every bounce. You fly. You soar. You're free."

Mom is still smiling at me, and she looks exactly as I remembered except she glows. She looks so happy and healthy and rested. "You look so beautiful, Mom."

"And you're beautiful, sweet pea. Not your face, but your heart. Never forget that. Never forget—"

"You're not going, are you?"

"I have to. And you have to fly."

I cry harder. "I've missed you."

Her smile is radiant and warm and everything I remembered. She looks at me with so much love. She looks at me the way she did when I was just a baby and she'd rock me in her arms, rock me to sleep. "You don't know how proud I am of you, Tiana. Your father and I couldn't be prouder."

"I miss him."

"Dad loves you. The girls love you. We all love you."

"I need to see you."

"You will, one day, and we'll be waiting for you. We'll be there when the time comes—"

"Don't leave! Mom!"

"I have to go. Just remember, enjoy this, enjoy every moment of it."

And then she's gone and I'm still in the jet and it's still shuddering and shaking and the woman next to me isn't my mom. I have been crying, though, and I reach up to wipe my eyes and then tighten my seat belt. As the jet drops again, I close my eyes and do what my mother said.

I feel.

I breathe.

I focus on the miracle of being.

Later, I open my eyes and it's dark; the room is dimly lit and quiet. There are no bright lights or metallic clinks or whispered voices.

My throat hurts when I swallow, and my face feels numb and thick. I try to reach up to my face, but my right arm is strapped down and I have tubes taped to my left. Everything aches.

I try to remember what happened, but nothing's clear. I was flying. There was an accident. Michael came.

No. I was flying, leaving Michael, and then my mom came.

No. There was an accident, and my mom and Michael both came, but I don't know what happened then. It's too confusing. I hurt too much.

I give up and close my eyes and let go of everything to sleep.

Something's poking me, touching me, and I open my eyes. I'm still in the same room. It's dim, not dark, and quiet. But this time I'm not alone. Michael's here, next to my bed, leaning over me and examining what lies beneath the gauze on my face.

He sees that I'm awake, and his expression is strange. It's all closed up, like a doctor's face, but not my Michael's face. I want my Michael's face. "Don't look at me like that," I croak. "Smile."

He tries to smile, but it doesn't reach his eyes. "Hello."

"Thank you for coming." The words scratch my throat. I'm so thirsty. I look around for water but see vases of flowers instead. A massive marble vase of dark pink roses dwarfs the table at my elbow. I look past the roses, looking for something to drink.

"There's nowhere else I'd rather be."

"Then don't look so miserable," I say.

He reaches for a water bottle sandwiched between tulips and lilies. The plastic bottle has a long straw in it, and he holds the straw to my lips. I drink, but swallowing still hurts.

"I feel like a truck ran over me," I rasp.

"It was a Pontiac, but those are just details."

I try to smile, and it feels weird. Lopsided. My face is numb near the edge of my lips. "What time is it?"

"Around one. One-thirty."

"What's wrong with my mouth?"

"You'll be numb on that side for a while."

"How big is the scar?"

"Not bad, and it'll lighten over time. Later we can always talk about laser resurfacing if need be."

I reach up blindly, grab his hand, and hold it. Hold it so damn tight. Tight like the pain in my heart. Tight like the fear in my gut. He's telling me I've changed. He's telling me it's going to be different, but I don't know what that means. I don't know anything other than I need someone right now to do what Michael's doing. I need to be touched. I need to know I'm not alone.

"I'm scared," I whisper.

"I'm here."

"You left."

"But when you needed me, I came."

Chapter Eighteen

⋆⋆⋆

The flowers keep arriving. They fill my room. Dozens of vases and arrangements, baskets and balloons. The scent is almost overpowering, and the profusion of colors and blooms reminds me of the arrangements that arrived after Keith died.

I tell my day nurse Saturday afternoon to give most of the flowers to patients on the floor who don't have any flowers in their room. The nurse goes through the cards and tells me again which arrangement is from whom. Most are from industry professionals, and after plucking the cards from the bouquets, she sees that the flowers are dispersed to those who could use some cheer.

I wake up and discover Shey sitting in a chair next to my bed, leafing through a magazine.

"Hey," I say, blinking and trying to clear the cobwebs from my head.

Shey stands, leans over me, worry etched all over her face. "How are you?"

"Good."

"Yeah?"

"Yeah." I try to sit up but can't get leverage with my right arm in the cast and sling. I fumble around looking for bed controls, without much success. "What are you doing here, Shey?"

"What do you think I'm doing here, goofball?" She sits on

the side of the bed next to me. "You were nearly turned into roadkill, and it's big news. All over the country, every channel, every news program."

I giggle at the roadkill part, and Shey takes offense. "Honey, this is serious. I've seen the footage on TV. It's a miracle you weren't killed."

I reach for her hand and give it a squeeze. "That's twice now," I say. "God must have some big plans for me."

She squeezes my hand back. "Or maybe He's scared to let you into heaven. Afraid of all the trouble you'll bring."

"There is that," I agree, muffling a laugh because it still hurts to smile too big. My face still doesn't feel like mine.

Shey's eyes search my face, and her expression is so full of love and worry. She's worried about my face.

"So how bad is it?" I ask, my fingers linked with hers. "On a scale of one to ten, how upset am I going to be?"

"You haven't seen it yet?"

I shake my head.

She swallows hard, wipes her hands on the thighs of her snug faded Levi's. "You want to see?"

I nod.

"I'll get you a mirror. I've got one in my makeup bag."

It feels like forever while she crouches next to her suitcase, rummaging around. As Shey looks for her makeup bag, she tells me that Russian John picked her up from the airport and drove her straight to the hospital a few hours ago. "He wouldn't let me pay," she says, looking at me over her shoulder. "He was all choked up. Told me to tell you to get better soon."

"That's nice of him."

"Marta's sick that she can't be here," she adds, straightening, compact in her hand. "But the doctors won't let her fly right now, so I promised her I'd have you call. We're going to do that soon, okay?"

"Okay," I agree, suddenly nervous as she carries the mirror to the bed. I want to see. I don't want to see. I want to see. I'm terrified to see.

Oh God, just let me see.

Shey opens the compact and holds it out to me. I take it, lift it, try to see my face, and just get my cheek with the line of bruising and dark threads. The cut is longer than I expected. It goes from the edge of my right eye down over my cheekbone, stopping short just shy of my mouth.

I tilt the mirror this way and that, trying to get perspective, trying to see my entire face. "That's some scar."

"What has the doctor said?"

"That it'll fade with time. And later we can discuss other things like another surgery or resurfacing." I hesitate, nose wrinkling. "It's worse than I expected."

"I'm sorry."

"No. Don't be sorry." I look again, studying the scar and my face, and it's shocking. Strange. But I'm also glad I've seen it. I know the worst now. It's only going to get better. It'll heal, shrink, fade. "Thank you." I give back the mirror.

"What are you thinking?" Shey asks.

What am I thinking?

I'm thinking it's a pretty big scar for television. I'm thinking it's a bad time to get hurt, particularly when I'm without an agent and without a contract in just a few weeks.

I look at Shey. Her blue eyes are so sad.

I'm thinking that I'm lucky I'm facing this with Shey here.

"I'm glad you're here." I smile up at her. "And I'm glad you know I've been through so much worse. I've got a broken arm and some cracked ribs and a cut on my face. But I'm not paralyzed, not ill, not dead. You know?"

She bends over, wraps her arms carefully around my shoulders. "I love you."

Her warmth surrounds me, and I inhale, breathing in her familiar fragrance. She's worn Calvin Klein for years, and I can't smell it without thinking of her and sunshine. "I love you, too."

Shey's arms are still around me when a knock sounds on the door. The door opens and Max steps into the room. He's carrying an enormous vase of red roses. "How are you doing, doll?" he asks, closing the door behind him.

"How did he get in?" Shey mutters. "You have a no visitors policy."

"I don't know," I answer back, not at all happy to see him.

"I thought you fired him."

"I *did*."

Max introduces himself to Shey. "Max Orth, vice president, Allied Talent Management."

"Shey Darcy." She shakes his hand. "We've met before. But it's been a while."

I can tell Shey's not happy to see Max here. I'm curious as to why he's here. Shey excuses herself so we can talk. "I'm going to grab a cold drink and make some calls. I'll be back in a half hour."

Max takes the chair next to my bed. "You gonna be okay, kid?"

I smile crookedly. "Of course."

He doesn't say anything for a while. Seconds pass, and then more. Finally he takes a deep breath. "You're going to discover things are different for you now."

"The scar will fade and with makeup it'll be barely noticeable."

He shakes his head. "Doll, I'm worried about you and I have to be honest. This is going to be difficult for viewers to get around."

"Is that what you think, or is that what the heads at HBC have said?" I ask.

He doesn't answer directly. "Every time folks turn on the TV they'll see you're hurt, and it'll remind them that bad things can happen. And bad things will happen, and I can pretty much guarantee the studio doesn't want that. Folks tune in to *America Tonight* to escape real-life problems."

Wincing, I drag myself higher in bed with my left arm. God-damn, but I feel as if I've been run over by a garbage truck. "You haven't talked to Glenn. Glenn wouldn't say that, not about me, not right now."

"No, he might not say it, but the studio execs, the mon-eymen, they're not going to renew your contract. You're an expensive talent. Your image is your talent—"

"Correction, Max. My image supports my talent, but my talent has nothing to do with the outside packaging."

"I know that, doll. You don't have to sell me. I've been your fan from the beginning. I believed in you then, and I believe in you now, and that's why I want to help you."

I'm dumbfounded. Can't think of a single thing to say.

"We're going to get through this, and we're going to make it work to your advantage. There are lots of opportunities out there. It's just a matter of finding the right one."

He sounds so warm and enthusiastic that I'm wondering if maybe I've misjudged him, if maybe I do want him on my team again, representing me.

Max reads my silence as permission to continue, and does so. "I will get you work. Maybe not on one of the major networks, but there might be some opportunities on cable, especially in production. It'll be a move behind the cameras instead of in front, but it'll be work. Work you're lucky to get."

"Lucky?" I choke, pouncing on the last word to try to drown out the panic flooding me. Did he really just say I'd be *lucky* to get work?

"You were already at a crossroads, doll. The studios were nervous about your age. Now this"—he breaks off to point at my face, finger gesturing—"this just compounds the problem."

I've had issues with Max for a while now, and I fired him for a reason, but he's just done something marvelous for me. He's thrown down the gauntlet. He's given me the ultimate challenge, and I vow then and there to prove him wrong.

I am not going away. I will not disappear. And I will not be made invisible just because I'm not perfect.

Gripping the bedrail, I lean forward. "My face might be cut, Max, but my mind's the same. My personality's the same. And it's my mind, my personality—my grit—that makes me Tiana Tomlinson, *not* my face." I point to the door. "Thanks for the flowers. Good-bye."

"This isn't the time to let pride cloud your judgment," he says, rising to his feet.

I'm practically trembling with rage. "That's where you're wrong, Max. I'm keeping my pride, and my self-respect."

"I think that car broke something inside your head—"

"Better than my heart," I interrupt fiercely.

"Then protect your heart, doll, because you're going to discover that without me, your ass is grass."

*   *   *

When Shey returns ten minutes after Max's departure she finds me sliding out of bed, but it's difficult to get to my feet and find my balance with an IV tangled on the sides of the bed.

"What are you doing?" she demands, dropping her purse on the chair and charging toward me.

"I need to get up. I have to get up." I tug on the IV cord. "I want to go to the bathroom and then get out of here—"

"I'll help you to the bathroom, but you're not going home until tomorrow or the next day."

"No, it's tomorrow. I'm not going to stay here anymore. I'm not sick. I'm fine. I'm fine."

"Things go badly with Max?"

"He's an asshole and a prick." My voice shakes. "A first-class prick."

"Hope you're not talking about me," Michael's voice comes from the doorway.

"Hey. Hi." I flush and, still gripping my IV pole, sit down heavily on the edge of my bed, my pulse beating like mad. "I was talking about Max. He just left."

"That's a relief." He enters the room and he's wearing one of his expensive dark suits and I drink him in.

Shey's watching Michael with considerable interest, and I nervously make the introductions. "Shey, this is Dr. Michael O'Sullivan. And Michael, this is Shey Darcy, one of my best friends."

Michael extends a hand to Shey. "You're one of the boarding school friends."

"Yes." Her smile is warm and curious as she shakes his hand. "You're Tiana's doctor?"

Michael shoots me a glance, eyebrows lifting ever so slightly as if to say, *Is that what I am?*

I redden and my pulse races faster. "Michael's a plastic surgeon here in Los Angeles. And he was also in Zambia with Rx Smile while I was there."

She frowns, confused. "So he didn't do your surgery, then?"

"No, he did. But he's—" I break off, look at Michael, and my heart squeezes. "He's..."

What is he?

My heart.

He's my heart.

"A friend," I say out of desperation. It's been so long since I felt anything this strong. It's such a powerful emotion. Love. I do love him. If only he felt the same. In Katete I'd thought he felt the same.

I look at him now, and I feel positively naked, all my emotions right there on the surface. "I want to go home, Michael. When can I?"

"It's your arm keeping you here. But I can check with Dr. McBain, see if he'd be willing to discharge you early."

"Please."

Michael's beeper goes off. He glances down, checks the number. "I have to take this call. I'll step back in to say goodbye before I leave."

He exits through the door, and Shey's eyes dance as she approaches me. "Dr. McDreamy!"

I roll my eyes. "He's a good doctor."

"You lit up like a Christmas tree when he walked in. Haven't seen you look like that in years."

"I like him," I whisper. "Bad."

"That's good." She sits in the chair next to her purse. "How does he feel about you?"

I think about Michael during the Rx Smile mission. I can see him comforting parents, holding babies postsurgery. I see him stretched out beneath the lone tree, trying to get some rest. And then I see him on our last night. "I think he's attracted to me, but I don't think he wants anything serious."

Shey's expression gentles. "You're ready for serious."

"If it were with him. He just feels right to me...." My eyes burn and my heart aches. He feels too right. I can't imagine anyone else being so right for me. "I think I've fallen really hard. It scares me. I can't be hurt again. Can't."

"Maybe you won't have to be."

"You weren't there. You didn't see his face—" I break off as the door opens and Michael returns.

"Tomorrow," Michael says. "Dr. McBain said he'll get you discharged in the morning if you've got help at home."

"She has me. I'm staying for a few days," Shey volunteers.

"Good. You'll be on your way home, then." He smiles at me.

I smile back, yet this feels wrong.

It's empty. Strained. As though we're strangers.

And just when I think he's about to turn around and walk out, he asks about Max. "What did he want?"

"He was willing to take me back." My temper stirs just remembering. "He said without him my career's over. That with my face the way it is, no network will put me on TV."

"He is a prick," Michael agrees. "Wish I'd been here. Would have loved to put my fist down his throat."

I crack a smile. "Are you any good with those fists?"

"I'm Irish. We're street fighters."

"In that case, go. Tear him apart, Doctor."

Michael grins, and for a moment he looks so boyish, so free, and my heart's like butter. It melts.

Michael leaves moments later, and I look at the door, wanting it to open again, wanting Michael to return. If only.

Shey just watches me, and when I turn to meet her gaze there's a sheen in her blue eyes. "You're head over heels, Tits."

Tears suddenly fill my eyes. I put a hand to my mouth, covering my lips as if afraid of what they might say. Love, love, love. Love him. Want him. Need him. It's crazy how intense it is, crazy that I could feel this way again. Finally.

"I don't think he's oblivious to you," she says now. "Not at all."

"But there's a big difference between animal attraction and love and marriage and babies. And God help me, Shey, that's what I want. I want all the things I stopped believing in. I want the happy ending I gave up on."

"Who's to say it can't happen?" she answers briskly. "Now do you need to go to the restroom or was that just an excuse to get on your feet?"

Later that afternoon, Shey heads to my house to get things ready for me to come home. While she's gone I nap, and when I wake, I struggle to get up again, determined to make it on my own to the restroom.

I do, dragging my IV with one hand while trying to manage the door with the same hand. And in that hazy yellow light of the narrow hospital bathroom, I get a good look at me. My hair's dirty and lank. My face is swollen, stitched, and bruised.

I reach up and touch the right side of my face, buried

beneath stitches and thick gauze. My face will never be the same. Will that be okay?

Will I let this accident keep me from what I want and who I am?

No.

I refuse to let this accident change me. I refuse to let it change a thing.

Leaving the bathroom, I scoot my IV back toward my bed. The nurse sticks her head around the door to check on me. "You should be asking for help," she admonishes me.

"I'm fine," I answer crossly, and then I smile because I realize I mean it. I am fine. I'm going to get better. I'm going to be great.

I'm dreaming, replaying the accident over and over in my head. If only I hadn't been watching that little boy drink his smoothie off the table. If only I'd been looking out the window and seen the old woman behind the wheel of her old Pontiac.

If only…

I wake. It's dark and my eyes feel heavy. Why am I waking? What time is it?

And then I realize why I'm awake. I hurt. The pain's penetrated my sleep. I didn't take any pain meds earlier and now I'm suffering for it.

I shift carefully, trying not to put pressure on the ribs or arm as I reach for the call button to summon the night nurse, but I jar myself anyway and cringe with pain.

"Need something?"

The voice comes from the dark, close to my bed, and I startle. It's Michael.

"How long have you been here?" I ask hoarsely.

"Not long. Just arrived. I'm sorry I woke you."

I can't see him, but I can feel him, large and silent and very strong. "You didn't. The pain woke me. I hurt."

"Where?"

"My arm. My ribs. But mostly my arm."

He steps outside the door, retrieves my chart, and after turning on the light by my bed, he flips through it, reading all the notations. "You didn't take any pain medicine before bed."

"I'm trying to cut back."

"You're not taking much, and pain management is an important part of recovery." He leans over my bed to examine my face, his hands gentle as he tilts my jaw higher to see the wound from different angles. "This looks good."

His touch is firm. His skin is warm. "Yeah?"

"I'm very pleased."

"And I'm very grateful. Thank you."

"You don't have to thank me."

"Yes, I do. You said you'd never touch my face—"

He laughs softly. "I wondered if you'd remember that."

"I remember everything you've ever said to me."

He smiles, yet the smile doesn't reach his eyes. "In your discharge packet you'll find instructions on how to take care of the wound. If you see anything that doesn't look right, call me right away."

I won't see him again, then, for days. Maybe a week or more. My heart falls, hard, so hard. My arm throbs. My eyes burn.

Michael rings for the night nurse, tells her I need Vicodin. I don't protest. Right now I'd take anything to make the pain go away. And I'm not talking about my arm.

As we wait for the nurse, I study Michael's face. He looks tired. It must have been a long day. "You're not sleeping, are you."

He smiles crookedly, his skin still tanned from the trip to Zambia. "Not a lot, no."

"Why not?"

His shoulders shift. "I always seem to have too much on my mind."

Now is the time to tell him that he and I need to talk. Now is the time to ask about Katete and our dinner and our kiss. Now is the time to find out just what happened between us. But I can't ask any of the questions I'm dying to know. He's tired. And I'm scared.

I'm scared to find out that I was just a dalliance, an escape, a game.

I'm scared to learn that he's already seeing someone else, someone new.

I'm scared to compare myself with the flawless women he creates, those women of perfect body and face.

Thankfully, the nurse arrives with two pills in a little white paper cup. She hands the cup to me, and I knock back the pills and chase them with water. "Is there anything else you need?" she asks me.

"No, thank you. I'll sleep better now."

"Well, just ring if you can't." She nods at me and smiles prettily at Michael before leaving.

Of course she'd smile prettily at him. Michael is ruggedly handsome, a brilliant surgeon, and successful beyond belief. He's the ultimate package. He could have any woman at any time.

My eyes sting, but I won't cry.

Michael gazes down at me for an endless moment, his dark blue gaze shuttered, his jaw hard, and then the edge of his mouth lifts. "You call if you need anything."

I nod.

"I'll see you on the thirteenth—"

"Are you serious?"

His eyes crinkle. "I'll check the wound, and depending on how it looks, I'll either remove the stitches or we'll go another couple days."

"Okay."

"Any questions? Concerns?"

Are we ever going to figure this thing out, whatever this is between us?

I shake my head.

For a split second, I think he's going to lean over and kiss me good-bye. I hold my breath, hoping. But then he steps away. "Good night, Tiana," he says, his voice deep, husky. "Sweet dreams."

It's the good night he'd say to me in Katete. Sweet dreams. My throat's raw. My heart aches. I smile to hold back the tears. "Good night, Michael."

Chapter Nineteen

The nurse steps into my hospital room. "I know you're getting ready to be discharged, Miss Tomlinson," she says briskly, "but you have a visitor."

I've been sitting in the wheelchair by the window, savoring the Los Angeles sunshine as I wait to be wheeled down to the elevator where Russian John is waiting. Shey's taking care of my discharge papers and insurance forms so that I can go.

"Do you know who?" I ask the nurse, smoothing the hem of my chocolate velour sweat jacket over the waistband of the matching sweatpants, an outfit Shey brought from the house for me to wear home. I have one arm in the jacket and the other arm in a sling outside. It's not the most stylish look, but it works.

"She says she's your friend. She has her child with her."

It can't be Marta, I think, and Christie's already been here, but I nod agreement.

It's Shelby who walks in, and she's holding a little boy.

"Are we interrupting?" she asks uncertainly. "They told me you're just about to go home."

"It could be a long wait, so come in."

Shelby steps closer to the wheelchair. She's still tawny

blonde and tan, but in person she's small and very thin. TV always makes us look so much bigger and more impressive than we really are.

"I don't think you've ever met my son," she says carefully, even as she gives me her wide TV smile. "His name is Jason, but we call him Jay-Jay."

I look at the child in her arms. He's slim and dark blond and has her olive skin. He's a beautiful boy. "I didn't know you were a mom."

She flushes. "I thought it best for the career to keep it quiet. Working mothers don't get promoted as much. But I wanted to come see you, and I usually drop him at day care on the way to work. Hope it's okay."

"It's fine. And it's good of you to come. Thank you for the flowers you sent a few days ago. They were beautiful."

Jay-Jay stares at my face with its freshly applied gauze and tape bandage. "What happened to you?" he asks bluntly.

I suddenly think of the little boy drinking his juice off the table the day of the accident and I hope against hope he's okay. "A car hit me."

"Were you playing in the street?"

I'd laugh if it wouldn't hurt. "No. I was sitting inside a restaurant."

"How did the car get inside?" he persists, and Shelby tries to shush him.

I don't mind the questions, though. It's almost a relief to talk. "Went through the window."

"Why?"

"Because the door was too small," I say, trying to smile, but it's next to impossible. I am somewhere in the middle of heaven and hell, and I guess it's called earth. And it's called life. It's just so intense. So wild and impossible and hurtful and beautiful.

Jay-Jay's narrowed eyes suddenly widen and his brow clears. He snickers into his hand. "The door was too small," he repeats, giggling as only a four-year-old boy could.

My heart is tumbling somewhere inside me, tumbling free, and I don't even know I'm crying until Shelby leans down and puts her arm around my shoulder. "I'm sorry, Tiana," she's saying, "I'm sorry you were hurt. I just wanted you to know how sorry we are—"

"Thank you."

She lifts her head, and the tip of her nose is pink. Her eyes are wet. "We're all so sorry."

"How is everything at the studio?" I ask, trying to regain my composure. "Everyone doing well?"

"Yes. It's hectic. Sweeps month. And tomorrow night we air the first of your Africa stories. We've been running the teases all weekend." She gives me a watery smile. "I've seen them, and they're wonderful. You did a great job."

"Thank you."

"Madison sends her love. Harper, too."

I wonder if Madison works for Shelby now. That causes a stab of pain and I'm tempted to ask if Shelby's taken over my office again, but I know that answer. I've been replaced. But isn't that the way the system works? We're all commodities, eventually replaced by the newest model.

"Thanks for coming to see me," I say as Jay-Jay shifts restlessly on Shelby's hip. "And keep me in the loop. Let me know what happens."

"Don't worry—"

"You don't worry."

"It's okay," we both say at the same time.

She smiles tentatively, nervously, and is gone.

I sit there after she goes, and my head swims. It really is Shelby's show now, isn't it?

The thought hurts. I hurt. I long for the Vicodin I took last night. Long for a painless escape. But such a thing doesn't exist. The only way to get through this is by going through it. Simplistic but true.

And I will get through this, I tell myself, reaching up to touch the gauze bandage on my cheek. I'll prove them wrong. Max, Glenn, Shelby, all of them. I'm not done working. I'm going to have a great career. There are plenty of opportunities in television out there.

And maybe I'll have to start at the bottom. Maybe there won't be a lot of money. Maybe there won't be a lot of prestige.

That's fine.

I don't mind hard work. I'm up for a new challenge. In fact, I live for a challenge.

A member of the nursing staff takes me down in the elevator to the hospital lobby, where Shey waits. As the elevator doors open, Shey moves toward me. "It's a zoo out there," she mutters. "Photographers everywhere." She pulls off her baseball cap and plunks it on my head, pulling the brim down low.

People shout my name as the nurse's aide rolls me toward the car. Russian John is there, acting like a first-class bodyguard, straight-arming overzealous photographers who push too close. The back door is open, and I transfer into the back of the limousine quickly, too quickly, jarring my arm in the process and letting out a yelp of pain.

Shey climbs in next to me. "You okay, sugar?"

I grimace, cradle my cast. "My arm keeps getting in the way."

Christie arrives with bags of groceries to cook me a welcome-home dinner. She plans to roast the chicken at my house, and she and Shey, who've never met before but certainly have heard plenty about each other, peel and quarter and boil the potatoes as they talk and enjoy a glass of wine.

I notice neither offers me a glass of wine. Probably wouldn't mix with the Vicodin in case I need one tonight. I shift on the living room couch, a little bored, a little uncomfortable. As the smell of roasting chicken wafts from the kitchen, I fidget with the remote control, flip through channels, watching nothing but endless commercials.

I'm lucky, I tell myself. I'm fine. What's happened is fine. This is life. This is just how the dice go.

I watch a Neutrogena commercial. Beautiful Jennifer Garner washing her face, lifting it to the camera, smiling, her skin as serene and radiant as her smile.

Heat explodes inside my chest. Little spasms of heartbreak.

What if my face doesn't heal properly?

What if I can't cover the scar with makeup?

What if I'll never be loved now?

And isn't that the real worry: What if I'll never be loved now?

I close my eyes but see Michael. Opening my eyes, I change the channel. Can't think like this. Can't dwell on the negative. Time will tell. Time will reveal all.

*   *   *

We're eating Christie's homemade apple pie, warm and à la mode, when the phone rings. I hope it's Michael. Christie reaches for my cell phone and hands it to me. It's Celia.

Celia wants to do a story on me for *People*. The piece would be a six-page spread at the minimum with photos, possibly even a cover story. They'd do a full photo session here at my house with whatever hair, makeup, and stylists I want.

"Celia," I interrupt, "it's Sunday night. Do we have to do this tonight?"

"Yes. Time is of the essence if we're going to run it in the next issue."

"I don't want to be in the next issue."

"We're talking a big story, Tia, and some big money, too." She goes on to assure me that the photographer will capture my new face in the best possible light, but they need to do the pictures soon, before the stitches come out.

"I'm getting a mixed message here," I tell her. "You say it's a tasteful piece and the photographer will capture my face in the best light, but you also want to do it now while my face looks the worst? No, thank you."

I hang up and look at Shey and Christie, who are concentrating on their pie. "She wants to do a story on the accident for *People*. With my 'new face' front and center."

"Are they going to pay you?" Christie asks calmly, cutting into her flaky crust.

"She mentioned money, but I didn't ask how much." I'm repulsed by the thought of exploiting the accident. It disturbs me that I'd be offered money in exchange for revealing my facial injury. I don't want pity, or sympathy, and I especially don't want money for something like this. "I won't be turned into a freak show."

Tuesday morning Shey has flown back to New York, and Maria, my housekeeper, is working somewhere in the house as I read the newspapers in the living room. I'm reading every free second I can. Don't want time on my hands. Don't want to think. I need to have a game plan for the future, but I'm not quite ready to do that.

The doorbell rings. I wait for Maria to come and answer, but she doesn't. The doorbell rings again.

I drag myself out of the chair and toward the front door. Glancing out the door's peephole, I see Celia standing there. She's immaculate. Her beautiful face is exquisitely made up. My chest tightens.

I open the door a crack, look out with my left eye, hiding my right cheek. "Hi."

"Can I come in?" she asks cheerfully.

"What do you want?" I ask, aware she's never been to my house before.

"Good to see you, too. Or at least what I can see of you."

I don't want to open the door. I don't want to reveal myself. Don't want to be vulnerable. Don't want…

I take a deep breath, stifle the terror at feeling so fragile and mortal, and open the door all the way. "Come in. Please."

She steps into my house, the heels of her boots clicking on the adobe tiles. "Beautiful house," she says, looking up at the dark beams and then into the living room at the tall, narrow French doors.

"Thank you."

"There are the most amazing little houses tucked back in the canyon," she adds, heading into my living room. She sits in the white-slipcovered chair that faces the seat I just vacated. She crosses one long leg over the other, folds her hands in her lap, and looks at me expectantly. "So. How are you?"

Vain. I'm vain. And scared. And sad. But I don't say any of this. I smile a small smile, sit down again, and curl my legs under me. "Good. How's work?"

"Great. Busy."

"As always."

And then the conversation dies there. Celia is studying me hard, her gaze examining my face, inspecting it as closely as one would with a magnifying glass. "There's going to be a scar," she says at length.

I'm so bruised, so terribly bruised, and her words are a blow to that tender place. "Yes."

Celia continues to study me intently. Her dark gaze is emotionless. "I phoned Max to get a quote, but he said he no longer represents you."

"So he didn't give you a quote?"

"Oh, he did. But it was as your former agent."

Silence stretches, and then Celia clears her throat. "What are you going to do, Tia? Your contract's up in days. You have no agent. And that cut is going to take weeks, if not months, to heal."

"I'll find something. Maybe in serious news, broadcast news—"

"There isn't much room at the top, though, is there? Even Katie's finding it rough going."

I shrug, wishing I'd dressed for the day instead of lounging around in my fleecy blue robe. "Why does it have to be at the top? Why can't I start at the bottom and work my way up?"

"There won't be money."

"But there might be opportunity."

She nods faintly, her sleek dark hair spilling over her shoulders. "Max thinks the only place you can go now is behind the camera. Writing, directing, or producing."

"That's Max's opinion."

Her lips curve. "You're still hanging tough."

"I'm a fighter, Celia. You know that. I'm going to be okay. You don't have to worry about me."

"Five hundred thousand dollars to you for an exclusive with a four-page photo spread—" She breaks off, looks me in the eyes. "Or a million to the charity of your choice."

A million to the charity of my choice?

Immediately, PSI and Rx Smile come to mind. Jean. Meg. The children.

"I'd do the interview," Celia continues calmly. "You could approve photos and text."

I want to tell her I'd never sell my story. I want to tell her I'd never let them photograph my face.

But I see the father crying in Katete, telling the doctors that if they didn't help his son, his son would die.

I see the young mother holding her baby postsurgery, astonished at the beauty of her daughter's new face.

I see the hospital where the children were dying because they didn't have clean water.

"Last night *America Tonight* ran your first segment from your Africa trip. The show ran the teaser about 'Tiana's Heart: Inside Zambia with Tiana Tomlinson.' HBC is going to promote the hell out of your two-week series, but you know not everyone watches *America Tonight*. You have fierce competition with *ET* and *The Insider*. Let's drive viewers to your story. Let's get your stories watched."

Celia holds my gaze, steady, unwavering, as if she were a boxer in the featherweight division. "Do the interview with me, and the story is our cover story for next week's issue, coinciding with the final week of your Zambia features. Your story not only gets told your way, but it reaches twice as many people. In the article I'll do a sidebar highlighting the charities you're featuring on your program. We can give contact numbers, Web sites, information. We can also promote the show itself so more viewers tune in."

She leans forward. "A million dollars, Tiana. A million dollars could change a lot of lives."

One million dollars would mean two hundred thousand surgeries. Two hundred thousand lives changed. All because an old lady lost control of her pale blue Pontiac.

Two hundred thousand children desperate to eat, drink, swallow, breathe.

Two hundred thousand mothers and fathers aching to have their child live.

If I suck it up and toughen up and let myself be seen as I am for who I am. Not Tiana the celebrity, but Tiana the real person. "Just for my story and photos?"

"They'd run pictures from the day of the accident, and they'd want one with you without makeup showing the scars"—she sees my expression—"but it'd be tasteful."

It's a lot to think about. There's no way I can make a decision this second. This could be either a great thing or a travesty. "I need some time to think about this. I'd love to be able to do something huge for Rx Smile, but I'm not sure this is it...." My voice drifts off, and I look past Celia, out the door at the hazy Los Angeles afternoon. It's been hot, and the smog hangs low and gray over the city.

"I've been promised full editorial control, Tiana, which means I'd do my damnedest to protect you." She reaches out, touches my arm. "I won't let you down. I promise."

"It can't be a pity party, Celia."

"We won't martyr you, I promise."

"Then why are you about to cry?"

Celia shakes her head. "This is just shitty. The whole thing is shitty. I'm so sorry it's happened—"

"You're martyring me now. Stop it."

"Okay." She smiles a lopsided smile. "Will you think about the offer? I've got to give an answer to the editor in chief tomorrow. I'd love your answer to be yes."

"I'll think about it tonight. Call me in the morning."

After she goes, I curl back up in the chair and mull over her offer. A million dollars to my charity of choice. I just have to sit down and tell the story of the accident and answer whatever questions Celia asks. No biggie.

But it is a biggie. I'm not just proud, I'm private. I don't want everyone knowing my intimate thoughts and emotions. It's scary.

I go to my bedroom, lean across the dresser, and look at my face in the bureau mirror. This morning after washing my face and cleaning the wound, I didn't reapply the gauze bandage, and the livid purple scar with the black bristle threads screams at me.

What scar is this?

Whose face is this?

Gingerly I touch the skin, still raised, still tender. I study my face that isn't my face. I'm still not used to it.

And as I trace the scar, I remember how my mother used to kiss our bumps and bruises, light kisses to help with the pain and healing.

Life happens. Bad things happen. But in life there's always more good than bad. Always.

Chapter Twenty

—— ✦✦✦ ——

I wake up and my first thought is that Celia will be calling soon. My second thought is Michael. I *miss* him. I miss his wit and warmth and humor. I miss his intelligence and that slightly mocking, very sexy smile that makes his eyes glint.

Three days until I see him. Three days until I can maybe get the stitches out. Please God, let my face heal properly.

Please God, let everything work out.

Please God, help me get back on TV.

And then as I'm cradling my morning cup of coffee, I hear a voice inside me say, *Why don't you get yourself back on television?*

I start to drink and then stop.

Well, why don't I? What am I waiting for? An invitation?

I'm Tiana Tomlinson. I don't need an invitation, I just need a story. And I have a story. I'm the story. I've always been the story.

Sunshine pours through the kitchen window, glazing the counters, making me blink.

Getting me back on TV is important, as is picking up the threads of my career. Producers and agents aren't going to decide if I work or where I work; I'm going to decide. I'm in charge. It's my life, my career.

I call Harper and tell her I have an opportunity to be interviewed by *People*, and I propose that we approach *People* magazine and suggest we have *America Tonight* tape the interview. Harper could work with Celia to produce a segment that would run on *America Tonight* in conjunction with the *People* release and the Rx Smile stories.

Harper totally embraces the idea. She promises to get in contact with Celia ASAP to see if they can't work out a deal. "This would be huge," she says to me, "a cover article in *People* with exclusive interview clips on *America Tonight*. I love it. You're brilliant. I'll let you know what happens."

By the end of the day, and with financial details not disclosed to me, *People* and Horizon Broadcasting work out a deal. We're going to do the interview tomorrow in one of the empty soundstages at the HBC tower. Harper will be on set acting as producer with our lighting and sound guys and Howard as the cameraman. I'm glad it'll be Howard, too. We developed a close working relationship in Zambia, and I'll feel comfortable with him zooming in.

Celia is providing wardrobe along with the hairstylist and makeup artist. After the interview, we'll do photos back at my house with the *People* photographer. Howard's going to tag along with his camera there, too.

I'm awake early, and as always it's a struggle to take my bath without getting my cast wet. I wash my face carefully, too, using a wet washcloth to clean what I can. At this point, having use of only one arm, and my left arm at that, is far more problematic than my face.

Russian John picks me up and helps me into the car, treating me with kid gloves.

Since the interview isn't being done on the *America Tonight* studio stages, I step off on a different floor today. Harper is there and waiting, though. So is Madison. "I had to see you," she says, giving me a hug and yet being cautious not to hurt me. "Are you okay?"

"I'm great. How are you?"

"Good. Working with Shelby a lot, but she's okay. Not you, of course."

We chat about work for a minute or so, and then she says she has to go, that everyone thinks she's on a Starbucks run.

I smile. Some things never change.

After Madison goes, Harper and I have a chance to talk while we wait for Celia and her crew to show up. Harper confides that she's interviewing elsewhere, that *America Tonight* just isn't the best fit for her. She prefers a different news format, but she's enjoyed having the opportunity to work on *America Tonight*.

"If you find something else, please be sure to let me know where you go. I'll want to stay in touch with you," I tell her.

"I'm keeping ears and eyes open for both of us. I'm hoping I'll have the chance to work with you again. I know there's a lot of interesting things we could do together."

Celia arrives with her team, and then it's just busy. I'm in the hair and makeup chair and then meeting with their woman handling wardrobe. She's brought an off-white Calvin Klein jacket and skirt, a scoop-neck navy velvet top and oyster silk slacks, and a slim St. John suit in a nubby teal knit. The only problem is that I can't get my cast inside any of the shirts or jackets.

No one thought of that. Harper and Celia confer. Harper promises to go raid *America Tonight*'s wardrobe and see what she can come up with.

She's back in ten minutes, arms full of clothes. A black

beaded halter top, a white sleeveless cotton dress, a red one-sleeve vintage Indian top with silver embroidery, a short strapless pink satin dress. I put my foot down on the pink satin dress. Not going to wear pink. That's Shelby's color. But I like the red Indian top, especially if I can wear it with my slim dark denim jeans. Celia thinks we should go with the white dress, and that's what we go with in the end.

They have a simple gold necklace to wear and diamonds in my ears. With my hair blown out and my eyes made up and the bandage peeled off my cheek, I look like me, only vulnerable. I'm uncomfortable with my vulnerability written all over my face, but this is what I have to overcome. I have to connect with the audience anyway. I have to get them to see past my wound to my lips and eyes and voice.

Harper has provided Celia with some questions of her own, questions designed to tie in to my Africa trip. I thought we'd end with those questions, but Celia decides to start with them.

"Tell me about Zambia," Celia says, beginning the interview.

Just hearing the word *Zambia* does something to me, and my expression relaxes. "Amazing. Incredible. Life-changing. Going to Zambia to film Rx Smile was the best thing I've ever done."

As the interview kicks off, I'm aware of Howard behind the camera and Celia across from me and Harper with her clipboard and the sound and lighting men standing around. But as the questions continue, everything but Zambia fades away, especially when Celia asks me about my heartbreaking hospital tour in Lusaka, where babies were dying from diarrhea and dirty water.

"It blew me away," I answer, my voice dropping. "Wards filled with dying toddlers because children don't have access to clean water. And it's all preventable. That's what hurt so much."

The questions go from personal to professional, then return to very personal with the morning of my accident. "What were you doing the morning you were hurt?"

"Enjoying a rare free morning before catching an afternoon flight to Tucson," I answer.

"You didn't see the car coming through the window?"

"No. I was looking away, watching a little boy and being distracted. I don't think I even knew it was a car coming through the window until later. I just saw this blur of silver and blue and then the sound of breaking glass."

"You're lucky you weren't killed. Witnesses said the impact sent you flying."

"I'm very lucky. God clearly has a plan since He's keeping me around."

"You've been through a tragic accident before, haven't you?"

I blink, caught off guard. I didn't expect my past to be introduced, and I've never publicly discussed the car accident that took my family. I glance at Harper, who is clueless, and then at Howard behind the camera and then back to Celia. "When I was fourteen, yes."

"Four people died in that accident."

I flinch. "My entire family." Celia says nothing, and the silence stretches. Uncomfortable, I add huskily, "Both my parents and sisters died. I was the only one not wearing my seat belt and was somehow thrown free."

"You've been an orphan since you were fourteen."

I look at Celia, my expression pleading. Why is she bringing this up here and now? She'd promised not to martyr me. She'd promised to protect me. "Yes."

"Where did this happen?"

"On the Cape in South Africa. We were coming back from a day at the beach."

"Your mother was South African?"

"That's right. My father was American and my mother was South African." My eyes burn and I struggle to keep the edges of my lips lifted so the tears won't fall.

Celia is efficient if nothing else. "She wasn't just a South African, Tiana, she was a former Miss South Africa. Took second at Miss World. We have a picture of her." And she lifts a photo from her lap. It's my mom at nineteen, wearing the tiara. The camera zooms in.

My lip quivers. I'm fighting like hell to keep my composure.

"You're the spitting image of her," Celia says. "It's uncanny."

And then the camera's on me again right as I grind my teeth to keep tears from forming. I'm clenching my jaw so hard that pain shoots through my forehead.

"What was it like having Miss South Africa as your mother?" Celia persists. "And which of your sisters would have gone the pageant route? Willow, your eldest sister, who was undeniably beautiful—"

"Time out," I choke, struggling to my feet and unhooking the microphone. "I need a moment."

I stumble off the stage and out into the hallway, one hand to my brow to press back the pain.

I'm livid. Revolted. Betrayed. I had a deal with Celia, and this wasn't the deal. This is a dig through a heartbreaking past.

What is she going to do now? Bring up Keith? Show the photo from his funeral? What kind of dog-and-pony show is this?

Harper appears in the hallway. "You okay?"

I keep walking. "Yeah."

She leans against the wall, watching me. "You didn't see the questions coming?"

"Not about my family, no. I didn't think anybody knew."

"I didn't know."

"No one knew. And no one's known for good reason. How did she find out?"

"I don't know."

I stop and look at her. "I don't want to use any of my family's accident on the show. It's personal—"

"It's powerful."

"But it's not for everybody to know. It's my life. It's *my* family."

"But this is what people want to know, Tiana. This is what we do. It's what we're all about. Letting people know that no one is immune from pain or suffering, that beauty and fame isn't the end-all, but just another complication."

"I just don't want Willow and Acacia to be turned into a footnote. They were more than a footnote. They were real and they had dreams and they died too young, died before any of their dreams came true."

"Then maybe it's time you talked about them. Made them real to others. Maybe your grief doesn't have to just be your grief. We all lose people we love. Perhaps by sharing your losses, you'll help others know they can cope with loss, too."

I swallow, nod, wipe away the moisture clinging to my lashes.

"So what do you want me to tell Celia?" she asks.

"Tell her I'll be there in a moment to finish the interview."

And when I return, the makeup artist touches up my makeup and then I'm back in my chair. Taking a deep breath, I begin: I talk about Willow and how she was so beautiful that people routinely approached her, wanting to represent her, offering modeling contracts. But she wasn't interested in modeling. She loved the violin, and her dream was to be a member of the Cape Town Symphony. I talk about Acacia and how she was still just a little girl when she died, but she was strong, brave, braver than the rest of us, and she wanted to be a vet when she grew up. She was always nursing injured birds and mice and baby monkeys, and she didn't know the meaning of fear. I talk about being the middle sister of such extraordinary siblings and how lucky I was to be part of a family that encouraged our individuality.

"So how do I cope with my hurt face?" I ask, managing a smile, although unshed tears shimmer in my eyes. "It's nothing. And it certainly won't stop me from achieving what I want to achieve, and being who I want to be."

"And what is that, Tiana?"

"Fulfilled."

The taped interview was the hardest part of the day. The photos at my house are easy. I get to wear the pretty red Indian top and my jeans for the photographs, so that's a high point. I love the exotic blouse and dangly silver earrings and smile as I pose in the living room curled up with a book, in the kitchen slicing fruit, and in the garden gathering lavender.

After the photographer gets the shots he needs, everyone leaves and I'm trying to figure out what to do next when the phone rings.

"May I speak with Tiana Tomlinson?" the female voice asks.

"This is Tiana."

"Tiana, I'm Betsy Richmond with the Tucson Arts Guild. Is this a bad time?"

"No. Not at all." The Tucson Arts Guild is the group that was honoring me with my lifetime achievement award, and they were among the first to send flowers. "What can I do for you?"

"How are you doing?"

"I'm good," I say, and I mean it. I'm good. I feel strong and fierce and alive.

"Recovering?"

"Yes."

"We've all been very worried about you."

"Well, I'm healing and am getting out and about more and more."

"That's wonderful, and that also leads to the reason I'm calling. The guild is still very interested in recognizing your outstanding contributions to television arts and sciences, and we are hoping to have the opportunity to formally present you with your award."

Surprised, I don't say anything.

"You have inspired many in our industry, and it would mean a great deal to have you join us for a reception," she continues. "As you know, we held the actual dinner last week—it was impossible to cancel the event at the last moment—but we'd like to schedule a cocktail reception to present you with the award, and to minimize the stresses of traveling, one of our members would send his jet for you. He felt traveling by private plane would be far less exhausting and intrusive. The date we're considering is Saturday, March fourteenth, a month from now. Are you by chance available on the fourteenth?"

I have absolutely nothing on my calendar. It's never been so wide open. "Would I speak?"

"If you're willing to say a few words, we'd be delighted to have you speak. We're all fans—"

"I'd love to come."

"Yes?"

"Yes."

"Wonderful!" She lets out a cheer. "Fantastic. I'll send you an e-mail confirming details, but I'm speaking for everyone when I say I'm delighted you're able to join us. Thank you."

Off the phone I do a little spin, and prisms and sparkles splash on the wall, the sunlight bouncing off the silver embroidery of my blouse.

I have something on my calendar. I have an event scheduled. I'm going to speak again.

My life's not over. My life's just beginning.

I feel a welling up of excitement, the kind of excitement I used to feel when I was just starting out in the business and everything was new. Everything is new again. I get to shape a new path for myself, carve out a new niche for me. Maybe I'll pursue broadcast news. Or maybe I'll start my own production company, writing and directing documentaries. Or freelance for the various cable networks producing specials and programs relevant to women.

I can do anything.

I am free to be anything.

There's nothing and no one holding me back, because this time around I'm not holding me back. There's no image to maintain, no role to fill.

I should get an agent, though. I'll ask around—Harper and Christie might have suggestions—and this time the agent will work for me.

I smile, stretch out my arms, and take a huge breath. Relief washes through me. Relief and a new sense of adventure, something I haven't felt in a very long time.

I'm not falling asleep. I've been lying in the dark for nearly an hour trying to relax, but my mind races and I keep getting ideas and I sort through those, and then just as I think I can fall asleep, another idea comes and I'm wound up all over again.

I don't want to work for anyone. I want to work for myself. I want to call the shots. But I don't know if that makes financial sense.

But I have savings. Other than my house, I have no debt. I bought my car for cash two years ago with my end-of-year bonus. My savings could support me for a year—

Stop.

Go to sleep, I tell myself, exhausted by the frenzied pace of my thoughts. In two days you see Michael about getting the stitches out.

Michael.

And there I go again. Thoughts spinning helplessly, hopelessly, out of control.

Two days later, with my right arm still useless, Polish John drives me to my appointment at Michael's office. My heart's beating a mile a minute, too. I'm scared and yet excited. I think about inviting Michael to attend the Tucson Arts Guild reception with me. The event is undoubtedly formal, if not black tie, which would mean fancy dress. Hair. Makeup. The whole shebang. A date would be great. We'd have the jet. It could be romantic....

I feel a flutter of nerves in my stomach, and I suck in a breath. I'm so nervous that I'm queasy, but queasy about what? The event? My future? Michael?

All of the above.

But Michael did say if I ever needed a date, he'd clean up for me....

But if he means that, why hasn't he ever asked me out? Why doesn't he call me? Maybe we're just friends. Or maybe he's attracted to me but afraid I'd want a commitment, and that's one of those things he just can't do.

The town car turns from Santa Monica Boulevard onto Bedford Drive in Beverly Hills and stops in front of a white-marble-fronted building.

We're here.

The decor of Michael's waiting room is muted cream with accents in pewter and chairs upholstered in cobalt blue. My nerves just get worse, though. My hands are damp, and the cover of the glossy magazine sticks to my skin, lifting the ink from the paper.

Restless, anxious, I recross my legs, wondering if it's a bad idea to invite Michael to go to the reception in Tucson.

Looking up, I take in the massive modern oil painting dominating the wall, and then my gaze moves to the shiny silver sculpture in the corner. Funny, but this is exactly what I pictured Michael's office would look like. Tasteful. Elegant. Expensive.

Then the door opens and my name is called. Finally it's my turn. It's a short walk back to an equally serene exam room, but the soothing interior does little to soothe my anxiety. My heart is pounding, and I feel as if I'm going on a date instead of having a doctor's appointment.

There's a knock on the exam room door and then Michael opens it. "Ms. America," he says, walking in. "How are you today?"

He's wearing a white coat over dark slacks and a dress shirt. The coat is open, showing the blue shirt and buckle of his black belt.

"Great," I answer, pulse jumping. "How are you?"

"Very well." He grabs a rolling stool and takes a seat on it. "Sleeping okay?"

"Yes, Doctor."

"Not too much pain?"

"No, Doctor."

He grins at me, amused. "Then maybe I should just look at your cheek."

I sit, hands folded in my lap, breath bottled as he peels off the gauze and scrutinizes the sutured skin. "It looks really good," he says as he gently touches the seam. "Very, very good."

"You're pleased?" I murmur, trying to focus on his words instead of his hands and the warmth of his skin on mine.

"Yes." I see the corner of his mouth lift. "I think I can take the stitches out today."

"Really?"

He nods. "Ready for this?"

"Yes."

My heart pounds as he uses small, sharp scissors to snip the threads and pluck away broken bits with a pair of tweezers. When he's done, he hands me a mirror. The scar is a dark pink, but it's not nearly as thick as I feared.

"It'll flatten and fade as it heals," he adds.

"It looks good," I say gruffly, suddenly emotional because it's not as bad as I'd feared.

"And that's without makeup."

I can't tear my gaze from my cheek. It'll fade. It'll go. It's going to be nothing. A lump fills my throat. After the last week of worry, this is great. Better than great. "There's no reason I can't be on TV," I say. "Or do anything else I want."

"You're right."

I look up, blink against the threat of tears. There's no way to properly express my gratitude. "Thank you."

He smiles, blue eyes warm. "You're welcome. And I know it's a day early, but Happy Valentine's Day."

I've been trying hard to ignore what today is. The day before Valentine's Day. The day of Keith's and my anniversary. It would have been our eighth anniversary this year. I'd thought it'd be a nightmarish day. I thought I'd be sad, stricken, but I'm not.

I'm . . . happy.

I don't know if it's because the scar is less horrifying than I expected, or the fact that I escaped yet another accident with just this cut, or if it's the memory of the children in Africa, but I'm actually, surprisingly happy. Despite everything.

I loved Keith, but clearly, I'm ready to move on.

Surprised by the lightness inside of me, I gather my things, flash Michael a smile. "Happy Valentine's Day to you, too."

And I leave without asking him to go to Tucson with me. For one, it doesn't feel appropriate.

For another, I don't need a date for the event.

I don't need a date for life.

I'm doing good. I'm feeling great, bumps, bruises, and all.

*　　*　　*

I spend the weekend reading, researching start-up costs for a new business, and riding my exercise bike. I need to start exercising again, getting mentally and physically tough. There's no more invalid lifestyle. By the end of March, I want to be working again, and to have work again I have to be on my game.

Monday morning, I call Christie and ask her about her initial start-up expenses as well as the experience. If she had to do it over again, would she do anything differently?

Tuesday morning, Glenn calls. He'd like to meet with me if I have time in the next few days. I know my contract is up March 1. I've been on disability leave since the accident. I wonder if this is the meeting where I'm formally let go, told that my contract won't be renewed. "Do I need an agent present?" I ask him.

"It wouldn't hurt," he admits.

"How about end of the week? Friday at two?" I propose, needing time to find a new agent as well as wanting to put off the unpleasant as long as possible.

"Shall we meet here?"

"Great," I agree, but with a sinking heart. A meeting at the office never bodes well. When something's good, it happens at a fun restaurant. When something's bad, it's in Glenn's office behind closed doors.

An hour after Glenn's call, Harper phones to say that she has a copy of the new *People* magazine that will hit the stands tomorrow. She offers to bring me the copy after work so I can be one of the first to see it. Apparently, she got an advance copy so they could produce the story teases for the show.

"How does it look?" I ask.

"Great. You made the cover and you look beautiful,

although the scar is front and center. But you had to expect that."

"How about the text?"

She knows what I'm asking. "There are lots of really personal things," she admits.

"Ah." I was afraid of that. "Well, come on by. It'll be good to see you, and I'll open a bottle of wine."

It's nearly six when Harper shows up on my doorstep.

"Your stitches are out!" she exclaims as I open the door.

"What do you think?" I turn my right cheek toward her so she can get a good look.

"It's fantastic. Six months from now with some makeup no one will even know the scar is there."

"I think so, too." I smile, wave her in. "Thanks for taking the time to drive it over. Can you stay for a bit? I'd love the company."

"Definitely."

I open a bottle of wine, fill two glasses, and carry them back to the living room, where Harper waits. I hand her the wineglass and she hands me the issue. And there's my picture on the front. I'm in the white dress, smiling bravely at the camera while my scar curves along my cheek. The headline is even more graphic: TIANA'S TRAGIC ACCIDENT—AND THE DEVASTATING HEARTBREAK SHE'S KEPT SECRET UNTIL NOW.

"Oh God," I say beneath my breath, exhaling hard.

"She wrote fairly extensively about the car accident outside Cape Town," Harper says. "She also came up with some photos. I don't know if you gave them to her…?"

"No." My heart sinks. I start flipping through the magazine.

"Page one hundred and ten," she says.

I find the page, open the story, and there on the right side of the double-page spread is the photograph of my family: Mom, Dad, Willow, Acacia, and me. We're dressed up at some formal event or holiday event, and I don't even recognize the picture or the reason we were dressed up and smiling. Maybe it was a school function Dad had. Maybe a holiday party.

I flip to the next page and discover the photo of my mom, the one Celia had surprised me with during the interview. It's the photo where Mom's just been crowned Miss South Africa, and she has big hair, shiny happy eyes, and an endless smile. My stomach heaves. I close the magazine, press it against my chest, and take a deep breath to slow my crazy pulse.

"In Celia's defense, the story's well done," Harper says. "Strong writing, sympathetic storytelling. Nothing cringe-worthy."

"That's a plus."

"I think you'll see some positive feedback. And I think you'll like tonight's show. You're wonderful in an interview format. The public will just fall in love with you all over again."

I smile. But it's not the public I want to fall in love with me. It's Michael. And that's the one person I don't know how to reach. Not that I need to reach him. But if I did...

Michael calls me.

Wednesday night I'm eating macaroni and cheese for dinner—albeit Maria's mac and cheese, which is the home-made kind, which means rich and fattening with just a hint of red pepper—in front of the TV, waiting for *America Tonight* to start, when he phones. I wipe off my milky mouth and mute the TV's sound to take his call. "Hi," I say, thinking I sound far too breathless.

"Just saw the new *People*. Cover girl."

"What do you think?"

"I think they could have waited for you to get your stitches out. Other than that, it's great. You came across beautifully. Especially when you were talking about your sisters."

"Really?"

"Yeah."

"Thank you. I was worried about the story. Worried what people would think."

He hesitates. "I have to admit I was surprised by the photos and interview. It's not something I thought you'd do."

Was that a criticism? "They don't say it in the story, but they bought my photos and story. For a million dollars—"

"A million dollars?"

"—to go to the charity of my choice." I take another quick breath. "And I divided it between PSI Zambia and Rx Smile."

He doesn't say anything, and I wait, mouth dry, wondering if he heard me, wondering if he's shocked or upset. And then he laughs softly. "Good for you, Tiana. Well done."

Now is the time to invite him to the Tucson reception. Now is the time to ask him to go. But my mouth is so dry and my heart's beating too hard and I'm so nervous because I've been rejected once and don't want to be rejected again.

"My God, that's brilliant. Good for you," he repeats.

I glow a little, and caught up in the moment, I blurt out an invitation for Tucson. "I have an event on March fourteenth in Tucson, it's the lifetime achievement award I was supposed to get February seventh, the day after I was hurt, and they'd like me to come out so they can present me with the award. I'd say a few words, and I know it's a long way to go, but if you're free

I'd love it if you could go with me." I stop talking abruptly, realizing I was almost rambling.

"March fourteenth?"

"Yes. They're sending a jet for me. Kind of a fun way to travel."

"Tiana, I'm already booked that day. There's a medical conference in Boston and I'm speaking."

"That's okay," I say quickly, tone light. "Thought I'd ask."

"Glad you did. If things were different, I'd love to go."

But things aren't different, and he can't go. We talk about nothing for a moment and then say good-bye.

Hanging up, I look at my flat-screen TV, and there I am in high-definition, in my white dress, with my shiny dark hair, lush mascara lashes, big cast, and the stunning bristly scar. I watch me in mute, watch my face as I speak to Celia, answering her questions. I look not at the scar on my cheek, but at my eyes and my lips, and I see the fire and emotion I've spent my life trying to hide. But the fire and emotion aren't ugly. The fire and emotion are beautiful.

Hot emotion runs through me now, and I grab a pillow from the couch and press it to my chest. Even without a man, even without Michael, my heart is beautiful.

Chapter Twenty-one

———— ★★★ ————

The response from the *People* story and *America Tonight* segments has been overwhelmingly positive. I'm fielding calls right and left, ranging from interview requests to offers to make a guest appearance on talk shows. I need an agent, and a good one, but I'm not ready to rush into signing with an agent just because I'm feeling pressure. I'll represent myself until I find the right person—and it will be the right person, someone who respects me, my values, and my goals.

I say yes to an appearance on *The View* to discuss Rx Smile. Yes to an appearance with Ellen DeGeneres to discuss Zambia and the need there. And yes to Kelly and Regis, who want to chat about life now.

There are requests from magazines and newspapers, including *Redbook* and *O*, and the "Lifestyle" section editor from *USA Today*, and I promise to follow up with each in the next week.

In the meantime, there's the meeting with Glenn, and I prepare for it the way one would prepare for a boxing match. It's going to be tough, it's going to be painful, but it won't last forever.

I wear a silver tank with the gray Donna Karan suit skirt and drape the jacket over my shoulders to accommodate my cast. I'm wearing more foundation than I usually do, but it covers most of the scar and gives me confidence. With South

Sea pearls in my ears and a thick strand at my throat, I feel polished and confident and ready for whatever will come.

Russian John drives me, giving me a half hour to compose myself. One of three things will happen in this meeting. I'll be given walking papers, I'll be offered a new anchor contract, or I'll be offered part-time work. What do I want?

The front desk receptionist greets me as I step off the elevator. Libby rushing through the halls shouts a hello. Madison scurries to hug me before I disappear into Glenn's office. She's wearing pink, I notice, and I check my smile.

Glenn rises, puts a hand to my shoulder, and kisses my cheek. "You look wonderful."

"Thank you."

I can see him scrutinizing my face, searching for the horrific scar flaunted on the front of this week's *People*. "It's not so bad," he says, clearly surprised. "I expected much worse."

"*People* didn't want to wait for the stitches to come out."

"Shock value, of course." He gestures for me to take a chair and then sits once I'm seated. He looks at me for another long moment and then shakes his head. "This is difficult. This is really difficult. I wish the network heads were here now to see you, but they aren't, and they made their decision based on the photos they saw in *People*, as well as your appearance on the show this week, and it was felt that your accident was too traumatic for our viewers—" He breaks off, looks at me with sadness. "I'm sorry, Tiana, your contract won't be renewed."

I'm not surprised, but I'm disappointed. I expected a little more from the network. I expected at least an offer for part-time work, as a special correspondent or weekend anchor.

I meet his gaze directly. "So that's how it is."

"I fought hard for you."

And Glenn probably did fight. But I don't think his definition of hard matches mine. I can't imagine him wanting me to make many waves, not when his own contract is up for renewal in June.

"You'll continue to have temporary disability and then workers' compensation. Helen in human resources will be able to cover all that with you."

"Thank you." I get to my feet, square my shoulders, and smile. I won't leave here in tears. This is what I was looking for. New opportunity. Now I have it.

"Thank you," he answers.

I turn to go, but he stops me at the door.

"Tonight's the last of your Africa features, and I thought you should know that our ratings this week were our highest ever. Viewers loved your segments. I loved the segments. I'm proud to have had the chance to work with you. You're a gifted journalist, and you have a big future ahead of you."

He's right. I am going to have a big future. "Thank you, Glenn. All my best."

Russian John is waiting to take me home, but I'm not ready to go home. I'm dressed, I feel beautiful, and I want to celebrate. One chapter in my life is closing so that I can begin a new one.

"John, the Beverly Hills Hotel, please. I think I'll stop for a late lunch."

At two forty-five, there's no wait to be seated in the Polo Lounge. I order a salad and an iced tea and then take a deep breath to relax while I wait.

I feel a little brave and a little foolish sitting here on my own. This is a place where people come to make deals. To schmooze and to see and be seen. But I'm here for a reason. I'm making a statement. I'm making myself visible. I'm letting the industry know I'm not going away. This is my town. And I belong here.

Later that afternoon, I get an e-mail from Betsy in Tucson with details regarding the reception. As I suspected, it is black-tie and it'll be held at one of the swanky resorts in the desert. Apparently, every ticket has already been sold and the press have promised to attend in force. I call Shannon, my stylist. I haven't talked to her in five weeks, not since she dressed me for the Golden Globes back in early January.

"Tiana!" Shannon sounds genuinely delighted to hear from me. "How are you? God, it was good to see your name and number on my phone."

"I'm great. Thank you. How are you?"

We chitchat, and then I tell her about the Tucson award, how the accident happened the day I was to fly out and they're going to present me with the award now with a new event. "I need to look good. It's my first black-tie appearance since my accident and I want to be confident."

"I couldn't agree more. You need a great dress, a darling handbag, and your beautiful smile. What were you thinking of wearing?"

Having purchased virtually everything in my closet for me, she knows my wardrobe intimately and keeps an online album with photographs of my best pieces. "My black ruffled Oscar de la Renta gown. It's long, and except for the bare shoulders, rather demure."

"You love that dress and I love that dress, but on someone other than you. I think it's time to donate that dress, especially as I know a gown that would be amazing on you. I just saw it today at Neiman Marcus, and you'd look sensational in it. It's Monique Lhuillier. Long, silver satin, and paired with a modern silver collar or a chunky necklace you'd absolutely dazzle."

"Silver, in March?"

"Get a blowout and spray tan, just a touch of a golden glow. Almost naked makeup. A barely there lip with nude gloss. No earrings, no bracelets, and it'd be stunning but effortless. I'll run the dress over for you tomorrow."

The three weeks until the Tucson gala are filled with appointments, interviews, and appearances. I'm far busier than I expected, and it's gratifying to discover so much interest and support for the people and stories I covered in Zambia.

I get my cast off during the second week of March. My arm looks pale and a little shriveled, but I'm delighted to have it back. There's a scar on my forearm and the muscles are appallingly weak, but I'll get the strength back with use.

Three days after the cast comes off, and just two days before I'm to head to Tucson, I have a second meeting with agent Meredith Wochstein of Creative Talent. I like her very much and appreciate her energy and drive. She doesn't see my scar as a stumbling block; rather, she focuses on my experience and my charisma. There are a lot of opportunities for me, she tells me; it's just a matter of goal setting and priorities. I'm delighted to sign with her.

Finally, it's Saturday morning and time to fly to Tucson. I'm twitchy, aware that the last time I was headed to Tucson I came nose to nose with a car. It's a relief once I'm on board the Learjet, safely buckled in my seat with a glass of champagne in my hand. The flight is smooth and fast, and I'm on the ground before I've even finished going through my magazines.

With a half day looming before the reception, I indulge in body treatments and a massage at the resort's spa and then head to the salon at four for hair and nails. Back in my hotel room, I check my cell for messages and there's one from Meredith Wochstein, my new agent. She's just heard from Harvey Pearlman over at NBC, and he wants to set up a meeting for Tuesday to discuss the idea of developing an afternoon talk show with me as host. It's all very early, very preliminary talks, but Meredith says that Harvey's a huge fan of mine and would love to make something happen.

I listen to the message three times, my smile growing with every replay.

Even if nothing comes of the Tuesday meeting, the fact that Harvey Pearlman, one of the most influential men in the industry today, is a fan and wants to talk to me makes me feel amazing.

I am not just a face.

I am not just an image.

I am me, and I matter.

I call Meredith back, leave a message that I'd be delighted to meet with Harvey and my calendar's open, so any time, any place, is good. And then I hang up and it's time to dress for the party.

My hands shake as I carefully slide the new Monique Lhuillier gown over my head. Harvey Pearlman's a fan. NBC wants to talk to me. I have options. I have a very big, bright future, and there will be new risks to take, new crises as well, but I welcome them all. I love a good challenge and am up for a new challenge.

The silver dress is formfitting, and after zipping it up, I turn to see myself in the mirror. It's beautiful. *I'm beautiful.*

I smile, and leaning close to the mirror, I kiss my face where the scar is. The mirror is cold against my lips, but I leave my lips there until the glass warms and I feel the love, the same love I felt when my mother comforted me as a child. *I love you, Tiana. I'm proud of you. You're going to be wonderful tonight.*

The ballroom chandeliers are dimmed, and candles flicker on the twenty-some round tables and chairs. Even though this is supposed to be a cocktail reception, there is enough food at the buffet stations to make it a dinner. I mingle and visit and nibble a little and drink even less, as I'm aware that soon I'll be on the platform, accepting my award and giving a thank-you speech.

And then it's time, and the lights are further dimmed, and everyone takes a seat. I'm being introduced, my biography is read, along with a list of achievements I've heard before. Emmy Award–winning...

Top-rated show...

HBC's most popular TV host...

All those distinctions, all that recognition, usually it rolls right off me, but tonight I hear it all, take it in, savoring every honor, every achievement, realizing that I should have been doing this years ago. I've worked hard. I've accomplished a lot. I should enjoy it. But like other women, I never take time to savor my successes. I've always been too focused on what I haven't done right or what I still need to do.

No more.

Standing in front of the microphone, I have my speech there in front of me, but as I look out at the audience beneath the glowing chandeliers, I ignore the speech I've prepared and just speak from the heart.

I talk about my experience in television and how in the months leading up to my accident, I'd been increasingly cautious and fearful, worried that my career would end if I aged, worried I'd lose respect if I wasn't a flawless image. I tell them I didn't realize how strong I was and that my power was not in my image, but in my convictions and my drive.

"I craved change," I tell them, "but was terrified of change, clinging ever more tightly to what was familiar, to what I knew. But clinging to fear only increases fear. There's only one way to fight fear and that's by fighting back. Embrace change. Grab for the unknown. And believe in hope and joy and love.

"There isn't just one kind of love, either," I conclude. "And there's more than enough love to go around. So love yourself, and love your life, and even love fear, because it won't hold you back."

The audience is on their feet, applauding. I appreciate the show of support, but today's speech wasn't for them. It was for me. I have spent years not loving myself, not loving my life, not loving much of anything because I've been so afraid that no matter what I do, I'll never be successful. Never be valuable. Never really matter.

But I can't matter if I won't let myself matter, and not matter to others, but matter to me.

I have to be my first lover, my first friend, my first fan. I have to start with me because this is where it all begins.

As I step off the stage, the applause continues, and I smile and nod my gratitude. Tonight couldn't have gone better, and I go home with a gorgeous crystal award and a grateful heart. I'm ready for the next phase of my life, whatever it is.

I'm walking through the emptying ballroom toward the lobby when I see him. He's dressed in one of his gorgeous black Italian suits, hands in his trouser pockets, and he's handsome as all sin. Michael.

My heart flips. I walk slowly toward him.

He makes a show of looking around. "No date?"

I want to answer something clever, but I can't think of anything. He's so damn attractive, and he's made life very hard for me lately. "No."

"Why not?"

My temper stirs. "That's like asking how you always manage to get one. Really, Dr. Frankenstein, mind your manners."

He laughs softly, appreciatively, and closes the distance between us to kiss me on the cheek. "You look amazing, and you smell even better."

"Thank you." My calm voice belies the wild beating of my heart.

He puts one arm around me. "It was an incredible speech. You had everyone on their feet."

"Michael, what are you doing here? I thought you had to be in Boston."

"I was. But the moment I delivered my lecture I jumped on a plane and was able to catch your speech."

My gaze searches his. He looks completely unruffled, as if being here is nothing out of the ordinary. "You could have let me know."

"And ruin the surprise?"

"I hate surprises."

He laughs and wraps me in a hug, then drops a kiss on top of my head. "You're feisty."

"I don't understand you," I answer stiffly, not wanting to

get excited, not wanting my heart to get banged up, not again. Not by him.

"What don't you understand?"

"You."

"Oh, I'm easy enough to understand. I'm crazy about you. Very much in love with you and here to take you home and make you mine."

"Is that so?"

"That is so." And then he reaches for me, his arms sliding around my waist, pulling me close. I can feel his hard, warm body against the length of me. His head dips, his face blocking the bright lights, and then he kisses me. And this kiss, so hot, so fierce, so consuming, feels like home, too.

When he finally lifts his head, his eyes are darkly blue as they look down at me. "Convinced?"

"No," I say. "Can we do that again?"

And he does, and this kiss is even longer and hotter than the last. My knees buckle and I have to grab on to him.

"Ready to go?" he asks long moments later.

"Yes. If you'll fly home with me."

"I was hoping you'd ask."

On board the small, sleek jet, Michael and I sit next to each other in our leather seats, our fingers linked. It feels very glamorous and more than a little surreal with Michael in his suit and me in my gown. All we need is champagne and caviar and we could be posing for *Town & Country* magazine.

We're quiet during takeoff, but once we've reached cruising altitude, Michael covers my hand with both of us. "Can we get this right?" he asks.

"I hope so," I answer. For weeks I've craved this, wanting this, wanting him to love me, choose me, to say it's me he's always wanted, that it's me he can't live without.

Just as they do in romantic movies. Except I want it for real.

I want love that's huge and fierce and strong. I want a man who will love me and be with me and not disappear on me.

I want a man who will grow old with me. Who will be there as the creases deepen and the wrinkles lengthen and my hair goes from brown to gray to white.

I want a man who will hold my hand even when it trembles with age.

I want a man who will wait for me even if I walk slowly from the chair to the door.

I want a man who will sit with me on the winter days and we will face the pale sun together, faces lifted, pleased to still be alive, to still be together, to still just be.

That is my dream. And then he hands me my dream. "Do you remember asking me about my relationships, especially Alexis?" His eyes find mine and hold. "I couldn't commit to her, couldn't love her. I was already in love with you."

Goose bumps pepper my skin, and I shiver. "You're really in love with me?"

"Madly, ridiculously, although I didn't want to be."

"Why not?"

He reaches out, strokes my hair back from my face. "I don't know. I was certainly attracted to you, and have been from the first time I met you."

"Where did we first meet?"

"Max's house. Four years ago. He and Irene threw a huge party just before Christmas. You wore an emerald green dress and were unbelievably hot."

I wrinkle my nose but on the inside I'm beaming. Hot, huh? "You make it sound like a bad thing."

"Well, it was. Here's this gorgeous, sexy, very smart woman with the most ridiculous guy."

I'm giggling now but Michael ignores me, adding, "He was a painter. From Laguna. And he couldn't keep his hands off you. Even though I'd just met you I wanted to rip his head off. *I* wanted to be the one touching you."

"Matthew Breese," I say, remembering. We'd dated for five months, but it never felt right. "He was awfully touchy-feely, wasn't he?"

"Excessively."

"So if I was hot, and you were attracted to me, why didn't you ever ask me out? Why always give me such a hard time?"

The edge of his mouth curves and he smiles this slow, rueful smile that has to be the sexiest thing I've ever seen. "I just knew you deserved more than what I could give you. I'm married to my work. It's been a problem in all my relationships and I hoped that if I stayed away from you, someone else, someone better, would snatch you up."

My chest suddenly feels too tender and my happiness slips a notch. "But no one did."

"Thank God." He looks into my eyes and there's so much warmth and emotion there that it takes my breath away. "I was being stupid, and it took the trip to Zambia to make me realize that I didn't just want your body, but I wanted you, Tiana Tomlinson, forever."

"But in Katete, you knew I liked you. That last night I invited you to my room..."

"I know. I wanted to go. I wanted to rip your clothes off and devour you, but it didn't seem like the right time, or place."

"I can't believe you turned sex down."

"But I didn't want sex." Michael hesitates, struggling for words. "I wanted you. And I wanted more than one night, and God help me, I didn't want to screw it up. I'd been attracted to you for so many years and finally, here's this opportunity, but was it the right one?"

"I had no idea you were so old-fashioned."

"Not old-fashioned, just protective when it comes to you. I hated it when other jerks hurt you. I didn't want to become one of those jerks. So I gave us time."

"How nice of you," I drawl. "But what was the time for? Time to forget you? Get over you? Meet someone new?"

He grimaces. "There is that. And it did cross my mind. But then the accident happened, and before we had a chance to figure anything out, I was your doctor and I couldn't act on my feelings even if I wanted to."

"Your damn ethics!"

He laughs huskily and reaches for me, tugging me from my seat belt and onto his lap. "Don't think it was easy. Once you were at UCLA's Medical Center, I couldn't stay away. I'd go by twice a day just to see you."

Michael gently sweeps his thumb across my scar, soothing it. "This little thing complicated everything."

"How's that?"

"I worried that I'd scar you. Worried that you'd blame me. Worried that it'd change you. I needn't have worried so much. You're such a fighter. You've come through like a champ. You came out swinging, and I couldn't be prouder."

I slide an arm around his neck and press a kiss to his lips. "You should have just called," I whisper against his mouth. "I wanted you to call. I missed you so much."

His hand reaches up into my hair, letting the thick mass slide over and through his fingers. "Can we make this work?"

"Yes."

"How can you be sure?"

I touch my lips against his, close my eyes, and just breathe him in. He smells of soap and cologne, and his skin feels warm, and on his breath there's a hint of mint. This is what a man should feel like and smell like. This is what my man feels and smells like. "Because I've waited a long time to feel this way."

My eyes sting and I look up at him. "I love you. I've only said that to one other man, and I married him."

"You love me."

"Yes."

The corner of his mouth lifts. "This is working out pretty nicely, if I do say so myself."

I just shake my head. He's so impossible and awful and wonderful, and I don't think I could love any man more. "You make me a little crazy," I confess, "but I think that's part of your charm."

He kisses me with hunger, and desire explodes inside me, fierce and raw. Just when I think I have to tear his clothes from his back, he draws away, and he looks down at me with dark, intense eyes. "I don't want to screw this up, baby."

"How would you?"

He shakes his head. "I don't always communicate well. I work too hard. I can be preoccupied—"

"I know. That's part of you, part of what makes you the brilliant and gorgeous and maddening Michael O'Sullivan. The only man I want in my life."

He cups my face between his hands. "Say it again."

"The only man I want."

And then he's kissing me again, and things get a little hotter—well, a lot hotter—and clothes shift, and bodies move, and it's me who thinks this is absolutely the right time to make love. "We have to seize the day," I say, unbuttoning his shirt and then his belt buckle.

"I'm afraid in a moment you'll be seizing a lot more," he answers gravely, and he's right. Unzipping his trousers, I discover there's a lot of Michael, far, far more than I expected. It's an exciting surprise, even a little daunting.

Michael lifts my evening gown and makes quick work of my stockings, and I don't know if it's the altitude or the turbulence, but making love is beyond orgasmic. If it weren't for Michael's mouth on mine, even the pilot would have heard me scream.

After, he holds me on his lap, my face on his chest, and I sigh with pleasure and peace. That was so good. And so fun. I don't suppose we'd have time to try it again....

We do.

And I am not disappointed.

We're on our final descent into Burbank, and I'm back in my seat, clothes adjusted as best as they can be. My beautiful silver gown will never be the same, but isn't this what beautiful gowns are for? Falling in love? Making love?

As the plane touches down on the runway in the smoothest landing ever, Michael brings my hand to his lips and kisses it. "So what happens now?"

"I hope we go home together," I answer honestly.

"To whose house?"

"I don't care. Russian John's here to meet my flight. He'll take us wherever we want."

"Your house tonight. Mine tomorrow. And maybe one day we can find a place we pick out together…?"

"I like it."

He kisses my hand again and then reaches for his discarded coat and retrieves an envelope. He hands me the envelope.

I look at him, try to read his expression but can't, and pull a sheet of paper from the envelope.

It's an itinerary for an Rx Smile mission to Egypt. "It's the last weekend of April," Michael says. "I would love it if you could go with me."

"I'd love to go."

"I understand you have a career and you can't just follow me everywhere—"

I cut him off with a kiss, aware of the little half shiver at the mention of work. I'm so looking forward to Tuesday's meeting with Harvey, but I'm not ready to talk about it until there's something concrete to share. This meeting with Harvey might be only the first of dozens of meetings.

I tap Michael on the chest. "I'll worry about my work. You worry about your work, and knowing us, we'll always find a way to be together."

"I couldn't have said it better," he answers.

I grin. "I know. I'm good with words. It's my gift."

"Thank God, because you're a disaster at Yahtzee."

I laugh and laugh and tears fill my eyes, and it's the best feeling, this coming home, this returning to real life and all its challenges with the man I adore.

The jet brakes, slows, before turning to taxi toward the terminal. We both look out the windows at the lights and the activity.

"I wish we weren't back," I say wistfully as the lights of the terminal grow bigger and brighter. "Wish we could stay on this plane forever."

"You'd get bored," Michael says, "and we both have things we want to do. You have stories to tell, and I have people to heal. But I also know this: We're meant to be together. We're going to achieve amazing things together."

"I couldn't agree more."

He lifts my chin and studies my face with the crescent scar and then my lips that won't stop smiling and finally my eyes. "But I also promise right here, right now, to support whatever it is you want to do." His voice is so deep, it has a hint of a brogue in it. "I support whatever matters to you. You have my unconditional support, and my unconditional love. I just ask that whatever journey you choose, you include me."

And that's when I'm all his, completely, not just the broken pieces of me, but the whole heart, soul, and funny bone. Michael knows how to make me laugh and hope and believe in all the things I had stopped believing in. Best of all, he loves me, the real me, not just the pretty face on TV.

I lean forward and kiss him, and just like before, once I start I can't stop. I'm just happy, so happy.

"I love you," I whisper against his mouth, and it crosses my mind that I am complete and content. I have all I could want and more. Because youth is fleeting and beauty does fade, but the one part of us that never ages is our heart.

I don't need to be glossy and flawless. I don't need a pretty face. I just need my heart. It's a good heart, a beautiful heart, and it's a fighter. It knows how to forgive and knows when to make a stand, and most of all, it knows how to love.

Love.

Love is the real answer. Love is everything.

About the Author

I imagine God blessing me as a baby much the way the three fairy godmothers blessed the infant princess in *Sleeping Beauty*. I see God peering over my crib and, after much thought, bestowing on me three special gifts: humor, optimism, and tenacity. Of these three, He gave tenacity in the greatest abundance.

At nine I was tested by a prominent foundation that measures skills and aptitudes. Because they weren't used to measuring children my age, I came up lacking in vocabulary, and my test results showed that I lacked finger dexterity as well. I would never be a concert pianist. I would probably also struggle to thread the eye of a needle. But I did score off the charts in one area, and that was foresight.

Foresight meant that I could work for long periods of time to achieve a goal. Foresight meant that I could work alone for long periods of time. Foresight meant I didn't give up easily.

I suppose in the world of skills and gifts, there are more glamorous gifts, but industriousness—and that good old gift of tenacity—has helped me achieve the seemingly impossible. I didn't know any novelists growing up. I didn't know that I could publish. I just knew I loved books and stories, and I had to try to write them, too.

When people ask me today for writing tips or insights into

my success, I say, never give up. Don't accept defeat. And be willing to keep learning.

This mantra became my personal mantra while writing *Easy on the Eyes*. This book challenged me at every turn. I spent four months writing from 8 a.m. until 10 p.m. and then another two months tearing it apart and trying it again. And then another month attacking it yet again. And then again even in the copyediting stage.

In contrast, *Mrs. Perfect* rolled from my fingertips. The writing was smooth, taut, dreamlike, whereas writing *Easy on the Eyes* felt like open-heart surgery without anesthesia.

In this new novel, I had to work, dig deep, struggle for the story. And for the first time in a long time I felt like a writer, not an author. Writing became something active and alive, a fierce process that required all of my talent and all of my patience and all of my skill. *Easy on the Eyes* ended up being a gift. I rediscovered how much I love a good challenge and how even the most difficult work becomes rewarding if you keep a sense of humor and remain hopeful (there are those other gifts!).

The great thing about being forty-five instead of thirty-five or twenty-five is that I don't have to be perfect, and I don't have to know everything, and I don't have to get it right the first time, or all the time. I just have to try. And I just have to be myself.

In the five years I've written for 5 Spot, I've grown to not just like myself, but love myself. I love even all the bad stuff about me, the negatives like pride, and temper, vanity, willfulness, and ambition, because without the bad, I wouldn't have the good, and the good is very good.

Easy on the Eyes reminded me that I still have a few goals and dreams left. I want to be allowed to age gracefully. I want to be valuable even with wrinkles and extra padding. I want to be loved even though I'll always be flawed. And I want to keep counting my blessings.

Humor, optimism, tenacity.

Especially tenacity. Because as I've learned, as long as we don't quit, we don't fail.

5 Steps to Ageless Beauty

1 *Make Your Hair Look Great*
Play your hair up with a good cut and color and have fun. You don't have to cut your hair off after forty. Long hair is gorgeous at any age.

2 *Softer Makeup*
A lighter lipstick is more flattering as we hit our forties and beyond. Darker lip colors tend to age. Discover how softer, lighter colors can light up the face.

3 *Own Your Style*
Don't chase trends. Develop your own style and make it work for you. We're big girls now. We don't have to play follow the leader.

4 *Go for a Great Fit*
A perfect fit always flatters, and well-tailored clothes look gorgeous no matter the price.

5 *Be Happy*
There's nothing more beautiful than a woman who smiles. Enjoy being you!